THE RIVER
WE REMEMBER

ALSO BY WILLIAM KENT KRUEGER

Fox Creek

Lightning Strike

This Tender Land

Desolation Mountain

Sulfur Springs

Manitou Canyon

Windigo Island

Tamarack County

Ordinary Grace

Trickster's Point

Northwest Angle

Vermilion Drift

Heaven's Keep

Red Knife

Thunder Bay

Copper River

Mercy Falls

Blood Hollow

The Devil's Bed

Purgatory Ridge

Boundary Waters

Iron Lake

THE RIVER
WE REMEMBER

A NOVEL

William Kent Krueger

ATRIA BOOKS

New York   London   Toronto   Sydney   New Delhi

ATRIA
BOOKS

An Imprint of Simon & Schuster, Inc.
1230 Avenue of the Americas
New York, NY 10020

First Atria Books hardcover edition September 2023

ATRIA BOOKS and colophon are trademarks of Simon & Schuster, Inc.

For information about special discounts for bulk purchases, please contact Simon & Schuster Special Sales at 1-866-506-1949 or business@simonandschuster.com.

The Simon & Schuster Speakers Bureau can bring authors to your live event. For more information or to book an event, contact the Simon & Schuster Speakers Bureau at 1-866-248-3049 or visit our website at www.simonspeakers.com.

Interior design by Alexis Minieri

Manufactured in the United States of America

1   3   5   7   9   10   8   6   4   2

Library of Congress Cataloging-in-Publication Data is available.

ISBN 978-1-9821-7921-2
ISBN 978-1-9821-7923-6 (ebook)

To Peter Borland and Sean deLone, editors extraordinaire,
who so often have helped me see my way through the mist

Three things cannot be long hidden:
the sun, the moon, and the truth.

BUDDHA

- PART ONE -

BLACK EARTH COUNTY

PROLOGUE

THE ALABASTER RIVER cuts diagonally across Black Earth County, Minnesota, a crooked course like a long crack in a china plate. Flowing out of Sioux Lake, it runs seventy miles before crossing the border into Iowa south of Jewel, the county seat. It's a lovely river filled with water that's only slightly silted, making it the color of weak tea. Most folks who've grown up in Black Earth County have swum in the river, fished its pools, picnicked on its banks. Except in spring, when it's prone to flooding, they think of it as an old friend. On quiet nights when the moon is full or nearly so and the surface of the Alabaster is mirror-still and glows pure white in the dark bottomland, to stand on a hillside and look down at this river is to fall in love.

With people, we fall in love too easily, it seems, and too easily fall out of love. But with the land it's different. We abide much. We can pour our sweat and blood, our very hearts into a piece of earth and get nothing in return but fields of hail-crushed soybean plants or drought-withered cornstalks or fodder for a plague of locusts, and still we love this place enough to die for it. Or kill. In Black Earth County, people understand these things.

If you visit the Alabaster at sunrise or sunset, you're likely to see the sudden small explosions of water where fish are feeding. Although there are many kinds of fish who make the Alabaster their home, the most aggressive are channel catfish. They're mudsuckers, bottom feeders, river vultures, the worst kind of scavengers. Channel cats will eat anything.

This is the story of how they came to eat Jimmy Quinn.

CHAPTER ONE

IN 1958, MEMORIAL Day fell on a Friday. This was long before the federal government made the celebration officially the final Monday of May. Back then it was still referred to as Decoration Day. Like many rural communities, Jewel took its holidays seriously. The people of Black Earth County were mostly farmers, sensible, hardworking folks. Their days were long, their labor backbreaking. But when they could legitimately give themselves permission to relax and enjoy life, they did a pretty fair job of it. Decoration Day was the first real celebration after the relentless work of spring. By then, the ground had been plowed, harrowed, planted. The honey wagons had spread manure across the seeded fields, and near the end of May, that aroma, which is a peculiar hallmark of farm country, had pretty much disappeared. In its place was a different scent, the fragrance of green shoots and leafed trees and early-blooming wildflowers and, in town, lawns freshly mowed. What had come by the end of May was the smell of promise.

Jewel had always called itself "The Gem of the Prairie." The grand courthouse on the hill was built twenty years after the Civil War, constructed of granite quarried in the Minnesota River Valley seventy miles north. The shops that lined the main street were all family-owned, and proudly so. It was a small town by most standards. There were no stoplights and the only grocery store was Huber's, in business since before the turn of the century. If you came from the city, you'd probably have thought of it as sleepy. But in 1958, it was bustling, with lots of life in it. And death, too, as it turned out.

The Decoration Day parade was a grand affair. The veterans dressed up in their uniforms. The oldest was Gunther Haas, who served with Colonel James W. Forsyth's 7th Cavalry at the battle of Wounded Knee in 1890. The uniforms of the old vets were generally faded and ill-fitting, but a lot of the younger men, who'd fought in World War Two or the Korean War, still looked pretty snappy in their khaki and braid or their navy whites. The veterans were at the center of the parade, Gunther Haas among them, pushed along in his wheelchair, a frail wisp of a man with ill-fitting false teeth and barely enough strength to wave the little flag he held. Up front marched the Jewel High School Band in its final official performance of that school year. The fire department, as it did for every parade, rolled out its two engines and hit their sirens many times along the route, so that the spectators on the sidewalks screamed with delight. Jack Harris, the mayor, was there in a shiny red Edsel convertible that Wheeler's Ford dealership was still trying to get rid of. Near the end came the Black Earth Trotters, a group of local show riders, on their mounts, the horses decked out in ribbons and high-stepping proudly. The parade moved down the entire length of Jewel's business district—three blocks of shops and businesses—and turned at the corner of Main and Ash, where chairs had been set on a high platform so that Harris and a few others could speak, offering the kinds of platitudes expected on such a day. Afterward, in Veteran's Park, there would be picnics and fireworks.

In those days, Jewel's population hovered around four thousand. A lot of them turned out for the celebration, and a good many farm families came into town as well. Absent that year, as usual, was Brody Dern, sheriff of Black Earth County. Brody would have been among the most decorated of veterans had he chosen to march with the others, but Brody never did. He had duties to attend to, he would say as an excuse, and folks let it go at that.

On the Decoration Day when this story begins, Brody was, in fact, occupied overseeing the one prisoner the county jail held, Felix Klein. Felix wasn't the kind of man who needed much oversight. When he was sober, he was every bit as decent and peace-loving as the next citizen of Jewel. But Felix had demons inside him, or so he claimed when he'd been hitting the Wild Turkey, and these demons sometimes made him do things he regretted. He tried to set fire to the water tower once. When he sobered up and Brody demanded an explanation, Felix was stumped. And late on the previous New Year's Eve, Brody had found him wandering Jewel in his long johns, his feet bare. Brody had taken him to the emergency room of the little hospital, where, because of frostbite, they'd had to amputate a couple of toes on both feet. When Brody questioned him, Felix said he couldn't stand to be in his house any longer, not with Hannah there, crying like that. Hannah was Felix's wife. By then, she'd been dead a dozen years.

But get him off the bottle and Felix was a man who could carry his own in an intelligent conversation, and he was one hell of a chess player.

That's precisely what he and Brody were doing that afternoon when the Decoration Day parade was taking place on Main Street. Brody could hear the high school band and the cheers and the applause of those who'd gathered to watch, and now and again he heard the fire engine sirens. Later, when everything had moved to Veteran's Park, he planned to join his brother's family and his mother for some cold fried chicken. But at that moment, he was content to be right where he was.

Hector, Brody's golden retriever, lay on the floor not far from the men. Brody had named him for the noble hero of Troy, and when you looked into that beautiful dog's soulful brown eyes you knew why.

The sheriff was thirty-five years old, tall and lean. His hair was the color of acorns. He wasn't handsome, not in the way of Hollywood. In fact, the Amish of the neighboring county would probably have called him very plain and meant it as a high compliment.

With his queen, Brody had just checked Felix's king and had lifted his coffee mug for a sip when the door to the jailhouse burst open and Herman Ostberg rushed in, breathless.

Brody and Felix looked up from the chessboard, and Hector sprang to his feet. Ostberg was a small, excitable man. For several moments, he just stood there panting, his eyes opened impossibly wide.

"Brody," the little man managed when he finally caught his breath. "You'll never guess."

"No," Brody replied. "I don't suppose I will."

"Jimmy Quinn," Ostberg gasped.

"What about Quinn?"

"The catfish," Ostberg said. Then said again, "The catfish."

Brody was a man who'd seen things in war that had inured him to the shock of normal emergencies in a place like Jewel. No one knew the details of his war experiences but they knew of the medals. To settle the little man, Brody said, "Take a deep breath, Herman, then tell me about Quinn and the catfish."

Ostberg stared at the two men, one on either side of the chessboard, tried to calm himself, and finally, as if he couldn't quite believe his own words, said, "They ate him, Brody. They ate him right down to the bone."

CHAPTER TWO

"WHO'S THEY, AND who did they eat?"

The question came from Sam Wicklow, standing in the open doorway behind Ostberg. Wicklow was publisher and editor of the *Black Earth County Clarion*, a twice-weekly newspaper. He was dressed in a light blue denim shirt and khaki pants. He sported a full beard, something not many men did in the nineteen fifties, unless they were Amish or beatniks or Ernest Hemingway. Wicklow's facial hair gave him a gruff countenance, which was not at all the truth of who he was but came in handy when he had to defend an unpopular editorial or ask a hard question in pursuit of a story. Mostly he wore the beard to cover up some of his scars. He had a lot of them, all over his body. He'd been blown nearly apart on Iwo Jima, but the army doctors were able to sew him back together, except for the lower part of his left leg, which was scattered in pieces across a tropical hillside. He walked with a prosthetic attached to the stump of his knee, which gave him a stiff, awkward gait. On occasions that required him to attempt to run, he was sadly comic. He'd been taking pictures of the parade, and his Leica camera hung from a strap around his neck.

"Those damn channel cats in the Alabaster," Ostberg said. "They pretty near ate up Jimmy Quinn."

Felix Klein, interrupted in mid-move, still held in his hand the bishop he intended to use to defend his threatened king. "Where?" he asked.

"Near the bridge on County Seven."

"Good fishing under that bridge," Felix noted. "Nice deep water there."

"Quinn's dead?" Brody said.

"Hell, yes, he's dead," Ostberg said. "Ain't no living man going to let channel cats feast on his insides."

"You found him?"

"Not half an hour ago. I was planning on fishing. Then I spotted this jumble of driftwood kind of nudged up against the bank. And right there in the middle of it was Quinn. Or what's left of him."

"You're sure it's Quinn?"

"Them channel cats pretty near chewed off his face, but even so, he's a man it's hard not to recognize."

"You can show me where?" Brody rose from the small table on which the chessboard sat.

"I sure can."

"I'd like to come along," Wicklow said.

Without bothering to think about it much, Brody said, "All right." He went to the radio and tried unsuccessfully to raise his deputy, Asa Fielding, then looked back at his chess partner. "I'm going to have to put you back in your cell, Felix."

"I'd like to come, too," Felix said.

"I'll tell you all about it when I get back."

Brody pulled a ring of keys from a drawer in the office desk and led Felix through a metal door to the cellblock. Because his missing toes made balance a little precarious, Felix walked carefully to the cell, where he'd slept the night before after Brody had brought him in for being drunk and urinating in public in front of the Alabaster Inn. Felix couldn't go before a judge on a charge until court convened following the holiday weekend, so the cell was his temporary home. Which was not uncommon.

"You're proposing to leave me here alone?" Felix said.

"No choice," Brody replied.

"And what if there's a fire and I'm locked up?"

"The building is brick, Felix."

"Wooden floorboards and joists," Felix pointed out.

"Felix . . ." Brody began.

"Lots of wood furniture in this place. And you know yourself, Brody, that most deaths in fires are caused not by burns but smoke inhalation. You want that on your conscience?"

"All right, all right," Brody said, because he didn't want to keep arguing. "But stay out of my way."

Through the open window in the east wall came sunlight and a summer breeze and the sounds of the celebration. Brody thought about his deputy, who was walking the parade route, helping to maintain order. He considered whether he should wade into things and let Deputy Fielding know what was up. But that would mean he'd have to endure a lot of handshaking and backslapping and questions about why he was not in his army uniform and marching with the other vets, things he wanted no part of.

Back in the office, he found Herman Ostberg perusing the wanted posters and notices tacked to the bulletin board that hung on the wall. Sam Wicklow stood at the opened doorway of the jailhouse, staring outside down the street toward the hoopla. Wicklow was another man who opted not to walk with the veterans in the yearly parade. Brody wondered if it was because Wicklow was self-conscious about his awkward gait or if, like himself, he simply found the whole thing uncomfortable. He'd never asked. He figured he probably never would. A man made his own choices for his own reasons, and unless any of those choices put him in opposition to you, you simply let them be.

Brody wrote a note to Asa Fielding and left it on the desk. While he wrote, he said, "You parked out front, Herman?"

"Yeah. My truck."

"Go on out. We're right behind you."

When Ostberg had left, Brody said, "You just happen to be here at the right time, Sam? Happy coincidence?"

Wicklow shook his head. "Saw Ostberg speed into town behind the parade going way too fast. He almost clipped the rear end of the Co-op float. I watched him cut up Cottonwood Street and head toward your office. I thought it was worth the trouble of following."

"Jimmy Quinn," Felix said. "If it's true what Ostberg says, feeding those catfish is just about the only unselfish thing that man ever did."

"Come on, Hector," Brody called to his dog. To Sam Wicklow and Felix Klein he said, "Let's go see for ourselves what the truth is."

CHAPTER THREE

JEWEL WAS NESTLED in a crook where the Alabaster made a wide turn in its course. Brody followed Ostberg's dusty pickup over the bridge at the edge of town. They turned south and the road climbed out of the narrow river valley, and in a few minutes, they were driving through farmland, between fields striped green with rows of young corn. Outside Jewel, the road turned to dirt and gravel and became bone-rattling washboard. The air that day was still, and Ostberg's tires kicked up a thick cloud of dust visible for a mile.

Felix Klein sat in the back of Brody's cruiser, Hector beside him placidly gazing at the land sliding past. Wicklow sat up front and watched Ostberg churning up dust ahead. For a newspaperman, Brody thought he seemed awfully quiet.

"I saw Jimmy in church last Sunday. Him and the kids," Felix said. He spoke loud in order to be heard over the road noise.

"Not Marta?" Brody said, speaking of Quinn's wife.

Felix shook his head. "Too sick, apparently."

"Did you talk to him?"

"Only to say hello."

"How'd he look?"

"He didn't look like he'd be feeding catfish pretty soon."

Wicklow finally spoke. "I once saw a man chewed on by fish. Carp, most likely."

"Yeah? Where?" Brody asked.

"The Philippines. Leyte. A Japanese soldier. He'd been in the water awhile."

Some people might have asked for more, wanted the gruesome details. Brody simply said, "Wonder how long Quinn's been in that river."

Wicklow said, "I'm wondering if Marta's missed him yet." Then added, "Or ever will."

Under the warm afternoon sun, the land rolled gently into the distance, reminding Brody of a restless sea, and the scattered farmhouses were like ships riding those swells. A century earlier all this had been wild grass taller than a man. But every bit of that tall grass was now cropland, and the winding course of the Alabaster River, outlined on both banks by the dense growth of broad-leafed trees, was easy for the eye to follow.

Just before he came to the bridge on County 7, Ostberg turned his old pickup in to a couple of ruts that ran through wild oats and milkweed and timothy grass. He pulled into a turnabout, an area worn bare of vegetation. Brody was familiar with the place, a spot where a lot of fishermen parked and also folks planning to swim in a deep pool just upriver. Ostberg killed his engine and got out. Brody did the same and then opened the back door for Hector to hop out and Klein to follow. Wicklow maneuvered himself out the cruiser's passenger side.

"Bring your camera," Brody told him.

Which was an unnecessary directive, because Sam Wicklow's camera was as much a part of him as that prosthetic leg.

Hector trotted ahead of the men, sniffing his way, looking back periodically to check on Brody. After a hundred yards, Ostberg cut into the trees along a path that wove down to the Alabaster. It was a path Brody knew well, and he found himself thinking, *Not here. God, not here.* They came out on a little beach nestled beneath a sandstone cliff where the river curled in on itself, forming a deep, gently swirling pool. Dragonflies darted over the water and swifts shot into and out of little holes in the cliff face where they'd built nests. The pool was heavily shaded by cottonwoods, which loomed atop the high banks of the river. It was a beautiful spot, popular for swimming. And for skinny-dipping. For Brody, the pool conjured up a number of treasured memories in that regard.

"Over there," Ostberg said, pointing.

Brody saw the humping of driftwood and detritus caught where the current of the river nudged against the cliff. To Hector, he said, "Stay," and the dog settled himself patiently in the shade.

The sheriff walked slowly, taking note of the many footprints in the sand that edged the pool. People had been here, but there'd been no rain for a week, so probably no way of telling when. As he neared the woody tangle, he saw what Ostberg had seen, a body caught up among the limbs and branches. He also noted an indication of aquatic activity, ripples where the body met water.

Behind him, he heard the click of a shutter and the crank of film being wound. He glanced back and saw that Sam Wicklow was already shooting.

The body was positioned on its back, legs sticking into the current of the river. The head was turned to the side, so that Brody looked directly into the face, or what was left of it. The eyelids and eyes and nose had been eaten completely. So had most of the lips, which gave the face the grin of a Halloween skeleton. The skin was puckered and wrinkled. Brody could see a portion of the lower torso in the tea-colored water and could see the cavity below the ribs, where even as he watched, he caught the black flicker of a tail as a small catfish darted in and then out of the great gaping wound. Although there'd been a lot of carnage done, Brody, like Ostberg, could tell that he was looking at what was left of Jimmy Quinn. This was because of the great mane of red hair and the size of the body itself.

"Sam," he said over his shoulder. "I need you to document this."

He stepped back and let the newsman snap away. Ostberg kept his distance.

After Wicklow had shot the body from every possible angle, Brody said, "I could use a hand here, Herman."

"With what?"

"I want to get his body out of the river."

"Uh-uh," Ostberg said. "No way I'm touching him."

"I'll help," Felix offered.

"With those missing toes, you have trouble just standing up," Brody pointed out.

"Let me help," Wicklow said.

What they laid out on the sand was a gruesome sight. Except for a pair of striped boxer shorts, Quinn was naked. His chest, all rock-hard muscle in life, was no less massive in death, but it looked waxen, unreal. Wicklow began snapping photos again.

"Herman," Brody said without looking up. "I need a favor."

"What?" Ostberg replied with a cringing tone, as if whatever Brody was going to suggest was bound to be something awful.

"Would you go into town and find Deputy Fielding? Tell him what's going on and have him get Doc Porter."

"Doc Porter? Hell, Brody, the doc can't do anything for Jimmy now."

"He's the county coroner, Herman. I can't move Quinn until Porter has certified death."

"Certified? Brody, I never laid eyes on a man more certifiably dead. Hell, a moron could see Jimmy ain't coming back."

"Would you just do it, Herman?"

"This wasn't exactly the way I'd planned to spend my day," Ostberg complained. "I'll find 'em and send 'em back, but I'm done here, okay?"

"I understand, and I appreciate your help." As Ostberg headed away, Brody said, "Felix, will you go with him and give him a hand? But don't forget, you're still under arrest."

"Nothing I can do here?"

"Not at the moment. When you find Fielding, tell him to bring a body bag and his pickup so we can haul Quinn back to town. And don't say anything to anyone else about this, okay?"

"You can count on me," Felix replied.

"Not a problem," Brody told him. "When you're sober."

"If you'd suffered what I've suffered, Sheriff, bourbon would be your good friend, too."

It was a line Brody had heard often from the man. He could have replied that he'd seen plenty himself and knew a thing or two about suffering and that bourbon was not his answer to the night sweats, but Brody didn't. Like so much else in his past, this was a subject on which he chose to remain silent.

When Felix and Ostberg had gone, the sheriff asked Wicklow, "Anything like that Jap soldier you saw in the Philippines?"

"Big difference," Wicklow said. "That soldier wasn't my neighbor. What do you think? Drowned?"

"I'm guessing not. Drowned folks, their lungs fill with water and they've got no buoyancy. They stay under quite a while. Days."

"Jimmy'd still be on the river bottom then?"

"That would be my guess."

Wicklow considered this a moment. "So you think he went into the water dead?"

Brody nodded. "And floated until the current brought him here."

"Heart attack, maybe, and he fell in? The way he's dressed, he might have been getting ready to swim."

"Maybe." Brody stood up. "Once our coroner takes a look at him, we'll know more."

"What about Marta?"

"What about her?"

"When are you going to tell her?"

Brody looked up at the sky, a shattered blue among the boughs of the big cottonwoods overhead. "Soon," he said.

For the most part, after that, both men held to silence and their own thoughts. It might seem odd, the casualness of these two as they kept company with the grisly remains. But war does something vile and irreparable to the human spirit, leaves thick scars on the soul. For Brody, however, there was another reason for silence. He was feeling a burning resentment because this was a place that had meant much to him, that was almost sacred in its way. On many occasions in his youth, this placid pool had offered him the beautiful nakedness of the only woman he'd ever loved. Now it felt to him desecrated, ruined by that damn Jimmy Quinn.

CHAPTER FOUR

FELIX KLEIN RETURNED to the Alabaster River with Deputy Asa Fielding and Doc Porter, who officially declared Quinn dead. Porter said he'd do the autopsy in the morning, then headed back to the festivities in Jewel. The remaining men zipped up Quinn's corpse in a body bag, which they loaded in the back of Asa Fielding's pickup and drove directly to Brown's Funeral Home. Although it was Decoration Day, there was always someone at the funeral home, because, as Fred Brown was fond of saying, death never took a holiday.

Brown wasn't there, but Alice, his wife, was, and she supplied Brody with a gurney. They got Quinn into one of the funeral home's two prep rooms, where they slid him into the mortuary refrigerator to await the coroner's examination. Quinn wasn't alone in there.

"Who's that?" Brody asked when Alice opened the door to the appliance and he saw another body bag on a lower shelf.

"Ruth Coffee."

"Ruth?" Brody's heart gave the kind of painful twist it never would over the death of Jimmy Quinn. "How?"

"The folks at River Haven called us. We brought her in a couple of hours ago. She died real peaceful in her rocking chair this morning. They thought she was napping, until they tried to wake her for lunch."

"How come I wasn't called?"

"We tried your office. No answer."

Brody had known Ruth Coffee his whole life. She'd taught English forever at the high school in Jewel, and every kid in town passed through her classroom on the way to graduation. What Brody remembered best about his own time there was that she loved to read to her students from the classics and had a way of making even the most ancient of prose seem alive and relevant. It felt wrong to him that such a woman should have to reside in proximity to the monstrosity that had been Jimmy Quinn.

By the time Brody and the others returned to the jailhouse, the parade was long over and the festivities had moved to the park on the river. The town felt a little deserted.

Inside the jailhouse, Brody said, "I've got to lock you up, Felix."

He walked the man back to his cell, but Felix paused before he entered it, turned to Brody, and said, "It's my birthday today. I turned sixty."

"I didn't know that, Felix."

"After Hannah died, I stopped caring. Didn't seem much point to celebrating an empty life."

Brody wasn't sure he saw the point the man was trying to make.

"You know, I served in the Great War."

"I know, Felix."

"Every time I woke to a new day, I celebrated. That's because I never expected to come back alive. Amazing how in the middle of hell something as simple as dawn can be the most beautiful thing imaginable. I'm thinking about Jimmy Quinn and that I never saw a smile on the man's face. He had a wealth of blessings, but I never once saw him celebrate his life. And now he's lost his chance. Makes me think it's time I started celebrating again before it's too late."

"Hold on to that thought," Brody said as he closed the cell door.

When he stepped back into the office, he found young Scott Madison talking with Asa Fielding and Sam Wicklow. Scott's mother, Angie, one of the many war widows in Black Earth County, ran the Wagon Wheel Café. Because the county contracted with her to supply meals when someone was in lockup, fourteen-year-old Scott had become a regular visitor, dropping by with a tray of food or to check on what a prisoner might like. Brody had become fond of the kid, who spoke politely, stood up straight, and treated his elders with the respect people in Black Earth County expected from well-brought-up youths.

"Mom sent me over to see what Mr. Klein might like for supper," Scott told Brody.

"Why don't you ask him?"

When Brody brought Scott into the cellblock, Felix smiled and stood up from his cot. "What's on the menu, son?"

"Mom says you can have fried chicken or a hot roast pork sandwich."

"Nobody makes fried chicken like Angie," Felix said. "And maybe a little of her apple pie?"

"Yes, sir." Scott studied Felix for a long moment. "Are you okay, Mr. Klein?"

"Not so much, son. Spent much of the afternoon in the company of a dead man. Takes the wind out of your sails."

"Really? Who?"

"That's enough, Felix," Brody said. "Let's go, Scott."

"Don't forget the apple pie," Felix said.

In the office, as the kid prepared to leave, he pressed Brody, "Who was the dead man?"

"I can't tell you that, Scott. His name won't be public for a while."

"How'd he die?"

"I can't tell you that either." He could see Scott was disappointed. "I'm sure you'll know soon enough. The whole town will."

"Oh," Scott said as if he'd just remembered. "Mom wanted to know if you might like some supper, too."

Brody smiled. "Thank her for me but tell her I'm going to eat with my brother's family. Picnic in the park. Decoration Day, you know."

After Scott had gone, Sam Wicklow said, "I should get myself arrested.

Free meals from Angie Madison—that would take the sting out of lockup."

"I'm going out to Quinn's place and talk to Marta," Brody said to Asa. "I want you to cover here. I'm leaving Hector."

"And if anybody asks about you?" his deputy said.

"Until you hear from me that I've informed his family, don't say anything to anyone about Quinn. Am I clear?"

"As a bell, Brody."

"You, too, Sam."

Wicklow nodded. He accompanied Brody outside, where he stood a moment, writing on the little notepad he was never without. "So, Marta next?"

"Yeah." Brody had informed families of death before, but this one was different, and he was feeling the heavy weight of the duty that rested on his shoulders.

"Don't suppose I could go along."

"You want to talk to her, Sam, you can do it later, if she'll let you. I'll need those photos you shot."

"I'll develop them while you're at the Quinn place. They'll be at the *Clarion* office when you get back." Wicklow closed his notepad.

"Done with covering the Decoration Day celebration, Sam?"

"There'll be another next year. But Jimmy Quinn and the catfish?" Wicklow shook his head. "Once in a lifetime."

CHAPTER FIVE

ON HIS FATHER'S death, James Patrick Quinn had inherited a thousand acres, and in his time, he had added twice as much again. He was the largest landowner in the county, his holdings spread far and wide and managed by a slew of tenants, all of whom feared the wrath of Quinn. As a result, the farming of his land was like clockwork, the tilling, planting, harvesting all begun and completed in the best time frame that weather and the elements would allow. He saw to it that his own outbuildings and those of his tenants were in good repair and wore a clean coat of paint. His equipment was up to date, the most modern available. Jimmy Quinn was proud of what he'd accomplished. And he was always the first to tell you so.

The large acreage that he farmed himself required help, and for this Quinn relied heavily, as most farmers do, on family. Quinn had been married twice. Gudrun, his first wife, had died in her early forties, but she'd given him two children. With his second wife, Marta, he'd fathered three more. The two older children had grown up and gone on to lives of their own. Terence, the oldest, had bought land in Faribault County, a good distance east, and farmed there. The daughter, Fiona, had married her high school history teacher. It was a scandal because she'd only just graduated and less than six months after the wedding gave birth to their first child. Shortly thereafter, she and her new little family left Jewel for good.

The children from his first marriage were of no help to Quinn. They'd deserted him, or that's how he was prone to characterize it. So he demanded much from his second brood, especially the eldest, James Patrick Quinn, Jr., eighteen years old in that summer of 1958.

Over the years, Quinn had hired numerous men to work for him part-time, some of them young and hoping to save enough money to buy a farm of their own one day, some already small farmers in their own right who supplemented their income working for the big Irishman.

The Quinn farm was seven miles south of Jewel, along the banks of the Alabaster River. When Brody turned up the lane off the county highway, he could see activity near the barn, where Quinn kept a small herd of beef cattle. As Brody drove between the young fields—corn to his right, soybeans to his left—he watched three men trying to run down a big black bull that was making a mess of Quinn's tidy crop rows. Brody pulled into the yard and parked between the farmhouse and the great array of outbuildings. He stepped out, walked to the fence, leaned against the top rail, and watched the chase in the cornfield. He considered offering to help, but he knew about bulls, knew they were cantankerous creatures, and he figured he'd just stay put and see how things played out.

"Big Bastard."

He turned and watched a girl of fourteen cross the yard and come to where he stood. She was tall for her age, with dark red hair, which she wore long. She had on jeans and a blue work shirt with the sleeves rolled above her elbows. Her name was Colleen, and she was Quinn's daughter. She leaned against the same rail as Brody and looked where Brody had been looking.

"Big Bastard?" Brody said.

"The bull," she replied. "That's what J.P. calls him, anyway." She nodded toward her brother, who was one of the figures chasing the animal. "He hates that bull. Daddy named him Big Black, but I like J.P.'s name better. Fits that critter perfect."

"Looks like he's trying to make a break for it."

"He does that sometimes. He wants to get at the cows over there."

Colleen lifted a hand toward the herd milling about in the big cattle yard behind the barn.

"Always this hard to get him corralled?"

"Not if Daddy's here. Him and Big Bastard, they've got an under-standing. Or that's what Daddy claims."

"You don't help?"

"Men's work," she said. "Are you looking for my father?"

"Your mother, actually."

"She's in the house, resting."

"I need to talk to her. It's important."

"Come on then."

Colleen took one final look toward the mayhem going on in the cornfield, turned, and led the way. There was something melancholy about the girl, and Brody thought that maybe anyone whose father was a man like Jimmy Quinn and whose mother was bedridden might be prone to darker moods.

The farmhouse was an enormous two-story clapboard painted white, with gingerbread trim and green shutters. It was a good house, sturdy, built by Quinn's grandfather before the turn of the century. It had been modest then but had been added to and refined over the years, as the prosperity of the Quinns increased. Once inside the house, the girl offered him a seat in the parlor, then she mounted the stairs. On the mantel of the fieldstone fireplace sat an antique-looking clock flanked by framed photographs. One was of Jimmy Quinn alone. He was a huge man, with a great shock of red hair, hard green eyes, and enormous hands like an ape. He wore a three-piece suit and was posed in a way that might make one think of those great robber barons who so horribly misshaped America's history with their greed and hubris. A lot of farmers came into town in their faded, patched, and soiled biballs or dungarees, their boots crusted with barn muck. Not Jimmy Quinn. He claimed to be descended from Irish kings, and he always rolled into Jewel looking like gentry. The other photo was a family portrait with him and Marta and their children. Conspicuously absent was any evidence of Jimmy Quinn's first wife and the two children she bore him.

Through the doorway to his left was the kitchen, and in that doorway stood a girl eyeing him silently.

"Hello, Bridget," he said and smiled.

Quinn's youngest daughter was only eight. Like her sister and her father, she was a redhead, with long pigtails and deep-sunk eyes, which regarded Brody with a look he couldn't quite decode. Was it interest? Apprehension? Did his uniform intimidate her?

"I'm Sheriff Dern," he said. "Remember? I talked to your class last fall about what policemen do."

"I remember," she said, but that didn't change her demeanor. "Do you want some Kool-Aid?" she asked in a flat voice.

"No, thank you," he said.

She continued to stand in the doorway and eye him in a way that was, frankly, unnerving.

He heard boards creak, and a moment later Colleen appeared on the stairs, helping Marta Quinn descend. They came slowly. The effort it took was clear, and Brody offered, "We could talk upstairs, Marta."

She looked up from where she'd been considering each stair carefully before placing her foot. "No, this is fine, Sheriff." She still, after all these years, spoke with a thick German accent. "Just give me a moment."

She wore a pink housecoat buttoned nearly to her chin. On her feet were pink slippers. Her hair, Brody could tell, had just been brushed, probably with Colleen's help, so that she would not appear in complete disarray before her visitor. She wore no makeup, and her face, once quite beautiful, was pale and drawn. She wasn't even forty yet, but her illness made her seem a decade older.

She fixed Brody with dull eyes. "It's about James, isn't it?"

Brody glanced at Colleen, who stood behind the sofa, at her mother's back, with one hand laid gently on the woman's shoulder. "Could we talk alone?"

"Colleen," Marta said, "would you go and make some coffee for us?" She saw her other daughter watching from the kitchen doorway. "And, Bridget, you give your sister a hand, all right?"

"Yes, Mama," Bridget replied.

When the girls had vanished into the kitchen, Marta said, "Where is he this time?"

Jimmy Quinn suffered from insomnia. Everyone knew it. He often dealt with the affliction by driving somewhere in the night and drinking himself into oblivion. Sometimes it was on one of his own properties, sometimes on the land of another family, as if Quinn considered all of Black Earth County his rightful domain. Brody would get the call from an irritated farmer. He would pick up one of the hired men and they would go and collect Quinn. Sometimes the hired man drove Quinn home, and sometimes Brody would haul him back to the jailhouse in Jewel because, when Quinn was drunk, he might take a blind swing at those trying to help him. Brody had plenty to keep him busy as sheriff without such runs, but he did it because, like most folks who understood the circumstances, he had great sympathy for Quinn's family.

"He's in Jewel, Marta." Brody took a deep breath and gave her the rest. "At Brown's Funeral Home."

"The funeral home?" Marta thought about that a moment, then light flared in her dull eyes. "He's . . . dead?"

"Yes, Marta. Your husband's dead. I'm sorry."

Her face, which had already been pale, went even whiter. Her mouth opened, but nothing came out for a while. Then, in little more than a whisper, "How?"

"I don't know exactly. We pulled his body from the Alabaster earlier today."

"Where?"

"Near the bridge on County Seven. My guess is that he went in somewhere upstream and his body floated down."

Marta looked away, out one of the windows. "He went fishing yesterday," she said quietly. "Or at least that's where he said he was going. When he didn't come home all night, I just figured . . . well, you know."

"Yeah," Brody said. "What time did he leave?"

"I don't know exactly. Sometime near dark."

"Did he say where he intended to fish?"

"No."

"Did he take his truck?"

She nodded.

From the kitchen came the sound of a door opening and men's voices, and Colleen speaking words that Brody couldn't quite make out. Then James Patrick Quinn, Jr., strode into the living room. To avoid confusion with his father, most everyone simply called him J.P. He was eighteen and resembled his mother, with dark hair and a physical frame that would never equal Jimmy Quinn's massive build. He was dressed in jeans soiled at both knees, probably from falling in the effort to round up the bull. His boots were caked with dried mud. He wore a Western-style shirt, colorful and with pearl snaps. He carried a brimmed straw hat in his hands.

"Your shoes, Patrick," his mother said.

He didn't seem to hear her. He came straight at Brody. "Where is he? Where'd he pass out this time?"

"Your father didn't pass out," Marta said quietly.

"No? Then where the hell is he?"

"In Jewel," Marta said. "At the funeral home."

"What, he killed somebody?" It was meant as an angry joke, but when he saw the look on his mother's face, he understood. His own face took on a quizzical look. "He's dead?"

"Daddy's dead?" Colleen said from the kitchen doorway. Bridget stood behind her, almost hidden by her older sister.

Marta beckoned them. "Come in, children. Here, Bridget." She patted the cushion beside her. "And, Colleen, here," she said, patting the cushion on her other side.

The two girls did as they'd been told, moving mutely and with faces poised on the edge of some emotion, though Brody couldn't tell yet what that would be. J.P. remained standing. He was holding his straw hat with both hands and staring at the polished wood floor under his dirty boots.

"The sheriff has just informed me that your father is dead. He was found in the Alabaster River this morning."

"Was he swimming or something?" Colleen asked, then looked at Brody.

"We don't know yet exactly what happened," Brody told her. "We retrieved his body and took it to the funeral home in town. That's about it at the moment. I'm sorry."

There was a period of silence while Brody's words soaked in, then J.P. said, "Hell, I'm not."

"Patrick," his mother said, so harshly that even Brody jerked back a little.

J.P. looked down at the floor once more and again went silent.

"Your mother said he was going fishing. Is that what you all understood?" Brody asked of them in general.

"I dunno." Bridget shrugged, and Brody couldn't tell if her blank look was confusion or numbness in the face of such a sudden and overwhelming consideration as the death of her father.

"Bridget wasn't here last night," Marta said. "She was at a sleepover with some friends. At the Baldwins' house."

"I was asleep in my bedroom," Colleen said. "I didn't even hear his truck leave."

Brody glanced at Quinn's son. "Did he say anything to you?"

"I was out on a date last night," J.P. replied. "Wouldn't have mattered, though. He never tells me anything except that I'm not pulling my weight."

One of the hired men stepped in from the kitchen. "Coffee's perking, Mrs. Quinn."

"Remove it from the burner, Able, and then would you come in here for a moment? And bring Tyler with you."

The man stepped away from the door and reappeared a few moments later with the other hired hand. They came into the living room and stood beside J.P.

"Something's happened," Marta said. "Something terrible."

"Yeah, we overheard. Sorry, Mrs. Quinn, couldn't help it." Able Grange poked a thumb back toward the kitchen.

Grange was small but powerfully built, in his late twenties, and recently married. He farmed for both his father-in-law and Quinn, trying to bank enough money so he could someday buy and work his own land.

The other man was Tyler Creasy. He was in his mid-thirties, tall and gaunt, cheeks that were hollows in a horse face. He'd removed his hat when he came into the living room, an old red ball cap, exposing a scalp with only a few long wisps of hay-colored hair remaining. Brody and Creasy had a history; not a good one. The sheriff had known Creasy since they were both boys but never known him well. Creasy came from an extended family that lived along the river south of Jewel in a place folks called Creasy Hollow. They were a bunch that kept to themselves and Tyler, the youngest, was no exception. He'd been a quiet kid, a loner, as Brody recalled. Then, like so many young men, on graduation from high school he went away to war and came back changed. Darker. Harder. Brody had hauled him in a number of times for a variety of reasons, usually involving alcohol and fisticuffs. At the moment, Creasy's hostility was clear in the way he eyed the sheriff.

Brody asked, "Did Jimmy say anything to either of you yesterday about going fishing?"

"Didn't say anything to me," Grange said.

"Me, neither," Creasy said.

Brody looked behind the two hired men, as if searching. "Where's Noah Bluestone?"

"Jimmy let him go a couple of days ago," Creasy said.

"Why was that?"

"They had words," Creasy replied. "Jimmy said he didn't have no need for an uppity Indian and told him to get off the place."

"Any idea what they argued about?"

"Bluestone was stealing gas from the pump. Filling his own truck."

Brody looked at Marta and the children. "And his wife, Kyoko Bluestone? She worked for you, too, right? And Jimmy let her go as well?"

Marta nodded. "He said the girls could do Kyoko's work here in the house."

Brody tried to think if there was anything more he should ask, anything else he should say before he approached the final piece of the unpleasant business.

"I guess that's it for now, folks. Except . . ." Brody hesitated. "Marta, I'm going to need someone to come in and make a positive identification."

"I'll do that," J.P. volunteered.

"No," Marta said. "I'll do it. When would you like me to come, Sheriff?"

"Would tomorrow morning work?"

"Yes. And I'll talk to the people at the funeral home then, too, about the burial arrangements."

"What about his other children?" Brody asked. "Terence and Fiona? Would you like me to break the news to them?"

Marta shook her head. "I'll make those calls."

Brody stood. "Again, I'm sorry to have to bring such bad news."

But looking at those folks, Brody thought they didn't seem to be taking it badly. They were surprised, sure, but grieving? Not at all. At least not yet. Brody knew a thing or two about death and its aftermath and knew that it sometimes took a while for the grief to set in.

J.P. saw him to the door.

"I'll bring my mother tomorrow," the boy said. "Would ten do?"

Brody looked into the young man's eyes and didn't see any of Jimmy Quinn there—the bully, the brute, the blustering Irish giant. He found that reassuring.

"Ten'll be just fine," he said.

CHAPTER SIX

THE SHERIFF'S DEPARTMENT and county jail were housed in a long, narrow, red-brick building that in 1958 was already half a century old. The sheriff's office occupied the small front room. Behind a metal security door was a block of six cells. Upstairs was a living area that, while he wore the badge, was Brody's. The jail was seldom occupied for long. Most crimes in Black Earth County were simple affairs, and sentences usually lasted no more than a few days, or maybe a week or two. Lengthier stays were generally farmed out to the much grander jail in Worthington, a larger town in the adjoining county with, apparently, a more vigorous population of miscreants.

Brody parked on the street. When he entered the jailhouse, Hector leapt to his feet and came trotting to greet him, tail wagging like a crazy metronome. Deputy Asa Fielding was there, but not alone. Gordon Landis was with him. Landis had once been a police officer in Saint Paul. He claimed to have left the force of his own volition, but rumors circulated that he was let go because of his cruelty in handling offenders. He'd returned to Jewel and taken over the running of the Alabaster Inn, which his family owned. Brody didn't like the man. His official nickname was Gordy, but out of his hearing Brody and his deputies often referred to him as "Gory" because he was easily inclined to share publicly the unpleasant details of the car wrecks and other bloody incidents he claimed to have been involved with while in uniform.

"Heard about Jimmy Quinn," Landis said. "Heard you found him in the river, chewed up by catfish. True?"

Brody wasn't happy that Quinn's death was already public knowledge. He trusted Asa Fielding and Sam Wicklow, so he figured it had been Herman Ostberg who'd opened his big mouth. Brody simply gave Landis a nod.

"He kill himself or somebody do that for him?"

"We just got the investigation under way," Brody replied.

"Whoo-ee, this'll set folks back on their heels." Landis laughed as if it were an entertaining joke. "You need a hand, you let me know."

"Will do."

Landis looked toward the cellblock. "Klein giving you any trouble?"

"Felix? Only on the chessboard, Gordy."

"Well, listen good," Landis said, loud enough that Felix could hear from his jail cell. "Next time he decides to use the parking lot of the Alabaster Inn as his private toilet, I'll cut off his pecker and shove it up his ass."

"I'll keep that in mind," Brody said.

When Landis had gone, Asa said, "Fred Brown called from the funeral home. Wants you to call him back."

"Did he say why?"

"Nope. But I'm just the deputy here."

Asa Fielding was a strapping young man. He'd been a bit of a hellion in his teenage years, but he'd gone into the service during the Korean War, had served his entire tour of duty as an MP, and had come back with a respect for authority he hadn't shown before. He'd married Suzie Thorndike, former cheerleader and his high school sweetheart. When an opening had come up for a deputy, Brody had hired him. Asa had proved himself to be a man of restraint, and because of his size, he was good to have along when Brody was trying to subdue a guy who'd had too much to drink and was just itching for a fight. Asa was his deputy and his colleague, but Brody didn't think of him as a friend. In truth, Brody had few of those.

Asa stood up, offering the sheriff the desk chair. Brody sat, lifted the telephone receiver from its cradle, and dialed the number of the funeral home. When Brown picked up, Brody said, "You asked Asa to have me call."

"Doc Porter's doing an autopsy on Quinn tomorrow morning, is that right?"

"That's the plan," Brody replied.

"Is Quinn's family coming in to make funeral arrangements?"

"Marta will be there to make an official ID. She'll probably make the arrangements then. Plan on that for around ten."

"Hope you don't mind, but I took a cursory look at Quinn. Those catfish did a lot of damage, but it's still pretty easy to see what killed the man."

Brody waited.

"That wound's full of buckshot," Brown said.

"He was killed by a shotgun blast?"

"That's probably what tore him open and gave the catfish such a glorious meal. But don't quote me. Doc Porter'll want to give the official word."

After he hung up, Brody sat a few moments, mulling over what he'd just been told. He finally looked up to see Asa Fielding eyeing him curiously.

"Did I hear right?" Asa asked. "Somebody shotgunned Jimmy Quinn?"

"You repeat that to anyone, I'll rip that badge off your shirt, Asa."

"But it's true, right?"

"That's what Brown thinks."

"A murder?"

"Let's not call it anything until we know all the facts, okay?"

The jailhouse door opened, and Garnet Dern, Brody's sister-in-law, walked in, accompanied by her youngest child, Jack.

Garnet's maiden name was Olson. Even as a young girl, she was a

Nordic beauty—long, buttercup-yellow hair, eyes like little chips of blue sky. She came from a farming family, and although she grew up used to hard work, she possessed a softness of spirit that seemed rare and terribly ephemeral, and made you feel a little like grieving because you knew that the demands of a farming life would, over time, probably suck all of that loveliness out of her.

"Uncle Brody," seven-year-old Jack cried out happily. "We came to arrest you."

"Arrest me?" Brody laughed. "What for?"

"For promises unkept," Garnet replied. That Decoration Day she wore khaki shorts and a sleeveless blouse almost exactly the same ethereal blue as her eyes. On her feet were sandals, and you could see that the color of the polish on her toenails, a joyful red, matched her fingernails. She wagged one of those fingers at Brody. "You promised to picnic with us, remember?"

"Things have been busy around here today."

"I heard Felix Klein is your guest. Is he such hard work? Really?" She gave him a look of playful admonition.

"Jimmy Quinn's dead," Asa said.

Brody shot his deputy a killing look.

"Jimmy Quinn?" Garnet's eyes bloomed huge. "How?"

"We're still investigating that," Brody said.

"Don't be officious with me, Brody Dern. How did Jimmy die?"

"Honestly, we can't say for sure. He's at Brown's Funeral Home right now. Doc Porter intends to do a full autopsy tomorrow, and we'll know more. Until then, I'm really not at liberty to say anything, Garnet."

Her face took on a look of deep, genuine concern. "How's Marta?"

"I just came from talking with her," Brody said. "She's holding up."

"Uncle Brody, can I have one of these?" Jack stood at the bulletin board where Brody pinned the wanted posters.

"Not any of those, but I'll give you one of these." Brody opened the bottom desk drawer and pulled out an old circular, one for a man named Albert Jenkins, a.k.a. Arthur Jenks, a.k.a. Anthony Jurgens, wanted for several armed robberies in small towns across the Midwest.

"Wow," Jack said. "Is he dangerous?"

"Not anymore. He was killed last week in an exchange of gunfire with policemen in Waterloo, Iowa."

"Have you ever shot anybody, Uncle Brody?"

"That's not an appropriate question," the boy's mother said.

Brody answered anyway. "Not on the job, Jack."

"In the war?" the boy persisted.

"Jack, that's enough about killing." Garnet smiled apologetically at Brody. "Will we see you at all today?"

"Probably not."

Garnet looked down at the scuffed old floorboards and said quietly, "We hardly ever see you these days."

"I'll be by for Sunday dinner, as usual. Promise."

"You promised to picnic with us today, too."

"Can I see the jail?" Jack asked.

"I have someone in lockup right now. Another time." Brody met his sister-in-law's eyes. "Another time, promise."

"Come on, Jack," Garnet said, brightening suddenly. "Let's get you back to the park. You can show everybody your poster. Tell your uncle thank you."

"Thanks," Jack said and was out the door.

Garnet gave Deputy Fielding a lovely parting smile and followed her son outside into the bright sunlight. In that old jailhouse, which, across all the years of use had seen every kind of imaginable befouling, Brody's sister-in-law left behind only the overpowering scent of gardenia.

"You really skipping the festivities entirely?" Asa said.

Brody pulled his eyes from the doorway. "We still have Quinn business to see to."

"Oh? What's that?"

"We're going to find his pickup."

"What about Felix?"

Brody took the key ring from the desk drawer and turned toward the cellblock. Just then, Scott Madison entered the office carrying a covered tray and bringing in the enticing aroma of fried chicken.

"Mr. Klein's dinner," the kid said.

"Wait there," Brody told him.

Felix, who'd been lying on his bunk, sat up and swung his feet to the floor. "Dinner?"

"Nope. I'm springing you." Brody unlocked the cell door.

"Gordon Landis won't like this," Felix said.

"Let me worry about Landis. But, Felix, promise me you'll be at the courthouse Monday morning at nine. And no alcohol in the meantime."

"What about my dinner?"

"Scott's here with your fried chicken. Just go back to the Wagon Wheel with him and you can eat it there. Tell Angie it's still on the county's tab."

Although Felix left with Scott Madison, he didn't look particularly thrilled with the idea of freedom, probably not sure what to do with it, but he was clearly eager to dig into the dinner Angie had prepared for him. Asa Fielding glanced at the big round wall clock and said, "Lots of ground to check before dark. Maybe we should bring Connie in on this."

Conrad "Connie" Graff was the previous sheriff of Black Earth County. For nine years, Brody had served as his deputy, then Graff's wife had become seriously ill and Graff had decided that taking care of her was more important than being sheriff. In the election that followed, Gordon Landis ran against Brody for the office. Graff threw his support to Brody, who'd won easily. After Graff's wife died, Brody brought Graff back onto the force as a periodic deputy, often using him to cover when Brody or Fielding needed a little vacation time, or when some extraordinary event demanded additional law enforcement presence.

"Good idea," Brody said. "Give him a call."

Asa picked up the phone and dialed.

CHAPTER SEVEN

THE ALABASTER ALWAYS had a thriving fish population—those raven-ous channel catfish, of course, but also bullheads, carp, bass, shovelnose sturgeon, even the occasional walleye, and probably a lot more that savvy fishermen could name. There were fast channels in the river, deep holes, areas of snag, and where you fished depended on what you hoped to catch.

Brody didn't know what Quinn went fishing for on the day he disappeared. That left pretty much the entire Alabaster below Jewel to be checked.

It was still a few hours until sunset when he pulled his cruiser to the side of the road at the east end of the bridge on the old Soldier Highway. The road was so named because, when it was little more than a couple of ruts across prairie land, it had served as a major military route during the Dakota War of 1862.

Conrad Graff was already there, sitting on the flatbed of his old pickup, smoking a hand-rolled cigarette. Graff was tall, slender, as tough as jerky. His eyes were the gray of a gun barrel, and his nose was hawked, set in a face gone to leather from age and the summer suns and the bone chill of winter winds. He wore the khaki pants that had been part of his uniform as sheriff and above them a faded blue Pendleton work shirt rolled up to his biceps, which still had the look of steel. A beat-to-hell gray Stetson shaded his face.

Brody exited his cruiser. Hector jumped out behind him and shot toward the high wild grass that edged the pavement, where he lifted his leg to pee.

"Where's Fielding?" Graff said as Brody approached.

"I told him to check the trestle on his way out. Good fishing spot."

Graff let out a stream of smoke the color of his Stetson. "Jimmy Quinn. Shotgunned." He shook his head. "Pissed off half the men in this county at one time or another, but a shotgun? Hell of a way to take care of a slight."

Brody put his hands on the flatbed, lifted himself, and sat beside Graff. "We don't know what's happened, Connie."

Graff laughed. "Yeah, officially. Me, I'm well and truly done with 'officially.' I can say whatever the hell I please."

Initially, Brody had asked Graff to come back as a part-time deputy out of affection and loyalty because he thought he would be doing his old boss a favor. As a widower, Graff had seemed a little lost, uncertain what to do with himself. But Brody had found the older law officer to be full of sage advice and helpful in so many ways that he annually budgeted a significant sum to ensure Graff would continue to be a presence on the force when needed.

"You're still officially a deputy, a sworn officer of the law."

"You want my badge?" Graff grinned from under the shadow of his hat brim.

"I want your discretion, Connie."

After finishing his business, Hector dashed to the bridge and began sniffing his way around the abutments.

"You talk to his family?" Graff said.

"Of course."

"How'd they take it?"

"Stoic, I'd say." Brody's eyes scanned the line of trees that marked the Alabaster's course all the way to the southern horizon. "When Asa gets here, if he didn't find anything at the trestle, I figure we'll work our way south down to the pool where Quinn's body got hung up. You and Asa take the east side of the Alabaster, I'll take the west."

"A lot of river to cover with a lot of foliage that could hide a truck. Might take a good long while."

"Got something better to do?"

Graff took a final drag off his cigarette and flicked the butt onto the gravel just as Asa Fielding's pickup appeared down the road. The deputy parked behind Brody's cruiser and walked to where the two men sat.

"Anything?" Brody asked.

"An old hobo camp in some trees near the trestle. Whoever they were, they're gone now. No truck or any other sign that Quinn had been there. Hey, Connie," he finally said in greeting.

"Asa," Graff replied with an almost imperceptible nod.

"So what now?" Asa asked.

Brody explained his plan, and the three men separated. Half an hour later, Brody found Quinn's truck.

The Alabaster, like every river, follows the line of least resistance. Seven miles south of Jewel stood a geologic uplift called the Fordham Ridge. Fourteen thousand years ago, during what is known as the New Ulm phase of that glacial period, a lobe of thick ice stretched down into Iowa all the way to the area occupied now by Des Moines. In its retreat, it left behind large deposits of drift, mostly sand and pea gravel through which the Alabaster early and easily cut a course. But the glacier also left behind a number of gently curving ridges and knobby hills composed of more solid rock, which the ice couldn't bulldoze and around which the river found its meandering way. Fordham Ridge was a long, worming uprise that caused the river to almost reverse itself in a tight curl. In its shadow, on the finger of land circumscribed by the curling course of the river, lay Inkpaduta Bend, an area of open land owned by the county. It was a lovely spot, especially at sunset, when Fordham Ridge caught the last, amber-colored light of day and the terraced farmlands on the slopes looked as if they were covered in honey.

When Brody pulled up behind Quinn's pickup, there was still plenty of good light to see by. The truck was parked at the end of a lane almost completely overgrown with wild oats and goldenrod and blazing star and a dozen other wildflowers. It sat twenty yards from the Alabaster, grille toward the water. Brody approached the vehicle slowly and peered through the window on the driver's side of the cab. A pair of soiled calfskin work gloves lay on the seat and next to them an emptied pint bottle of Jim Beam rye whiskey. There was a gun rack affixed to the back of the cab. Like the liquor bottle, it was empty.

He went on toward the Alabaster, which in that particular section, was lined with birch trees. There was a wide break in the trees through which the surface of the Alabaster shimmered gold in the late afternoon light. From a distant field came the diesel chug of a tractor. But there were other sounds Brody heard: the rustle and sigh of the branches and leaves of the birches as wind blew through, and the calling of an oriole perched somewhere among all that shifting foliage. Brody stopped. Stopped because he knew without having to think it that what he was about to discover was something alien to the peace of that lovely place. It was an experience he'd already had that day, beside the pool whose beauty had been desecrated by the torn-open carcass of Jimmy Quinn. In life, Quinn was a man Brody had never much cared for. In death, he was a man Brody was beginning to hate.

He moved forward and found where Quinn had set up to fish, if fishing was, indeed, the reason the man had come to this out-of-the-way location. A rod lay on the riverbank and next to it an opened tackle box and a Coleman lantern. A pair of pants, a blue work shirt, and white undershirt, all large enough to have fit Quinn, lay in a careless pile near the rod and tackle box, and on top of these sat a pair of huge work boots and gray socks. In the middle of a large area of blood-soaked earth between the clothing and the fishing gear lay a shotgun.

Brody returned to his cruiser and radioed his deputies.

—

"QUINN'S SHOTGUN?" ASA Fielding asked. He stood well away from the blood-darkened earth.

"That'll be easy enough to check," Graff said.

"Came to fish, and then what?"

"Got no bites and maybe got frustrated and decided to end it all," Graff said. "Jimmy was not known for his patience."

Hector sat leashed to the door handle of Brody's cruiser. Every so often, he made a pleading sound or gave a short bark. Brody paid no attention. He stood at the edge of the river. The winter snow that year had been deep, the spring wetter than usual, and even on the threshold of summer, the Alabaster still ran high and fast.

"There's that pint bottle in the truck," Asa said. "Quinn was probably drinking. So an accident maybe?"

Graff thumbed his Stetson high above his wrinkled brow. "I hunted pheasant and wild turkey with Jimmy back in the day. That man knew his way around a firearm, even drunk. What are you looking at, Brody?"

"Just gauging the river. We got a deep, fast channel along here, so when Quinn's body entered the water, it would have been swept downstream pretty easy."

"And how'd he get into the water?" Asa asked.

"We need photos of everything," Graff said. "That old Brownie we got won't do. Asa, you mind going back into town to get Sam Wicklow and his Leica out here?"

Brody said, "No."

Graff gave him a puzzled glance.

Brody nodded toward the western sky, where the sun was a burning orange ball not far above the horizon. "It'll be going on dark by the time Wicklow gets here."

Graff eyed the sun and gave in. "Tomorrow morning then, first thing."

"I'll spend the night here," Brody said.

Asa said, "Who'll cover at the jailhouse?"

"Connie, you willing to sleep on a cot tonight?"

"Rather sleep out here."

Brody shook his head. "I've got this."

"All right, then," Graff agreed. "You have bedding for yourself?"

"A couple of blankets in the trunk of my cruiser. That'll do."

"What about dinner?" Asa said. "You're going to get hungry."

"One night without dinner won't kill me."

"Be happy to bring out a sandwich," Graff offered.

"Just cover the jailhouse."

Asa Fielding left first. After he was gone, Graff took a final look around and shook his head. "There's a lot that's not right here, Brody."

"Tomorrow, we'll see about sorting it out."

Brody waited until both deputies were well away from Inkpaduta Bend, then he returned to the riverbank. He stood a long time looking over the items Quinn had left there. He went to his cruiser and took from the trunk the chamois cloth he used to wipe the vehicle dry whenever he washed it. He started with Quinn's truck, wiping clean the door handles, the steering wheel, the dash, the whiskey bottle. He went to the riverbank and wiped down the tackle box, the Coleman lantern, and the handle of the fishing rod. He lifted the big shotgun from the middle of the great stain of blood and wiped that clean, too. Finally, he circled the whole scene searching in the wild grass for anything he might have missed. He found another empty pint bottle of Beam splashed with blood. He held it to the dying light and saw fingerprints all over the glass.

"God damn you, Jimmy Quinn," he said.

He cast the bottle into the middle of the river, where the current snatched it away, and he stood watching as it filled with the tea-colored water of the Alabaster and sank utterly from sight.

CHAPTER EIGHT

IN 1857, AN Indian named Inkpaduta led a small band of renegade Wahpe-
kute on a bloody raid that began in Iowa near Spirit Lake and extended
into what is now southern Minnesota. They killed many dozen settlers along the way and took four white women prisoner. They were
believed to have camped several days on the Alabaster River, at the
base of Fordham Ridge, hence the name of the point of land where
Brody, more than a century later, lay on a blanket, his head cradled on
a second blanket rolled into a makeshift pillow, and stared up at a black
sky powdered with stars. It was a warm night, full of life. From the tall
grass all around him came the chirr of spring field crickets. Tree frogs
sang in the birches that lined the river. From high up Fordham Ridge
came occasional yips and howls that he was pretty sure were coyotes.
He was about as far away from another human being as you could get
in Black Earth County, and he felt empty. This wasn't a new feeling. It
didn't come over him suddenly just because he lay alone under such a
vast night sky. Brody felt empty most of the time.

He'd never married, though he'd been in love. Once. Crazy in love.
It hadn't turned out well. Then he'd gone to war and had come back
a different man, his heart scarred by wounds far worse than any love
could deliver.

He'd been lying wide awake for an hour after hard dark when Hector, who'd been asleep in the grass nearby, lifted his head and gave a low

growl. Brody put out his hand and stroked his dog's back, which had gone stiff. "What is it, boy?"

Then Brody heard a noise, maybe the same one Hector had picked up. It sounded like soft crying, almost human. He strained to hear more clearly, but the noise was already gone.

Coyotes, Brody told himself. Coyotes that had come down to the river to drink.

Still, the land was mysterious. Two of the women taken captive during Inkpaduta's raid had been killed by the renegades in their flight, and there were those who believed that at least one of the murders had taken place on Inkpaduta Bend. No one really knew the truth, but the story in Black Earth County was that you could sometimes hear the woman crying. And Brody thought that if one of those poor women had, in fact, met her end there, then who knew? Everything that died became a part of the earth where it lay, and maybe more than just flesh and bone was involved in that kind of transfer. Spirit, perhaps. If so, what kind of spirit resided in a place where brutal death had occurred? A soul that still wept? Brody wasn't particularly superstitious, but he couldn't help feeling that something was on that bend with him.

But in almost the same moment Brody thought these things, Hector growled again and was answered by the low, distant growl of a car engine as a vehicle slowly made its way along the grown-over lane that led to the tip of Inkpaduta Bend. Brody looked at his watch. The luminous face indicated ten forty-five. Graff? he wondered. Or Fielding? Some trouble?

He threw off his blanket and stood. Hector was already up on all fours, looking in the direction of the engine noise. The headlights cut a wide swath in the dark, and Brody saw night insects dart across the beams. He couldn't tell the make of the vehicle yet but could see that it was a sedan of some kind. It drew up behind his cruiser. The lights died and the engine was turned off. The driver's door opened, and a figure emerged, black against the paler dark under the stars.

"Hello, Brody."

The voice was soft, melodious, playful, and Brody recognized it instantly.

"Hello, Garnet." He didn't bother to hide his pleasure.

"Brought you something," she said, walking toward him through the high grass. When she was near enough that he could smell her perfume, she reached out her right hand, which held a paper plate covered in aluminum foil. "When you didn't come down for the fireworks, I went to the jailhouse and found Connie Graff. He told me you were here and that you'd be hungry. I brought you some cold fried chicken and potato salad. Cookies, too. And I have a ham bone for Hector, if that's okay."

"Thanks."

He took the plate, laid it on the hood of the cruiser. "Does Tom know you're here?"

Tom was Brody's brother, Garnet's husband.

"After we packed up the picnic things at the park, I told him I wanted to stay behind and help the ladies' auxiliary clean up their area. I kept the car, and he took the kids and your mom home in the pickup. He's in bed by now, dead to the world." She looked toward the river. "So, you found the place where Jimmy died?"

"Pretty sure."

"How did it happen?"

"There's a lot of blood and his shotgun's in the middle of it. It's clear he did some serious drinking. So maybe a horrible accident. Or maybe he killed himself deliberately."

"Jimmy Quinn? Suicide?" She sounded incredulous.

"I've seen stranger things."

"Is it possible he was murdered?"

"Which of your neighbors do you want to accuse?"

She reached out her hand and ran her fingers slowly down the line of his cheekbone. "You'll get to the bottom of it, Brody. I know you will.

You're very good at what you do." She paused a heartbeat and added, "At everything you do."

Hector, who was well trained, waited patiently at Brody's side, but his tail was whipping the high grass behind him.

"Hey, there, boy," Garnet said. She held out a big ham bone with plenty of meat still on it. "Bet you could eat, huh? Here." She tossed the meaty bone a distance away. "Get it, boy."

But the dog didn't budge until Brody said, "Go on, Hector."

A cloud hid the face of the moon. "Awfully dark out here, Brody," Garnet said. "Luckily, I brought some light." She reached into the pocket of her shorts and took out a candle stub and a matchbook. She struck one of the matches, lit the candle, and tilted it above the hood of Brody's cruiser. After a few moments, she seated the stub in the melted wax that had dripped there. In the flickering light, she looked where Brody's blanket lay. "If you spread that out a bit more, both of us could fit."

The blanket had been folded in half, and Brody knelt and spread it out completely, smoothing the wrinkles into a uniform softness. When he stood up again and turned back to Garnet, he found that she'd already removed her blouse and bra. In the pale illumination from the single flame, her breasts were so beautiful that Brody's breath caught and he whispered, "God, Garnet."

She stepped to him, pressed herself against his chest, turned her face up, and kissed him with a hunger that was almost violent.

"It's been too long, Brody," she said. "You're cruel sometimes."

"Shut up," he said and drew her down onto the blanket.

"SEPARATE BEDROOMS?" BRODY said. "Your suggestion or his?"

They lay together on the blanket, in the warm night and dim light of the flickering candle. Brody cradled Garnet in his arms.

"Tom snores so bad I can't sleep some nights. And if I read in bed, he complains that my noisy page turning keeps him awake."

Brody wondered if Garnet and her husband still had sex and, if so, how frequently. But he didn't want to ask, didn't really want to know the answer. Instead he said, "Do you get lonely? Does he?"

"He says he likes it, that he never has to worry about keeping me awake or me stealing all the covers."

"And you?"

She was thoughtfully quiet. "If he just didn't snore." Then, as if eager to change the subject, she said, "Why would he kill himself?"

"Quinn? I don't know."

"He was such a bully. Bullies don't kill themselves. They kill other people."

"He had dark periods, Garnet. Terrible insomnia. He'd go off somewhere, isolate himself, drink until he was in a stupor."

"I know. Tom found him asleep in our barn once, drunk and all drugged up."

"He battled demons. Maybe this time the demons got the better of him."

"Who found him?"

"Herman Ostberg."

"I don't know him."

"Lives in Carthage, works at the gravel pit."

"He just stumbled onto Jimmy Quinn here?"

"Not here." This part Brody had known he would have to tell her, but he hated the thought of it. Still, it had to be done sometime. "We found his body at the swimming hole."

"No, Brody, you didn't."

"As nearly as I can tell, he went into the Alabaster here, drifted downriver, and finally got caught up in a snag of driftwood."

"Oh, Brody, I wish you hadn't told me. My memories of that place, of us there, are so special."

That swimming hole was the first place they'd ever made love. It had happened in the late spring before his father's death, before Tom had come home to take over the farm. Garnet had been Tom's girl, had been expected to marry him. But there'd always been a spark between her and Tom's wild younger brother, and in that final spring, it had blazed into the kind of passion that drove Romeo and Juliet to their fatal ends. But in Black Earth County, people didn't kill themselves over love. They went ahead and did what was expected of them.

She rolled away from Brody.

"It's okay, Garnet."

"No, it isn't. I don't have much of you, but I've always had those lovely memories. Now . . ."

"They're still lovely, Garnet. They always will be. And we're still creating memories."

She put herself against him, her back to his chest. "I hate this, Brody."

"Then leave him."

"I can't." Her breath caught a little, and Brody realized she was crying. "He's a good man, really. It's not his fault that I love his brother. And he's a wonderful father."

"And you're Catholic," Brody said, without trying to hide his bitterness at all the arguments she was able to mount against his wish.

From high up on Fordham Ridge came the howl of a coyote, and Brody and Garnet both fell silent, maybe listening for the call to come again. Or maybe it was something else they were hoping might come to them out of the night, an answer to an impossible situation.

"I should go," Garnet said.

She sat up. The candle stub had burned nearly completely down, and the wick had begun to sputter. Brody watched her dress in the last gasps of light. Just before she turned back to him, the candle flame died, and they were both in the dark again.

He drew himself up from the blanket and stood naked before her. "Stay."

"You know I can't."

"Someday?"

She kissed him, lingered in his embrace long enough to understand that he wanted more of her, and she finally stepped back. "Keep that thought, Brody. And don't stay away so long in the future. Bye, Hector," she called and returned to her car.

When the headlights came on, Brody felt naked and silly and vulnerable in the light. He stepped behind his cruiser and watched her maneuver a U-turn in the high grass.

"Bye, love," she called to him as she drove away.

When she'd gone, Brody picked up his clothes and dressed. He opened the door of his cruiser, reached into the glove box, and pulled out a flashlight. He clicked the beam on and searched the ground at the edge of the blanket until he found the condom he'd used and had discarded. Too often as he patrolled Black Earth County, he'd seen its like despoiling lovely, isolated places, and he didn't want to be guilty of the same. He took the collapsible spade he kept in his trunk, dug a small hole, and buried the condom where the wildflowers would grow over it. When he'd finished, he returned to the blanket and sat down. Hector trotted to him, bone in mouth, and lay at his side. After that, Brody sat wide awake for a very long time, thinking about that condom and wondering what, under other circumstances, might have grown from the seed it held.

CHAPTER NINE

BRODY WOKE WITH his back and shoulders sore from the night sleeping on the ground. The sun had just risen. The birds on Inkpaduta Bend were already singing and arguing. He rolled to his side, and there was Hector, breathing into his face, eyes open, blinking patiently.

Brody wanted to go back to sleep, but Hector stood up, gave a woof, and stared toward the county road several hundred yards down the Bend. Then Brody heard what the mutt had heard: a vehicle approaching. He threw off his blanket and got to his feet. In the fresh light of that early morning, Conrad Graff's pickup rolled toward him. Graff pulled the truck up beside Brody's cruiser and got out.

Brody looked at his watch. "It's not even six, Connie."

Graff wore his Stetson. He'd wedged a hand-rolled cigarette between his lips. He knelt and scratched Hector's head. He felt around for a moment, then pulled something from the dog's fur and studied it. He took his cigarette from his mouth and touched the ember to what he picked off the dog.

"Still tick season, Brody. Might want to check yourself."

"Who's at the office?" Brody asked.

"Asa came in early. Said he didn't sleep well last night. Looks like you didn't either, those bags under your eyes."

"The hard ground, this old body," Brody said.

"Old?" Graff smiled broadly. "Son, you tickle me. All you need is some coffee and a good breakfast. Why I'm here." He went back to his pickup and returned with a thermos and a ham sandwich wrapped in waxed paper. "Got something for Hector, too." He visited his pickup again and brought back a brown paper bag. Whatever was in it had Hector dancing on his paws. "I chopped up some round steak I decided I wasn't going to eat. Okay if I give it to him?"

"I think he'll bite you if you don't."

Brody ate the sandwich, the two men drank coffee, and Hector chomped the raw beef.

"Talked with Sam Wicklow last night," Graff said. "He delivered the photos he shot of Quinn's body. I told him we'd appreciate him being out here this morning. He'll be joining us pretty soon."

"Any trouble during the night? Any calls?"

"Nope. Quiet as the grave. How 'bout you two? Any excitement?"

"Heard a woman crying," Brody said. "That or it was the coyotes."

"Inkpaduta Bend. Pretty out here, but it's always had a reputation." Graff's gaze fell on the riverbank, the place where it was stained with blood. "And now this. Who would've thought?"

Brody's radio crackled, and Asa Fielding's voice came over the speaker. "Base to Unit One. Do you read me, Sheriff?"

Brody slipped inside his cruiser and lifted the mic. "Unit One. Go ahead, Asa."

"Just got a call from Ed Swallow, Brody. He says somebody with a pellet gun put holes in the window of his gas station last night. He wants me to find 'em and shoot 'em if I can. Pretty steamed."

"He has a right to be. Does he have a suspect in mind?"

"Every kid in the county with a ducktail haircut. I'm heading out to take a look. I'll keep you posted. Quiet on Inkpaduta Bend last night?"

"Yeah, but the ground was like concrete. My back's killing me."

"You and Connie okay working the scene out there without me?"

"Yes, then I'll meet the Quinns at the funeral home for an official ID."

"Ten-four. Anything else?"

"Nope, but good luck with Swallow. Unit One, out."

Graff was grinning when Brody finished. "What's so funny?" Brody asked.

"Ed Swallow. He's a son of a bitch. I've been tempted on occasion to shoot out his windows myself." He nodded toward the overgrown lane. "Here comes Wicklow."

Sam Wicklow drove a brown and white Studebaker station wagon. The tall grass and wildflowers bent with the push of the front bumper, and the car approached with the soft grating of stalks against metal. He parked behind Graff's pickup, got out, and brought his Leica with him.

"Thanks, Sam," Brody said.

Wicklow looked toward the birches and the Alabaster. "This is the place, huh?"

"Yep," Brody said, then offered, "Coffee?"

Wicklow shook his head. "So, when do we get started?"

"You coffee'd up enough?" Graff asked Brody.

"Let's do it," Brody said.

He popped the trunk of his cruiser, pulled out two pair of leather gloves, and tossed a pair to Graff. They tugged them on as they approached the riverbank.

"What do you want me to shoot?" Wicklow asked.

"Everything," Brody replied.

Brody and Graff slowly walked the perimeter of the scene, just as they had the day before, trying to get a general sense of things, while Wicklow shot photo after photo. Of the large area of blood-soaked earth with the shotgun dead center. Of the discarded pants and shirt and undershirt and boots and socks. Of the opened tackle box and the rod and reel lying on the ground nearby. Of the Coleman lantern. Of Quinn's pickup from every angle. Of the seat with the soiled calfskin gloves and the empty pint of Beam lying beside them.

After half an hour, Wicklow said, "I've used up two rolls of film, Brody.

I can't see anything I haven't photographed seven ways from Sunday."

Brody said, "Just stay over there by my cruiser until I say it's all right to join Connie and me."

Brody brought out a number of paper evidence bags and a clean tarp from the trunk of his cruiser. He laid them on the ground and then he and Graff entered the scene.

Brody said, "Let's start with the shotgun."

It was a double-barrel, eight-gauge Tolley, a big, expensive piece. Brody cracked the breech and found one spent shell and one unfired. The shotgun still carried the smell of exploded powder.

He said, "Let's wrap this in the tarp and dust it for prints back at the jailhouse."

They handed the wrapped firearm to Wicklow with instructions to put it in the trunk of the cruiser and continued their investigation. Brody went through the pockets of the discarded clothing. He pulled out a wallet, checked the driver's license, confirmed it belonged to James Patrick Quinn. The wallet contained $116, a lot of cash to be carrying around in those days. In the right front pants pocket, Brody found a prescription bottle of Seconal, not a surprise. But from the left pants pocket, he pulled a silver ring set with a gemstone. He held it in the palm of his glove, and he and Graff considered it.

"Looks like sapphire," Graff said. "Real, you think?"

"I don't know jewelry," Brody said.

"Too small and feminine for Jimmy Quinn. Unless he was going to wear it on his little toe."

Brody bagged the ring, then the discarded clothing and work boots. They examined the opened tackle box and the rod. The end of the fishing line had nothing on it, no leader or lure or hook.

"Think that's because he wasn't really intending to fish when he came here?" Graff asked.

"His tackle box is open," Brody said. "That Coleman lantern would indicate he was probably planning to stay well into the dark. For a man who wasn't intent on fishing, he came prepared."

"Maybe got too drunk to fish. But was he fishing and drinking alone?" Graff said.

Brody studied the riverbank, especially the area soaked with blood. "No shoe prints anywhere. No other evidence right now to suggest somebody was here with him. So it's either suicide or an accident." He positioned himself on the bank with his back to the river. "If it was suicide, to end up in the Alabaster, he'd have to be standing here, holding the shotgun like this." He posed in the way he'd described Quinn.

"It would take a long pair of arms to reach that trigger," Graff said.

"Quinn was a big man," Brody replied. "Arms like an orangutan."

"So he pulls the trigger, and the blast sends him reeling back into the river."

"And at the same moment, he drops the shotgun," Brody said, completing the scenario.

Graff eyed him. "You buy that?"

"I'm not dismissing anything at the moment. So, what about an accident? How would that have happened?"

"He's been drinking heavy," Graff said. "And maybe doping himself with those tranquilizers we found. He's brought out his Tolley in case he spots a pheasant or a big wild turkey or maybe a prairie chicken."

"It's not hunting season for any of those birds, Connie."

"Since when did a consideration of the law keep Jimmy Quinn from doing what Jimmy Quinn wanted to do?"

Brody accepted that and continued with the speculation Graff had begun. "He sees something that causes him to grab for the shotgun. But the Jim Beam and Seconal make him clumsy. He drops the Tolley, the butt hits the ground, the damn thing discharges. He falls back into the river, and there the shotgun lies."

Graff thought it over and said quietly, "Bullshit."

Brody nodded. "That Tolley was loaded with buckshot, not bird-shot. Whatever Quinn planned on shooting, it wasn't prairie chickens." He knelt and touched the stained earth. "All this blood, Connie. The shotgun blast opened him up wide. Big hole for blood to run out of."

"But if the force of the blast sent him into the river, that's where he would have bled out, right?" Graff argued. "There'd be some blood here, sure, but not like this."

"So you're saying he bled out right here? Then how did he get in the river?"

"The sixty-four-thousand-dollar question." Graff eyed the dark-stained ground, the flow of the Alabaster, the terraced slope of Fordham Ridge. Then he said, in a voice too low for Wicklow, who was standing near the cruiser, to hear, "When I was a patrolman in Kansas City back during Prohibition, I helped keep gawker crowds away from a couple of places where some of the local gangsters caught it. A lot of those lowlifes were shotgunned, just like this. I left K.C. after the Union Station Massacre. Didn't care to work law enforcement in such a violent place. Here, when somebody's been killed, it's always been suicide or some kind of obvious accident or in front of witnesses, usually during a bar fight. Never had anything wasn't pretty clear cut." He drilled Brody with his hard gray eyes. "This is different, Brody. This is like K.C."

"Ah, come on, Connie," Brody said. "Don't go there."

"I don't think it was an accident. And I don't think it was suicide." Graff looked down at the big dark area around his feet. "And I'm thinking more and more that Quinn wasn't alone here when he died."

"Look, let's just finish up, and then we can figure this thing out," Brody said.

They closed the tackle box and took that into evidence, along with the fishing rod and the Coleman lantern, and they placed everything they'd gathered in the trunk of Brody's cruiser.

"So?" Sam Wicklow said. He'd been helpful and he'd been patient, and that simple word was his request for some kind of payback. He was, after all, a newspaperman.

"Okay, this is for print," Brody told him. "What we know is that James Quinn was found yesterday in the Alabaster River. He'd sustained gunshot trauma to his torso, but we won't know the official cause of death until after the autopsy is completed later this morning. His family reported that he'd left his farm Thursday evening, indicating that he intended to go fishing. He didn't return. After his body was discovered—"

"Okay if I print Herman Ostberg's name?"

"Yeah. It'll probably make him a local celebrity, at least for a while."

"Go on," Wicklow said.

"Last evening at around eight-thirty p.m., sheriff's personnel found Quinn's pickup parked on Inkpaduta Bend. Preliminary indication is that Quinn had come here to fish and that, while he was here, his shotgun discharged and the blast killed him. But, again, we need to have the coroner officially confirm cause of death."

"Was he alone?"

"We've found no evidence that someone was with him, so, yes, we believe he was alone."

"Had he been drinking?"

"It appears so."

Wicklow's eyes flicked to the riverbank. "I watched your pantomime over there. Were you trying to visualize a suicide?"

"That's one of the possibilities we've been considering."

"Could it have been an accident?"

"It could have been. Another possibility we're not discounting."

Wicklow's pen poised over his little notebook, and his eyes studied Brody's for a moment. "Could it have been murder?"

Brody replied quickly and a little sternly. "At this point, we're not officially considering foul play at all, Sam. I don't want to see anything like that in your paper."

"Is it all right if I interview his family now?"

"If they'll talk to you. I'm meeting Marta and J.P. at Brown's at ten for the official ID. I suppose you could approach them after that's done. Just keep in mind what they're going through."

Wicklow said, "I'd be very interested to know what they're going through. I've been trying to imagine myself in their situation. Honest to God, I don't know if I'd be broken up or dancing."

Graff pulled a pouch of tobacco from his shirt pocket, drew a leaf of cigarette paper from the pack he kept in that same location, and commenced to rolling himself a smoke. He said, "Human beings are a complex species, Sam. I think it's entirely possible for the Quinns to be doing both those things at the same time. Jimmy's absence will be a great hardship in some ways, but a profound relief, I imagine, in others. One thing's for damn sure. For quite a while, it'll be giving folks in Black Earth County something to talk about besides the weather."

Wicklow said, "Anything else here?"

Brody shook his head. "We'll be wrapping it up. When you have those photos developed, you'll drop them by the jailhouse?"

"I'll get on them first thing. And you'll call me with the results of the autopsy? I want to get this story right."

"I will. Thanks for your help, Sam."

Brody offered his hand and Wicklow shook it. The sheriff and his deputy watched as the newspaperman maneuvered himself into his station wagon, made a laborious U-turn, and drove away.

Graff lit his cigarette and let out a slow snake of smoke. "I'm thinking I ought to check all the farms nearby, see if anyone saw or heard anything."

"All right. I'm heading back into Jewel, meet the Quinns for the ID."

"What about his truck? Can't just leave it here."

"When I meet with the family, I'll talk to them about getting it back to the farm."

"Want to dust it for prints?"

"What would be the point? It's pretty clear what happened. He killed himself, Connie. Or it was a tragic accident. Besides, I've seen Quinn and J.P. and every one of his hired men driving that truck at one time or another. It's covered with prints, I'm sure, so what would they tell us? Seems to me our time would be better spent in other pursuits."

Graff walked to his pickup, but he didn't get in immediately. Connie Graff was always a man to see the broad perspective, and he stood looking at the wildflowers and the tall green grasses, then he squinted toward the sun and studied the distant cultivated fields beyond the eastern curve of the river, and finally his eyes climbed to the top of Fordham Ridge. "Remember your history of Black Earth County, Brody? The Stephen H. Long expedition?"

Brody said, "Early eighteen hundreds. Legend has it that Long named the ridge after one of his superiors, a man he disliked intensely. From what I understand, he hoped this Fordham would see it as an honor, but Long actually meant it as an insult because he thought everything along the Alabaster was nothing but wasteland."

"That's right. Stephen H. Long stood up there and declared that this whole area was unfit for cultivation. Said this was all part of what he called the Great American Desert."

"What's your point?"

"Just thinking how a man can be looking at a thing and not see at all its true nature."

Brody said, "Is the fault in the man, Connie?"

Graff dropped what was left of his cigarette to the ground and crushed it under the heel of his boot. He gave Brody an indecipherable look and said, "Depends on the man, I suppose. I'll see you in town." He got into his truck and left Inkpaduta Bend, following the narrow trail broken through the prairie grass.

CHAPTER TEN

CONNIE GRAFF WAS sixty years old and had always expected to be dead by then. Or at the very least, glued to a rocking chair on the porch of an old folks' home waiting to be fitted for a coffin. Growing up, he hadn't seen many men make it to the age of white hair and a face full of wrinkles. Guys like Gunther Haas, that leathery old veteran of one of the last Indian campaigns, were a rarity in Black Earth County, where the men were mostly farmers and working the land killed them early. Which was one of the reasons Graff had chosen to wear a badge as a way to make a living. A lawman's life could be cut short by a bullet, sure, but Graff had seen far more death from inattention or drunkenness around combines and balers, or the errant kick of a draft horse or mule, or the suicides that came with the uncertainty and worry of trusting in the Lord to deliver just the right combination of weather. Or a man simply worked himself to death. His father and his grandfather had been farmers, and Graff had seen the land suck all the life right out of them. He wanted no part of that.

He drove away from Inkpaduta Bend, drove the threads of back roads and gravel lanes that knitted the farms and hamlets of Black Earth County together in a loose fabric of commerce and community. It was a lovely summer day, the sky a blue blade that seemed to cut off the rest of the world along a green horizon. Occasionally the approaching rattle of his pickup flushed a pheasant from the tall grass and weeds at the roadside.

The flight and cackle of the birds made him think of Myrna and those days when he'd ride with her on horseback down these country roads and the pheasants would fly up at their coming and take to the safety of the tall corn. She'd been born a city girl, but she knew how to sit a horse proud. God, he missed her.

He spent a good part of the morning catching farmers in their barns or in their fields, questioning them briefly. They were, to a man, ignorant of anything that might help crack the mystery of Jimmy Quinn's death. This was exactly what Graff had expected and mostly his questioning was done for the sake of thoroughness, just good cop work. Because Connie Graff had an idea about Inkpaduta Bend and about Quinn, and before long he was driving up a very narrow lane to a farmhouse that stood in the shadow of an enormous Dutch elm just a stone's throw from the Alabaster.

The farmhouse was small and built of lumber hand-hewn around the turn of the century. There was a modest barn, old but recently refurbished; a newer construction of corrugated metal that was probably a garage or machine shed; a chicken coop full of strutting, bobbing hens; and a pen where pigs lay sleeping in the morning sun. Graff drove his pickup into the farmyard, killed the engine, and got out. On most farms, a dog would have come bounding out, barking a greeting or warning, but here there was only the quiet of the countryside and the occasional grunt from one of the pigs and the cluck of hens. The man who owned the place drove a red Ford pickup, but the pickup was nowhere to be seen. Graff walked to the farmhouse door and knocked. When no one answered, he knocked again, with the same result. He stepped out of the shade, nudged the brim of his Stetson up a bit higher on his forehead, and scanned what he could see of the property.

The place was tiny compared to the vast majority of the farms around it, eighty acres at most. Behind the house, a small orchard had been planted in neat rows, the trees still too young to bear fruit. Graff drifted around to the back of the barn. In the field there, amid green shoots rising up from the black earth, a figure with a hoe stood bent, working the area between two rows. Whoever it was wore a broad-brimmed straw hat that cast a dark shadow, so that Graff couldn't see the face clearly. The figure was tiny, an adolescent, most observers might think, but Graff knew differently. He walked into the field, and as he approached, an old Saint Bernard lying near the figure stood up and barked a warning.

The woman had been singing quietly to herself as she worked. When the dog barked, the song died on her lips, the hoe paused in its chopping, and the woman looked up out of the shadow of her straw hat. She was young, pretty, Asian. Japanese, Graff knew. Hell, everyone in Black Earth County knew. Word had gone out within days of Noah Bluestone's return to Minnesota that he'd married a Jap. Although the war had been over for more than a dozen years, many folks in Black Earth County still considered her one of the enemy. Graff had seldom seen her, and then only briefly on those few occasions when she accompanied her husband into town. Usually, she sat alone in the truck while Bluestone conducted his business. Did she speak English? He had no idea.

And so, when she eyed him from the shadow of her hat, he didn't know if she would be able to understand his question.

"Mrs. Bluestone, I'm Deputy Graff. I'm looking for your husband."

Her dark brown eyes studied him briefly, then she lowered her gaze again to the earth she'd broken with her hoe and said, "He's not here." She spoke quietly but clearly, with only a little accent that harked back to her origins.

"Do you know when he'll be back? I'd like to talk to him."

She shook her head.

"Do you know where he is?"

"At the Quinn farm."

"Jimmy Quinn's place?" Surprise was in his words and on his face;

she'd have seen it if she'd lifted her eyes to look. "You know that Mr. Quinn's dead?"

She nodded.

"It was my understanding your husband had been fired."

"They asked him to come back to work. They said they needed him."

Graff felt his shirt sticking to the damp of his back. He could tell that the day would be unusually hot and humid for so early in the summer. He saw sweat trickling down the side of the woman's smooth face, following the lines of a few long black hairs that had escaped her hat and lay clinging to her temples.

"A lot of work," he said, noting the great number of planted rows where the ground still needed breaking with her hoe, if that was her intent. It was the kind of job most farmers in Black Earth County would have used a tractor and cultivator to accomplish.

"It's good work. I don't mind it," she said.

Graff knelt on one knee and touched one of the shoots in the line that had risen from the black dirt to a height of nearly six inches. The leaves felt soft but resilient in his callused hand.

"What is this?" he asked.

"This field is amaranth."

"Amaranth. Never heard of it. Sure it'll grow here?"

"My husband believes that it will. It is one of the most ancient and versatile of grains." There was a little iron in her voice now, a thread of defiance, as if she was fully prepared to defend her husband's crop choice.

Graff stood and brushed the soil from the knee of his pants.

"At Quinn's, you say? You worked for the Quinns, too, didn't you?"

"Three days each week. I cooked, cleaned, washed."

"Why aren't you there with your husband now? Not one of your days?"

"It's summer. The children are out of school and can help. Marta told me she didn't need me now."

A moment passed with nothing between them except the silence of that empty land.

"Amaranth," Graff finally said. "Well, Mrs. Bluestone, I wish you a fine harvest."

"Thank you."

Graff tipped his Stetson. "I appreciate your time."

"Good day," she said. Then she added, "Deputy Graff."

He turned and left her alone with her old Saint Bernard. But in the way a magnet is always drawn toward the north, the old deputy could feel the pull of her presence at his back.

CHAPTER ELEVEN

BRODY STOOD AT the screen door of the funeral home, waiting for the Quinns to arrive. Brown's was a lovely building, an old Victorian that nearly forty years earlier had been turned to its current use by Fred's father, Carl. The Browns had not always been Browns. Until World War I, they'd been Brauns. The anti-German sentiment abroad in America during and after the war had compelled Karl Braun to Anglicize his name. In the same way, Schmidt's German Bakery on Main Street had become simply Smith's Bakery.

It had been Carl Brown who'd prepared Brody's father for burial. Brody rarely thought about Robert Dern, but when he did it was with a mixture of sadness, anger, and regret. His father had died young, at the age of forty-five, from the explosion of an aneurysm in his brain that had sent him tumbling from his tractor while harrowing the fields for spring planting. The back wheels of the John Deere had rolled over him. The discs of the harrow that followed had sliced his legs into pieces. Brody, who was eighteen at the time, had witnessed all this from near the barn, where he was mucking out the cattle yard, a chore he hated but one his father forced on him. Brody had raced across the field, stumbling on the broken earth. He'd caught up to the tractor, killed the engine, and turned to see to his father. There was no point. The man was stone dead. Brody's older brother, Tom, had been away at college in Ames, studying modern agriculture, but he returned to Black Earth County to take over the running of the farm, which, in his will, Robert Dern had left entirely to his older son. Brody had known this would be the way of things, that Tom would inherit everything. It wasn't only because this was the tradition, to pass the land intact to the eldest. It was also because Tom had been the favorite, the good son. Brody had been the wild one. Irresponsible and reckless as hell, his father had often ranted. In retrospect, Brody knew this had been true. But at the time it struck him as simply one more example of the low esteem in which Robert Dern had always held him. And what son, even the most reprobate, wants to be seen as worthless in his father's eyes?

"J.P. told me they'd be here by ten," he said. "They're running a little late."

Fred Brown, who'd been sitting at a desk in what had once been the living room, rose, walked to the door, and stood beside Brody. The mortician wore a dark suit and round wire-rim glasses, and was bald as an egg.

"This is hard enough on a family when it's only about the funeral preparations," Brown said. "Add to it the situation and the need to make an official identification and I imagine it becomes even more difficult. Understandable that they might be dragging their feet." He removed his glasses, took a folded handkerchief from the breast pocket of his suit coat, and cleaned the lenses. "Ruth Coffee's family was in earlier today. A much simpler affair."

"Oh?"

"Ruth had everything in order, right down to the hymns she wanted sung at the service. The funeral's on Thursday. I imagine a good part of Jewel will attend, a lot of us who were her students."

Brody thought about James Patrick Quinn and wondered who would turn out for that burial.

Brown, as if reading his thoughts, said, "And I imagine there will be a lot of people at Jimmy's service, too. He supported Saint Ignatius pretty substantially. A good portion of our parish will undoubtedly feel obliged."

Brody interpreted this as a diplomatic way of saying that Quinn had bought himself a crowd of mourners.

"Here they come," Brody said.

"Do they know?" Brown asked.

"Know what?"

"That Jimmy was shot?"

"I haven't told them yet, no. I'd appreciate it, Fred, if you didn't say anything either."

"As you wish."

The car was a two-tone Chrysler Imperial, white and robin's egg blue, new within that year. James Patrick Quinn, Jr., was at the wheel. He pulled into the parking lot and got out. He wore a dark blue suit and tie, as if this were church or some other formal occasion. He walked around to the passenger side, opened the door, and helped his mother climb out. She, too, was dressed formally, all in black. She leaned heavily on her son's arm as they came up the front steps of the funeral home.

Brown opened the door. "Marta, J.P. Won't you come in?"

Sometimes her illness made Marta Quinn look far older than her late thirties. This day, however, she had carefully prepared herself, put on makeup and fixed her hair, and Brody saw that despite her ailment and the hardship of the current situation, she was still a beautiful woman.

After the greetings were made, the mortician said, "This way."

He led them down a long corridor to a room near the back and opened the door. He slipped inside, turned on a light, and moved away so the others could enter.

They found themselves in an immaculate preparation room that smelled of bleach. Brody had been there on several occasions, because it was the room where all official autopsies for Black Earth County were conducted. Since completion of the new hospital three years earlier, the autopsies could have been done there, but Brown had a long-standing contract with the county, and Doc Porter was comfortable with the working relationship.

On the ceramic table at the center of the room, a sheet had been draped over the body. Brody was amazed that the sheet was so white, so completely unstained, and he figured that Brown must have placed some kind of barrier between the great raw hole in Jimmy Quinn's torso and the material that now cloaked it.

Brody said, "Marta, I need to warn you. When he was in the water, your husband was chewed on a good deal by fish. His face is not pretty."

Marta Quinn thought this over, then gave a ghost of a nod.

Brown reached to the top of the sheet and drew it back, only enough to expose the head. In the antiseptic glare of the ceiling lights, Quinn's widow and son took in the face that was hardly human anymore—the eyes and eyelids and nose eaten away almost entirely, the skin pale and puckered, the teeth and gums exposed in a kind of snarl where the catfish had feasted on Quinn's lips. It was a mask from a horror movie, and Marta Quinn, when she saw it, fainted dead away.

"HOW DID HE die?"

A breeze came through the window screens in Brown's office. On a telephone wire outside, two cardinals sat, a brilliant red male and a drab female, calling to each other with a few lilting notes. Randy Swope, the boy Brown paid to keep the grounds neat, was cutting the front lawn. As the reel of the push mower spun and paused and spun, the rhythmic sound reminded Brody of breathing. To folks in Black Earth County, the seasons were living things, and each had its own peculiar voice and smell and personality. Early summer in Jewel was a season that usually breathed promise.

Brody replied, "We located your husband's pickup last night, Marta, parked on Inkpaduta Bend. It appears that's where Jimmy went to do his fishing Thursday evening."

Quinn's widow spent a moment taking this in, then asked, "What was it like?"

Brody wasn't sure what she was asking. "You know Inkpaduta Bend?"

"Of course," Marta said. "I mean, could you tell what happened?"

"I won't know the exact cause of death until after the autopsy."

"Autopsy?" she said.

"In any death in which the cause is uncertain, an autopsy is required, Marta. It's the law."

"You have no idea how he died?" She seemed surprised. "You said you found him in the river. He didn't drown?"

"I'm pretty sure not."

"Then what?" J.P. asked. "Was it those pills he takes to sleep?"

He sat next to his mother and held her hand, as if to give her some of the strength that was his simply by virtue of his youth.

"Not the pills." Brody paused a moment, then said, "It was a shotgun blast."

J.P.'s face went slack as the young man absorbed this piece of information. Marta may have paled, but her makeup made that hard to see.

J.P. responded carefully, "Someone killed my dad?"

"He sustained a gunshot wound, J.P. That's all I can say for sure. I can't tell you that's what killed him. Not yet, not officially. And I can't tell you exactly how he got that wound either."

"Did you find the shotgun?" J.P. had let go of his mother's hand and was leaning forward toward Brody.

"Yes. It was an unusual piece. A fine old Tolley, an eight-gauge."

"That was one he was especially proud of." J.P. sat back and stared at the floor and then lifted his eyes to Brody again. "Could he have done it himself?"

"I can't say for sure at the moment. But possibly."

Marta appeared as if she were about to faint again. "A mortal sin," she whispered.

The Quinns had a family plot in the Catholic cemetery in Jewel. But if he'd committed suicide, which was, as Marta observed, an unforgivable sin, James Patrick Quinn would not be allowed to be buried there. His remains would have to reside in the town cemetery, separated from the rest of his family.

"Until I know all the facts, I can't say anything for sure." Brody waited a moment, then asked, "When Jimmy left the farm Thursday evening, how did he seem?"

Marta thought the question over. "I was inside, resting. He came in and told me he was going fishing. That's all. He didn't seem anything."

"Did you smell alcohol on his breath?"

"Yes, but that wasn't unusual."

"Did he say anything about fishing with someone?"

Marta frowned in thought, but J.P. said, "He never fished with anyone. It was something he liked doing alone. He said it relaxed him and was the one time he could count on no one bothering him."

"You never fished with him?"

"When I was a little kid," J.P. said. "But not since I was ten. I don't much care for fishing."

"Marta, did your husband seem unusually troubled lately?"

The cardinals had flown from the telephone wire, and Randy Swope had left off his cutting. In Brown's office, an uncomfortable silence settled.

"If you don't tell him, Mom, I will," J.P. finally said.

Brody said, "Tell me what?"

Marta stared at her hands.

"My father tried to kill himself once before," J.P. said.

"When?" Brody asked.

"Last fall, not long after harvest," J.P. said. "He's got this shack near where our creek runs. He keeps a supply of liquor there. It was one of the best harvests in years, so I'm not sure what was going on, but when November turned gray, Dad went into that hole in himself, that place he goes sometimes. He started drinking in his shack and didn't come back to the house and when I went to check on him, I found him standing on a chair with a rope around his neck and a bottle of whiskey in his hand. He was drunk out of his mind. Just standing there, swaying. I figured he was maybe waiting to fall and hang himself that way, or he was trying to build up his courage to step off the chair."

J.P. had started this piece of information angry, but as he told it, his emotion changed, and by the time he'd finished, he seemed resigned.

"You talked him down?" Brody asked.

J.P. shook his head. "When he saw me, he, I don't know, changed his mind. He smashed the bottle against the wall, took off the rope, and got down from the chair. He told me that if I ever said anything to anybody, he'd beat me until I was bloody. So I never did."

"Except your mother," Brody said.

"That's right. But not until yesterday, when you found him in the river. I figured maybe he'd drowned himself."

Brody looked toward Marta. The window was behind her and the breeze that came through and blew over her carried to Brody the pleasant fragrance of lilac soap and bath powder. "Do you have any idea why your husband might have tried to kill himself?"

She shook her head. "He kept things to himself."

Brody felt as if he was torturing them with his questions, but he had one more that needed asking. From his pocket, he drew the sapphire ring he'd found in Quinn's clothing on the riverbank. He held it out to Marta.

"Have you ever seen this ring before?"

She stared at it blankly. "No."

"You're sure?"

"Absolutely. It's lovely."

"It was in the pocket of your husband's pants," Brody told her.

"I don't know what it was doing there. As I said, I've never seen it before."

"J.P.?" Brody said.

The kid shook his head. "Nope."

Brody returned the ring to his pocket and decided that was enough for one day.

"Thank you for your time and your patience. You've been helpful." He stood. "I'll send Fred in, so that you can discuss the burial."

Marta Quinn's blue eyes were soft, wet, confused. "When . . . ?"

"I'll release your husband's body as soon as the autopsy is finished. That will probably be later today. You can schedule the funeral whenever you think is best." He looked to J.P. "Your dad's pickup is still out at Inkpaduta Bend."

"Okay if we drive it back home?"

Brody told him it was.

"I'll get one of our hired men to help me," J.P. said with no enthusiasm. "Sometime this afternoon or this evening."

Brody left them and found Doc Porter waiting for him in the hallway outside.

"Ready for me to begin?" the coroner asked.

"He's all yours," Brody said.

CHAPTER TWELVE

YOUNG SCOTT MADISON stood back and admired his work. He'd lashed together the frame of a lean-to using twine and several long cottonwood branches he'd scrounged from the banks of the Alabaster. He tested the joints, shook them as if a fierce wind were attacking, and he was pleased with the way they held. He stepped into the middle of the structure and sat down. Although he was on the grass of the yard behind the Wagon Wheel, his family's café, seated under the shade of an enormous oak, in his mind's eye, the lean-to was on a mountainside, with a clear stream running nearby and tall pines rising all around him except right in front of his shelter, where the vista was clear and he could see a hundred miles. He'd seen a postcard once, a photo taken from the top of Pikes Peak in Colorado. He imagined himself on that mountaintop, looking down at the plains stretching away before him, a place where he could just about see the whole world.

His dreaming was interrupted by the *grrrrr* of a small engine approaching, and he knew what that meant. A moment later, Del Wolfe appeared on his homemade motorbike and shot up the gravel drive to the yard, where Scott sat inside the lean-to. Del was tall and thin, almost a year older than Scott, but in the same grade, which, come September, would be their freshman year in high school. He had jet-black hair, always in need of cutting. It hung down over his forehead so that Del's dark eyes seemed to peer from under the shadow of an awning.

"Hey, Madman," Del cried, killing the little engine he'd scavenged from an old lawn mower. He hopped off and laid the motorbike in the grass of the yard. "Did you hear?"

"Hear what, Wolfman?"

"Jimmy Quinn's dead. And get this. He was eaten by catfish in the Alabaster."

"Mr. Quinn? No."

"I swear it. I heard it from Creasy, and he heard it from the sheriff himself."

Del joined Scott under the lean-to, sat down, slid a knapsack from his back, and cradled it in his lap.

"How'd he die?" Scott asked.

"Shotgun blast opened a big hole in him." Del used his hands to illustrate the size of the wounding. "And those catfish, man, they ate all his guts."

"Somebody killed him?"

"Naw, an accident probably. But who knows? Bastard like him, maybe somebody got fed up. Creasy says he's wanted to kill the son of a bitch lots of times."

Creasy had married Del's mother, but he was not Del's stepfather because Del had refused to be adopted. The man worked for James Quinn, on the farm. Creasy was his last name. His first name was Tyler, but Del, who didn't much care for him, always called him Creasy.

"What was he doing in the river?"

"Search me." Del finally seemed to notice the lean-to, reached out, and touched the framework. "What's with the log cabin?"

"We've got a Scout jamboree coming up end of June. Just practicing my lashing techniques."

Del gave the construction a good long assessment and said, "Cool, Madman."

Delbert Wolfe had come to Jewel the year before. He and his mom and Creasy had traveled around a good deal prior to that, and Scott had a sense that the nomadic life had been tough. A new kid and an odd one, Del hadn't made friends easily. Scott Madison was another kid who was different, and their differences attracted. When their acquaintance ripened into deep friendship, Del rechristened them both, gave them names that, because no one else addressed them in that way, created an intimacy Scott had never experienced before and, having found it, enjoyed greatly. Del Wolfe had become Wolfman. Scott Madison had become Madman.

"Got something to show you." Del lifted the flap on the knapsack and pulled out a book. "Dig this."

The book was *Peyton Place,* Grace Metalious's exposé of small-town life in New Hampshire. Because of the furor it had created on publication, even Scott Madison in isolated Black Earth County knew about the book. Or knew enough to understand that it was, for someone his age, forbidden fruit.

"Where'd you get that?" Scott asked, awe and admiration in his voice.

"Gowen's Book Store."

"They let you have it?"

"My mom wrote a note telling them it was okay for me to buy whatever I wanted. She doesn't care as long as I stay out of trouble and don't bother her. And I used my own money." Del opened the book to a page he'd dog-eared. "Read this."

The text was underlined in red pencil, and Scott began to read. Sentences about nipples and hot throbbing flesh. About a woman wanting sex in a way that would hurt her a little. About a man with his hand on a woman's most private place. About them actually doing it.

"Hot stuff, huh?" Del said.

"You better not let anyone catch you with this."

"It's just a book, Madman." Del smiled. "But what a book."

"You read the whole thing?"

"Fuggin' right. Twice."

Fuggin'. That was a word Del had pulled from one of his all-time favorite books, *The Naked and the Dead,* a story about combat soldiers in World War II.

"Scott!"

He looked toward the café, where his mother stood at the screen door that opened into the kitchen. She wore a flowered apron over a blue skirt and a yellow blouse. She gestured him to her and Scott got up. Wolfman stood with him and slipped the book back into his knapsack.

"Hello, Del," Angie Madison said, offering the boy a warm smile. Her hair had fallen over her forehead and threatened to cover her right eye. She brushed it back with a casual gesture. "Nice to see you."

"Thank you, ma'am," Del replied.

"Scott, I need you to take this to the jailhouse for the sheriff." Angie held out a brown paper bag. "It's lunch."

"Someone in the clink?" Del asked.

"It's for the sheriff," she replied. To her son, she said, "It's a busy day for him, and I know he doesn't eat right."

"Did you hear about Mr. Quinn?" Del asked.

"Yes, Del. Tragic. And that's why I think our sheriff could use a little help today. If you want to go along with Scott, that would be fine."

"Thanks, Mrs. Madison, but I've got things to do. Later, Madman." Del gave his friend a slap on the shoulder and returned to his motorbike.

Through the screen door at his mother's back, Scott could hear the sounds of the busy kitchen as the lunch crowd gathered—meat sizzling on the grill, pans and platters clattering on steel counters, the hiss and bubble of deep fry, the call of orders.

When Del had gone, Scott's mother gave her son a quizzical look. "Madman?"

Scott shrugged. "It's just a nickname."

"From Madison?"

"Yeah."

"Madman." She thought it over and seemed amused by it. "Well, Madman, scoot yourself over to the jailhouse. And I'll need you back here this afternoon. Your grandma has a doctor's appointment."

"Yes, ma'am."

"Angie!" came a cry from inside.

"Off with you now." She spun away and disappeared into the clatter and sizzle and roiling aromas of the kitchen.

THE WORLD TO Scott Christian Madison was Black Earth County. He'd seen pictures of other places—New York City, the California coastline, the mountains of Colorado, the Florida swamps—postcard images. But his own experience was limited. He knew the way the tar on the streets of Jewel turned to putty in the hot summer sun. The feel of the Alabaster when he swung from a rope and dropped into a cool, tea-colored pool. The scents as he walked the alley behind Main Street—the sweet yeasty aroma of Smith's Bakery, the clammy smell of the steam that shot from the back of Myers Dry Cleaning, the chemical odor of perms emanating from Marie's Beauty Salon. His world in Black Earth County was bitter blasts in the winter that threw sleet into his face like needles or brought great curtains of snow that fell and lay in drifts for months on end. It was summer storms he could see coming from a million miles away and the wet-earth scent that came before them on the wind. It was also loneliness.

Scott Madison had been born with a hole in his heart, what in those days was sometimes called a "blue baby." He had no father—well, he had a father, didn't everyone?—but Scott's father had been killed in the war, and all he knew of the man were the photographs his grandmother kept in profusion and the stories she told again and again in a way that made the remembrances feel like ritual. Scott even thought of his grandmother's repetitions as a kind of transubstantiation, a word Father Gregory had explained in his Lutheran catechism class when talking about how Roman Catholics viewed the Eucharist. It seemed to him his grandmother's words and remembrances, in repetition, became flesh and blood to her, just like the wine and wafers did to the Catholics. But not to Scott. He didn't mind hearing the stories, but they remained to him just that, stories.

His grandfather had died when Scott was five, and the boy had only the vaguest recollections of the man. So he'd been raised by women, his mother and grandmother. Because of that hole in his heart and because they'd lost every man they'd ever loved, these women fussed over him and were full of cautions that made him feel sometimes as if he couldn't breathe.

There were men in his life, sure, but only peripherally. Wendell Moon, who worked for his mother and grandmother in the café. The Lutheran pastor, Father Gregory, but only so far as religion was concerned. His scoutmaster, Mr. Sorenson, who was nice enough but had sons of his own. And more and more, there was Sheriff Brody Dern, whose eating habits his mother had recently taken a particular interest in. The sheriff was often at the café around mealtime, and if he was not, Scott sometimes caught his mother gazing across the rooftops of town and up the hill toward where the jailhouse stood. What he saw in her look made him think of his own loneliness, and that of his grandmother, who'd lost both son and husband, and even that of Father Gregory, whose face reminded Scott of a camel's, long and thick-lipped, with enormous nostrils, and who, though he was Lutheran and could have taken a wife, never had. Very early in his life, Scott Madison had come to believe that loneliness was the normal condition of people, and he didn't think of it, his own or that of others, as a terrible thing.

He reached the jailhouse and tried the door. It was locked. He didn't know where Sheriff Brody Dern was or when he might be back. But he'd been given a duty to perform, so he sat down on the curb in front of the jailhouse to wait. Although it was only the town of Jewel in front of him, he imagined himself on a mountaintop in Colorado, and in his mind's eye, he could almost see the whole world.

CHAPTER THIRTEEN

AFTER HIS MEETING with the Quinns, Brody spent an hour or so with Mayor Jack Harris reviewing some logistical issues with the parade the previous day and possible changes for the next year's celebration. Then he went back to the jailhouse, where he found Scott Madison waiting. The boy sat cross-legged in the shade, his back against the door, idly tossing bits of gravel into the street. As soon as Brody pulled up to the curb, the kid stood. In his hand, he held a brown paper bag.

"Hey there, Scott. What's up?"

The boy showed him the bag. "Lunch. Mom thought you might be hungry."

"Did she now?"

"She worries about you."

Brody came around his cruiser and stood smiling down at the boy. "She told you that?"

The boy nodded.

"Worries about me? Really?"

"She says you don't eat right." The boy looked down at the old concrete under his sneakers, and Brody understood that he was embarrassed to be saying such a thing to a grown man.

"Well, come on in," Brody said. "Let's see what's on the menu."

Brody had left Hector at the jailhouse. As soon as they entered, the dog came bounding to greet them. He and Scott were old friends, and their mutual affection was obvious.

Brody looked inside the paper bag. "Turkey sandwich, potato salad, and an apple. How'd your mom know I'd be hungry?"

"Deputy Graff told her your refrigerator never has anything in it that's less than a month old."

"What do you say we put this food in my refrigerator—I promise it won't be there a month—and head over to your mom's café. I'd like to thank her in person, and maybe get a hot meal for lunch. Would that be all right?"

Before the boy could answer, Gordon Landis threw open the jailhouse door and swept in with an air of outrage. "I heard somebody shotgunned Jimmy Quinn."

Brody's gut clenched, not only because of Landis's abruptness, but also because someone Brody trusted must have divulged this important piece of information.

"What do you want, Gordy?"

"You and I both know who did it."

"I don't know anything of the sort."

"Everybody knows who did it. Bluestone, that Indian son of a bitch."

"I'm warning you, Gordy. You go around spreading that kind of rumor, I'll lock you up so fast your head'll spin."

"Maybe so, but it won't keep folks around here from doing what needs to be done."

"What's that supposed to mean?"

"If I was you, I'd lock that Indian up right now. Otherwise, he might never make it before a judge."

Brody tried to breathe out his anger, and he spoke carefully. "Just last month, I heard you call Quinn the biggest son of a bitch in southern Minnesota because he got you kicked off the town council. If somebody killed Quinn, maybe I ought to be looking at you. Or any of the other folks in this county with hatred toward Jimmy Quinn in their hearts."

"Big difference between us and Bluestone, and you know exactly what that is."

"I want you out of here, Gordy. And if anything happens to Noah Bluestone, I'll come looking for you first, understand?"

"I'll be watching you, Dern. We'll all be watching you."

Landis turned and left as abruptly as he'd entered. Scott Madison stood by, apparently not surprised by what he'd just heard.

"You knew?" Brody asked.

The boy nodded. "Tyler Creasy told my friend Del Wolfe, and Del told me."

"Can I trust you not to spread that rumor any further? It's important."

"Yes, sir," the boy promised.

Brody took a deep breath and let it out slowly. "Let's go get some lunch."

THE WAGON WHEEL Café was a simple place with a counter and ten booths. By 1958 it had occupied that spot for twenty years. Angie's in-laws, Ida and Harvey Madison, had started the place near the end of the Great Depression. They served standard fare and did all right. But when Angie married into the family, things changed. She was from bayou country, and the folks in Black Earth County had never seen the likes of what she could do with food. Odd as it was for Minnesotans to embrace anything with a kick to it, they couldn't get enough of Angie's cooking. Eggs with Cajun spices. Blackened catfish. Hot pepper meat loaf. Gumbo. Fried okra and fried green tomatoes. Coffee strong and rich, the way no Scandinavian would ever make it. On Saturday evenings, she served barbecued ribs that drew folks from as far away as Lake Okoboji and Worthington and Fairmont. They came for the food, sure, but they also came for Angie, who was flamboyant in expressing her Southern roots.

"I got bayou in my blood," she would say, "and gator in my gait."

She was a war widow; had met her husband, Christian Madison, when he was in Texas, training to be a navigator. They'd married, he'd been shipped off to Europe and had never returned. Angie had come north to deliver her child and to live with Ida and Harvey. In the opinion of most folks in Black Earth County, Jewel became a better, far more interesting place the minute she arrived.

It was well after lunch and the café was no longer busy. The place smelled of the barbecue that, come four o'clock, would be bringing in folks from all over. There was a jukebox at the other end of the café and someone had tapped in "The Purple People Eater," a recent popular song whose charm Angie had never quite understood. Wendell Moon, who was cook, bottle washer, general handyman, and anything else that Ida or Angie asked of him, was seeing to the few lingering customers while Ida, Angie, and a third woman sat talking over cups of strong brew.

The third woman was Charlotte Bauer, who preferred to be called Charlie. Angie Madison liked this woman enormously. She saw Charlie Bauer as a kindred spirit, independent, strong, and outspoken. She was nearing sixty, an attorney, mostly retired though she still did some pro bono work in Black Earth County. Charlie was fond of whiskey, although she didn't drink to excess. She sometimes allowed herself the pleasure of a cigar, an oddity that Angie knew was also true of Gertrude Stein and George Sand and was a habit Charlie claimed to have acquired early in her life while defending striking farm laborers in the San Joaquin Valley of California. Most often she wore jeans and work shirts, except in the courtroom, where she dressed smartly but without flair. Angie suspected that Charlie had more in common with Gertrude Stein than just a taste for cigars, but it was a subject they'd never broached and that made no difference in how Angie thought of her friend.

Across several years over coffee at the Wagon Wheel, Charlie had shared a good deal of her history with Angie. She'd left Jewel when she was eighteen, had attended Mills College in Oakland, and afterward had read for the law. She'd spent most of her career representing the downtrodden in California but had returned late in life to Jewel and had qualified to practice in her home state. Although Angie had never actually seen her at work in the courtroom, she'd heard plenty of stories from others of how valiantly Charlie defended the defenseless.

They had already talked about the high cost of food—"Eggs, sixty cents a dozen! Milk, a dollar a gallon!" They'd commiserated about the death of Ruth Coffee, whom they'd all loved and admired. They'd discussed Jimmy Quinn's death at great length, though they didn't have a lot of details yet. And now they were on to Brody Dern.

"I heard," Ida said, "that she got tired of waiting for Brody to pop the question, and she up and ran off with a piano salesman from Saint Paul."

"It was Saint Louis," Charlie said. "But Brody doesn't seem all that broken up about it."

They were talking about the mysterious woman Brody had been dating for a lot of years but no one in Jewel had ever seen. For a good long while, Brody had been leaving town on Saturday nights and would be gone for hours. His mother had let on that he was seeing a girl in Worthington, a teacher, she thought, though she seemed a little uncertain about that. In his personal life, Brody was circumspect at best, even with his family. But for several Saturdays now, Brody hadn't made his usual disappearance, and folks had begun to wonder and to talk.

"The door's wide open," Ida said to her daughter-in-law.

Angie set her coffee cup down and said levelly, "What's that supposed to mean?"

"You and Brody have been dancing around each other for ages. But there's always been that Worthington girl in the way. Not anymore."

"You make me sound like some kind of vulture waiting to swoop down."

"Honey, I can't imagine a more delectable morsel than Brody Dern."

"Speak of the devil," Charlie said.

The three women watched as Brody and Scott walked toward the café from the direction of the jail. Scott split off to the house, but Brody came in. He said his hellos to the few diners finishing their meals and to Wendell Moon, who wore an apron around his waist and was wiping down a table. The sheriff took a stool at the end of the counter where Angie, Ida, and Charlie sat.

"Ladies," he said.

Before Brody even asked for it, Angie got up, poured coffee from the pot on the burner, and set the mug in front of him.

Charlie Bauer wasted no time on small talk. "True about Jimmy Quinn?"

"Is what true?" Brody reached for the sugar on the counter.

"You found him in the Alabaster, all chewed up by channel cats?"

Brody stirred sugar into his coffee. "I didn't find him, but the other part's accurate."

"Drowned?" Angie asked.

"I can't say yet. Doc Porter's doing an autopsy right now."

"Drunk?" Ida asked.

"It appears that he'd been drinking. I don't know if that contributed to his death."

"Well, it probably didn't help him any. How's Marta taking it?"

"She seems to be holding up."

"This on top of everything else for that woman," Angie said. For a moment, her face was full of sympathy, then she looked at Brody and gave him a playful scowl. "Didn't want the turkey sandwich I sent over?"

"I'm thinking that'll be dinner. I wanted something good and hot for lunch."

Ida said, "Meat loaf maybe?"

"Now you're talking."

"Be right back," she said and left.

Angie cocked her head and gave the sheriff a long, penetrating look. "What kind of job is it, Brody, where you find and dissect dead men?"

Brody said, "Dissecting is Doc Porter's job."

"You know what I mean. What you deal with, it just seems so hard. Why would anyone want a job like that?"

"Didn't want to be a farmer and I had no education or training for anything else."

It was true, in a way, but it was a flippant answer, and he could see on Angie's face that it didn't satisfy her. The real truth was that he'd hadn't considered the question before. Maybe had even avoided it. But because Angie was waiting for an answer, he thought about it now.

"In the war, all I saw was senseless destruction, just total chaos. It seemed to me it was pretty much caused by people who paid no attention to laws. When Connie offered me the job as his deputy, I thought that maybe with a badge . . ." He hesitated because what he was thinking sounded grandiose.

"With a badge you could make a difference," she finished for him.

"Sounds stupid, I know."

"No, it sounds perfectly sensible. And admirable."

She smiled, and because he felt suddenly embarrassed by his honesty and by her praise, he concentrated on drinking his coffee.

The diner door opened and Garnet Dern entered. She looked over the faces inside, all upturned at her entrance. She spotted Brody and beelined.

"Here you are. I've been looking for you." She took the stool beside him and offered him a red-lipped smile. She nodded to Angie and Charlie. "Afternoon."

"What brings you in, Garnet?" Angie asked. There was just a bit of frost in her voice. "We don't often see you in the Wagon Wheel."

"The truth is I need this man's help." She laid a hand gently on Brody's arm and spoke to him directly. "The ladies of Saint Ignatius have put some food together for the Quinns, meals and such, so that Marta won't have to worry about fixing anything for a while. I'm wondering if you'd mind going out with me to deliver it."

"You need an official police escort?" Charlie said.

Garnet kept her response directed toward Brody. "It's just that I could use a good strong pair of arms and someone who's already made an appearance there. I don't want to overwhelm them with a lot of needless folks milling around. Would you do that for me?"

Brody shrugged. "Sure."

"I have everything in my car."

"I was just about to have some lunch."

"There's potato salad out there, Brody. I'd hate to take a chance with it sitting too long unrefrigerated."

"All right, then."

Ida came from the kitchen. "Meat loaf will be out in two shakes, Brody. Afternoon, Garnet."

"Hello, Ida. How are you?"

"Fine and dandy, thank you."

Brody said, "Got to cancel that order, Ida."

"Oh?"

"My help's been requested."

Garnet smiled. "We're delivering some food to Marta Quinn on behalf of the ladies of our church. One less thing for Marta and those kids to worry about. You understand, Ida."

"That's mighty Christian of you," Ida said.

"Garnet, why don't you go on outside?" Brody suggested. "I'll be there directly."

"Not too long," she said. "The potato salad." She lifted a hand in a silent parting gesture to the women and headed outside.

"Any chance that meat loaf will still be here when I get back?" Brody asked.

"Can't promise anything, Sheriff. A popular menu item." Ida looked straight into Brody's eyes. "That woman smells awful nice for this Christian mission of hers."

"No law against smelling nice, is there, Ida?"

The three women watched him leave, get behind the wheel of the station wagon, and drive away with Garnet Dern.

"Whoo-ee," Charlie said and waved her hand to clear the air. "Any idea what that girl was wearing?"

Angie poured herself a little more coffee. "No idea, but Brody better stay upwind of her or that smell will knock him right out of his jockey shorts."

Ida laughed, then leaned near her daughter-in-law. "So like I said, door's open. If you don't pounce on Brody, somebody else will."

CHAPTER FOURTEEN

THE AFTERNOON WAS lovely and warm, the kind of early summer day that makes southern Minnesota—or anywhere for that matter—feel like a small part of heaven. Brody followed the crooked course of the Alabaster south out of Jewel, passed areas of wetland full of cattails and the flutter of red-winged blackbirds. Fordham Ridge lay on the distant horizon, a sleeping giant overlaid with a quilt of plowed and planted fields.

"Have you been thinking about me?" Garnet asked.

"I've got a lot on my mind."

"I hope I'm in there somewhere. Because I think about you a lot, Brody. You do get under a girl's skin." She reached out and moved her hand seductively over his thigh. "So. Angie?"

"What about Angie?"

"Brody Dern, don't tell me you don't notice."

"What?"

"That little piece of southern hospitality's got her eye on you."

"You think so?"

"Don't go getting a big head, Sheriff. Or ideas. A woman raising a child alone, she's bound to have her cap set at most any man without a wedding band."

"I'll keep that in mind."

Garnet laughed. "Oh, Brody, I do love you. You're still such a kid." Her fingers squeezed his thigh.

Brody thought it was an odd thing for her to have said. He couldn't recall ever feeling like a kid. All he seemed to remember of childhood was doing the backbreaking work of a man day after day alongside his father and brother. And before he was out of his teens, he was in the middle of the slaughter of war. But he did love hearing Garnet laugh.

He turned onto the lane that led to the Quinns' farmhouse and outbuildings. When they pulled up to the house, Brody spotted Connie Graff's truck parked near the barn.

Garnet noticed it, too. "What's Connie doing here?"

"Good question. Only one way to find out."

"Before you run off, Brody, will you help me get the food inside?"

There were several covered boxes in the back of the station wagon. While Garnet went to the front door and knocked, Brody lifted the first box and joined her on the porch. Colleen appeared behind the screen door. The teenager studied them a moment, as if trying to make sense of their presence, then said, "Hello, Mrs. Dern. Sheriff."

"Hello, Colleen," Garnet replied. "Is your mother here?"

"She's resting," Colleen said.

"Well, you just let her rest, dear. I'm here on behalf of the ladies of Saint Ignatius. We've put together a few things to take some of the worry off your shoulders. Some casseroles and whatnot. May we bring them in?"

"Sure, I guess. Thank you."

The girl opened the door, and Brody followed Garnet inside. He made several trips carrying boxes filled with enough prepared dishes to feed the whole Quinn clan and their hired men for a week. On the final trip, he found that Marta Quinn had come downstairs herself. She was sitting beside Garnet on the living room sofa. She still had on the black dress she'd worn to the funeral home. Garnet held both of the widow's hands in her own and leaned toward her in a compassionate way.

"Whatever you need, Marta," Garnet was saying. "We're all here for you."

"Thank you."

"Do you need help with the house?"

"No. The girls are good."

"J.P., does he need a hand around the farm?"

"No, we have men."

"All right."

Brody put the final box on the table in the kitchen, where Colleen was already busy finding room in the refrigerator.

"Everything okay?" he asked.

"There's a lot," Colleen said.

"You know how folks are."

Which was, Brody thought in retrospect, an odd thing to say to the girl. How would she know how folks are when you've lost a father? It had never happened to her before.

But she said, "Yes," as if she understood perfectly and the kindness of these rural women was something for which she was, in fact, grateful.

Brody returned to the living room, where the two women were in deep conversation. Garnet had buried both her parents and a brother and knew firsthand about death and its aftermath. Marta seemed intensely interested in her perspective. Brody excused himself to go find Graff.

"Don't go far, Brody," Garnet said. "We'll be leaving shortly."

He wanted to tell her that they would leave when he was done, because Graff's presence had changed the nature of his visit, but he said only "I'll be around."

The barn, an enormous structure painted white, stood on a rise fifty yards from the house, along with the other outbuildings and grain silos. The barn's lower level had been dug into the hillside. It contained feeding troughs and opened onto the large cattle yard behind the barn. The main level, above, contained a number of stalls that had once been occupied by draft horses but now held various implements. Above that was a great loft stacked with bales of hay.

Except for its enormous size, the structure was little different from most barns Brody had been in.

As he climbed the dirt lane, he caught the dry scent of hay and the underlying smell of manure. Just inside the broad, open doorway, he found Graff standing beside a John Deere tractor, talking with Noah Bluestone. The two men stopped their conversation when Brody appeared.

"Hey, Connie," Brody said.

"Sheriff," Graff replied in a formal way. Which signaled to Brody that what was going on between the men in that barn was all business.

"Afternoon, Noah," Brody said.

"Sheriff," Bluestone responded.

"I thought Jimmy fired you," Brody said.

"Mrs. Quinn asked me back. Said they could use an extra hand, especially now."

Noah Bluestone was not particularly big—a full head shorter than both Brody and Graff—but what there was of him was all hard bone and thick muscle and tough sinew. His hair was panther black, short-cropped. His dark face was the legacy of both his long days in the sun and the Sioux blood that ran through every one of his capillaries. His eyes were heavy-lidded, so that he looked at the world through slits behind which mostly darkness showed. He was a difficult man to read.

"Mind telling me why Jimmy let you go?" Brody said.

"I just finished explaining that to your deputy," he said.

"How about explaining it to me."

"We didn't see eye to eye," Bluestone said simply.

"On what?"

"You name it."

"I heard that you and Quinn had words before he fired you. What was that particular argument about?"

"His drinking."

"What about his drinking?"

"I told him I didn't like it."

"And he fired you."

"Not right away."

"What happened in between?"

"He accused me of stealing gas from the pump."

"Did you?"

"No."

"You tell him that?"

"Once Jimmy had something in his head, no use trying to convince him otherwise."

"So you had words. About his drinking and his accusation of theft. Is that all?"

"One more thing."

"What?"

"He threatened to beat the hell out of me."

"Over the gas thing or his drinking?"

"Neither."

"What then?"

"Because I told him exactly what I thought of him, which wasn't much."

"Was he drunk when you told him?"

"He'd been drinking."

"What did you say?"

"I told him I'd like to see him try."

"Did he?"

"He was a big man but he had a small spirit. He fired me instead."

"And then he ends up in the Alabaster River," Graff said.

Bluestone's face changed not at all. "I heard he shot himself."

"We found his truck out at Inkpaduta Bend," Graff said. "That's not all that far from your place."

"Not all that far from a lot of places, including Quinn's."

"Where were you Thursday, Noah?"

"Home."

"All day?"

"Most of it."

"Didn't happen to go to Inkpaduta Bend, did you?" Brody asked.

"Yes."

The forthrightness of the answer surprised Brody. "When?"

"Just before dark."

"Why?"

"It's a place I go sometimes."

"Why that night?"

"I told you it's a place I go sometimes. A spiritual place."

"Did you see Jimmy?"

"No one was there."

"Quinn wasn't fishing?"

"I told you. No one was there."

"How long did you stay?"

"Until the sky was all stars. An hour maybe."

"And you didn't see Jimmy?"

"I didn't see a living soul. But I heard something."

"What?"

"You won't believe me."

"Try me."

"A lost spirit."

Brody did believe him, believed him absolutely, because he'd heard the same thing and had tried to convince himself it was the sound of a coyote.

Bluestone's eyes shifted. So did Graff's. Both to something behind the sheriff.

"Brody?"

He turned and found Garnet smiling pleasantly at all the men.

"Hello, Connie. Noah," she said.

"Ma'am," Bluestone said.

Graff tipped his Stetson. "Afternoon, Garnet."

"Mission accomplished," the woman said brightly to Brody. "Shall we go?"

"I need to stay. I'll get a ride back with Connie. You understand," he said.

"Of course." She smiled as if she understood perfectly, but Brody saw the frosty look in her eyes. "Gentlemen." She turned and left.

"Anything else, Sheriff?" Bluestone said. "I've got a tractor here that's not running right. And there's lots of other chores to be done now that Jimmy's not around to help."

"Why did you work for him?" Graff asked. "You and your wife both, if you didn't like anything about him?"

Bluestone took a red rag from where it hung out the back pocket of his jeans and wiped grease off his hands. "I was in the Marines for more than twenty years. I worked for a lot of men I didn't particularly like. In my experience, liking is usually at the bottom of the list of why folks do what they do."

"Let me ask it another way," Graff said. "You've got a good pension coming from the service. You have a nice little place out there the other side of the Alabaster. Why work for Quinn at all?"

"I have my reasons," Bluestone said. Which meant it was a question he would not answer. At least not at the moment and not in this way.

"Does it ever gall you?" Graff went on. "Working the land that should be yours but Quinn had the deed to?"

This was a question that came from an understanding of the long, difficult history that existed between the whites of Black Earth County and those in whom the blood of the Sioux ran. It was, at its heart, about an old war and wounds that had never really healed.

Bluestone blinked twice, then replied, "My father worked for Jimmy

Quinn and I did, too, before I became a Marine. I never liked the man. Sometimes I even wanted to kill him. But it was never about the land."

Brody stared into the dark eyes, trying to read what little of the man they revealed. All the while, the stink of the cattle pen below rose up and enveloped them.

"One last thing," Graff said. "The Quinns asked you back, but not your wife. Any reason they didn't want her?"

"It was me. I didn't want her back here," Bluestone said. "I need her at home. There's a lot of work to be done."

"Thanks for your time, Noah," Brody finally said. "We'll let you get back to that tractor. Come on, Connie."

"WHAT THE HELL were you doing at Quinn's?" Brody said.

They sat in Graff's truck, paused at the junction of the highway and the lane that led to Quinn's place. The sun was in their faces, and Graff lowered the visor to shade his eyes. He rested his wrists over the top of the steering wheel and considered Fordham Ridge in the distance, and then the course of the Alabaster, which ran behind a field on the other side of the road, a field that, like much of what they could see, belonged to James Patrick Quinn. Or had.

"I stopped by Bluestones'," Graff replied. "One of the farms in the area I had to check. Pretty near Inkpaduta Bend."

"No, you've figured it was murder from the beginning and from the beginning you pegged Bluestone for it," Brody said. "You and everybody else in this town, it seems. Gordy Landis was in this morning, threatening to string up Bluestone."

Graff shrugged. "Bluestone has a legitimate grudge. And I'm not talking just about this recent thing with Quinn. Goes way back. We both know it. Everyone in this county knows it."

A big rig rolled by on the highway, heading toward Spirit Lake or

Lake Okoboji in Iowa. Graff waited until it had passed and the wind in its wake had died.

"Bluestone killed men in a couple of wars," he said. "I'm thinking killing one more wouldn't be much of a stretch."

"You kill anybody when you fought in the First World War, Connie?"

Graff didn't respond immediately. It was a question Brody had never asked him, and the kind Graff, for his part, had never asked of Brody.

"Because I did," Brody said. "And I'll tell you, when I walked away from the service, I was sick to death of killing."

"Yet here you are, son, in a job that might require you someday to draw a bead on a man. You telling me you couldn't do that if the time came? Because if I'd thought that when I hired you, I'd never have given you a badge."

"It's different," Brody said.

"I'd like to know how."

"Talking about Bluestone and Quinn, you're talking about something that might be cold-blooded murder."

"Killing is killing, Brody. You can justify it seven ways from sundown, but it's still the same thing in the end."

"The law says different, Connie."

"Screw the law. You know exactly what I'm talking about." Graff stared across the empty highway toward the Alabaster. He spoke slowly and quietly. "I remember a night in Belleau Wood. We're hunkered down in a big shell crater, the three of us left in our platoon. Me, I'm scared, but I'm so used to being scared it's second nature. Kid next to me is green. From Oklahoma. Preacher's boy. Brought a little Bible along with him. He's holding it next to his heart and he's praying. Real quiet, real desperate. I want to offer him some kind of comfort, but honest to God I got nothing. Because it's hell and there's no way around that. All the trees in the woods are nothing but jagged stumps. We can hear stuff going on around us, but it's so dark we can't see anything clear. Next thing we know, a couple of Jerries come diving into that crater, bayonets fixed. The guy next to the preacher boy, he gets a bayonet through his throat. Preacher boy, this scared kid, throws down his Bible and launches himself at the first Jerry. They go down. I've got my rifle up and put two rounds into the second Jerry. The preacher kid, he's on top of the first one and they're going at it hand to hand. I can't shoot cuz I'd hit the kid. But it's over pretty quick. Kid stands up and the Jerry's lying there with his belly open and his guts spilling out. Somehow that kid had managed to draw his own bayonet, and let me tell you, Brody, I never saw a more effective use of that particular weapon. When it's done, the kid pukes. All over his Bible. He never did pick it back up." Graff swung his eyes from the course of the river to Brody. "Do I think Bluestone's capable of killing Quinn in cold blood? You bet I do. And under the right circumstances I'd say the same of you. Or me."

"How come you never told me that story?" Brody said.

"Lots of stories I never told you. Probably never will."

Brody rubbed his eyes, trying to push away a headache that was just starting. "Did you talk to his wife?"

"A nice young woman. Quiet, respectful. Wouldn't meet my eyes, though."

"Did she tell you anything? Other than that her husband was at Quinn's place?"

"She said the reason she wasn't working for the Quinns now was that they didn't need her. Bluestone told us it was because he didn't want her there. A difference in their stories. It's small, but something to consider."

"There's nothing to consider, Connie. Look, why would Quinn go out to Inkpaduta Bend, take his fishing gear and that Coleman lantern, if he wasn't actually planning on a little night fishing? It's clear that man shot himself, and it was either suicide or a terrible accident."

"Why'd he disrobe?" Graff asked.

"Maybe he was going to swim. Or maybe he thought about drowning himself instead of using that Tolley."

Graff gave him a long look. "You're trying awful hard to see this in only one way."

"The Quinns told me Jimmy tried to kill himself once before. J.P. talked him out of it."

"You don't say." This clearly caught Graff by surprise.

"If we call it suicide, the Catholic Church won't let them bury Jimmy with the rest of the family. So I'm telling you right now, unless that autopsy turns up something I can't even imagine, I'm going to call Quinn's death accidental. And unless you've got something that points beyond a shadow of a doubt to murder, you're not even going to whisper that word. Are we clear?"

Graff let a few breaths go by. "You're the sheriff," he said.

CHAPTER FIFTEEN

THERE WAS A note on the jailhouse door. Lester Henning, the town cop in Jefferson, fifteen miles north, wanted Brody or one of the deputies to take a look at a break-in that had occurred at the Catholic church there. Nothing missing, but there'd been some vandalism. Henning thought it was similar to incidents that had occurred in two other towns in Black Earth County recently. Brody told Graff to cover it, and the deputy took off. Brody unlocked the jailhouse and stepped inside. Hector leapt up to greet him, then looked a little plaintively toward the open door.

"Guess we better go, huh?"

They went down Cottonwood Street, making a round they both knew well. Hector had been Brody's since the dog was a pup, given to him by Connie Graff.

"You'll need some company in that jailhouse," Graff had said. "Gets lonely there at night. Unless you're planning on taking some bride I don't know about."

There was no bride and no prospect for one, and Brody soon recognized the older lawman's wisdom. Hector was the best of company, a companion who never complained, who listened without reply, who was always overjoyed to see Brody, and whose constant presence was not only easy to tolerate but also greatly appreciated.

People didn't walk their dogs back then, not like they do now. But Brody was sheriff and didn't want anyone complaining about Hector running wild. They were a familiar sight on the streets of Jewel, and most folks felt comfortable offering the dog a friendly pat in greeting.

On this particular outing, they walked past the courthouse lawn, where a couple of girls were playing with Hula Hoops. It was a recent fad, one Brody didn't quite understand, but it had been a long time since he'd been a kid and had the freedom to kill time in frivolous ways. When he turned down Main Street, he was stopped again and again by people wanting to know about Jimmy Quinn. He dropped into Bennett's Jewelry Store to check on the sapphire ring he'd found in Jimmy Quinn's pocket. He was just leaving when the door of the *Clarion* office opened and Sam Wicklow stepped out. The newspaperman crossed the street and approached Brody. "I gave Asa all the photos from Inkpaduta Bend this morning. You had a chance to look at them?"

"Not yet, Sam. Thanks again for the favor."

"No problem. Also, Loretta wanted me to let you know that we're all still on for the Prairie Blooms tomorrow night."

The Prairie Blooms was the reading group Ruth Coffee had formed years before in her never-ending effort to bring culture to Jewel. She'd named it as a kind of play on the Bloomsbury Group, the fabled collection of English writers and literati that included the likes of Virginia Woolf and E. M. Forster. The Prairie Blooms met one Sunday evening each month to discuss a book, or collection of poetry, or a play, anything that Ruth Coffee believed would elevate conversation to a level that dealt in Ideals, "with a capital *I*," she was fond of saying. It was an honor to be invited by Ruth to join the group. Because of her death, Brody had figured that was the end of the Prairie Blooms.

"Where?" Brody asked.

"We're hosting. Loretta's fixing up a special dinner in Ruth's honor. Wants us all to dress nice."

Brody said, "I'm pretty busy with this Quinn thing, Sam, but I'll see what I can do."

"You going over to the Wagon Wheel anytime today?"

"I could drop by. Why?"

"I'm wondering if you could let Angie know. Loretta tried calling, didn't get an answer."

"I'll do that, Sam. What time?"

"Six-thirty."

On his desk at the jailhouse, Brody found the manila envelope containing the photographs Wicklow had taken that morning. Graff was right. There were a lot of troubling aspects about the scene, but nothing for which he couldn't come up with a plausible explanation. When his phone rang, he put the photos down. It was Doc Porter on the other end of the line.

"I figured you'd want to know as soon as possible what I found in Quinn's autopsy. I can give it to you simple, then I'll start putting together the official report."

"Thanks, Doc."

"It was pretty much what I expected, Brody. That shotgun blast killed him. No water in his lungs, so he was dead before he went into the Alabaster."

"The shotgun we found out there on Inkpaduta Bend was an eight-gauge. You get pellets out of him?"

"Yep. Not sure they're eight-gauge. You'd have a better idea of that than me. But they're big."

"Any idea how long he was dead before he went into the river?"

"Can't say."

"There was a lot of blood on that riverbank. Did he bleed out there, you think?"

"Again, I can't really say."

"Was he drunk? Heavily sedated?"

"I'll have to run tests before I can give you anything on that."

"How are you going characterize it?"

"Jimmy's death? I'm just going to say what killed him. Massive trauma from a gunshot wound. The characterization, as you call it, I'll leave to you."

"Okay, Doc. Thanks."

Brody turned his attention to the evidence they'd collected on the Bend and which he'd stored in a couple of lockers. He put on leather gloves and brought out the tackle box and rod, the empty whiskey bottle, the pill bottle, the Coleman lantern, the folded clothing and boots, and the shotgun. The last item he placed on the desk was the silver ring set with a sapphire, which he'd pulled from his own pocket.

He considered the bottle of Seconal first. The date on the prescription was only two weeks earlier, but the bottle was already less than half full. Considering that Quinn often ended up dead to the world on another man's land, it was a miracle he hadn't been shot earlier. Maybe the insomnia was a medical condition, Brody considered. Or maybe it was simply the plague of a man with terrible sins weighing on his conscience. That was something Brody could understand.

He put the pill bottle aside and picked up the ring. At the jewelry store, Myron Bennett had looked at it through a loupe and assured him the stone was real. He'd said it probably sold for a couple hundred dollars, maybe a little more, and that it hadn't come from his own stock of merchandise. He said the size of the ring made him believe it was probably meant for an adolescent or a small woman. Brody set the ring aside.

He studied the shotgun next. It was a beautiful firearm, English-made, double-barreled, with a polished walnut stock. Lots of men in Black Earth County owned shotguns. It was great pheasant-hunting country, with a sizable population of wild turkeys as well. Most of these men owned standard American issues—Remingtons, Marlins, Winchesters—and they hunted with smaller-gauge firearms. For the past twenty-five years, it had been illegal in Minnesota to hunt fowl with an eight-gauge. Leave it to Jimmy Quinn to go shooting with an outlawed British classic.

Brody still had the piece on his desk when the jailhouse door was thrown open and a tempest blew in. The storm had a name: Terence Timothy Quinn. He was Jimmy Quinn's eldest child, born to Quinn's first wife, but he hadn't lived in Black Earth County for years. On those rare occasions when his father begrudgingly mentioned him, Jimmy Quinn had spoken of Terry as an ungrateful son who'd forsaken his duty to the family.

"Dern," Quinn huffed, offering no other greeting. There was also no acknowledgment of Brody's position or authority. Jimmy Quinn would have used the title, called him "Sheriff," but not because the elder Quinn really believed he was subject to the same laws as everyone else. It was a deigning of sorts, as if Brody served not at the will of the rest of Black Earth County but somehow because of Quinn's own generosity.

Terry Quinn stormed toward the sheriff's desk. Hector, who'd been lying quietly on the floor at Brody's side, stood, and a low growl rumbled from his throat.

"It's okay, boy," Brody said. He patted the dog and Hector sat, still alert. "Afternoon, Terry."

"I came about my father."

"I figured. Have a seat." Brody indicated the old office chair that Asa Fielding usually occupied.

Terry Quinn ignored the offer. He stood looking down at the items Brody had laid out on the desk. "What are you doing?"

"Police work."

"Is all this evidence?"

"Maybe."

"Of what?"

"I won't know exactly until I've gathered all the facts. I'm still working on that, Terry. And by the way, I'm sorry for your loss."

Quinn very much resembled his father. He was a couple of years older than Brody, every bit as big as Jimmy Quinn had been and with

Jimmy Quinn's mane of flaming red hair. He was a farmer, as his father had been, though he had a long way to go before he farmed on the same scale. The land Terry Quinn had bought was two counties to the east.

Quinn said, "Murder, I heard. Noah Bluestone. Is that true?"

"I don't have all the facts, but I'm not thinking it was anything like murder."

"Dad fires Bluestone and the next thing you know someone opens him up with a shotgun? Come on, Dern, only an idiot wouldn't see the connection."

"I don't even have an official autopsy report yet. So, Terry, I'm going to ask that you don't go jumping to any conclusions or making any accusations. When I have more, I'll let you know. That's a promise."

"Bluestone's always hated us Quinns. Accused us of stealing his family's land. Everybody knows that."

"I don't."

"Then like I said, you're an idiot."

Brody slowly sucked in a breath. "Is there anything else, Terry? Because I've got work to do here."

"You screw this up, Dern, I'll see that you never wear a badge again." Which was something Brody could imagine Jimmy Quinn saying.

Quinn's eyes settled on the shotgun in Brody's gloved hands.

"You recognize it?" Brody asked.

"My father's pride and joy. His Tolley. What are you doing with it?"

"I think it's the firearm that killed him."

"It was a special piece. He usually only took it when he was going to shoot with someone he wanted to impress. What the hell was he doing with it out on Inkpaduta Bend?"

"Like I said, Terry, we're still investigating."

"And you'll let me know what you find out?"

"I'll let you know."

The jailhouse door opened and Connie Graff walked in. "Well, now. Terence Quinn. How're you doing, son?"

"My father's dead. What do you think? I'm here to see what you're going to do about his murder and about that damn Bluestone."

Graff came to the desk and stood near Quinn in a relaxed way. "You really want to know what I think, Terence? I'll tell you what I think, since you asked. I'm thinking that if I were you, I'd be mighty upset. And I'm thinking that it would be best to let cooler heads work out the truth of your father's death. And I'm thinking that it does no one any good to be making accusations at this point. Again, since you asked." Graff removed his Stetson, hung it on a wall peg, and smoothed back his grayed hair. "Have you talked to your sister Fiona?"

"I've talked to her. What of it?"

"Just wondering how she's doing with this."

"How do you expect she's doing? Sick with grief."

"I'm sure," Graff said. "And I'm sorry for her loss."

"My loss, too."

"Of course," Graff said.

Brody said, "Anything else, Terry?"

"Nothing, I guess. For now. But I expect you to keep your promise."

"What promise was that?" Graff asked.

"You'll keep me in the loop," Quinn answered for Brody. "What you know, I'll know."

"You promised that, Brody?" Graff gave the sheriff a look that wasn't hard to interpret.

"I did."

Graff swung his gaze to Terry Quinn. "Well, sir, I've never known Sheriff Dern to go back on a promise. So I guess you have your answer."

"I guess I do." Quinn turned and, without any formal words of parting, left the jailhouse.

In the quiet and calm afterward, Graff said, "They don't fall far from the tree, do they?"

"He told me he'd heard it was murder and that it was Bluestone." Brody shot his deputy an accusatory look.

"Small town, Brody. People are going to talk, you know that."

Brody's stomach growled, long and low.

"You get yourself any lunch?" Graff asked.

"Meant to. Got distracted."

"You want me to take care of this? Dust for prints?" Graff nodded toward the shotgun and other evidence Brody had been examining. "You are planning on dusting for prints, aren't you?"

"Of course," Brody said.

"You can go on over to the Wagon Wheel. Bet Angie might have a little something for Hector there, too."

Brody stripped off his gloves, said, "Let's go, boy," and left the old lawman to the work of dusting for prints, work Brody knew would yield nothing.

CHAPTER SIXTEEN

BRODY AND HECTOR returned an hour later. Graff was still at the desk but appeared to be finished with what he'd stayed behind to do.

"I got a call from Bob Magruder out in Lincoln Township," Graff told him. "Says he parked his truck at the edge of his cornfield when he was cultivating this afternoon. Somebody stole it. Asa's out there now. He'll take the report, then he's going to call it a day."

"How do we stand with things here?"

Graff sat back, stared at the evidence on the desk, then gave Brody a long, penetrating look. "There's nothing."

"What do you mean?"

"No fingerprints. Not a one. Not on anything."

Brody shrugged. "Those pigskin gloves we found in Quinn's truck. He probably wore those."

"There'd be residual prints on something, Brody. All this stuff was wiped clean. Somebody went to a lot of trouble to make it look like a suicide or an accident. And if they did that, I'm thinking they probably made sure they left nothing behind that'll point to them."

Graff waited for Brody to reply, but nothing came.

"There was a lot of blood on that riverbank," the old deputy said. "The man bled out there and died. Then he went into the water. A dead man doesn't move himself."

"Why would someone kill Jimmy Quinn?" Brody knew it was a stupid question, and it came out limp.

"A long list, that one," Graff said. "Jimmy knew it. Maybe that's why he had the Tolley with him."

"Terry told me his dad only used it when he wanted to impress someone. Who was he trying to impress? And why tell his family he's going fishing?"

"Something going on he didn't want them knowing about?" Graff said. "Something to hide? Something out on Inkpaduta Bend maybe?"

"We looked that place over pretty good."

"Never hurts to look again," Graff said, rising from his chair.

Brody had no choice but to follow.

Fifteen minutes later, they stood on the Bend, near the great stain of blood. The sun had dropped behind Fordham Ridge, and Brody and Graff were engulfed by the blue shadow of that dramatic formation. Except for the sound of the birds in the birch trees along the riverbank, the evening was quiet. In Brody's thinking, this was a lovely and peaceful place, one of the most beautiful in all of Black Earth County.

Graff said, "A spiritual place. That's what Bluestone said about the Bend. Now tell me what could be spiritual about a place where a white woman was killed by renegades?"

Hector was sniffing around in the grass not far away, his tail going crazy as he picked up a world of scents.

Graff slid his hands into the pockets of his jeans and scanned the whole area. "What brought Quinn here? Why was he wearing only his boxer shorts when he was shot? This place is far from prying eyes. Was he meeting someone he didn't want his family or anyone else to know about? A romantic meeting, maybe?"

"The sapphire ring would go along with that," Brody offered. "But why bring the Tolley? Kind of kills the idea of a romantic meeting."

"Aren't women impressed by a man with a big gun?" Graff said with a grim smile. "Maybe it was a confrontation with someone he thought he might need protection against. That Tolley's pretty intimidating."

"When it's pointed right at you, any gun is intimidating. It's an expensive piece. Maybe he planned to give it as a gift."

"I cracked the breech," Graff said. "Still one unfired shell in there. Quinn came here with both barrels loaded. He might have been intending to give someone a surprise, but probably not a gift." The deputy shook his head. "At the moment, nothing makes much sense. What are we missing?"

Brody walked around the place where everything seemed to point to Quinn bleeding his life out onto the dirt of the riverbank. He knelt and carefully studied the ground between the blood and the Alabaster. "No sign that he was dragged into the river. Jimmy Quinn was a giant. If someone killed him and threw him in the Alabaster, unless they were just as big as he was, wouldn't they have had to drag him? Wouldn't there be some indication of that in the dirt here?"

"Kind of lends a little bit of credence to the suicide theory, I guess," Graff said, but clearly with reluctance. He thought a moment, then said, "Or maybe Quinn met more than one person out here. A couple of people could throw him in easy enough. And if he was worried about the nature of the people he was meeting, that Tolley of his would be a good friend to bring along."

"Okay, let's be thorough." Brody stepped to the edge of the blood-stained dirt. "Let's assume he's drunk and drugged up on tranquilizers. He's got his Tolley out, for whatever reason. He either decides to shoot himself or fumbles the shotgun, drops it, blows a hole in his guts. Would the force of the blast itself knock him into the river right away, you think? Or is it possible that in fact he did stand here and bleed out, then, as he took his last breath, stumbled back into the river?"

"Died by himself out here, you're saying?"

"Not saying, just mulling over the possibility. Because all things considered, I'd just as soon believe that Jimmy Quinn didn't have any help passing out of this life. It would make everything easier."

"You wanted easy, you should've been a shoe salesman." Graff looked Brody in the eye. "We both agree Jimmy didn't die alone out here."

"I haven't said I agree."

Graff ignored his objection. "So the question is why? Was Quinn set up? Did he set up something that somehow got turned around on him? And what was he doing getting himself undressed?"

In the tall grass a dozen feet from where the men stood, Hector began digging furiously. Brody walked over to see what had so taken the dog's interest. As soon as he bent above Hector, he called the dog off sternly, and the mutt backed away.

"What is it?" Graff said.

Brody crouched in the grass. "Come on over and see for yourself."

Graff joined him. "What the hell?"

"More blood," Brody said.

It was not nearly so much as the big stain on the riverbank, but it was blood, spilled across a small area, staining the grass stalks and the ground out of which they grew. Brody looked from there to the larger spill, then stood and slowly walked a line between the two, carefully studying the ground.

"Nothing between them," he reported to Graff. "It's like two different incidents, two different woundings."

"The person who was out here with Jimmy?"

"Get the evidence bags," Brody said.

They collected samples of the bloodstained grass and dirt of the smaller spilling, then gathered the same from the large blood spill on the riverbank.

"Going to send these to the BCA for analysis?" Graff asked when they'd finished. He was talking about the state's Bureau of Criminal Apprehension.

"That might take forever. I'll give Doc Porter a call, see if he'd be willing to look at them."

It was nearing sunset. The two lawmen stood beside the Alabaster River, under a sky empty of clouds. The air was still, in the way it often became in southern Minnesota when the day prepared to yield to darkness. Brody breathed in the scent of the tall grass and wildflowers, and below that, the heavy smell of the river and the mud, and under it all, the fecund aroma of the deep, black earth from which the county drew its name.

"What now?" Graff said.

"Back to the office," Brody replied. "I'll give Doc a call. Then I've got a turkey sandwich in my refrigerator and some cold beer, so unless something comes up that needs my attention, I'm going to settle down for the night. Welcome to join me. For the beer, anyway."

Graff shook his head. "I got me a couple of horses to feed. And I've got my own beer, thank you. And I've also got a lot of thinking to do." He took one last, long look around the scene. "I know you've been fighting against this as a homicide, Brody. And I think I know why. There's a reason they call us peace officers, son. But there'll be no peace in this county for a while. Everybody's going to be talking about Jimmy Quinn's death, and everybody's going to have a theory. There's going to be fingers pointing in a lot of unfortunate directions. And you're going to be in the middle of it and making no one happy. Would have been a whole lot easier if you could just write it off as a terrible accident, or even suicide. And I'll tell you one more thing, a little bit of a confession."

Brody waited, then had to ask, "What's that?"

"I'm glad it's you and not me wearing that sheriff's badge. And good luck sleeping nights. Because any hope of a peaceful life for you in Black Earth County was blown to smithereens with that shotgun blast."

CHAPTER SEVENTEEN

CONNIE GRAFF'S PLACE was a few miles north of Jewel, an acreage looking west toward the narrow dip in the farmland where the Alabaster had long ago cut its course. His property included a house and lawn; a combination garage and workshop; a horse barn and corral; and some pastureland with a small, clear stream running through. He kept two horses in that pasture—Bogie, named for the movie star, and Honeydew, who'd been his wife's mount.

He'd fed the horses and brushed them and stood now in the open doorway of the little barn. He'd rolled himself a cigarette and had punched open a can of Pabst Blue Ribbon. He smoked and sipped the beer and watched the light dying. It was that time of day when he and Myrna might have sat in the glider together, holding hands. Myrna had always been one for holding hands. When he thought about her, which was often, it wasn't the big things he missed, but the small, intimate moments. Like those in the glider.

When he finally crossed the yard to the house, there was nothing to light his way but a dim afterglow in the west. Inside, he turned on a lamp, and the living room seemed to leap at him in the way of a stranger whose appearance was sudden and unexpected. It was the same room he'd shared with Myrna for more than thirty years, and yet it wasn't. There was no place Myrna had been that was the same. From the moment his wife died, Connie felt as if he'd entered an unfamiliar land.

He was no stranger to death. He'd seen it on the battlefield, young. He'd seen it in the warehouses and dirty streets and shabby neighborhoods of Kansas City as a uniformed cop. He'd seen it in Black Earth County as both deputy and sheriff, seen it amid a tangle of twisted metal and shattered glass on highways, in the bloodied cogs and blades of farm machinery, in the sweat-stained, rumpled bedding that was the end of a long, drawn-out battle with some terrible illness. He and death were well acquainted, he'd thought. Until Myrna.

He boiled a hot dog and ate it with some potato chips and another beer while he sat in an easy chair in the living room and listened to Wagner on the RCA phonograph. That was Myrna's influence. The city girl, whose father had been a wealthy doctor. By the time the record was finished, tears streamed down his cheeks and he had no further appetite.

He scraped the plate and washed it and turned out the lights. He went to the bathroom and brushed his teeth and washed where the tears had dried to salt on his face and stripped out of his clothing down to his boxers and undershirt and stood in the doorway of the bedroom that had been his and Myrna's. He no longer slept there. Instead, he used what had always been the guest room. He couldn't bring himself to sleep in the bed where he'd shared so much with Myrna. Where he'd seen the end of her life, a death for which he felt responsible.

Murderer, he thought to himself, then turned away and went to the bed in the guest room, where he was alone now, always, and where, he knew, if sleep came, it would come after a long struggle.

IN THE JAILHOUSE, above the office and the cells, was the apartment Brody called home. He had a small living room, a kitchen larger than he needed, a bedroom that was more than adequate for his simple needs, and a bathroom with a toilet, a pedestal sink, and a claw-footed tub. He'd lived there since he'd taken the job as Connie Graff's deputy. It was as much a home as Brody felt he needed. He hadn't really decorated. There was little from his past that he cared to be reminded of, so no framed photographs on the walls, nothing from his days growing up on the farm or his time in a military uniform. No sweetheart. No children. He'd hung up a print of a painting he kind of liked by a guy named Hopper. It showed a diner in some big city at night and there were only a few people inside and they all looked like they had nowhere to go and no one who cared where they were or if they were lost.

He did have a photo of Hector, which he'd taken when they were out hunting. The dog was sitting alert in prairie grass, one tall dead tree at his back, the Black Hills of South Dakota in the distance. A brace of grouse that Brody had shot lay on the ground beside him. Although Hector was in the middle of nowhere, he appeared more content than anyone in the painting by Hopper. Whenever Brody looked at the photo, he remembered that outing and how good it was to be out there alone with his dog, and he almost always felt comforted.

After he returned from Inkpaduta Bend, Brody put some Purina in a bowl for Hector. For himself, he pulled from the refrigerator the turkey sandwich Angie had made for him earlier that day but he hadn't eaten. He grabbed a can of Hamm's beer and punched holes in the top with a church key. He sat in the easy chair and tried to watch *Gunsmoke,* but his heart wasn't in it. He turned off the television, switched on the radio, picked up WOW out of Omaha, and listened to the Everly Brothers singing "All I Have to Do Is Dream." His chair faced the south window. The sky beyond was already dark. He could see the lights of Jewel—the marquee on the Rialto Theater, the streetlamps along the three blocks of businesses, the lit windows of houses beyond that. It was Saturday night, and folks were up a little later than usual, and so there were headlights moving along the streets, and every once in a while, Brody caught a snatch of conversation from the sidewalk below his window.

He used to be gone from Jewel on Saturday nights, and Asa Fielding or

Connie Graff would be on duty. Long ago Brody had created a girlfriend for himself. He'd let on that she was a teacher in Worthington, a safe forty miles away. Her name was Lilah. That's all he would say. Except he made sure folks in Jewel knew that on Saturday nights he and Lilah had dinner together and took in a show or went dancing. Everyone in Jewel understood that Brody didn't talk marriage, but the reason or reasons were a little fuzzy. It didn't matter. It kept people from asking the wrong kinds of questions and kept his relationship with Garnet Dern, who was the only soul who knew the truth of the lie, safe. But he'd got tired of that particular story, of keeping up the pretense, and he hadn't been gone on a Saturday night for weeks. He knew folks were talking. He'd let out that he and Lilah had parted ways, though he never said exactly why. One lie to kill another. Where all this was leading, he still didn't know.

When he finished his sandwich and beer, he turned off the radio and took his guitar from where it sat in the corner near the kitchen table and began to pick out the chords of the Everly Brothers tune. After that he strummed a little Hank Williams, and finally, in honor of Elvis Presley, who'd been drafted into the army a few months earlier, he ended with "Love Me Tender."

He put his guitar away and picked up the book he'd read for the Prairie Blooms, *Catcher in the Rye*. It was about a kid named Holden Caulfield who'd lost his way in life pretty early. Holden didn't think much of the adults he knew. In his daydreaming, he imagined himself standing at the edge of a great cliff where a field of rye grew. There were children playing in the rye field, and it was his responsibility to keep them from falling off the cliff. Brody didn't much like the book, but one thing he understood well was Holden Caulfield's desire to protect the innocent. In a way, that's how he saw himself now. And at heart, it was the reason for the part he was playing in the death of Jimmy Quinn, something he hated himself for even as he moved ahead with it. He put the novel aside and got ready for bed. But sleep eluded him. He lay for a while thinking about the pill bottle in the evidence locker downstairs and wondering if anyone would notice a couple more capsules of Seconal missing. Eventually he fell asleep on his own. Then he dreamed.

He'd thought the nightmares from the war were behind him. It had been years since the screams of the burning men had jarred him awake. But they returned that night and woke him with a cry that leapt from his own throat. He lay in sheets damp with sweat, breathing hard and fast, staring up at the ceiling. Along with the screams and the nightmares of war, he could still see the ghost of the man he'd murdered. He sat up and swung his feet off the bed, so twisted up inside he was afraid that he might puke.

Graff had been right. Jimmy Quinn's death would make his life hell and sleep impossible. What he feared wasn't the return of the nightmares. It was the knowledge, always there like a knife in his heart, that he was not what he seemed, not what people thought, not at all the man he wanted to be. Brody understood that the life he lived was nothing but a rickety framework of lies. As he sat sweating on that warm summer night, sick to his stomach, he knew he wasn't just a liar but a coward, too. Worst of all, a murderer. And what had awakened him wasn't just the ghost of the man he'd killed or the nightmare of the other terrible things he'd been a part of. It was the nightmare of that moment yet to come when all his cobbled-together lies would fall apart.

THE WAGON WHEEL was closed. Angie Madison had long ago tallied the day's take. In the house behind the café, Scott and Ida had finished their game of cribbage or hand and foot or some other card game they played together in the evenings and had gone to bed while Angie completed the business of the day. She sat at the counter, in the light of a single overhead lamp, a little pool of illumination. She was smoking the rare cigarette she allowed herself. It was a habit she'd picked up in

Madame Justine's house in Houston. As with so much of her life there, she'd been able to put it behind her. Or almost. Like the single cigarette, she held on to certain things as reminders of a past she'd escaped. She knew she was one of the lucky ones, and she didn't ever want to lose that sense of blessedness. What did she do to deserve a second chance? Nothing. It came to her in the form of a kid who was not really a kid, but who wasn't a man yet either. What he offered her was a different way of seeing herself. What he offered her, in all her brokenness, was hope.

She was remembering her dead husband, Christian Madison, as she often did at night, alone like this. But she was also thinking about someone else: Brody Dern. He'd returned to the café that afternoon and had taken a seat at the counter. He'd confessed that he still hadn't eaten lunch and had asked was there any meat loaf left. She'd poured him coffee and had started away to get the food, but he'd called her back. In an odd and rather flustered rush, he'd explained about the Prairie Blooms and the dinner at the Wicklows' and needing to be dressed nice and that he'd be happy to give her a lift. *If she'd like,* he'd finished, and didn't quite look at her. She'd been asked out before by men in Jewel who were widowed or still bachelors, and they'd often approached her in this same stumbling way. She had never accepted their offers. Her life was all about Scott. And in truth, none of the men who'd asked had interested her. But this offer from Brody Dern, which was really just the offer of a ride but felt like much more, intrigued her. She'd told him very simply and without any real thought, "Of course."

She'd been busy after that with the usual Saturday rush, and she'd had no time to think about what had occurred with Brody Dern. But now she thought about the exchange and wondered if it really meant anything at all, beyond Brody's polite offer of transportation and her polite acceptance. And to her own pleasant surprise, she found herself hoping that it did.

She was taken from her reverie by a tap at the diner door. The face of Felix Klein gazed at her through the glass. She put her cigarette down in the little saucer she used as an ashtray, went to the door, and opened up. The smell of bourbon came in with the night air.

Felix looked at her, shame in his bloodshot eyes, need in his voice. "I saw the light, Angie. Wondered if you might have some coffee. And maybe a bite to eat. I'm a little . . . uh . . ."

"Yes, you are, Felix." She shook her head, but not in judgment. "Come on in. I'm sure I can rustle up something."

She took his arm and gently guided him to the counter, to the stool next to her own. He had trouble walking, not just because of his inebriation, she knew, but also because of those toes that had been amputated.

She helped him get seated. "A little late for an evening stroll, isn't it?"

He took a deep breath, let out a heavy, liquor-scented sigh. "It's my birthday today."

"I didn't know that, Felix. Well, happy birthday. And I can see that you've been celebrating."

"I thought I'd try." He shook his head and looked miserable. "But I walk in that house and it's like walking in a museum. Everywhere I look, there's Hannah. You must know what I mean." He looked into her eyes for understanding. "You lost a husband."

Not really, she thought. What she'd lost was a friend who'd never had much opportunity to be a husband to her. But for Felix's sake, she said, "I understand. I'll heat up some water and make you a little Nescafé, And I think I've got some sliced turkey for a sandwich. How does that sound?"

"You're an angel, Angie."

She went to the kitchen, ran water into a pot, turned on a burner of the big stove, and set the pot over the flame. By the time she'd finished making the sandwich, the water was hot, and she stirred in the coffee crystals. Finally, she cut a slice of carrot cake and put a small lit candle atop. When she returned to the café counter, Felix sat slumped forward, his head cradled on his arms on the countertop.

She woke him gently. "Dinnertime."

Felix came up as if from a depth of water. He looked around, got his bearings, smelled the coffee, spied the sandwich and the cake with the candle, and smiled.

"Happy birthday," Angie said.

He ate greedily. He closed his eyes while he drank the instant coffee and said, "Ambrosia." Then he added, "Jimmy Quinn."

"My coffee reminds you of Jimmy Quinn?"

"It's just I've been thinking." Felix turned his face from her and went quiet, staring at his reflection in the glass of the diner window.

"Thinking what?" she finally prompted.

"Jimmy Quinn. There was one unhappy man."

Which was one of the most generous assessments of James Quinn that Evangeline Madison had ever heard. The thing was, she happened to agree.

"People who make other people unhappy are generally pretty unhappy themselves," she said.

He gave a small nod of agreement, then turned to her. "What about people who make other people happy? That's you, Angie."

"Well, I'm glad you think so."

"Why?" he asked.

"Why am I glad?"

"No, why are you so happy?"

"Maybe it's because I know how blessed I am."

"That must be something," he said.

She put her hand over his on the counter in the pool of light they shared. "You're blessed, too."

"No, what I am is broken."

"We're all broken, Felix."

"Broken but blessed, huh?"

"That's what I believe. You want to know one of the things I love most about you, Felix? There's not a vindictive bone in your body."

"Yeah, but I've got a hell of a fondness for Wild Turkey."

"The drinking never makes you mean."

"You've forgotten I tried to burn down the water tower?"

"I haven't forgotten. And I've always wondered why."

"You know, I still wonder that myself." He grinned for a moment, then got serious again. "Why do you suppose he was?"

It was a leap, but she thought she understood. "Jimmy Quinn? Why was he so unhappy?"

"He was the richest man in Black Earth County. Hell, maybe all of southern Minnesota. Had himself a fine family. Two of 'em, when you think about it. Marta is such a decent soul. I mean, that man had every reason to feel good, but all he ever did, every step he took, was to sow seeds of discontent."

He finished the last of his coffee and stared into his empty cup.

"You want to know something, Angie? Every so often, I get it in my head that I'd be better off dead."

"Oh, Felix, no."

"Mostly it's the Wild Turkey talking. I never made a move to go through with it. I probably never will. But hasn't everyone thought about it at one time or another? Or am I just odd and pathetic?"

"I believe it's something people think about sometimes, some of them, when life is really hard."

"But Jimmy Quinn went ahead with it. What makes a man take that final step?"

"I don't know, Felix. You'd have to feel awfully alone, I think."

"Alone." He thought about that, then looked at her and smiled again, though there seemed a shadow of sadness over it. "Jimmy should have spent more time at the Wagon Wheel. Who could ever feel alone with you around?"

"For a German, Felix, you sure have a lot of blarney in you. Come on," she said, taking his hand. "Let's get you home."

She walked him the three blocks to his small one-story on Gilbert Street. The homes of his neighbors were all unlit, the citizens of Jewel long ago abed. Felix stood on the walk staring at his own dark house.

"It's haunted," he said.

"No, Felix. That would be you."

She took his arm and urged him gently to the door. She lingered with him at the threshold. "You're on your own from here. But promise me something. No more Wild Turkey tonight, and you'll go straight to bed."

He held up three fingers in a sign that she recognized. "Scout's honor," he said. He smiled at her a final time that night, his face peaceful. "Angel. It's in your name. Evangeline."

"Off with you now," she said, but waited to leave until he'd closed the door and she saw a light wink on inside.

She walked back to the Wagon Wheel and to the house behind it that was home to her now and had been for nearly fifteen years. Her mother-in-law had left a light on in the hallway for her. Angie turned it off and mounted the stairs in the dark. She passed Ida's bedroom, where the door was closed, and then her son's, where the door was not. Scott lay asleep on his bed, the sheet kicked aside. Above the bed hung a poster of the Grand Canyon, a place Scott wanted badly to see someday. His guitar stood leaning against the bedpost. He'd probably practiced some before he went to sleep. She'd given him the instrument for Christmas, and Wendell Moon, who was amazing with a guitar, had been teaching him chords and picking and strumming. Scott would listen to the radio or to the 45s he bought and try to play along. Other boys had baseball, but Scott would never have that. He might have the guitar and music, however, and that made Angie happy.

Blessed, she thought.

In her own room, she prepared for bed, but she didn't immediately slide under the covers. As she usually did, she turned on the lamp that sat on her writing desk. A small key hung from a gold chain around her neck. She bent and used the key to unlock one of the desk drawers, from which she removed two journals. The cover of the first was old and worn and bore no title or other indication of the contents. She'd been given that volume of blank pages when she was twelve years old. Across the next few years, she'd filled that journal, then bought herself another, and then another. She kept them all in her desk under lock and key. She made several entries per week. Sometimes she wrote only a line or two, sometimes more. In a way, it was her testament to what Felix Klein had said about his own life and was, she believed, an apt characterization of the lives of most people: They were broken and they were blessed.

Every time she sat down to write in a newer volume, she would begin by reading from that old, worn first journal, to remind herself of the place she'd come from and all that she had to be thankful for now. She leafed through the pages, and her eyes fell on an entry composed more than fifteen years before, written in small, careful script.

March 11, 1943 . . . I don't know why, but I still count the men who come to me. Today they were numbers 88, 89, and 90.

CHAPTER EIGHTEEN

BRODY ALMOST NEVER attended Sunday Mass anymore, using his duties as sheriff for excuse. But what he couldn't get out of was Sunday dinner with his family.

Brody didn't look much like his older brother. Tom was taller and broader and, in the stern aspect of his face, very much resembled their father. Brody took after his mother, a softer look. Tom was also a good deal heavier than his brother, but that was due in large measure to Garnet's fine cooking. He'd begun to bald early, a worry for him. He usually wore a seed cap—to protect himself from the sun, he said—but Brody suspected it was due equally to his brother's vanity.

Tom and Garnet had three children: Mary and Rita, ages twelve and ten, and Jack, age seven. They were great kids and loved their uncle Brody, and he loved them in return. But there was always that knowledge in the back of his mind of what he and their mother shared but shouldn't, so even as he enjoyed them, he understood that if the truth were ever known, he'd hurt them all terribly. Like so much of his life, it was something he didn't understand and had stopped trying to.

Brody's mother still lived in the farmhouse where she'd raised her children and where now she helped raise her grandchildren. In the only wedding photograph Brody had ever seen, she was a girl of sixteen in a simple white dress, a bouquet of flowers in her hands, staring up at her new husband with a look that said he was her world now and she knew absolutely that it would be the best of all possible worlds. It had and hadn't been. His father was not a communicative man. Sentiments such as *I love you* or *You look lovely today* never fell from his lips. He spoke in concretes: *Rain again today, Em. Looks like I'll be getting those beans in late.* Or *Tore this shirt on a nail. Needs mending, Em.* Or if he was feeling particularly loving, *Good pot roast, Em.* From that beaming young girl, his mother had grown into a farmer's wife, thin and quiet and busy sunup until well after sundown, with hands every bit as hard and cracked as her husband's and a face plain as barn wood. And, as nearly as Brody could tell, happy. She'd been widowed early and had never remarried. When Tom and Garnet had tied the knot, she moved into one of the smaller bedrooms and gave the big one she'd shared with her husband to the newlyweds. When the children had come along one by one, she'd moved again and again, until finally, she lived in the attic, which Tom had made into a cozy living area for her, a small place of her own in a house that had once been all hers. And still, as nearly as Brody could tell, she was happy.

Gatherings always included Brody's younger sister, Amy; her husband, Sean Cassiday; and their son, Benny. Amy was one of the soft spots in Brody's heart and was much of the brightness in his memories of life on the farm.

Sunday dinner was always at one. When Brody and Hector pulled off the highway and onto the short lane leading to the farmyard, he could see the kids on the grass in front of the house, playing a game of croquet. The dogs came barking, and as soon as Brody opened the car door, Hector bounded out and the animals greeted one another with yips and nips and sniffings and wagging tails. Brody was greeted with shouts from his nieces and nephews and pleas to join in their croquet game. He begged off for the moment but promised that after dinner it would be a different story.

Inside, the men had changed out of the clothes they'd worn to church and were dressed in clean khakis and sport shirts. Garnet and Amy and Brody's mother were in the kitchen. Brody shook hands with his brother and brother-in-law, then went to the kitchen and kissed each of the women in turn on the cheek. They gave him a glass of iced tea and shooed him out, and he joined the other men in the cool of the living room.

Tom, as always, sounded so much like Brody's father that the minute he spoke, Brody felt himself go tense.

"Catfish ate Jimmy Quinn. True?" Tom's tone indicated that he thought it had to be an outrageous story someone had concocted.

"They nibbled on him some," Brody replied.

"I heard he killed himself," Sean said quietly, as if speaking of a sin. Which, in the Catholic tradition they all shared, it would have been.

"We're still sorting things out," Brody said.

"A lot of people are going to be very interested in how they get sorted," Tom said.

"I also heard that it might have been something else," Sean said. "That maybe someone killed Jimmy."

"Like I told you, Sean, we're still sorting it all out. Something like this, you have to be careful. You understand."

"Noah Bluestone, we heard," Tom said.

"You know, Tom, an accusation like that does nobody any good."

"Only saying what others are saying."

Brody could hear the children in the front yard, and the honest to God truth was that he longed to join them in their game, to forget about Quinn for a little while.

"Word is he was shotgunned," Tom said. "Hell of a way for a man to die."

Tom had been exempted from service in the war from which Brody had come home a hero, and Brody was tempted to tell his older brother about all the horrible ways there were for people to die, but he held his tongue and said instead, "Where's all this information coming from?"

"Church this morning," Sean said. "Everybody's talking about it."

"Something not right in what we've heard, Brody?" This was said as a kind of challenge, spoken in the way Tom often addressed his brother.

"Don't listen to gossip," Brody advised. He was relieved when his mother came into the dining room and announced, "Dinner's ready. Call the children."

AFTER THE MEAL ended and the dishes were done, Brody joined the women, who were going for a walk. They left Tom and Sean sitting in the shade on the front porch, talking crop prospects and complaining of the ever-rising cost of fertilizer and seed.

There was a long, grassy lane that ran past the outbuildings and between planted fields all the way to a creek that was spanned with a narrow wooden bridge built by Brody's grandfather. As a kid, Brody had spent a lot of summer days on this lane. Because it was lined with all manner of wildflowers, the lane was always aflutter with a host of butterflies. When he was very young, Brody would simply chase them. But as he grew older, he became fascinated by them in many ways—the differences in the colors and patterns on their wings, their sizes, the flowers they were particularly fond of. He wanted to study them. So his mother had made him a butterfly catcher from an old pillowcase that she sewed around a hooped coat hanger and affixed with tape to a sawed-off broom handle. Brody caught his butterflies and put them in a jar with a little rubbing alcohol to asphyxiate them, then mounted them on white cardboard with a label under each telling its common name and its Latin name. He hung the cardboard posters on his bedroom walls. He recalled a day when he was bent to this work and had looked up to see his father standing in the bedroom doorway, watching him. Brody had smiled, hoping for some encouragement, or maybe that very rare word of praise. Instead, his father simply shook his head and said, "I don't see the point."

Garnet walked with Brody's mother and Brody walked with Amy. They talked of the children and what summer held for them all. Eventually, Brody's mother stopped and turned to him and said, "You look so tired."

"Not sleeping particularly well these days, Mom."

"This Jimmy Quinn business?"

She was only in her mid-fifties, but her face was deeply lined, the skin pulled taut at the corners of her eyes and mouth. Her hair, which had always been a rich walnut color, was becoming dull gray.

"It's terrible," Amy said. "Such a tragedy."

Brody's mother said, "I don't know."

"What do you mean, Em?" Garnet said.

"Me, I married a good man," Brody's mother replied. "He could be a hard man sometimes, but he was a good man. He never raised a hand to me. Brody, did your father ever once strike you?"

Yes, but not with his hand, Brody could have replied.

Instead, he said, "No."

"I'm not sure the same could be said of Jimmy Quinn," his mother said. "I knew both his wives and all his children, and I swear every one of them feared that man. I never saw any bruises, but that doesn't mean he didn't abuse them. He liked his drink, too, and I've never seen alcohol do anyone any good. So, I'm just saying that in some ways life'll be hard going forward without him, but in others, I imagine, it will be a profound relief for those folks."

"Maybe we'll see more of Marta now," Amy said.

Marta had married James Quinn on the eve of the Second World War, and because she was from Germany, folks in Black Earth County hadn't been especially welcoming. As a result, Marta generally kept to herself on the farm, except for Sunday Mass at Saint Ignatius. Although the war was long over, her German accent could still raise hackles, and some people in the county insisted on referring to her as "Quinn's frau."

Garnet bent and picked a wild daisy. She studied the blossom. "Did Noah Bluestone kill him?"

"You, too?" Brody said.

"It's what everybody's saying."

Brody spoke harshly. "I don't know enough to say how it was that Jimmy died, and if I don't and I'm closer to this thing than anyone, then I can't understand how anybody else can be so ready to accuse somebody of murder."

"I agree, Brody," Amy said. "I heard that Bluestone's still working for the Quinns, and if they're not worried about him, why should the rest of us be? Right?"

Garnet put the daisy under her nose as if taking in a fragrance. "They weren't in church this morning, but Father O'Gara read a nice note from Marta thanking us all for the food you and I took over yesterday, Brody, and asking us to pray for them in this difficult time." She tossed the flower away. "I've always liked Marta. I never liked her husband one bit."

Brody could hear the distant voices of the children still in the farm-yard and, from somewhere down the lane, the call of a meadowlark. He wanted to be done with this conversation.

"Father O'Gara announced that the visitation and funeral are sched-uled for Friday," his mother said. "I expect it will be well attended." She glanced toward the farmhouse. "We'd best be getting back."

When they came to the house, Brody said, "I should be going. Lots to do."

He kissed his mother and sister goodbye, then whistled and called for Hector, who came running.

Garnet said, "I'll walk you to your car."

At his cruiser, Garnet said quietly, "I thought about you last night, Brody, alone in my bed."

"What do you want me to say to that, Garnet?"

"That maybe alone in your bed you think about me, too."

"You know I do."

"Good."

She leaned to him and kissed his cheek, then turned away and walked slowly across the grass toward the house. Brody watched her go, and he thought he understood now his father's feeling about those butterflies long ago, that once their wings were pinned to cardboard they lost their spirit and ceased to be what had so captured your eye and heart and became something instead that you might study forever but never really know.

CHAPTER NINETEEN

GRAFF WAS WAITING for Brody in the jailhouse, drinking a cup of coffee from the pot he'd brewed on the hot plate. The hand-rolled cigarette he smoked was as much a part of who he was as the old Stetson he wore everywhere.

Brody closed the door behind him. "Afternoon, Connie."

Hector trotted over for some generous petting from the deputy, then settled into his favorite corner.

"How's everybody out at the Dern place?" Graff asked.

"Good," Brody said. He poured himself a cup of Graff's brew, sat, and, like Graff, put his feet up on the desk. The windows of the jailhouse were open to let in the breeze, and sunshine poured through, laying bars of gold across the scratched wooden floor.

"Quiet out there," Graff said.

"Sunday." Brody sipped his coffee, which was a little on the weak side, and because Sundays were typically Brody's watch alone, he said, "So what're you doing here, Connie?"

Graff said, "Been thinking."

Brody said, "Jimmy Quinn?"

Graff blew smoke into the still air of the jailhouse, and it drifted slowly in the sunlight. He said, "I've been thinking about what could've taken him out to Inkpaduta Bend at night if he wasn't really interested in fishing."

Brody drank his coffee and waited.

"Everybody knows Jimmy Quinn was a man of excessive appetites. Land, power, money. I'm also guessing his libido might be added to that list."

"Okay. So?"

"He's got himself a wife who's been sickly for quite a while, so probably no way of satisfying that particular appetite." Graff took the cigarette from his lips and studied the ember. "In a situation like that, what does a man like Jimmy do?"

"He looks for satisfaction from someone else."

"Exactly."

"You're thinking he was out on Inkpaduta Bend to meet a woman. Why would he bring that big Tolley to a romantic meeting?"

"Who said anything about romance? Maybe this was strictly a business proposition. Or maybe . . ." Graff paused.

"Maybe what?"

"Maybe some coercion was involved."

"You mean rape?" Brody said.

"Or extortion or who knows what. One way or another, Jimmy Quinn usually got what Jimmy Quinn wanted."

"Give me a name."

Graff said, "Kyoko Bluestone."

The jailhouse was dead silent. Brody watched the smoke circle and rise and circle some more above him while he considered the name Graff had given him.

Graff said, "She worked for the man, so was right under his nose. She's a pretty little thing. And think about that sapphire ring we found in Jimmy's pocket, made for a small finger. That woman's hands are not much larger than a child's."

The phone rang and Brody answered. It was Lyle Anderson, who ran a gas station at a crossroads north of Jewel. He was irate, calling because he'd repaired a tire for a customer who'd taken off without paying. He knew the customer and gave the name. He wanted Brody to, in the words of Anderson, "arrest his ass." Brody said he'd be out to get the full story.

After the sheriff hung up and explained, Graff looked at his watch and said, "What time are you picking up Angie for that date of yours?"

"It's not a date, Connie. I'm just giving her a ride to the Prairie Blooms."

"If you say so. What time?"

"A little before six."

"Lyle's cantankerous. He's pissed off customers before. He's also a man likes to paint the truth a bit, so getting down to what really happened might not be simple. This could take some time, and I'd hate to have you late in picking up your"—Graff smiled—"traveling companion. I'll see to Anderson."

"What about Kyoko Bluestone?" Brody said.

"It's just speculation. We need more to go on, and there's always tomorrow. You just worry about having a good evening, okay?"

Graff headed off and Brody went upstairs, Hector at his heels. From his bedroom closet, he pulled his one and only suit, which was dark blue, and a white shirt, and the blue tie he always wore with the suit. He picked up his good black shoes from the floor of the closet and figured he should give them a shine. He busied himself, trying not to think about the evening ahead. He didn't want to look at this approaching time with Angie Madison as a date. He was simply doing her a favor, giving her a lift. But it had been a very long time since he'd felt so nervous about being with a woman. When he thought this, in the middle of buffing his black shoes, he stopped and considered his times with Garnet. What he shared with his brother's wife was all that he would ever share, and although in the end it always left him feeling lonely, even the loneliness was familiar and safe. Evangeline Madison, on the other hand, was an unknown in so many ways. He supposed that was true for her of him.

Two people who didn't really know each other; what might come of that? Brody put the thought aside and went about getting ready for the evening while Hector lay on Brody's bed patiently observing the sheriff's every move.

WHEN BRODY ROLLED up his in cruiser, Angie Madison said, "He's here, Ida."

Ida Madison had left the Wagon Wheel in the hands of Wendell Moon. Scott was there to give him a hand, and also Vivian Shaw, one of the part-time waitresses. Ida wanted to be available to help her daughter-in-law prepare for what she insisted was a date, Angie's first since coming to Jewel a widow with her womb full of Ida's unborn grandson.

"Nervous?" Ida asked, peeking through the curtains at the cruiser that had pulled up to the curb.

"It's not a date," Angie said for the umpteenth time. "He's just giving me a lift."

Ida turned from the window and appraised Angie a final time. She was, herself, a smallish woman who'd gone heavy with years of preparing food and liberally sampling everything she made. She studied Angie with loving eyes and said, "You look real good. A man wants two things from a woman: fine food and fine curves. You've got no worries there." She took her daughter-in-law in her arms and kissed her cheek and said, "Knock his socks off, girl."

"Ida!" Angie said with a laugh. "How many times do I have to tell you—"

"It's not a date. I know. But that doesn't mean you can't enjoy the company of the man. And make sure that he enjoys yours, you hear?"

There was a knock at the screen door. Ida released Angie and sent her off with a wink.

Brody told her she looked nice and opened the door of his cruiser for her and they headed away. And she was . . . happy.

CONNIE GRAFF STOOD at the open door of the jailhouse watching the sun drop in the west. He'd taken swift care of Lyle Anderson, whose story had changed as Graff pressed him with questions, and who, in the end, had agreed to deal with the matter of the repaired tire on his own, without the complication of legal complaint. When Graff returned to the jailhouse, Brody was gone.

Driving out to Anderson's and back, the old deputy had continued to mull over the question of Jimmy Quinn's presence on Inkpaduta Bend. Now, as he watched the sun set beyond the narrow valley where the Alabaster River ran, his thinking kept bringing him back to the same place, the same well of possibilities, and finally he said to the dog at his feet, "Sorry, Hector, got to leave you on your own for a while." He brought the dog inside and took from a desk drawer the printed sign that gave his telephone number and the number of Asa Fielding in case of emergency, posted it on the door of the jailhouse, locked up, and headed south out of town toward Fordham Ridge.

BRODY AND ANGIE arrived at the Wicklow home at the same time as Charlotte Bauer, the retired lawyer who preferred to be called Charlie. Loretta Wicklow breezed in from the kitchen to greet them at the door, wearing a little apron over her black velvet dress, bringing with her the scent of something Italian, the rich aroma of thyme and rosemary and garlic. She wore a string of pearls. Her shoes were black high heels. She'd had her black hair done in an elaborate bouffant. On the whole, the effect was probably meant to resemble Jacqueline Kennedy, whose photograph, even before she would become First Lady, was in all the magazines.

The talk at first was of Ruth Coffee, inspiration and mentor over so many years, a woman who loved Balzac, Jane Austen, Charles Dickens, Mark Twain, and, most recently, J. D. Salinger. She'd not only organized the Prairie Blooms but been almost single-handedly responsible for the Prairie Lights Playhouse, the community theater, which put on three productions every year, many of which Ruth herself directed. The group toasted her memory, and then, because she would have wanted it, discussed *The Catcher in the Rye*. The general sentiment was that Holden Caulfield whined a good deal and made bad choices, for which he refused to accept the responsibility or the consequences. Sam Wicklow offered a different perspective. He'd listened quietly and had commented only reservedly, but finally he said, "He's a kid who's never been shown the way to manhood. He has no one in his life to initiate him."

"Initiate?" Loretta Wicklow said. It seemed spoken with such clear disdain that for a moment the conversation stopped.

Loretta was a woman who wanted more than life in Jewel offered her. Brody had always suspected she blamed Sam for not having it. Her father had been a successful businessman and a senator in the state legislature. After graduation from high school, she'd planned to go to a university in the East. The war had intervened, and before he went into the service, she'd married Sam, whose family published the *Clarion*. She'd told everyone that when her husband came back, they were going to move to New York City and start an exciting life there. But when he returned, he was terribly changed in body and spirit. That prosthetic leg, those startling scars, these were things she hadn't counted on when she stood at the altar and said, "I do" and "for better or for worse." While Sam was away at war, his father had died and Sam, on his return, took over the running of the newspaper. Loretta settled for working with him, contributing items on cultural happenings and social events and taking on the responsibility of dealing with advertisers and subscribers. She was a woman with a ready smile that somehow never seemed to fit quite right. They were childless, and Brody always wondered if it was because of the particular nature of Sam's wounds or the nature of their marriage.

Sam replied to her in what seemed to Brody a practiced calm. "Most cultures have a rite or ritual of some kind that marks the end of childhood and the assumption of the responsibilities and standing of an adult. In the tradition of the Sioux or the Chippewa, our native tribes here in Minnesota, that's a vision quest. At a certain age, a boy leaves his village and goes alone into the wild to seek a vision that will guide him for the rest of his life. When he's received that vision, he returns to his people and is welcomed as a man. The Aborigines of Australia do this in what's called a walkabout. Some other cultures bury their children and then dig them up in a ritual resurrection. Holden simply doesn't know the way to manhood."

"I never underwent any kind of rite of passage," Gordon Landis declared.

Landis was someone Brody figured Ruth Coffee would never have invited to a book discussion. But he was courting Mimi Fowler, the town librarian, who was one of the Prairie Blooms, and she'd insisted he be allowed to accompany her.

"You fought in the war, Gordy," Sam replied.

"Wounded at the Battle of the Bulge," Landis said proudly.

"Boot camp, that was your initiation. And the battleground, that was your proof."

"Were you given visions, Sam?" Loretta said. "Because all I hear is the crying when you have one of your nightmares."

The room experienced a moment of rather stunned silence, then Landis asked, "How do you know about all this initiation stuff, Sam?"

"I've been doing some research for a book I'd like to write about the Great Sioux Uprising."

"Samuel, sweetheart," Loretta said, laying a hand on his arm. "This book you're going write, if you ever do, I wouldn't count on it being a bestseller. Believe me, no one cares about the Indians here. Why don't you write a mystery instead? Everybody loves a good mystery."

Once again, an uncomfortable quiet settled over the room. Into that quiet, someone said, "So, Brody, do you think Noah Bluestone killed Jimmy Quinn?"

IT WAS TWILIGHT, and Connie Graff sat in his truck near the long dirt lane that led to the simple farmstead where Noah Bluestone lived with his Japanese wife. He was parked at the edge of the Alabaster River, in a blind of cottonwoods. His window was down, and he listened to the call of the birds among the trees and the fallow strips that outlined the land cultivated by Bluestone, and before him by Bluestone's father and grandfather and great-grandfather. Graff had been watching the farmhouse with a pair of field glasses he kept in the truck. He had no intention of questioning the Bluestones again. He simply wanted to scrutinize the place unseen and, if he was lucky, observe the man and wife together when they believed themselves to be alone. He was curious about how they were with each other. He wanted to know especially how Bluestone treated this pretty, quiet woman from another country, another culture. He'd wondered that since the day before, when he spoke to her among the rows of amaranth, where, as nearly as Graff could tell, she worked long days like a common field hand.

Someone left the house. Graff lifted his glasses and saw that it was Noah Bluestone. The man walked slowly across the newly planted fields, a dark figure against the dying light, moving in the direction of Fordham Ridge, where the river curled back on itself to create Inkpaduta Bend.

Graff rolled a cigarette and smoked awhile and the light grew thinner. Then he saw the woman leave the house with her old Saint Bernard and disappear behind the barn, walking across the field in the direction opposite to the one her husband had taken. He crushed out the cigarette in the truck ashtray, started the engine, pulled out of the trees and onto the dirt lane. He parked near the pen where the pigs were kept. His presence disturbed them, and they grunted and moved about restlessly. The door of the small barn was open and Graff entered. His eyes were used to the dim evening light, and he had no trouble making his way around inside.

He'd come on impulse and wasn't sure what he was looking for. He opened a door to an area in one corner that was squared off by interior walls. Inside was clearly a slaughter room. A metal crossbar hung from a pulley attached to a ceiling beam. The floor below was stained with old blood. A tarp, also stained with old blood, hung on a wall peg. A shelf along one wall held the instruments of a butcher—a hacksaw, two great cleavers, sharpened knives of several sizes and shapes. There was an enormous metal basin that Graff figured might have been for the capture of entrails. Except for the bloodstains, all the materials looked clean and the area itself freshly washed down. Graff understood this was where Bluestone butchered his hogs. He left the barn and opened the door to an outbuilding that was both a garage and a workshop. Bluestone's pickup was parked there. The workshop was a well-organized area with tools and sawhorses and a workbench. Graff moved to the pickup and peered over the tailgate. The truck bed was empty and exceptionally clean, he thought, for a farm truck. A sudden bark at his back brought him around. The woman and the dog stood in the doorway.

"Good evening, Mrs. Bluestone." He tipped his Stetson.

She didn't reply.

"Deputy Graff," he said. "You remember me?"

"I remember," she said.

"I'd like to talk to you, if that's all right."

The woman looked up at the sky, which was beginning to salt with stars. "Would you like to come into the house?" It was said with disciplined politeness.

"Thank you," Graff said.

She offered him tea and he accepted. He'd never been inside the farmhouse before. Given her heritage, he'd expected some Oriental influence, but he saw none. Nor did he see anything that hinted at Bluestone's own Native heritage. The little house was old, but all the furnishings looked recently bought, and Graff wondered if the couple intended it as a way to leave their pasts behind them.

The dog, who was really a rather gentle creature, lay on the floor watching the woman as she prepared the tea.

Graff said, "Where are you from in Japan?"

"Okinawa." She brought the tea on a tray. The tea set was fragile porcelain, and the small cups had no handles.

"I don't know Japan at all."

"It's a beautiful land," she said, pouring tea for him and then herself.

"Have you always lived in Okinawa? I mean before now?"

"No." She didn't elaborate. She seated herself and waited for Graff to go on.

"You speak very good English."

"I had good teachers. Nuns."

"In Japan?"

"I grew up Catholic."

Which surprised the hell out of Graff. "I'm Catholic myself. I don't recall ever seeing you at Saint Ignatius."

"I went once, Deputy Graff. It was made clear to me that I wasn't welcome there. I say my prayers here now."

He felt bad about that and didn't know how to reply. "I was hoping to speak with you and your husband together."

"My husband isn't here."

"When do you expect him back?"

"I don't know."

"Do you know where he's gone?"

"Yes."

"And that would be?"

She set her tea down and folded her hands in her lap. "To the river."

"Anyplace special?"

"Inkpaduta Bend."

"Does he go there often?"

"Yes. In the evening."

"Why?"

"He says it's a special place for him."

"Special in what way?"

"He says it is a spiritual place."

"How long is he usually gone?"

"It depends. Sometimes he comes back soon, sometimes he's gone quite a while."

"During the day, when he's working for the Quinns, he's usually gone a long time, yes?"

"Yes."

"And when he's gone, you're here all alone?"

"Yes."

"Do you mind that?"

"It's the way it is."

"Do you ever have visitors?"

She hesitated. "Not often."

"You worked for the Quinns."

"To help Marta. You know she's sick."

"Of course. What kind of relationship did you have with Mr. Quinn?"

"What do you mean?"

"Did he ever come and visit you here?"

He watched her hands, folded on her lap, squeeze together. "Sometimes."

"Did he ever come when your husband wasn't here?"

He saw that she'd begun to breathe more rapidly. "Sometimes."

"What did you think of him?"

"He was . . ." Her eyes searched the room, as if the ghost of Quinn might be hiding in a corner there. "I thought he was not a happy man."

"Mrs. Bluestone, I have a very serious question to ask you, and I need you to tell me the truth. All right? Did James Quinn ever touch you?"

She didn't answer. But Graff saw that the fingers of her clasped hands had gone nearly bloodless and her body rigid. Her gaze had left his face, and she stared at the floor.

"Would you look at me, Mrs. Quinn?"

It took a moment, but her eyes slowly rose, and in them he saw fear.

"Did he ever touch you?"

She said in a firm voice, "I don't want to talk about that man."

The door opened at Graff's back and he knew, even before Noah Bluestone spoke, that he'd gotten all he was going to get from the Japanese woman who was so clearly afraid.

A GOOD DEAL of the Prairie Blooms' dinner conversation centered on Jimmy Quinn's death and on Noah Bluestone, who, it was obvious, had become the talk of Jewel.

"As I understand it, one of Bluestone's relations far back had been a homesteader," Jack Harris said. He was the mayor of Jewel, had been for three terms, and things were looking pretty good for him being reelected in November. He and his wife, Abigail, had been part of the Prairie Blooms from the beginning. "Maybe a half-breed or something. When the Sioux Uprising occurred, he was warned by his Indian relatives and went off himself to warn some of the white settlers. He never came back. They found his body hanging from a tree. He'd been . . . Well, things had been done to him. It was never clear who killed him, white or Indian. Anyway, after the fighting ended and the Sioux were rounded up, his wife and kids were taken, too. Everyone was marched off under army escort to Fort Snelling and eventually to South Dakota. When they were finally allowed to return, years later, one of Jimmy Quinn's ancestors had taken possession of the Bluestone land—good land, it was—and there wasn't a thing those folks back then could do about it."

"Hell, the Quinns started out in this county by stealing land, and they got rich through bootlegging," Gordon Landis said.

"Bootlegging?" Abigail Harris said, looking to her husband for confirmation.

"Rumors, dear, just rumors."

"The hell," Landis said. "During Prohibition, Jimmy's father supplied most of the booze for the illegal joints in this part of Minnesota. Used his money to buy up the property of his neighbors who couldn't meet their mortgages. Jimmy didn't bootleg, but he built his holdings off the poor bastards whose farms got foreclosed."

"The Quinns have always recognized a good opportunity," Mimi Fowler offered diplomatically.

"They're thieves, you mean," Landis said.

"Anyway," Harris went on, "Bluestone's people homesteaded that bit of property they've got now on the Alabaster. Not the best piece of land but one nobody else wanted. Never productive enough to sustain a family, so the Bluestones always did other work as well. Noah's father worked for Jimmy Quinn. Noah, too. An ironic situation, working for the family that basically stole the land from you."

"Noah Bluestone, he's worked for Quinn all these years?" asked Abigail, who hadn't grown up in Black Earth County.

"Not all these years," her husband said. "Noah joined the Marines before the Second World War broke out and made a career of it. He was gone twenty years. In that time, his old man died. The Bluestone farmstead kind of fell to ruin. Then last year Noah turned up, married to a Japanese woman, and started farming again. He also went back to work for Jimmy Quinn. His wife, too. We were all a little amazed, but the Bluestones have always been folks who kept their distance and so were kind of hard to understand. Maybe it's the Indian in them, I don't know."

"And then James Quinn ends up dead," Mimi Fowler said. "If you wanted to make that book of yours a mystery, Sam, this seems to me a perfect setup for murder."

Brody said, "I don't want anybody using that word, Mimi. We're still investigating."

"Everyone I talk to thinks Bluestone killed him," Landis said.

"Whatever happened to innocent until proven guilty, Gordy?" Charlie Bauer shot back.

The lawyer had been quite vocal during the discussion of the book but had been noticeably quiet in the conversation about Bluestone. Brody liked this woman, who was so different from most of the women he knew. He had seen her at work in the courtroom, valiantly defending the defenseless.

"Look, it's just talk," Harris said.

"The wrong kind of talk can be a virus, Jack," Charlie said. "It spreads and it poisons."

"Yeah, but in this case it's not far off the mark, Counselor," Landis said.

"You really think Noah Bluestone did it, Gordon?" Mimi Fowler looked troubled by the idea. "When he checks out books from the library, he's always so polite."

"He's Indian," Landis replied. "Let me tell you two things you need to know about Indians, Mimi. They haven't got an honest bone in their bodies. And never turn your back to 'em. They carry knives."

"I think that's enough of this kind of talk," Loretta said. "It's time for dessert."

—

IT WAS DARK when they left the Wicklow home. Brody drove slowly through town, as if reluctant to end the evening.

"That Gordon Landis, there's a piece of work," Angie said. "I don't know what Mimi sees in him."

"She's forty, never married," Brody said. "Maybe she thinks this is her last best shot."

"You shouldn't get married just to get married. Especially to a man like Gordon Landis. Even when you marry for love, there are no guarantees."

"I know what you mean. Just look at Sam and Loretta," Brody said. "My God is she hard on him."

"If they're so unhappy with each other, why don't they just divorce?"

"Catholic," Brody said.

Angie smiled, a little wickedly. "I hope he does write that book, just to show her." Then she said, "What do you think about Noah Bluestone and Jimmy Quinn?"

"I think we'd all be better off not talking and gossiping about it."

"You don't have an opinion?"

"I think it was a terrible accident, and I think it doesn't do anybody any good to speculate differently at this point."

She felt the anger in his words and didn't quite understand where it came from, but it was obvious he preferred to steer clear of the subject. Which was fine with Angie. She didn't want the evening to end on a sour note.

The Wagon Wheel was empty and unlit, but lights blazed in the house behind it. Brody pulled to the curb, got out, and opened her door. He escorted her up the walk, and they stood together a long, awkward moment, until she finally took the bull by the horns, leaned to him, and kissed his cheek.

"I had a lovely evening," she said. "Thanks for the ride."

"My pleasure." But he didn't leave. He looked away briefly, then back, His face was illuminated by the glow from inside the house, and a little fire from that glow danced in his eyes. "Would you like to do this again? Not this, I mean, but another evening out together, just the two of us?"

"I'd like that very much," she said.

"Good," he said. "Good."

And then, in that last moment before he left her, he did it. Kissed her gently, full on the lips. He turned without another word and strolled back to his cruiser.

Inside, she found Ida sitting in the living room looking pensive.

"What's wrong?" she asked.

"Scott," Ida said.

All of Angie's happiness fled in an instant. "What about him?"

"He should have been home long ago." Ida broke into tears. "Oh, Angie. He's gone, and I don't know where."

CHAPTER TWENTY

JEWEL HAD A movie theater on Main Street called the Rialto, which had been operating since the days of silent films. By the late fifties, the Rialto was open four days a week, Thursday through Sunday. Every Sunday night, after the final showing had begun, Scott Madison met Del Wolfe in front of the theater to change the marquee for the next week's offering. Neither boy received money for this. Instead, they were allowed to watch any movie they wanted as often as they liked for free. This included the Saturday matinees, which tended to be Scott's favorites, since they were often war movies or Westerns or grade-B horror films like *The Creature from the Black Lagoon* and *The Thing from Another World*. The matinee offerings never shared the marquee, which was devoted to first-run films—*The Bridge on the River Kwai, Gunfight at the O.K. Corral, Jailhouse Rock* (Del's favorite), *Old Yeller* (which had made Scott cry, and he was glad Del wasn't there to see him)—but the boys always knew what the Saturday morning showings would be and sat in the balcony together, munching on popcorn and Necco wafers. Lots of households in Jewel had television sets, but neither boy's home had one. Scott's mother believed television was a waste of time and preferred that he read instead or occupy himself with hobbies. Del's family couldn't afford a set. So it was movies that gave them the broader world. Movies and books.

That Sunday evening in early June of 1958, two days after Jimmy

Quinn's body had been found in the Alabaster River, the boys met on Main Street in front of the theater and went about their business. They removed the display for the current film, *The Long, Hot Summer.* They'd both seen it, but neither had much liked it. They put up the marquee for the next film, *The Proud Rebel,* which Scott thought might be okay because it was a Western that starred Alan Ladd, who'd also been in *Shane,* one of his favorite movies.

After they'd finished and stood looking up at their work, a pickup truck pulled to the curb. Tyler Creasy got out. He swayed a little as he stood with them looking up at the marquee.

"You know about him, right?" Creasy said. "That Alan Ladd?"

Scott didn't like Creasy. Some of it was because of all the rotten stories about him that he'd heard from Del. But Scott didn't need those stories to be repulsed by the man. Anger came off Creasy like a foul cloud.

"He's just a little prick of a guy, no bigger than a midget."

"What do you want?" Del said.

"Taking your mom dancing."

"Drinking, you mean."

"Watch that tongue, boy. We'll be out late. She wanted you to know. Thinks you'd be worried."

"I got the message," Del said.

The two of them stared at each other in a way that made Scott think trouble was on the way. But Creasy finally returned to his truck and drove off. Del watched him go and said, "Fuggin' Creasy." He turned to Scott. "So what do you want to do now, Madman?"

"I don't know. What do you want to do?"

"Funny you should ask."

Del shouldered the knapsack he always carried with him and smiled huge. It was clear to Scott that what he had in mind might well land them both in hot water.

—

THE LITTLE MOTORBIKE kicked up dust behind them. Above Fordham Ridge, the light in the sky was pale blue-white, as thin and fragile as a dusting of frost. There were already stars in the east, and the air was cooling into night. Scott knew they'd never make it back to town before hard dark settled over Black Earth County. He worried about this, but perched on the back of Del's motorbike with the wind in his face and his heart, that imperfect organ, thumping hard with excitement, he put away his concern and gave himself over to the promise of adventure ahead.

Del turned off the road onto the overgrown lane that led to the end of Inkpaduta Bend and guided the motorbike along one of a pair of tire tracks barely visible in the weeds and tall wild grasses. Scott could see the line of trees that marked the course of the Alabaster at the end of the Bend, nearly a quarter mile distant, and he felt the thrill of anticipation. When they reached the trees, Del braked to a stop; he killed the engine, and they dismounted.

"Come on," Del said and began to move toward the river.

The evening was quiet, the birds already roosting. The air was still and smelled of the river and mud. From high on Fordham Ridge came the glimmer of scattered yard lights on the farmsteads there.

"Jesus!" Del stopped suddenly and pointed. "Will you look at that."

Scott saw it, too, a black staining of the bare earth near the river's edge, dramatic even in the descending dark.

"That's his blood, Madman."

Del spoke in a whisper, and Scott thought it must be because Del felt exactly what he felt, that they were in the presence of some enormity, something both holy and wholly terrifying. A man had died here—*right here*—and not just died. Died brutally. At their feet was the evidence, that great soaking of blood.

Del began to walk slowly around the black stain in the dirt until he'd circled it completely. Then he looked into his friend's eyes, his own eyes round with wonder and excitement, and said, "Do you fuggin' believe this, Madman?"

"Maybe we should go," Scott said.

"Not yet." Del knelt and touched the blood-fouled earth. He drew his hand back and studied it. "Creasy says it wasn't any accident and he didn't kill himself. Creasy says Quinn was murdered."

"By who?"

"Some Indian who worked for him. Guy named Bluestone."

Scott knew who Bluestone was. Every once in a great while, the man sat at the counter of the Wagon Wheel and drank coffee. Always just coffee, always alone, and never saying much.

"Why?" he asked.

Del stood and wiped his fingers on his jeans. "Creasy says Quinn caught the Indian stealing and fired him. Creasy says Indians are like that."

Scott didn't know much about Indians. Mostly he knew what he'd seen in the movies at the Rialto, and if what he saw there was true, an Indian might certainly be capable of exactly what Creasy claimed. Scott knew something else, too.

"Know why this place is called Inkpaduta Bend, Wolfman?" he said. "It's named after an Indian. He was Sioux or something. Him and his band massacred a bunch of people down at Spirit Lake. They captured lots of white women and went on the run with them. They camped here, and while they were here, they killed one of those women."

"How?"

"I don't know."

"They usually raped the women they took captive, Madman." Del said this as if he knew it to be God's truth.

"They say that you can sometimes hear the dead woman crying out here," Scott offered.

"No fuggin' way." Del seemed delighted. "Let's build a fire."

"Now? We should be getting home, Wolfman. I'll be late as it is. Mom'll be worried."

"Yours maybe. Not mine. Come on. It's getting dark, and this place is spooky. A fire'll be good."

Scott was already going to be late getting home. And what would a few more minutes add to whatever his mother said or did as a result? Del pulled a cigarette lighter from his knapsack, they gathered sticks from along the riverbank, and in no time at all, they had a small fire burning, giving modest illumination to the scene.

Del gazed up at the sky, at the Milky Way, which was emerging in the growing dark, a vast vaporous highway across the heavens. "I miss *Sputnik,*" he said of the satellite that had fallen back to earth and burned up months earlier. "It was cool watching it, one little moving light, one little human thing in all those stars. I used to imagine what it would be like, up there in space looking down at the earth. Wouldn't that be something, Madman?"

Scott said, "I think it would be lonely."

Del looked down now, at the stained earth on the far side of the fire. "A lot of blood. Creasy says he heard that the Indian put a hole in Quinn the size of Kansas. Probably died quick."

Scott hadn't thought about that before, the actual dying. He did now. "Probably," he said and nodded in considered agreement.

"Do you know how your father died, Madman?"

Scott had a long stick in his hand, which he'd stuck in the fire so that flames had begun to spread up its length. "The plane he was in was shot down. He was the navigator. I guess he couldn't get out. What about your dad?"

"I don't know how exactly. Mom told me that him and a bunch of other guys were trying to hold a hill against a whole swarm of Chinese somewhere in Korea. They did it, but most of them ended up dead. He got a Silver Star. Or my mom did anyway. They sent it to her." He stared beyond the fire at the great black stain. "There's this guy in *The Naked and the Dead*. He craps himself when his platoon lands on this island in the Pacific where the Japs are dug in. Goes running down the beach looking for clean pants, gets shot all to hell."

Scott wondered why Del said this. Was he afraid his father had died like that? Scott had watched his share of war movies, and in them most guys died pretty bravely and pretty quick. There wasn't a lot of blood, not like that black soaking on the other side of the fire. He hadn't expected to see anything like this when he and Del came out, and it was working on his thinking in a way that confused him. When his grandfather died of a heart attack, Scott had seen him in the coffin, waxy looking but peaceful. He couldn't help trying to imagine what James Quinn must have looked like to have spilled all that blood in the dirt. And he couldn't help wondering what it must have felt like to die that way. Which was something he'd never considered when thinking about the death of his father.

But now he thought about it as he watched the flames on the stick in his hand crawl toward his fingers. To fall from the sky. To be trapped inside the burning belly of a great plummeting bird. How long did that fall take and was his father alive and was he scared? Scott pulled himself out of the imagining, his whole body rigid, his stomach taut, and he realized Del was asking him a question.

"You remember your dad, Madman?"

"He died before I was born. What about you?"

"He was big. Smelled like leather. You know, like from a baseball glove. Mom says he was a star pitcher in high school before he became career army." Del studied the fire and seemed to be thinking. "Your mom, she never remarried. Why?"

"I don't know. She just never did."

"You're lucky, Madman, let me tell you." He tore some grass from the ground beside him and tossed it on the fire. "Fuggin' Creasy."

"Listen." Scott held up his hand for silence. "Hear that?"

"Coyotes," Del said.

"No, I've heard coyotes before. This is different." He listened again. "It sounds like someone's crying."

Del gave a low eerie wail. "W-o-o-o-o. I'm the ghost of Jimmy Quinn. I'm coming to get you."

The crying sound died, but it left Scott feeling unsettled and anxious.

They heard no approach but instead felt the presence behind them. They both turned in the same moment, and there he was, illuminated by the flames of the small fire, surrounded by a dark that seemed unfathomable.

"The man's dead. You think that's funny?" he said.

Scott was so caught off guard by Bluestone's appearance that his voice failed him, and he couldn't reply. Del, on the other hand, said, "No, sir. Not funny. Not him. We just . . ." But under the hard glare of Noah Bluestone's eyes, charcoal in the dim light but full of reflected fire, Del trailed off before he could answer fully, before he could try to explain what was probably inexplicable.

"Put out that fire," Bluestone said. "Then get yourselves home."

"Yes, sir," Scott said.

He stood quickly and kicked the burning sticks apart, then he and Del tossed loose dirt onto the flames until the fire was dead. They turned back to where Bluestone had materialized from the night and had stood menacing above them. To their great surprise, he was gone. It was as if the night had simply closed the door on Noah Bluestone.

"Let's get out of here," Del said.

The boys hurried back to the motorbike and away from Inkpaduta Bend, the fierce growl of the little engine drowning out every other sound around them.

SCOTT LAY IN bed that night, after his mother and grandmother had had their say. They'd been more worried than angry, and they'd reminded him, as always, of his heart, his less than perfect heart. Now he stared up at the ceiling and thought about the great stain that was the lingering shadow of brutal death, and he thought again about the death of his own father and Del's. These things had been myth before, stories told to them, meaningful but, in the end, weightless. That soak of blood had made death terribly real and terribly heavy. In a way, it connected Scott with his father as nothing else ever had. His father had been more than a story. His father had been flesh, bone, blood. Scott's own flesh and bone and blood and even his imperfect heart were gifts his father had given him. Then his father had died, fallen from the sky, probably scared and probably burning and probably in great pain. And absolutely human. Like Scott. Like Del. And even like James Patrick Quinn.

CHAPTER TWENTY-ONE

THE CALL FROM Doc Porter came the next day, Monday, midmorning. Because Brody was in the process of arresting the culprit who'd stolen Bob Magruder's pickup two days earlier, Asa Fielding took the message. A little later, Brody brought the offender in—a seventeen-year-old named Douglas Anderson. The kid was surly and also scared. Anderson's father had called Brody out to the farm and shown him the stolen pickup parked behind the equipment shed. He hadn't seemed at all upset when Brody explained that he had to take the kid in and book him.

"A night or two in jail, do him some good," the father had replied, giving his son a cold look.

When Brody had the kid in a cell, Asa said, "Did he explain himself?"

"Says he stole the pickup because Magruder won't let his daughter date him. Thinks Douglas is too wild."

"Can't date the daughter, so he steals the father's pickup?" Asa shook his head. "Kid logic. Want me to call Williams?" He was speaking of the county attorney, Alexander Williams.

"Yeah," Brody said and sat down at his desk to get the paperwork done.

"Oh," Asa said as he lifted the phone. "Doc Porter called. Wants you to call him back. Says it's about Quinn and it's important."

"Did he tell you anything?"

"Nope. Apparently wants to tell you himself."

Brody waited while Asa talked to the county attorney.

"Williams wants to see the kid in his office," Asa said when he hung up.

"When?"

"He says now's just fine."

"You mind taking him?"

"Happy to."

Asa went through the door to the cells, and when he returned, he had Douglas Anderson in tow. The kid looked like he might have been crying.

"When you both come back," Brody said to his deputy, "get Douglas some lunch from the Wagon Wheel."

"Lunch?" the kid said.

"We try not to starve our prisoners," Brody told him.

Asa left with the kid, and Brody made the call to Porter. As he was dialing, the jailhouse door opened, and Connie Graff strode in. Brody lifted a hand in silent greeting, then spoke to the coroner.

"Asa said you wanted to talk to me, Doc. About Jimmy Quinn."

"I took a look at those blood samples you brought me."

"Are they Quinn's?"

"Nope, Brody, not Jimmy Quinn's."

"Who then?"

"Not who. What."

"I don't get you, Doc."

"That blood didn't come from a human being. I asked Mike Kearney to take a look."

"Kearney's a veterinarian," Brody said.

"Exactly. He says it's pig's blood, Brody. Every sample you brought me was pig's blood."

"You're kidding me. How the hell—" But the sheriff didn't finish. He simply sat there, dumbfounded, holding the phone to his ear.

"You still there, Brody?"

"I'm here, Doc."

"When you get this one sorted out, you'll let me know?"

"I'll let you know," Brody said. "Thanks."

Graff took the other chair and waited for an explanation.

Brody finally said, "Pig's blood, Connie. That was pig's blood we collected out there on Inkpaduta Bend."

"Pig's blood?" Graff seemed surprised for only a moment, then he said, "It's Bluestone, Brody."

Graff related his visit with Bluestone's wife the night before. How the woman had become agitated when he spoke about Quinn. How Bluestone, when he returned from Inkpaduta Bend and found Graff in his home, had pretty much thrown the deputy off his property.

"I'd been thinking that Quinn went out to the Bend to meet a woman," the deputy explained. "It's an isolated place, not a bad spot for what Quinn might really have had on his mind. And, consider this, Brody. He'd removed his shoes and socks and shirt before he was killed. What was that all about? Swimming in the Alabaster? I don't think so."

"It was Bluestone's wife he was meeting?"

"Had to be. Think about it. Think about that ring in Quinn's pants pocket. A ring for a small finger. Maybe a gift for a woman with a small hand. Mrs. Bluestone, hell, she's hardly bigger than a girl. You ever taken a good look at her hands? And another thing, proximity. Easy walk to Inkpaduta Bend from the Bluestone place."

"Bluestone told us he goes down there at night. Why would his wife agree to meet Quinn where her husband might be?"

"I had a couple of thoughts on that, Brody. First of all, maybe Bluestone lied to us. Maybe he doesn't visit Inkpaduta Bend as much as he led us to believe. But maybe he was there that night, and he was there because his wife was there. So either he followed her and something bad went down. Or . . ." Graff paused dramatically.

Brody bit. "Or?"

"It was a setup. Bluestone's wife lured Quinn there on purpose, and Bluestone was in on it."

"Like an ambush? Why in heaven's name would they do that?"

"Old grudge because of the land. New grudge because of the firing. Or it might have been something darker. When she wasn't working for Quinn, Mrs. Bluestone was alone a lot on her husband's place. Most days, Quinn would have known where Bluestone was and how long he'd be gone. In fact, he could have structured Bluestone's work in any way he wanted to make sure the man was away from home when he wanted him to be away."

"So that he could visit Bluestone's wife? Come on, Connie."

"I'm not saying it was necessarily something consensual. Quinn was a giant and the kind of man who might feel inclined to do that kind of thing. She's so small, Brody."

"Okay. But why the pig's blood on Inkpaduta Bend?"

"Maybe whatever happened that night didn't happen on the Bend. Maybe it happened out at the Bluestone place. I don't know the how of it exactly, but that pig's blood is the connection. Bluestone raises and slaughters his own hogs."

"So do a lot of other folks in Black Earth County," Brody pointed out.

"They don't all have reason to hate Quinn."

"I'm sure some do."

"Brody, that woman when I talked to her was afraid down to her bones."

"Cops scare people, Connie." Brody sat back and gave a good deal of thought to all that Graff had laid out and finally said, "Okay, I'm having trouble believing that Bluestone's wife would be involved in some kind of dalliance with Quinn. But I can buy that Quinn might have tried to force himself on her, especially drunk. Maybe he went out to Bluestone's place that night with something else in mind. He took that Tolley, so maybe it was really Bluestone he wanted to see, wanted to scare. Hell, maybe he even had murder on his mind. But he finds the woman alone, and, like you said, he's a man with a big appetite in all ways, and his wife is sickly, and he's been drinking, and so maybe he does decide to take advantage of Bluestone's wife. If that's the way it went down, maybe she defended herself with that Tolley. Or maybe Bluestone intervened and it was him that pulled the trigger. That's a scenario I could imagine, I suppose. And then Bluestone hauls Quinn's body to the Bend in the bed of his truck and pours the pig's blood there so it looks like that's where Jimmy died." He thought a moment. "But Bluestone admitted to being out on Inkpaduta Bend that night. Why?"

"Might be he figured that if he denied it and someone had seen him drive his truck out there, it would make him look pretty guilty. So he admits he was there but says he left before Jimmy arrived. Bluestone's got it all, Brody. Motive, opportunity, and that pig's blood is a reasonable connection."

"Let's take it to the judge," Brody said. "See if he thinks we've got enough for a search warrant."

CHAPTER TWENTY-TWO

WHEN THEY CAME bearing the search warrant authorized by Judge Kevin Eide, Kyoko Bluestone was at work in the field. They drove to the farmstead in two vehicles: Graff in his pickup, Brody and Asa Fielding in the cruiser with Douglas Anderson, the truck thief, in the backseat. They'd brought the kid because Brody wanted the help of both his deputies in the search and didn't want to leave Douglas in the cell of an otherwise empty jailhouse. Hector was also with them, riding in back with Douglas. The big dog and the kid got along well. The lawmen parked their vehicles in front of the farmhouse, and Brody walked out into the field. The old Saint Bernard with the woman stood and barked a couple of times, then wagged its tail. The woman wore a broad-brimmed straw hat that cast her face in shadow and she held a hoe. Without expression, she watched Brody approach.

"Mrs. Bluestone, my name is Brody Dern. I'm the sheriff of Black Earth County, and I'm here to execute a search of your property. Here's the warrant."

He held out the document. She glanced at it but didn't reach out to take it. He explained to her what he and his deputies were about to do and, generally speaking, why. He expected that she might lodge an objection, at least to the reason for the search if not to the search itself, but she said nothing.

"Do you understand what I'm telling you?" he asked.

She nodded.

"I'd like you to accompany me back to the house."

Graff and Fielding and the kid were waiting under the tall Dutch elm tree in the yard, beneath which sat a little bench of ornamental wrought iron. The woman turned her face toward Graff as she passed, and the old deputy looked sorry to have to invade her privacy in this way. At the door of her house, she stopped and finally spoke.

"Would you men like lemonade? It's already made and is chilling."

This was said quietly and calmly, with the kind of Oriental accent Brody had expected but with a clarity and command of the language he had not.

"Thank you, ma'am, no," Brody replied. "We need to be about our business."

Her eyes settled on the kid. "Would you like something to drink?"

"Lemonade would be good," Douglas said eagerly. As an afterthought, he added, "Thank you, ma'am."

"My name is Kyoko," she told Douglas and turned to go into the house.

"Asa, go inside with Mrs. Bluestone. Make sure she confines herself to the lemonade."

They began with the barn. Considering what Graff had told him about the butchering room there, Brody figured that might yield something. They took all the tools and utensils they found in the room. Brody gathered long splinters of the blood-soaked wood from the floor.

Graff said, "I'd swear there was a bloodstained canvas tarp hanging on that wall peg when I was here last night. Looked military issue."

"Maybe it'll turn up yet," Brody said.

Fielding came in and reported that the woman and the kid were outside now, drinking lemonade under the Dutch elm tree, and the dogs were with them.

The lawmen searched the barn and garage and work area. The only thing they found that might have been relevant was in a freezer that Bluestone kept in the garage, which was filled with meat from a butchered hog.

"Must've been recent," Graff said. "Looks like the whole pig's still there."

They went to the house and moved through room by room. Brody examined the floors carefully, looking for dried blood, scraping the blade of his pocketknife along wood seams and cracks that might have been overlooked in a desperate cleaning. They checked drawers and closets, hoping to find bloodstained clothing or linens or shoes with blood still clinging to the soles. They entered the cellar, a small, dank place without windows, and used a flashlight to scan the dirt floor and dirt walls and some old wooden shelving that held only empty Ball jars.

At the end of the long search, except for what they'd taken from the butchering area, they had nothing.

"What do you think, Brody?" Asa said as they stood in the tiny living room, looking around a final time.

"I don't know," Brody said. "Connie?"

"We're not wrong," Graff said. "It was Bluestone, I know it. We just . . ." He turned in a full circle, then shook his head. "We just missed something, somehow."

"What?" Brody said. "Where?"

"I don't know," Graff said. "Maybe there'll be something on those items we pulled from the slaughter room. And I'd like to know exactly when that pig was butchered."

Brody said, "Let's go see what Mrs. Bluestone has to say."

Outside, they found the woman and the kid talking amiably on the wrought-iron bench as if they were old friends or longtime neighbors. It was late afternoon by then. A breeze had come in across the fields, and a line of clouds had gathered along the horizon far to the west. It felt to Brody like a storm might be brewing. The woman watched the officers approach, and there seemed a calmness about her that was not at all what Graff had described in relating his visit with her the night before.

"May I ask you a few questions, Mrs. Bluestone?" Brody said.

She nodded.

"She likes Buddy Holly and Jerry Lee Lewis," the kid threw in. "She's all right, Sheriff."

"Thanks, Douglas. I appreciate the input. Asa, would you escort our young miscreant to the cruiser?"

"Come on, kid," Asa said.

Douglas rose and said to the woman, "Thank you for the lemonade, Kyoko."

She smiled. "You're welcome, Douglas."

The dogs had bounded away. Hector was using his nose to investigate the acreage, sniffing the perimeter of the house, trotting about the yard, moving farther and farther afield. Brody knew Hector would stay within earshot and didn't worry. The Bluestones' old dog kept him company.

"Mrs. Bluestone," Brody began, "that freezer in your garage is full of hog meat. Did your husband do the butchering?"

"Yes."

"Can you tell me when?"

She hesitated. "Last week sometime."

"Can you recall exactly when?"

She breathed twice. "Thursday."

"All right," Brody said, as if it meant nothing, though Quinn was killed that same night. "When my deputy visited you, he asked you a couple of questions that you never answered. I'd like answers now."

She waited, her face lifted from where she sat on the bench so that she could look at Brody's face.

"Did James Quinn ever visit when you were here alone?"

She stared into his eyes. Was it defiance he saw there?

"Yes," she said.

"What was the nature of his visits?"

"Sometimes he was looking for my husband. Sometimes he just seemed lost."

"Lost? James Quinn drank, Mrs. Bluestone, sometimes heavily, and he sometimes took a drug to help him sleep. It made him wander, get himself lost. Is that what happened?"

"He was not lost that way."

Brody waited, but she didn't elaborate.

"Did he stay long?"

"Sometimes he came into the field where I was working and talked to me a long time."

"About what?"

"Nothing, really."

"Jimmy Quinn just shot the breeze with you?"

"I think he didn't talk to many people."

"But he talked to you?"

"Didn't I just tell you he did?" It was said quietly, but there were splinters in her voice.

"Did he ever touch you?"

The night before it had been a question out of the blue and, if Graff had characterized her reaction correctly, had been one that frightened her. Not this time.

She said, "No. Never."

"There was bad blood between James Quinn and your husband. Quinn fired him last week. How did your husband feel about that?"

"My husband didn't like Mr. Quinn. Mr. Quinn didn't like my husband. But many people in this world don't like each other and still they find a way to work together."

Hector and the Bluestones' dog had wandered into the young orchard, and Hector had begun to bark. Brody glanced that way, then back at the woman.

"That doesn't really answer my question," he said.

"My husband wasn't upset about being dismissed."

"But he was upset about something."

Brody could see tension entering her face now, the shadows of lines forming at the corners of her eyes.

"Wouldn't it be better for you to ask my husband these things?" she said.

"Right now, I'm asking you. What was your husband upset about?"

"Mr. Quinn accused him of being a thief."

"Of stealing gas?"

"Yes, that."

"That's hardly reason to kill a man," Brody said.

She looked at him, then at the troubled sky behind him, then where the two dogs had become interested in something in the orchard.

"Was James Quinn here last Thursday night, the night before Memorial Day?"

The woman hesitated, then shook her head.

Brody said, "Look at me, Mrs. Bluestone."

The woman did but with obvious reluctance and with something else. Fear? Anger? Brody couldn't tell.

"Did your husband and James Quinn see each other that Thursday night?"

Her jaw clenched and her mouth went into a thin line. She clasped her hands tight on her lap in exactly the way Graff had described from his own questioning of her. And she did not answer.

Brody looked at her hands. "Mrs. Bluestone, I see you're wearing a wedding ring." He reached into his pocket and drew out the ring he'd found on Jimmy Quinn. "Would you put out your right hand?'

She seemed puzzled by the request but complied. Brody slid the ring onto her finger. He looked at Graff. "Perfect fit, wouldn't you say?"

As Brody took the ring back and returned it to his pocket, Kyoko

Bluestone's eyes locked fearfully on the orchard where the dogs had begun to dig at the earth in canine earnest, their paws kicking up sprays of loose dirt. Brody wondered if it was the strain of his questioning that was upsetting the woman or if it was the activity of the dogs.

"Connie," he said. "Go see what's up with those two."

The deputy walked into the orchard. The trees were saplings and their limbs sparsely leafed, and, against the vast, threatening sky, they seemed small and fragile, their existence precarious. Graff reached the dogs, knelt, shoved Hector and the old dog away, and dug into the earth himself. He stood and hollered, "Brody, you'll want to see this."

Brody looked down at the woman on the iron bench, and her face was crestfallen. He left her and joined Graff in the orchard. The deputy had cleared soil from what was obviously a freshly dug hole into which a canvas tarp had been thrown. The tarp was badly scorched, as if it had been exposed to significant flame. Brody pulled it up and held it open.

"Is this the one you saw hanging in the butchering room last night?"

"Military issue," Graff said. "I'd be willing to swear it's the same one. Appears that someone tried to burn it."

"Highly flame resistant," Brody said. "God bless the military. So Bluestone buried it." He touched a large stain the color of plum juice, clearly visible in one corner despite the scorching. "Pig's blood?"

"Maybe. Or maybe this was how Bluestone hauled Jimmy's body out to Inkpaduta Bend."

Brody looked back at the farmyard where the woman sat under the Dutch elm tree and stared west at the mounting clouds. Behind her, a plume of dust rose against the trees along the course of the Alabaster River, and Brody watched Noah Bluestone's pickup truck race toward the farmstead.

Graff said, "This'll be interesting."

They met Bluestone where his truck skidded to a stop in the dirt between the barn and house. The man leapt out.

"What the hell do you think you're doing, Dern?" He went immediately to where his wife sat alone on the iron bench. "Are you okay?"

She nodded, but he must have seen something in her eyes that told him more. He looked toward Brody and then at Graff, who held up the tarp.

"Found this in your orchard, Noah," Brody said. "Care to explain why you'd bother to bury a tarp out there?"

Bluestone didn't reply.

"Got any idea what this bloodstain is all about?"

Bluestone sat down beside his wife, and the two of them became like the iron of the bench.

"Noah, I'm taking this tarp and I'm going to have that stain analyzed, and if it's Jimmy Quinn's blood, I guarantee you I'll be back with a warrant for your arrest. You could make this a lot easier for yourself, your wife, me, and the citizens of Black Earth County if you just tell me the truth now."

Noah Bluestone took his wife's hand and didn't speak.

"Mrs. Bluestone? Do you have anything you'd like to say?"

She squeezed her husband's hand and followed his example.

"All right then. I think we're finished here."

Brody took the tarp from Graff and put it in the trunk of his cruiser. He called Hector, who came running. Douglas and the dog got into the backseat, and Brody and Asa Fielding got in the front. Graff climbed into his truck and headed toward Jewel. Brody did the same, giving his deputy enough lead that no one in the cruiser would have to eat his dust. As he drove away, Brody looked in his rearview mirror. Across the sky behind him, huge thunderheads had risen, and from them lightning sparked as if something terrible were being forged on the anvils of heaven. Against that great darkness, the farmstead seemed small and vulnerable. On the tiny iron bench beneath the Dutch elm, Bluestone and his wife sat together, staring at the approaching storm.

CHAPTER TWENTY-THREE

AS BRODY SUSPECTED, the blood on that tarp matched the blood type of James Patrick Quinn. In the absence of airtight confessions or reliable eyewitness testimony, justice, as has so often been the case, had to rely on speculation accompanied by a preponderance of circumstantial evidence.

Graff and Brody went together to make the arrest. Brody had called the Quinn home to find out if Noah Bluestone was working for them and, if so, where. Marta Quinn told him that Bluestone had requested the day off. She asked what it was about, and Brody said that he would explain to her later. Brody and Graff drove to the Bluestone farmstead in the cruiser. They spotted the couple in the field of amaranth, working together. The storm the night before had soaked the earth, and Brody and Graff followed in the couple's clear footsteps to the place where husband and wife stood together with the old Saint Bernard sitting patiently beside them.

It was an uneventful arrest. This was many years before the *Miranda* decision made mandatory the reading of a suspect's rights. Brody said simply, "Noah, I've got a warrant for your arrest for the murder of Jimmy Quinn. You ready to go with me?"

Bluestone said, "Can I change my clothes? I'm pretty dirty."

Brody said, "Sure."

The couple put their tools away in the barn and went into the house, accompanied by Brody and Graff. Brody was amazed at the calmness of the woman, who waited silently with them until her husband emerged from the bedroom in chinos and a white shirt and polished Red Wings. He kissed his wife and said, "You'll take care of things?" She nodded and, tearless, walked beside him to the cruiser.

"Backseat, Noah." Brody opened the door for him.

To Kyoko, Graff said, "Would you like to come?"

She shook her head.

Brody said to her, "He'll need a lawyer."

She stared at Brody as if she didn't understand English, though he knew she did.

"All right, then," Brody said. "Afternoon, Mrs. Bluestone."

He'd just put Noah Bluestone in the back of the cruiser when he spotted a pickup approaching on the lane. The truck pulled to a stop and Gordon Landis got out, followed by two other men from town—Avery Simpson, who owned the hardware store, and Melvin Crabbe, who worked for the county driving snowplows in the winter and dump trucks the rest of the year. All three men carried rifles.

"Heard you came out to arrest the Indian," Landis said. "We thought you might need a hand."

Brody eyed their weapons, his jaw tight. "It's been a peaceful arrest, Gordy," he said trying to keep his anger under control. "You men can put those rifles away before you accidentally shoot someone."

"Hell, someone's already been shot," Crabbe said. "Jimmy Quinn. We just want to make sure the redskin responsible don't cause any more trouble."

"I've got this in hand," Brody said. "I want you all to return to that truck and go on back to town."

"What about her?" Landis said. "She have any part in killing Jimmy?"

"Mrs. Bluestone is not a suspect, Gordy. Go on. Do like I told you. Just drive away."

The three men didn't move. Landis's companions looked to him for some sign of what to do next. Finally, Landis said, "Come on, boys. We'll leave the sheriff to his job. At least for now."

Brody watched until they'd driven the full length of the lane and turned onto the main road. When he turned back, he saw the terror on Kyoko Bluestone's face.

"It's okay, Mrs. Bluestone," he said. "I'll see to it that those men don't come back." But even as he said it, he feared it was an empty promise.

Graff, who'd moved to stand near her when the men arrived, said, "Is there someone who can stay with you or that you can stay with?"

The woman shook her head. Then she seemed to reach deep inside herself and draw up steel from somewhere. She held herself erect and said, "I will be fine."

"Good day, ma'am." The deputy tipped his Stetson to her and joined Brody at the cruiser. "She's hardly more than a kid," he said quietly. "I don't like the idea of leaving her alone here. Word's already out that we've arrested Bluestone for killing Quinn. A lot of folks beside those three goons are going to get their hackles up."

"What do you suggest?"

"We keep an eye on her, especially at night."

"You volunteering, Connie?"

"I got nobody waiting for me at home."

Brody gave a nod. "Don't be obvious."

"I'm nothing if not discreet." Graff looked back at the small woman. "She'll never know I'm watching."

AT THE JAILHOUSE, Fielding stood up from the seat behind the desk, and Brody said, "Let's book him, Asa."

They took Bluestone's fingerprints and mug shots and took from him his wallet, locking it in the safe they kept for prisoners' personal articles.

Brody said, "Someone you want to call, Noah? A lawyer, maybe?"

Bluestone said, "No one."

"You intend to represent yourself in all this?"

"I'm not going to do anything in all this," Bluestone said.

"I'm not sure what you mean by that, Noah."

"I mean exactly what I said."

"The court will appoint a lawyer for you."

"The court will do what it has to do, I guess."

Douglas Anderson had gone to court that morning, been arraigned and released into the custody of his parents, so Noah Bluestone became the sole occupant of the jailhouse cellblock. He sat on the metal-framed cot and put his back against the wall. The only window was at the far end of the cellblock. All he could see there was a small patch of evening sky.

"It'll be suppertime soon. What would you like?" Asa asked.

Bluestone said, "Doesn't matter."

"Makes it easy," Asa said.

The lawmen left him and joined Graff at the jailhouse desk.

"He's going to need counsel," Graff said. "And it doesn't sound like he's inclined to get his own."

"I'll apprise the judge and our county attorney of the situation," Brody said. "Guess we all know who they'll bring into this."

And less than an hour later, Charlie Bauer got the call.

- PART TWO -

THE RIVER WE REMEMBER

CHAPTER TWENTY-FOUR

CHARLOTTE BAUER'S FATHER had been a banker in Jewel, a relatively wealthy man who'd invested in land. For as far back as anyone could remember, he'd called his daughter Charlie. When Charlie finally returned to Black Earth County after the man's death, she sold most of those holdings but kept the property on which she'd been born and raised, a few acres along the Alabaster River a mile north of town. The house looked across a field that her father and his before him had planted in alfalfa for hay they sold to others. When the land became Charlie's, she left the field fallow so that the natural wild plants of the prairie would take root there, things like goldenrod and milkweed and clover and coneflowers. Beyond the field, along the bank of the Alabaster, stood a line of trees, mostly cottonwoods and box elders. Charlie had been a lawyer and though retired, still took on a case now and then if it interested her. When she wasn't busy with legal work or other things, Charlie Bauer often sat on her porch and enjoyed the view, most often in the company of a good book and a little Johnnie Walker Black and occasionally, with a cigar.

The afternoon when Judge Eide called and explained Noah Bluestone's situation and asked Charlie to represent the man's legal interests, she'd been sitting on the porch reading *The Grapes of Wrath* yet again. She'd met Steinbeck, had encountered him in California in 1937. Some of the migrant workers she was trying to help in one of their many attempts to organize themselves took her to a small shack where a tall, very serious man with a thin mustache was temporarily living. He introduced himself as John. Only that. They shared some wine and bread and cheese and talked about the terrible situation of the itinerants who worked the fruit ranches. When Charlie left, he gave her a copy of a book he'd recently published titled *Tortilla Flat,* which she kept in a place of honor among the many volumes on her bookshelves.

After talking with the judge, she returned to the porch and stood for a long time looking across the wild grass and flowers. The trees that sheltered the Alabaster were green against the washed blue of the late afternoon sky. Beyond them to the east, the land rose in a series of swells quilted with young, cultivated fields, and Charlie thought that Steinbeck might understand and appreciate the complications of the heart that such a place as this engendered.

"IN HERE," BRODY said and opened the door to the cellblock.

Charlie had read the formal complaint against Noah Bluestone. The prosecution's assertion was that Bluestone had shot and killed James Patrick Quinn at an as yet undetermined location, but most probably the Bluestone farmstead. He'd wrapped Quinn's body in a tarp and had transported it to Inkpaduta Bend, where he'd attempted to make the death look like a suicide. At the moment, the only solid evidence against him was the blood on the tarp, which he'd attempted to burn and then to hide by burying it in his orchard. But there was also the hog's blood on Inkpaduta Bend and the evidence of the slaughtering at the Bluestone farmstead, which Mrs. Bluestone admitted had been carried out on the same day as Quinn's death.

According to the prosecution, that death had most likely occurred in the heat of anger as a result of two circumstances. The first was the argument with Quinn over the accusation of theft and the firing that followed. The second was the attention, unwanted or not, that Quinn was paying to Bluestone's wife. The evidence of this second assertion was the sapphire ring found in Quinn's pants pocket, a ring that perfectly fit the finger of Kyoko Bluestone. It was all circumstantial, but damning enough, especially in light of the fact that both Noah Bluestone and his wife refused to answer any questions related to Quinn's death. Because there was no indication of premeditation in the crime, the county attorney was indicting on a charge of murder in the second degree. But Charlie knew that could always change if additional evidence came to light.

No one had told Bluestone that Charlie was coming, but he knew who she was, and when she entered the cell, he knew what she was doing there.

"I don't need a lawyer," he said before she had a chance to open her mouth. It was spoken politely.

"Mind if I sit, Noah, and we can talk about that?"

There was only the cot, and he slid to one end to give her room.

Charlie studied him. He was only forty years old, but like most men who've worked the land, his face held deep creases, the results of long hours squinting against a blazing sun. His eyes were narrow, the irises dark brown. Bluestone seldom looked her way as they spoke, choosing instead to stare at the sky outside the window at the end of the cellblock.

"Murder, Noah. That's as serious a charge as anyone can have leveled against them," Charlie said. "But you don't believe you need a lawyer?"

"I don't intend to fight it."

"Because you're guilty?"

He didn't reply.

"Our legal system is complicated, Noah, and terribly flawed, and even in simple cases things can be very difficult. Murder isn't a simple case."

It was as if he hadn't heard. He just stared at the tiny, framed patch of sky.

"Do you intend to represent yourself?"

"I don't intend to do anything," he said.

"Just accept what happens to you, is that it?"

No reply and he still would not look at her.

"If you didn't kill Jimmy Quinn, why not say so?"

"Who in this county would believe what an Indian says?"

"I would."

He laughed, which surprised Charlie. "That'll get me sprung for sure."

She smiled. "Yeah, neither of us'll ever get voted citizen of the year here. In a way, Noah, that makes us a good pair."

He finally looked at her. "How do you figure?"

"We're both seen here as folks who don't quite fit in. We begin with some understanding of each other."

He lost his good humor. "You don't understand me."

"All right. But I do understand the situation you're in, and I know you'll need help if you want to get through this."

"I'll get through this my own way."

"Is that what your wife wants?"

"Leave my wife out of this."

"Impossible, Noah. Going forward, she'll be hit with a storm of questions. Our sheriff will press her for what she knows. Our county attorney will do the same. Questions will be coming from all kinds of folks, one way or another. She doesn't have to answer, but wouldn't it be better if someone were with her and on her side when that happens?"

Bluestone thought on that awhile. "Maybe," he said.

"So you'll let me represent you?"

He gave a nod, though she could see his heart wasn't in it.

"Good. Now, let's get down to business. Remember that everything we talk about is confidential. It stays between you and me. In this country, not even God can pry it out of me. Do you understand?"

"Yes."

"Brody says you had good reason to want to see Quinn dead. Tell me about that."

"You knew Jimmy Quinn."

"Yes."

"You didn't want to kill him on occasion?"

It was Charlie's turn to laugh. "Okay. Lots of people aren't shedding tears over his demise. But tell me about your situation. I understand he accused you of stealing gasoline and fired you. Is that true?"

"He accused me of stealing gasoline. But that was only part of the reason he fired me."

"The rest?"

"He couldn't scare me."

"I don't understand."

"Jimmy Quinn liked to believe that he was a powerful man, but he had no power over me. In his heart, he was small and afraid, and I knew that, and he understood that I knew."

"So his firing didn't anger you?"

"No."

"Did something else anger you?"

He turned his eyes away.

"If I'm going to defend you, Noah, I need to know the truth."

"I didn't ask you to defend me. You said you would represent me."

"In my book, that means a defense."

"You'll need a different book, I guess."

"The complaint says you killed Jimmy Quinn, shot him with his own shotgun, carted his body to Inkpaduta Bend, and tried to make it look like he killed himself there. What do you have to say about that?"

"Nothing."

"The buried tarp with Quinn's blood? You have nothing to say about that?"

"Nothing."

"Everybody knows Jimmy had insomnia and sometimes trespassed at night. Is it possible he wandered onto your property and you just mistook him for a burglar?"

Again, all she got was silence.

"You're not making this easy."

"I didn't ask for your help."

They sat there, Bluestone at his end of the cot and Charlie at the other. Between them was something unseen and, she was beginning to suspect, absolutely impenetrable.

"Are you a drinking man, Noah?"

"Not much," he said.

"Well, I drink." She reached into her purse and brought out a small flask. She took a long swallow of Johnnie Walker and held the flask out to Bluestone.

He eyed it a moment, accepted the flask, took a sip, then handed it back.

"We're a funny lot, you know?" Charlie indulged in another swallow and returned the flask to her purse. "We have this amazing ability to communicate. And what do we say to one another? 'No' or 'Nothing.' Not much more than the grunts of lesser beasts. 'This above all: to thine own self be true.' Know who said that, Noah?"

"Shakespeare."

"What I'm thinking is that your *no*s and your *nothing*s are simply less eloquent rephrasing of Shakespeare. So this is what I'm going to do. At your arraignment tomorrow morning, I'm going to plead you not guilty."

"I don't want to plead one way or the other."

"You wish to remain mute when you face the ogre we call justice?"

"Yes."

"All right then. How about this? You don't plead. I will plead on your behalf. The response will come not from you, but from me."

"What's the point?"

"I'd like to have a chance to defend you. A plea has to be entered for that to happen. I could plead nolo contendere, which means that you don't want to contest the charge. It's looked upon as an admission of guilt without actually having to say it."

"That's not what I want."

"I figured as much. So if I enter a plea of not guilty on your behalf and am clear that this is coming from me, not you, you will have neither admitted your guilt nor denied it, but you will have your day in court."

"I don't want my day in court. I want this to be done with as quickly as possible."

"Then plead guilty."

"No."

"Or nolo contendere. Which, as I said, will be seen as the same as guilty, but will get all this over with."

"No."

"Then let me tell you what might happen with a day in court. I might be able to get a jury to think about the kind of man Jimmy Quinn was. I might be able to remind them of all the harm he's done across the course of his life here in Black Earth County. I might even be able to get them to understand a scenario of self-defense, which just might get them to acquit you and set you free. Is that something you'd like?"

His eyes, which throughout the interview had been so intent on that little square of sky at the end of the cellblock, turned to Charlie. They were dark and narrowed to squinty, sun-beaten slits with deep lines at the corners, but she saw in them the first glimpse of something hopeful, something she could use. Noah Bluestone wanted to be free.

CHAPTER TWENTY-FIVE

IT WAS EVENING in Jewel. All that day the sun had drawn up from the earth the wetness left by last night's storm, and the air had been full of a scent that made Scott Madison restless. Although he didn't have a name to pin on it, the smell seemed one of promise, of possibility. He felt as if there were an important thing that had to be discovered, to be experienced. All day he'd been waiting for something to happen.

He'd just put a bag of trash into one of the cans behind the Wagon Wheel when he heard the growl of Delbert Wolfe's motorbike and watched his friend swing around the corner and into the yard, and lay the little machine on the grass next to the lashed-together lean-to.

Del greeted him with "On KP duty?"

"Yeah. And grounded."

"But it was worth it, Madman," Del said with a grin. "We talked to a murderer. You heard, right?"

"Heard what?"

"That Indian. Bluestone. They arrested him."

"I didn't hear," Scott said.

"Creasy told me Bluestone lit out from the Quinn place yesterday like a bat out of hell. He didn't come in to work today. And the Quinns got a call from the sheriff saying that the Indian had been arrested for the murder of their old man, for killing him in cold blood."

Noah Bluestone had sat at the Wagon Wheel's counter. Scott had spoken to him, not much, but pleasantly. This same man had blown a hole in James Quinn, had spilled all that blood on the ground next to the Alabaster River, had scared the bejesus out of him and Del as they sat by the fire on Inkpaduta Bend. Now he was a prisoner in the jailhouse. Black Earth County, which had always seemed to Scott one very particular, familiar thing, had quickly become something entirely different. He wondered, was this what he'd sensed, what he'd been waiting for?

"What's with the black eye, Wolfman?" Scott asked, because Del's left eye carried the shadow of a bruise.

"Fuggin' Creasy," Del said. "He's always been a bastard, but lately he's been getting worse. He has these nightmares. Wakes up screaming. It didn't used to be so bad, but since we came here, something about this place seems to have set him off. Mom says it's because his old man used to beat him pretty bad when he was a kid. Whatever it is, it gives him the shakes, even during the day sometimes. Drinks like a fish, and when he's sloshed, let me tell you, you better stay out of his way. He's scaring me, Madman."

"Can't you leave?"

"Me, I'd take off in a minute. Mom says she has to stand by him. I don't get it, but that's the way she is. How long you grounded?"

"Not really grounded. I just have to work extra hours at the Wagon Wheel."

"Not so bad," Del said. He looked around furtively, then reached under his T-shirt at the small of his back and brought out a pistol. "What do you think?"

"Whoa. Where'd you get that?"

"It's Creasy's."

"You just took it?"

"Yeah. He keeps it in the closet in their bedroom. He has rifles, but he almost never takes this out. It's a twenty-two. I've been sleeping with it under my pillow in case some night Creasy really goes nuts. I thought maybe when you're not on your mom's shit list anymore, we could do some target practice. It'll be a kick, Madman."

The pistol was small but looked dangerous in Del's palm. Although Scott felt a profound sense of menace coming from it, he also found it mesmerizing.

"Scott!" his mother called from inside the café.

At the sound of her voice, Del shoved the firearm back into the waist of his pants and hid it again under his T-shirt.

Scott's mother opened the screen door. "Hello, Del." Scott knew she was upset with Del for his part in keeping them both out so long beyond curfew the night before, but she nonetheless gave him a gracious smile.

"Evening, Mrs. Madison."

"Del, I'm afraid Scott has work to do."

"Sure. I just stopped by to ask if he could help me entertain my cousin and her friend who'll be visiting this weekend."

Which was news to Scott, though he tried his best not to show it.

"When are they coming?" Scott's mother asked.

"Friday."

"That would be all right, if it's all right with Scott. What are you planning on doing?"

"I thought we'd take them tubing on the river."

"Okay with you, Scott?" she asked.

"Sure," her son said.

"Great." Del slapped his friend's shoulder and said, "Later, Madman." He went to his motorbike, righted it, pulled the cord to engage the engine, and rode off.

Scott's mother watched him go with a troubled look on her face. "Was he in a fight?"

"I don't think so. Why?"

"That bruise," she said.

He could have told her the truth, but that might lead to other questions and then he might not be able to go shooting with Del. So he said, "Probably just fell off his bike."

She said, "Hmmmm," as if not completely convinced, but turned her attention to her son. "You need to take some supper over to the jailhouse."

"Mr. Bluestone?"

"So, you heard." She glanced where Del had gone, then back to Scott. "Yes, Noah Bluestone."

MURDERER, SCOTT THOUGHT as he walked with the tray toward the county jail, and he wondered exactly what that meant. He'd seen John Wayne and Audie Murphy kill Indians and Japanese and Germans by the thousands on the screen at the Rialto, but that wasn't called murder. There was glory in what they did, or pretended to do, for the camera. Noah Bluestone had killed only one man, the kind of man who, when speaking about him, a lot of good people used a lot of bad language. Yet Noah Bluestone was locked up behind bars. In cold blood, Del had said about the killing. What did that mean? And he wondered, as he walked along the storefronts, his reflection keeping him company, what it felt like to kill someone. Did what you feel depend on the reason for the killing? John Wayne seemed pretty happy with himself. Was that how Noah Bluestone felt?

His wondering was interrupted by an amiable greeting.

"Hello there, Scott."

He looked up and found Mr. Wicklow standing in front of the *Clarion* office, smiling down at him.

"Hi," Scott replied.

The newspaperman nodded toward the tray in Scott's hand. "For Noah Bluestone?"

"Yes, sir."

Wicklow stroked his beard and shook his head, as if he found something unacceptable, but Scott wasn't sure what that might be.

"Mind if I walk with you a bit?"

"That would be okay," Scott said.

The newspaperman fell in step beside him. Wicklow moved with an odd, rhythmic gait, a normal stride followed by the stiff swing of his artificial leg. Scott had never seen that leg, and now it was a part of his wondering. He wanted to ask the man about it, about what had happened in the war that caused him to lose it, about what it felt like to be torn apart and put back together.

"Terrible business," Wicklow said.

Business? An odd word, Scott thought, for something that dealt with one man killing another. It was a word that suggested handshakes and agreements and civil exchanges, not the giving and receiving of a load of buckshot.

"Yes," Scott said with his most serious voice. "Are you going to write a story about it?"

"Absolutely. Several probably. Nothing quite like this has ever happened in Black Earth County. It's news with a capital *N*, Scott."

"Why did he do it?"

"I don't know that he did."

"Sheriff Dern arrested him."

"You know the phrase 'innocent until proven guilty'?"

"Yes, sir."

"That's how we operate here. Until a jury of his peers finds him guilty, we should presume that Noah Bluestone is innocent."

Which was the way it was supposed to work, Scott knew, but listening to Del and hearing what Creasy said, he figured that wasn't the way it really was.

"I heard Mr. Bluestone was a professional soldier," Scott said.

"Career Marine, yes."

"And he fought in World War Two and Korea both."

"That's right."

"He must've killed a lot of men."

"I don't know that he did, Scott, but if so, that's a very different situation. A soldier kills because—" Wicklow stopped suddenly and looked where the sun was just about to set in the west. His face was orange with the glow, and he closed his eyes nearly shut against that last flaring of the light. "A soldier kills . . ." he said slowly, as if it was something he'd never really thought about before, as if he was only just now working out the reason. He thought some more and finally looked down at Scott, and the boy could see along his jawline under the hair of his beard the jagged scars where his exploded skin had been sewn back together. "In the end, a soldier kills because all the circumstances of a moment drive him to it. It isn't for freedom or God or for the people back home. It's because he has no choice but to kill. And in that moment, he's not thinking of it as a good thing or a bad thing. He's not thinking about ethics. He's thinking about keeping himself alive and keeping his comrades alive. And in all that mess, the only thing he wants is for it to end and for him to be alive to see that end."

Wicklow peered deeply into Scott's face, and the boy understood that the man felt he'd communicated something important, some truth that was essential to Scott's grasp not just of Bluestone's situation but of what it was to be a man, to be a soldier. And those scars on his face and his missing leg were all testaments to his ability to bear witness to that truth.

But Scott was only a boy, and a boy with an imperfect heart that would keep him out of whatever war might erupt in his future. So what he said, he said only to please the man. "I see, sir."

Wicklow smiled, but it was a sad thing, as if he knew he'd failed in what he'd tried desperately and sincerely to pass down to the boy. "Come on then, son. Bluestone's supper must be getting cold."

WHEN SCOTT AND Sam Wicklow arrived at the jailhouse, the sheriff checked the tray and unlocked the cellblock door.

"Go on," the sheriff said to Scott. "I want a word with Mr. Wicklow."

Noah Bluestone was sitting on his cot with his back against the wall, staring at the little window at the end of the cellblock. The smell of the meal Angie Madison had prepared brought his attention quickly to where Scott stood outside the cell door.

"Supper, Mr. Bluestone," Scott said.

"Smells like fried chicken."

"Yes, sir. And mashed potatoes and gravy, and some corn with red peppers. There's a slice of apple pie, too."

Bluestone got off the cot and came to the door, where there was a narrow rectangular opening down low designed to allow the tray to slide through. Scott passed the food to the prisoner. Bluestone took the tray, set it on the cot, and turned back to the boy.

"You and your friend, you made it home okay the other night?"

"Yes, sir."

"I was hard on you out there."

"It's all right."

"I heard you laughing is all. It's not a place for laughter."

"I know. A man died there."

"Not just a man. A good man, a man worthy of respect."

Which surprised Scott Madison, because that was the first time he could recall hearing anyone speak highly of Mr. Quinn. The first time, and it had come from the mouth of the man who'd murdered him.

"So how does this work?" Bluestone asked. "Do you wait until I'm finished eating and take the tray back?"

"Usually, yes, sir."

"Then I better get about my business."

Bluestone sat on the cot, uncovered the tray, and began to eat. Scott felt uncomfortable simply standing there, watching, so he said, "I'll be back when you're finished."

Mr. Wicklow was just leaving, and the sheriff looked lost in thought. He stared at the floor and didn't seem to notice Scott.

"He's eating," Scott said.

Brody looked up. "Good. Thanks."

"He said something that I don't understand."

"What was that?"

"He said Mr. Quinn was a good man. He said he was a man worthy of respect."

"Noah Bluestone said that?"

"Yes, sir."

"Well, I'll be."

"If he thought that, why did he kill him?"

"That's a very good question, Scott. And I intend to ask him."

Hector drifted over, and Scott knelt down to pet him. "Good boy," he said. "You're a good boy." He wanted a dog himself, but his grandmother was allergic to them and to cats as well. He'd had turtles and fish and he'd had a canary once, but they weren't the same as having something with soft fur that you could run your hands over, and when you talked to them, they looked at you as if they were listening and understood.

Then a question popped out of his mouth that he didn't even realize was coming until it was too late. He said, "Have you ever killed anyone?"

The question seemed to startle the sheriff, and the boy was immediately sorry he'd asked. But it was done. Scott watched as so many painful changes crossed the man's face. "That's okay, you don't have to answer," he said. "I shouldn't have asked."

"It's all right," Brody said. "And the answer is yes. And also the answer is that I would undo it all if I could."

"That was in the war, right?" Scott said.

"The war," Brody confirmed.

Scott knew that Brody had come back a hero. Everyone in Jewel knew. He didn't know the whole story, but it had something to do with a daring escape from a Japanese POW camp in the jungle somewhere. He longed to hear the story, the true story, but he knew that would be asking too much. So he simply nodded as if Brody's response—*the war*—had been enough.

"I better see if Mr. Bluestone's finished," Scott said and returned to the cellblock.

Bluestone slipped the tray through the slot in the door. "That was good. Thank your mom for me, okay?"

"Yes, sir. I will."

Bluestone smiled at him, then looked toward the window. When Scott passed through the office on his way out, the sheriff was staring out a window, too. And Scott had the sense that these men were looking at things he didn't understand yet. But no matter how awful those things might be, he wanted to know what they were and to understand them, too. And then maybe, even with a hole in his heart, he might feel like he was finally a man complete.

CHAPTER TWENTY-SIX

BEFORE THAT EVENING, Charlie Bauer had seen Kyoko Bluestone only from a distance. When she arrived at the Bluestone farm, the sun had already set, and although the land was lit only with a peach afterglow, Charlie found the woman still working in one of the fields. Until the old Saint Bernard rose from where he'd been lying in the dirt, Kyoko didn't notice the lawyer's approach. When she looked up from her hoeing, her face was so calm and so beautiful Charlie was actually startled. She was much younger than Charlie had imagined, mid-twenties at most. She wore dungarees and a faded blue work shirt and a broad-brimmed straw hat. Her eyes were amber.

"Mrs. Bluestone, I'm Charlotte Bauer. I'm your husband's lawyer."

"My husband has a lawyer?"

"He needs legal representation, and I've offered my services. He's accepted."

Kyoko Bluestone waited, her face a picture of patience.

"I'd like to talk to you, if I may," Charlie said.

"We should go inside then. Come, Fuji," she said to the dog.

She walked back toward the house and outbuildings, Fuji and the lawyer following. She laid the hoe against the barn and crossed the yard. From the branches of the tall Dutch elm came the song of a meadowlark, but Charlie knew it was too late in the evening for that. Kyoko stopped and listened.

"Mockingbird," she said. "It pretends to be so many things it isn't."

Inside, she invited her guest to take a seat. She washed her hands and prepared tea and only when she'd poured two cups did she finally sit and say, "How do I know this to be true?"

"I beg your pardon?"

"You told me that you are my husband's lawyer. I didn't know my husband had a lawyer. I didn't know that a woman could even be a lawyer. So I am asking, how do I know this to be true?"

In those days, Charlie Bauer had an old leather satchel, worn and scuffed, that she carried with her on business. She opened the satchel and took out a folded note that Noah Bluestone had given her to deliver. He'd told Charlie his wife would be distrustful and the note would explain everything. He'd asked Charlie not to look at it, and she had respected his wishes.

While Kyoko read what her husband had written, her face showed no emotion. Then she raised her amber eyes and said simply, "Yes."

"Your husband is being charged with a very serious crime."

"The killing of James Quinn."

"In order to defend him, I need to know everything I can about Quinn's relationship with you and your husband."

"He was my husband's employer," she said, as if that was the end of it.

"He fired your husband."

"Yes."

"Did that make Noah angry?"

"No."

"Why not?"

"A wise sailor gets used to the stormy sea."

"Quinn accused Noah of stealing from him," Charlie said.

"My husband didn't steal from James Quinn."

"And it didn't anger him to be accused of being a thief?"

"He was accused by a man who himself could be accused of things much worse. It didn't trouble him."

"The complaint against Noah states that he killed James Quinn here on your farm, took his body to Inkpaduta Bend, and staged what was supposed to look like a suicide."

Bluestone's wife didn't respond but sat with her hands folded on her lap, relaxed, as if this were simply an evening tea and her husband was not at that moment behind bars with his freedom very much in peril. Charlie stared at those hands, saw how small and delicate they were, and considered how a sapphire ring might look on one of those fingers.

"Could you tell me what happened that night?" Charlie said.

"My husband, in his note, asked me to say nothing to you about James Quinn's death."

"I can't defend him if I don't know the truth of what happened, Mrs. Bluestone."

"My name is Kyoko. You may call me that," she said.

Charlie lifted her cup and sipped her tea. The cup was Japanese, fragile-looking, hand-painted, with no handle. She had drunk tea from similar cups years earlier in Northern California when, following the end of the Second World War, she'd worked on behalf of a number of Japanese-American families whose possessions—their land, their savings, their whole livelihoods—were taken from them while they were forced to live behind the barbed wire of internment camps.

"Your husband told me that he's unwilling to offer a plea to the charge against him. He won't say that he's guilty or not guilty. But he also won't agree to what we call a plea of nolo contendere."

"No contest," Kyoko said, then nodded as if her husband's response, inexplicable to Charlie, was perfectly understandable to her.

"Kyoko, why would he want to do that?"

"I can't say anything more."

Charlie pressed her, which was uncomfortable because Kyoko was so polite in all her refusals. When she knew it was useless to proceed, Charlie said, "News people may come out here and harass you. Say nothing to them. Say nothing to anyone about your husband's situation unless I'm with you. And I'd like you in court tomorrow when your husband is arraigned. Will you do that?"

"Yes," she said. Then she said, "I don't drive."

"I'll pick you up." And they settled on a time.

Before she left, Charlie offered Kyoko a caution about another danger, one the lawyer was only too familiar with over all her years fighting for what she thought of in those days as justice. She said, "Alone out here, you may not be safe."

Kyoko gazed at her calmly, and Charlie wasn't sure that she'd made herself clear.

"People, they get upset about things, about Jimmy Quinn's death, and some of them may be tempted to come here and give you trouble." Charlie took a breath and said the other part of this because it needed saying. "And you're Japanese, Kyoko. The war is still being fought in the minds of some folks here."

"I understand."

"If you're threatened, call me. But be careful what you say on the phone. It's a party line, and folks listen."

Kyoko offered her small hand in parting. She was no more than a wisp of thing, and as Charlie left, she felt a great concern for the young woman's safety, because except for an old dog who would be no threat to an intruder, Kyoko Bluestone was completely alone and unprotected.

CHAPTER TWENTY-SEVEN

NOAH BLUESTONE'S ARRAIGNMENT was as well attended as a church Christmas service. People showed up that morning who'd never seen the inside of the Black Earth County courthouse. Charlie Bauer had picked up Kyoko, who was dressed in a white blouse, gray skirt that came to midcalf, and black shoes with short heels. Her hair was washed, brushed silk smooth and shiny, and she wore it long. The look of her was unadorned but attractive. Per Charlie's instructions, she brought a clean shirt and tie and sport coat for her husband to wear at the proceeding. Noah Bluestone sat with his attorney at the defendant's table. Kyoko sat directly behind them, on the other side of the railing that separated the jurists from the public who'd come to watch.

When, after Charlie Bauer's long absence from Minnesota, she'd returned to Jewel and had begun to defend the defenseless there, she was looked on as a kind of freak. People in Black Earth County didn't think of women as lawyers. Or doctors or bankers. They could be teachers or nurses. Or wives and mothers. But competing on a playing field that was traditionally male made Charlie an item of consternation and even disapproval. Which she always thought odd, considering that not many years earlier, when men on that prairie were either giving up or going crazy because of the hard work the land demanded, it was often the iron-backed pioneer women who endured and saved the homesteads. So not only did the disapproval in Black Earth County not bother her, but Charlie rather reveled in it.

The county attorney, Alex Williams, didn't arrive until moments before the arraignment was to begin. Charlie guessed that this was by design. She'd faced Williams many times in the courtroom, and he was a man who liked a good show. Charlie suspected that he was preparing to play a part in Minnesota's larger political arena, building a reputation, and the murder of James Quinn was a blessing that had fallen into his lap.

Brody was there, of course, and Connie Graff. Sam Wicklow, too. Right up front, staring nails at the back of Noah Bluestone's head, sat Terry Quinn, who'd come into town that morning for the proceeding. But Charlie noted that his sister, Fiona McCarthy, was absent. This wasn't necessarily surprising considering the cloud of scandal that had hung over her in Jewel. Charlie was gone when Fiona had become pregnant and quickly married her high school history teacher. Still, twenty years later it continued to be an occasional topic of gossip in Jewel. Since Jimmy Quinn's death, it was part of all the juicy tidbits, old and new, that were making the rounds. What was more telling for Charlie that day was the absence of Marta Quinn and her children.

Judge Kevin Eide was then in his final years on the bench. He hadn't been challenged in his bid for reelection in forever. He was a fair man and ran his courtroom in a relaxed but judiciously responsible manner.

Things began in the usual way, then came time for the judge to ask Bluestone how he pleaded to the charge of murder.

Charlie stood. "On behalf of my client, I would like to enter a plea of not guilty."

"On behalf of my client? That's an interesting phraseology, Counselor." Eide wore little half-glasses for reading. He peered over the top of the rims at Noah Bluestone. "Is that your plea, Mr. Bluestone?"

Bluestone, from the outset, had held himself erect in his chair. It struck Charlie as perhaps a holdover from his long military life. "No, sir," he said.

"No?" Eide looked at Charlie. "I don't understand."

"My client refuses to enter a plea on his own behalf, Your Honor. I'm entering the plea for him."

The judge's eyes shifted again to Charlie's client.

"Mr. Bluestone, is there a reason you won't speak for yourself in this?"

"Yes, sir."

The judge waited and finally said, "I wouldn't mind hearing from you sometime today."

"My reasons are my own, sir."

"If it please the court," Charlie said, "in this and all other related proceedings, I intend to be the voice of my client in every respect."

"In every respect." Eide rolled this over in his thinking. "This is what you want, Mr. Bluestone?"

"Yes, sir."

"Do you understand the seriousness of the charge against you?"

"I do."

"And yet you intend not to participate in your defense in any way."

"Yes, sir."

Eide said, "So be it. Let the record show that on behalf of her client, defense counsel has entered a plea of not guilty." He eyed Charlie, then Bluestone, and said, "But I'm going to order a psychiatric evaluation."

"On what grounds, Your Honor?" Charlie said.

"The crime he's accused of is a particularly heinous one, Charlie. Yet here he sits, and as nearly I can tell, he's about as moved by all this as a tree stump. And in addition, he refuses to participate in his own defense. I think it would be unwise to proceed with everything that a trial is bound to entail without first having a good, expert opinion of your client's current mental state."

"I concur, Your Honor," Williams said.

The judge gave the county attorney a mildly withering look. "Well, hooray for that, Counselor."

Charlie considered objecting but decided to let it pass. Noah Bluestone seemed unaffected by the idea. And the judge was right. Nothing so far had seemed to have any effect on him.

The county attorney stood. "Your Honor, I'd like to recommend that bail be set at one hundred thousand dollars."

"A hundred thousand dollars?" Charlie leapt to her feet. "Come on, Alex."

"I know that this seems like an extraordinary amount, Your Honor, but in my opinion, Mr. Bluestone represents a significant flight risk, and perhaps a continuing danger to the citizens of this county, particularly in light of his questionable mental state."

"Your Honor—" Charlie began to protest. But Eide cut her off.

"Go on, Counselor," he said to Williams.

"Some folks here might think of Noah Bluestone as a longtime resident of Black Earth County. Although it's true that he was born and raised here, he's spent most of the last twenty years gallivanting around the globe. He's a seasoned traveler, a man comfortable on the move. His holdings in the county aren't significant. I'm not sure what brought him back, but he has no family remaining here, so no roots that strike me as deep enough to hold him if he's of a mind to run. I'm also concerned that a soldier, a veteran of two wars, a man as used to killing as you and I are to picking up our morning newspaper from the porch, a man accused, as you yourself say, of a particularly heinous crime, would be running free on the streets of Jewel and on the roads of Black Earth County. I've heard it said that after the first time, murder is easy. I'm just thinking here of the safety of our citizens, Your Honor."

Charlie saw clearly that this wasn't just an argument for setting bail. It was the opening salvo in Williams's prosecution of Noah Bluestone.

They were Midwesterners in the courtroom, stolid folks normally about as emotional as tools hanging in a garden shed, but Charlie saw a ripple of approval run through them, saw a wave of nodding heads. She could see that in the court of public opinion, the verdict had already been rendered. She thought it was interesting that many of these same people, only a month earlier, had been at a meeting of the county commissioners bashing Jimmy Quinn for his efforts to muscle through a proposal that would pave the way for him to dump the foul waste of a hog operation he owned into a creek that fed the Alabaster.

"Your Honor," Charlie said, speaking calmly and reasonably, "you've already ordered a psychiatric evaluation of my client, which will take time. It will delay the setting of a trial date. If you accede to the prosecutor's request, it will effectively keep Noah Bluestone behind bars during some of the busiest months for anyone who earns a living from the land.

"Yes, it's true that Noah Bluestone has been gone for a long time. But remember, his absence was in valiant service of our country. He is a decorated veteran. Since his discharge—his honorable discharge—and his return here, he's been a model citizen, not only successfully revitalizing his own property but also helping the Quinns manage their vast holdings. He's done nothing to warrant the kind of monstrous picture our prosecutor has painted this morning and to which I strongly object on the grounds that it has no foundation and is unconscionably prejudicial."

The judge said, "Your objection is noted, Counselor. Bail will be set at fifty thousand dollars."

Which would still require the posting of a bond outside the ability of Noah Bluestone or almost anyone else in Black Earth County to post. Effectively, Judge Eide had acknowledged the validity of Charlie's argument while still giving Alexander Williams what he wanted. That was the kind of action that had kept him unopposed in reelections for so long.

When the proceeding was finished, Brody and Connie Graff took Bluestone back to the jailhouse. Kyoko and Charlie followed. Brody gave the couple time together in Bluestone's cell, and he and Graff and Charlie gathered around the desk outside.

"That Williams is some piece of work," Graff said, rolling himself a cigarette. "A man risks his life in war—two wars—and Williams uses it against him. Hell, Bluestone's no more a threat to the citizens of this county than you or me, Brody."

"You don't think he's guilty?" Charlie said.

"He might have killed Quinn, but that doesn't make him crazy and it doesn't make him dangerous to anyone else. You plumb the hearts of a lot of folks in this county and the truth you'll find is that if Bluestone wasn't an Indian and if he didn't bring home a Japanese bride, they'd be thinking of him as a kind of hero."

"Easy, Connie," Brody said.

Graff sealed his cigarette and shook his head. "Charlie, you got a defendant who refuses to defend himself. How the hell are you going to do this?"

"Every bit of evidence is circumstantial, Connie."

"Still pretty compelling," Brody said.

"You have no real evidence that places him at the crime scene."

"Somebody wiped everything down," Graff said. "Noah doing the smart thing."

The radio on the table in the corner crackled, and Asa Fielding called in.

Brody, who'd suddenly looked a little troubled, went to respond.

Graff spoke to Charlie in a quiet voice. "I do think Bluestone killed him. But the real question here is why. I think absolutely that if you can get Kyoko to open up to you, you'll find out the reason, and it'll be one that might fill a jury's heart with forgiveness."

"What are you thinking?"

"That Quinn might have raped her or tried to rape her. To me, it's the only thing that makes sense. Brody won't say as much, but I'm guessing it's what he thinks, too."

"Why are you telling me this?"

"That girl's young enough to be my granddaughter. Breaks my heart to think of what a man like Quinn might have done to her, or tried to do. I could surely understand the temptation to open him up with a load of buckshot." Graff struck a match, touched the flame to his cigarette, and blew smoke at the ceiling. "Charlie, you and I both know that justice isn't always about what the law dictates. Hell, maybe it never is."

CHARLIE RETURNED KYOKO to her home. The old dog came out of the shadows to greet them. Charlie intended to walk the woman inside, but Kyoko turned and offered her hand in parting. "Thank you, Miss Bauer."

"It's Charlie, Kyoko."

"I'm grateful for your help."

"I could be of a lot more help if you'd let me. All the evidence indicates that Jimmy Quinn was out here on the night he died. I'd like to know why."

"It's not my place to speak of this. It's for my husband to say."

"He killed Jimmy Quinn for good reason, I think."

Kyoko's face showed not a ripple of emotion. "Forgive me," she said. "There's much work to be done." She turned and went inside with Fuji at her heels.

Charlie stood a moment, looking the small homestead over. The pigs were lounging in their pen with no sign of being hungry. The chickens in the hen yard pecked and cackled and seemed unperturbed. To put these things in order and still be ready when Charlie arrived to take her to town for her husband's arraignment, Kyoko Bluestone had to have risen well before dawn. Charlie was fairly certain that if she returned that evening, she'd find Kyoko still at work in the fields after the sun had set.

Noah Bluestone had married a remarkable woman. And Charlie thought that Connie Graff was right. If Quinn hated the man and was intent on doing him harm, Kyoko offered the best way to pierce Bluestone's heart and crush his soul. If she could just get some piece of evidence indicating that was exactly what had brought Jimmy Quinn out the night he'd been murdered, Charlie knew she could win over a jury.

CHAPTER TWENTY-EIGHT

CHARLIE HAD TO wait a bit before anyone answered her knock on the screen door of the Quinn home. Colleen, the Quinns' fourteen-year-old daughter, finally appeared, wiping her hands on a dish towel. Charlie had seen her often in town in the company of her family, so even though they'd never been formally introduced, Charlie knew who she was. A dash of white flour lay across the girl's cheek like a streak of war paint.

"Yes?" she said.

"Hello, Colleen. I'm Charlotte Bauer. I'm an attorney. I'd like to speak with your mother."

The girl had blossomed young, the cut of her waist and curve of her hips womanly, her breasts already well defined. She wore a long calico apron, and her dark red hair hung limp from the humidity of the day and the heat of the kitchen. All of which made her look older than her fourteen years, almost matronly. "She's not here right now."

"Do you know when she might be home?"

"She's at a doctor's appointment. It could be a while."

A face appeared behind her. The Quinns' other daughter.

"Hello," Charlie said.

"Hello," she echoed back.

"You're Bridget, aren't you?"

"Yes, ma'am."

"My name is Charlotte. But everybody calls me Charlie."

"Charlie?" Bridget said. "That's a boy's name."

"It's my name, too." Charlie sniffed the air. "Is that cinnamon bread I smell?"

"Yes." Bridget smiled.

"You're baking it?"

"Me and Colleen. She's teaching me."

"It smells heavenly. You two must be good bakers."

"I don't bake so much," Bridget said. "But I cook a lot."

"You, too?" Charlie said to Colleen.

"Yes," the older girl replied.

Bridget had come outside now and stood beside her sister on the front porch.

"I used to do all the cooking in my house when I was your age," Charlie told them.

Bridget said, "Was your mom sick, too?"

"No, Bridget, she was dead."

"I'm sorry," the girl said.

"It was a long time ago," Charlie assured her. "How long before that cinnamon bread is finished baking?"

Colleen glanced back toward the kitchen. "A few minutes."

"Would you be willing to talk to me for those few minutes?"

From the moment she'd opened the door, Colleen had been reticent to speak. Now her eyes turned wary. "About what?"

"Girls, I'm representing the man accused of killing your father."

"Noah," Bridget said.

"Noah Bluestone, yes."

"I like Noah." It was clear from the distressed look on the girl's face that the whole situation confused and saddened her. "We don't think he had anything to do with what happened to Daddy, do we, Colleen?" When her sister didn't answer, Bridget went on, "Please do whatever you can to make sure he doesn't go to jail."

"Could we sit?" Charlie said, indicating the swing that hung from hooks in the porch shade.

Colleen thought it over and finally said, "Okay."

Charlie sat between them. "Your mom's pretty sick," she said. "Do you mind me asking what's wrong with her?"

Colleen smoothed the apron on her lap. "She has ALS, what a lot of people call Lou Gehrig's disease. My dad's first wife had it, too. She was Mom's cousin. I guess it runs in their family."

Bridget said, "She was supposed to go to the Mayo Clinic for some new kind of treatment."

"But now she's not?" Charlie asked.

"The treatment's been rescheduled," Colleen said. "With my father dead and all." She spoke politely, but there was a businesslike tone to what she said.

"You two do most of the cooking?"

"Mom does sometimes, when she's feeling strong enough. But mostly it's Bridget and me, now that Kyoko's gone."

"J.P. helps," Bridget said.

Colleen nodded. "Yeah, J.P. helps. He's pretty good with things like barbecue and chili."

"And pancakes," Bridget threw in.

"It must be hard around here with your father gone."

"It wasn't all that easy when he was here," Colleen said. Her voice was different now, more personal, as if her guard was dropping. "He never helped around the house."

"Before Kyoko came to help, did he ever consider hiring a house-keeper or cook, someone to give you all a hand?"

"He hired a girl last winter," Colleen said. "She didn't stay long. My father was kind of hard to get along with."

"Who was that?"

"Sissy Barrows."

"From Aetna?"

"Yeah, that's her."

Charlie knew of the Barrows. A hardscrabble family in the south of the county. Sissy was what folks called "slow."

"Could I ask you about the night your father was killed?"

Bridget said, "Not me. I was at a sleepover at Jan Baldwin's house."

"Colleen?"

She stared across the yard into the distance. "Sure, why not?"

"What time did he leave?"

"I don't remember. I was sleeping, but I think it was almost dark."

"And he was going fishing?"

"He took his fishing stuff, so I guess."

"He also took a shotgun. Did he usually do that?"

"I didn't see any shotgun," Colleen said.

"Would it have been unusual for him to take a firearm, especially if he was going fishing?"

Colleen reached up and brushed at the streak of flour on her face, smearing it into a chalky dusting across her tanned cheek. "I don't really know. He would just take off sometimes, and sometimes he wouldn't tell us where he was going or why. And then he'd come back later, a lot later sometimes, you know, kind of drunk. Or the sheriff would bring him back."

"Did he seem at all angry that night?"

"He was mad a lot," Colleen said. "So probably."

"Was he mad at Noah Bluestone?"

"Oh, yeah," Bridget said. "He was really mad at Noah."

"Why?"

"He said Noah was stealing gas from him."

"And that made him really mad?"

Colleen said, "There were other things, too."

"Like what?"

"Nobody stood up to my father, but Noah did."

"The night he was killed, it appears that your father had been drinking heavily. Did you see him drinking before he left?"

"He drank a lot before dinner that night."

"Did he say anything about Noah? Or maybe Kyoko?"

"Kyoko?" Colleen turned her face to Charlie, her look confused. "I don't think so. Why?"

"It's not important."

At the same moment, they all caught the scent of something burning.

"The cinnamon bread," Bridget cried and jumped from the swing.

"We need to get back to our work," Colleen said.

"I understand. Thank you for your time."

The two girls hurried inside.

Human beings are wired to remember. Struggle as we may to stuff the past out of sight and out of mind, nature has devised triggers that bring back even the most unwelcome memory. The smell of that baking cinnamon bread had done it for Charlie. Sitting in the porch swing, the scent of the sweet burn drifting through the window, Charlie was taken back nearly five decades. She felt her stomach tighten and the bile rise, as it had so often in those years after her mother died and Charlie replaced her in the house where she and her father continued to live together so unhappily, so at war.

Charlie left the swing and went to the porch steps, intending to leave. But she heard crying through the window screen, and if the sound of a child's weeping doesn't break your heart, nothing will. She turned back and, although she knew it was a trespass, went inside. She found the girls in the kitchen, where the smell of the burn was strong. The older girl sat in a chair at the table, her head laid across her arms. Bridget stood behind her, her hand on her sister's shoulder. The cinnamon bread sat on the stove still in the pan, charred.

"It's only bread, Colleen," Bridget said gently. "Only bread." She looked up and saw Charlie and said as if speaking of some great mystery, "Only bread."

Charlie pulled up a chair beside Colleen and put her arm around her shoulders and drew her close. The girl didn't resist but laid her head against Charlie's breast and wept, soaking her blouse with warm tears.

"My fault," she cried. "It's all my fault."

"Hush, child. The blame is mine. I distracted you."

"I never can do anything right."

"Not true," Charlie said. "Is it, Bridget?"

"Colleen can do everything."

"I can't," her sister cried. "I mess up all the time."

"Oh, sweetheart, we all do," Charlie said. "All the time. More than anything else, we're made of mistakes. But you know what? We always have a second chance."

"That's what the rainbow is about," Bridget offered.

"Exactly," Charlie said. Although she didn't necessarily agree this was the point of that particular biblical fable, she appreciated Bridget's effort.

Brody, when he told Charlie about his visit to the Quinns to bring them the news of Jimmy's death, had reported that the children showed no sign of grief. He didn't remark on it as a strange thing, necessarily, and there was good reason for this. Grief—both Charlie and Brody knew this well—doesn't come in the immediacy of the moment. Nor does it send a calling card for later. It arrives unannounced, springing from some unexpected incident, grabbing the heart in moments of total surprise.

That's what Charlie thought she was seeing in that hot, humid kitchen with Colleen's tears wetting her blouse. The ambush of grief.

"You don't get second chances with everything," Colleen said.

"Okay, maybe not everything," Charlie agreed. "But with bread, you get as many as you want. What do you say we take another shot at it, all of us together?"

And they did. They made the bread again, put it in the stove to bake, and Charlie sat with the girls in the kitchen and didn't ask them any more about their father or Noah Bluestone, but instead told them stories of mining towns and shantytowns, of battles with hired thugs, of the courage of common people in the face of great adversity. They listened as they might have to someone telling them Grimms' fairy tales, telling them stories of places far away and maybe even only make-believe. They listened as if they were the children Charlie never had.

WHEN CHARLIE LEFT them at the front door and started for her car, which was parked in the shade of a great beech tree beside the drive, their mother and J.P. still had not returned. As she crossed the yard, she heard the sound of a tractor approaching along a lane that cut between fields to the southeast. She watched it come, shading her eyes against the glare of the June sun.

The man who occupied the seat of the John Deere was no stranger to Charlie. Tyler Creasy had been her client on a single occasion, a little under a year earlier. She'd been appointed to defend him on an assault charge arising from a bar fight. She didn't like the man and had told him that the next time he got into trouble, he'd need to find other counsel. The problems with Creasy ran deep. He was one of the Black Earth Creasys, a notorious and unfortunate family that resided as a group in a low-lying area near the river a mile south of town, a place folks called Creasy Hollow. They ran a gas station and garage service along the road, which was backed by several dilapidated houses and a trailer home mounted on cinder blocks, set among trees that edged the Alabaster. The Creasy men tended to be gifted mechanics. They also tended to be drunks. Their wives were silent, sullen women, and their children kept to themselves and ran in packs, almost feral.

Like so many sons in Black Earth County, Tyler Creasy had been drafted in the Second World War. Charlie hadn't known him then, but

Brody had, and Brody had told her that Creasy had been a quiet, unre-markable kid. When he returned from his service, which had been mostly in North Africa and Italy, he was changed. He fought with everyone, including his own family, and he didn't stay long in Jewel. Brody had heard nothing about him until he'd shown up eighteen months ago, bringing with him his wife and her son, who was not Creasy's child.

Creasy drove the tractor to the gas pump near the big barn, and Charlie headed in that direction. He was just dismounting when she called his name. He wore a dirty cap with the insignia of the St. Louis Cardinals across the crown. He removed the cap, smoothed his wet, thinning hair, and put the cap back on.

"Counselor," he said. Although his face didn't show it, there was a sneer in his tone.

Long before she was close, Charlie caught the odor that emanated from the dark circles of sweat soaking the underarms of his work shirt.

"Good afternoon, Tyler," she said.

"Know what I heard, Counselor? I heard you're going to defend Bluestone. Is that true?"

"It is."

"You won't defend me if I get myself in a scrape with the law, but you'll defend a murderer?"

"He's been accused, Tyler, not convicted."

"Hell, good luck. Everybody knows about Bluestone."

"Knows what exactly?"

"For starters, he's a redskin. And a thieving one to boot."

Although he sounded like a character out of a John Wayne Western, the meat of his sentiment was one that was shared by others in Black Earth County. It came from an old wound, Charlie knew, unhealed and maybe unhealable.

"Mind if I ask you about the thieving part?" Charlie said.

"What do you want to know?"

"Quinn fired Noah for stealing gas, is that correct?"

"Damn right."

"How did Jimmy know he was stealing?"

Creasy stepped to the pump and grabbed a small notebook attached with twine. He opened it, and Charlie saw that it was a log of dates and gallons.

"We write it all down here, me and J.P. and Able Grange and Bluestone. Jimmy, too, when he was alive. Last time gas was delivered and Jimmy did the calculations, the numbers didn't match. He asked all of us about it. We all told him it was Bluestone."

"And you all knew this how?"

"Seen him put gas in his own truck when he thought nobody was around."

"You witnessed this?"

"Yep. And I told Jimmy."

"And Jimmy confronted Noah?"

Creasy laughed as if he was enjoying himself immensely. "Oh, yeah. That was something, let me tell you."

"An argument?"

"Knock-down, drag-out."

"Blows were thrown?"

"Well, no, but a lot of hot words got exchanged."

"What did they say to each other?"

"I can't tell you exactly."

"Why not?"

"I saw it from kind of a distance."

"But you figured you knew what it was about?"

"Oh, sure."

"The gas?"

"And more. That Bluestone, he was uppity. Moment he started working here for Jimmy, I knew it was only a matter of time."

"How long have you worked for the Quinns?"

"Year and a half now."

"Did you ever have a run-in with Jimmy?"

"Hell, everybody's had a run-in with Jimmy. Nothing serious. Jimmy was the boss, so you always knew who was going to have the final word."

"You ever think about throwing a blow at Jimmy?"

"And get my ass fired? You kidding?"

"Never had that deep burn in your gut, that hot voice telling you, the hell with it, just deck him?"

He studied Charlie, then he laughed. "Looking for another suspect? It ain't me, Counselor. Brody Dern, he arrested the right man. Now if you'll excuse me, I got me a job to do."

He turned back to the tractor.

"One more question, Tyler."

He removed the hose from the pump and began to fuel the John Deere. "Shoot," he said.

"Jimmy had a taste for liquor."

"No crime there."

"You ever see him drunk?"

"Hell, yes."

"Did he always drink alone?"

"Mostly. But on occasion he asked me to join him for a snootful out there in that little shack of his." Creasy pointed toward a small ramshackle structure a hundred yards up the lane he'd just driven. "Jimmy wasn't a sociable drinker, but everybody needs company now and again."

"Did he ever invite Able Grange or Noah Bluestone to join him?"

"Hell, Grange doesn't touch the stuff. Think he's Mormon or something. And no way would Jimmy ask that redskin to drink with him."

"What was he like drunk?"

"Depends. Drinking alone, he tended toward surly. But if he asked me to drink with him, it was usually cuz he felt like talking. Could talk your ear off then."

"Did you ever see him out of control? Dangerous maybe?"

"Out of control?" He seemed to give it serious thought. "He was a big man. It'd take a lot of whiskey. So, I guess no."

Charlie thanked him for his time, but he didn't bother to acknowledge it or seem to note her departure in any way. Creasy, when she'd defended him, was a man like used motor oil. If you tried to get a grip on him, he slipped through your fingers, leaving you with the feel of grit and dirt and a desire to wash yourself clean.

CHAPTER TWENTY-NINE

THERE WERE TWO funerals in Jewel that week. The first was on Thursday, for Ruth Coffee, who'd taught school in the town forever, who'd touched the lives of generations in Black Earth County, and who, in the end, had shared with Jimmy Quinn for a few hours a refrigerated space at Brown's Funeral Home, something Brody Dern still considered an assault to her dignity. The service was held at eleven o'clock in the morning at the Methodist church, which was crowded with family and other folks gathered to celebrate the life of a woman who'd given them so much. Afterward, a long procession of cars followed the black hearse to the cemetery on the hill, where a brief graveside observance was held.

Brody didn't participate in the post-service gathering for food and fellowship in the basement of the church. He had duties to see to. Asa Fielding, who'd gone through high school after Ruth Coffee retired and so didn't have the same level of affection as Brody, had volunteered to stay at the jail that morning, overseeing the one prisoner currently in residence and taking care of neglected paperwork. As for Connie Graff, Brody hadn't seen or heard from him in nearly a day.

Brody stopped at the jailhouse and checked in with Fielding, who was sorting through some wanted posters recently received and who reported that everything had been quiet. Brody asked if he'd seen Graff. Fielding told him that the deputy had dropped by and mentioned that he was on his way to Bluestone's place but didn't say why.

"Probably just checking to make sure she's safe, like I asked him to," Brody said.

"Ever since we brought Bluestone in, I've been hearing grumbles about Japs and Indians," Asa said. "I get the feeling we've put a pot on the stove and it's starting to boil. A good thing Connie's hovering like a mother hen out there."

Brody glanced at the door to the jail cells. "Probably a good thing Noah's locked up. Maybe the safest place for him right now. Think I'll head out and check on the Bluestone place myself. Couple of things I want to talk to Connie about, if he's still there."

He changed from his dark suit into his khaki uniform, called to Hector, and headed off in his cruiser.

The day was hot and humid, as summer days often tend to be in southern Minnesota. Through the thick lens of the wet air, the farmland took on a distant and dreamy look. Brody drove with the windows down, and Hector, in the backseat, stuck his head out and opened his mouth to the breeze.

Brody crossed the Alabaster and drove the long dirt lane toward the house and outbuildings. He spotted the small figure of Kyoko Bluestone at work with her hoe in her little garden beside the house. In a distant part of the amaranth field, someone sat astride a tractor, drawing behind it a cultivator. Brody had been worried about the young woman's ability to meet all of the demands of a farm in the absence of her husband, and he was glad to discover that she'd found some help.

Graff's truck was parked in the lane near the house. Brody pulled his cruiser up next to it, let Hector free, and walked to the garden. "Afternoon, Mrs. Bluestone."

"Good afternoon, Sheriff." She dropped her hands to her sides and bowed slightly at the waist.

It was, Brody recognized, an *eshaku* bow, a gesture of casual greeting common in Japan. During his time—his hell—in Shwenwa, an unofficial and undocumented Japanese POW camp in Burma, he'd had ample opportunity to observe the customs of his captors. Although Kyoko had not meant it as such, to Brody it felt like a hard slap that awakened old angers, old hate, that ripped open old, deeply painful wounds. Until that moment, he'd been able to separate Kyoko Bluestone from those of her kind who'd nailed the hate to his heart, but that simple, respectful gesture, which he'd seen accompany so many moments of mindless butchery in Shwenwa, shattered his restraint. Under the glare of the sun, he stared down at her coldly, and her face, in the shade of the broad-brimmed straw hat she wore, changed. Fear was stamped there, a terrible fear, a look that said she was prepared for Brody to do something unspeakable.

The sound of the tractor nearing made Brody wrench his eyes away from her. What he saw surprised the hell out of him. At the wheel sat Connie Graff.

WHEN CHARLIE BAUER drove up to the Bluestone farmhouse, she saw Graff sitting alone on the wrought-iron bench in the shade of the big Dutch elm tree, drinking lemonade. She stormed out of her car, angry because she was certain he'd come there against her express wishes, come to question her client's wife without counsel present.

"Relax, Charlie," Graff said when she flung the accusation at him. "I don't work for the sheriff anymore."

"What?"

"I tendered my resignation half an hour ago. See all that horsepower by the barn?" He nodded toward Bluestone's old tractor. "I jockey that now."

"I don't understand," Charlie said. "Where's Kyoko?"

"Inside," Graff said. "Getting herself cleaned up, and then I'll take her into town to visit Noah."

"You're really not a deputy anymore?"

"Not at the moment. We'll see what happens after all this Jimmy Quinn mess is settled."

"You quit to help out here?"

"The quitting part Brody pretty much insisted on," Graff said. "The day we arrested Bluestone, we had some men show up here with rifles. Brody assigned me to keeping an eye on the farmstead in case someone got it in their head to make another visit. It became obvious to me pretty quick that she needed a hand with the place." He shrugged. "Seemed like the least I could do."

"And Brody didn't like it," Charlie concluded.

"Told me it wouldn't look right, me fraternizing with the Bluestones while wearing a badge. He's right, you know." He looked toward the house. "She's hardly more than a kid. Can't help thinking that if I had a daughter, I'd want someone looking out for her." He swung his eyes back to Charlie. "You out here on a social visit? Or are you on the legal clock?"

"I just came from talking with Sissy Barrows."

The name meant nothing to him.

"She worked for the Quinns briefly last winter, Connie. Briefly, for good reason."

Graff patted the empty area beside him on the bench. "Have a seat and fill me in."

Charlie told him about her visit with the Quinn girls and her subsequent visit to the Barrows' home, where she talked not just with Sissy but with the girl's parents as well. At the Christmas Eve service at Saint Ignatius months before, Jimmy Quinn had approached them with a proposition. All the parishioners knew about Marta's illness or knew as much as anyone did. Quinn explained his need and asked if Sissy, who was eighteen, unmarried and with no prospects in that direction, might consider working for him, helping with the upkeep of the house and with the cooking responsibilities. The children, he explained, were a great help, but there was so much. He quoted them a wage, which was a little outlandish in its extravagance. Sissy accepted. Or rather, they accepted on her behalf because Sissy, though grown, was not a young woman fully capable of making her own decisions. But she knew well how to take care of children and housework and was good in a kitchen. She'd looked pretty on that Christmas Eve, they remembered. And she'd seemed happy.

The problems with Quinn began a few weeks into her employment. The first time Quinn approached her—"in that way" was the phrase they'd used—Sissy didn't understand. The children were in school. Marta was upstairs in bed, as she often was. Sissy had been at work on the pot pie that would be the evening meal. Her hands were covered with flour as she made the dough, and she was intent on her labor when Quinn stole up behind her and— Charlie had to pause in her telling to choose the right phrasing. She could have said "grabbed her ass," which was how Sissy's father had put it. Instead she said, "He touched her derriere inappropriately."

"Grabbed her ass?" Graff said.

"It got worse after that," Charlie went on. "It finally reached the point where Sissy was afraid to be alone in the house."

"She told her folks?"

"Not until he actually attacked her."

Charlie explained it in the way that it had been explained to her. Quinn came in for the noon meal smelling of whiskey. Usually the hired men were with him and Sissy fed them all. But that day it was just the two of them, Sissy and Quinn, in the kitchen. She'd sometimes smelled alcohol on his breath, but it had never been that strong before. He reeked. When Sissy set his plate in front of him on the kitchen table, he'd grabbed her and had pulled her down to the floor and then he'd begun to unbuckle his belt. She'd screamed and fought, but Quinn was a big man. He pinned her under him so that she couldn't move. He would have done something terrible, except that Marta came into the kitchen and, small and frail though she was, shoved her husband off the terrified girl. Quinn had stumbled out into the cold, vanished toward the barn. Marta had helped Sissy up, had tried to comfort her, told her it was best if she did not come back. She'd given Sissy a check for a lot of money and had pleaded with her to say nothing of this to anyone. Though Marta was not at all well, she'd driven Sissy home.

"The Barrows didn't think of reporting this to Brody?" Graff said.

"There was the money Sissy had accepted," Charlie told him. "And nothing really had happened except that Sissy got a terrible scare. But the next Sunday after church, Sissy's father pulled Quinn aside. Jimmy denied everything and threatened that if they pursued the issue, he'd sue them for all they owned. And you know that with Jimmy it was no idle threat."

"So the whole thing was dropped and nothing ever said." Graff shook his head. "Then Kyoko began working out there." He gave Charlie a long, meaningful look.

"If Noah or Kyoko would just tell me the truth, I could help them, I know I could," Charlie said.

"Too afraid, I'm guessing. And with good reason. You know how big the human heart is?" Graff balled his hand into a fist. "About that size. I continue to be amazed at how much hate such a small thing can hold, even in people who think of themselves as decent and Christian. There are a lot of folks in this county with a lot of hate stored up, and those small hearts of theirs are just ready to burst from it. You can work miracles with a jury, Charlie. I've seen you do it. But I'm afraid you'd have to be God himself to get a fair hearing for Noah Bluestone. And he knows it."

Kyoko stepped out of the house and smiled when she saw Charlie. "I have never had so many visitors. This is becoming like . . ." She thought a moment, then said, "Grand Central Station. Did I say that right?"

She looked small and delicate, and Charlie hoped that Graff was wrong about the hatred locked up in the hearts in Black Earth County, because she was afraid that if whatever restraint held it in check was removed, the great rush of all that enmity might easily shatter Kyoko Bluestone.

CHAPTER THIRTY

BRODY DERN WASN'T much of a drinking man, but he sure wanted a drink now. He wanted something that would cool the burn in his gut, stanch the raw bleed of his emotions. He wanted not to be angry and hurting and confused and betrayed. He wanted not to be a part of his own past.

He drove away from the Bluestone farmstead, away from his confrontation with his friend, mentor, and part-time deputy Connie Graff. He hit the steering wheel with his fist and cried, "Damn you! You were just supposed to make sure she was safe, not farm the goddamn land for her." He balled his fist again but this time swung at the empty air in front of him. "I never wanted this to be murder. That was all your idea."

The absolute truth was that from the beginning Brody hadn't cared who killed Quinn. How many times after some superior slight or further demonstration of Quinn's heartlessness had he himself been tempted to shoot the son of a bitch? But someone had finally had enough of Quinn's cruelty, and the truth was that, however it had occurred, Brody was certain the killing was justified, and he'd done his best at the scene of the crime to wipe away any evidence of who that might have been. Because, when he was being true to himself, he felt like a coward for not having taken Quinn down himself long before.

It was Noah Bluestone who'd done that. Brody was certain of it. He knew the why of the killing didn't matter. In Black Earth County, justice would be meted out by a jury of people already thinking in their hearts that the Indian was guilty. There was no way Bluestone would walk free. And that was all Connie Graff's doing.

At the farmstead, Kyoko Bluestone's *eshaku* bow, a simple, respectful Japanese gesture, had torn Brody wide open. Now his anger spilled out, and as he drove toward Jewel he didn't see the road. In a blind fury, he saw what he saw in the terrible dreams that had been giving him night sweats ever since he pulled Quinn's chewed-up body from the Alabaster: the burning men, the Asian girl whose smile had betrayed him, the ghost of the man he'd murdered long ago. He saw the true coward he was and had always been. He saw a darkness before him that was a kind of vortex threatening to suck him in, body and soul. And then he saw that he was pulling into the empty gravel parking lot of the Wagon Wheel.

He let Hector out of the cruiser. He didn't speak to the dog as he normally would have, didn't tell him to be good and that he would be right back. He didn't say a thing as Hector stared up at him with those patient brown eyes.

He walked into the Wagon Wheel, walked without clear thought. The place seemed deserted. He sat at the counter and heard noise in the kitchen, and a moment later, Wendell Moon appeared, wiping his hands on his apron.

Wendell was tall and lean, somewhere in his late fifties, his hair gray and curly, his skin the color of mahogany. His face looked like the Devil had stepped on it, but his eyes were always full of welcome. He hailed from Oklahoma and had hit the road in the days of the Great Dust Bowl. His left eye was disturbing to look at. It never moved, the result of a beating he'd taken nearly a decade earlier, when he'd first arrived in Jewel. He'd drifted into town with only an old guitar and knapsack to his name and had asked Ida for work. She didn't have anything and had sent him on. He made a little camp for himself on the bank of the Alabaster and that night was set upon by some local toughs who'd been drinking and who were never identified, though most folks figured they were some of the Creasys out of the hollow. When Ida found out, she visited Wendell in the tiny community hospital, paid his bill, and gave him not only a job but a place to stay. He lived above the garage behind the Madison house, a little apartment the elder Madisons had planned to occupy when their son and his family took over the big house. He'd become like family to Angie and Ida and Scott, but because Wendell was a Negro, many of the patrons of the Wagon Wheel, before ordering, would ask who was cooking that day. If the answer was Wendell Moon, they would order soup or some other food item they believed his hands wouldn't actually have touched.

"Sheriff," he said in greeting.

"Where is everyone?"

"Still out to Ruth Coffee's funeral, I imagine. Folks'll be gathered a long time talking about that fine woman. Angie came back early, though, to give me a hand here. She's out back. You want, I'll get her."

"Thanks, Wendell."

The man eyed Brody with concern. "You sick or something, Sheriff?"

"I'm fine."

Wendell made a sound in his throat that clearly communicated he didn't believe Brody. He walked into the kitchen and Brody heard his deep voice calling Angie's name. A minute later, she was in front of him, behind the counter. She came smiling, but when she saw the look on his face, her own face changed. "It's true," she said. "You do look sick."

She put her hands over his, and he stared at them, at the nails that were clean and unpolished. He wanted to let go of the burden. He wanted to tell her about the terrible memories that the dark magic of Jimmy Quinn's blown-open and chewed-on body had brought back to him and that he couldn't shake from his thinking. He wanted to let her know how confused and scared he was.

"I could use a cup of coffee," he said.

She brought it quickly and watched his hands tremble while he drank.

"Do you believe in ghosts, Angie?"

"I pretty much believe in the possibility of everything, Brody. It saves me a lot of needless fuss. Why?"

"I see them."

He was staring into his coffee mug, but her fingers slipped beneath his chin and gently tilted his face upward so that he looked into her eyes.

"We all see them, Brody."

She leaned across the counter and kissed his cheek as a mother might have.

"Connie quit me," he said.

"Quit? You mean handed in his badge?"

"Yeah."

"Why?"

"Says he needs to be out at Bluestone's place, helping Bluestone's wife with all that farmwork."

"That's awfully nice of him. But did he have to quit?"

"I insisted. Told him it wouldn't look right."

"I understand," she said.

He'd been staring down again into the black of his coffee, but now, on his own, he raised his head and studied her face. He could see that she believed it, believed she understood his reasoning and was willing to accept it. She couldn't possibly look into him and see all the way down into the cave of his heart.

"Have you had any lunch?" she asked.

"No."

"Let me fix you something. I sent Scott over a while ago to the jailhouse with a cold pork roast sandwich for Noah Bluestone. How does that sound?"

"Good. Thanks."

The door of the diner opened, and in walked Gordon Landis. He saw them together at the counter and took the stool next to Brody.

"It's like a ghost town here today," he said. "You two skip out on Ruth Coffee's funeral?"

"We attended the service," Angie answered. "We didn't stay for the meal at the church afterward. Work to do. I didn't see you there, Gordon."

"Ruth Coffee nearly kept me from playing football in high school. Flunked me in her class. Told me Shakespeare was more important than carrying a pigskin."

"You think she was wrong?" Angie said.

"Reading Shakespeare never helped me run down a suspect."

Brody said, "Did you ever actually run down a suspect, Gordy?"

Landis ignored him and said, "How about a piece of your pecan pie, Angie, and maybe some coffee to go along with it?"

"All right. And, Brody, I'll have your sandwich ready in a minute." She disappeared into the kitchen.

Landis watched her go with an obvious appreciation of the view of her from behind. "Mind if I ask you a question, Brody?"

"It's a free country."

"Anything between you and Angie?"

"Between?"

"She your girl now?"

"I wouldn't say that, no."

"So you wouldn't mind if I asked her out sometime?"

"I thought you were dating Mimi Fowler?"

"Not married to her." Landis glanced toward the kitchen. "So, you mind?"

"Gordy, you do whatever you want to do."

"Looks like you nailed Bluestone good. That's one Indian can kiss his ass goodbye."

"He gets a fair trial, Gordy."

"Right." Landis laughed as if it were a joke. "It's in their blood, you know. There's a reason they're called savages."

Everything in Brody wanted to hit the man. Instead he said, "I have to go. Duties to see to." He stood up, walked the length of the counter, and called into the kitchen as he passed, "Gotta run, Angie. I'll take a raincheck on that sandwich."

SHE MET HIM that night in a place where they'd sometimes met before. It was in the loft of the barn on the old Zimmerman homestead, abandoned but not so long ago that everything had fallen into disrepair. It was a good place for a clandestine affair, set back from the road and with no other farmhouse near. When they met this way, it was always at night, and Brody always brought a little kerosene lantern and kept the wick burning low so that they could see each other, but only dimly.

Her lovemaking that night was fierce. There was something almost animal in everything she did. It was exciting, but it wasn't what Brody had wanted from her exactly. When they'd finished, they lay on the blanket Brody had spread across a bed of old straw, both of them sweating, panting, together yet apart.

For a long time, neither of them spoke. Brody was trying to work up the courage to tell her some of the things he'd never told anyone, some of what he'd wanted to tell Angie that afternoon but had, in the end, been too afraid to. Across the rest of the day, he'd chewed on it mercilessly and finally decided that if anyone could accept the truth of him, it would be the only woman he'd ever loved. What they shared, he thought, went deeper than all the places their naked flesh had touched.

She spoke first. "Did you have a good time?"

"I love being with you like this. You know that."

"I mean the other night. At Loretta Wicklow's party."

"Oh. That. It was fine."

"I heard she was pretty."

"Who?"

"Your date."

"It wasn't a date. I just gave Angie a ride."

"I think you enjoyed yourself quite a bit for just a ride."

"What makes you think that?"

"I know you, Brody. I can tell. So, did you kiss her good night?"

"Garnet—"

She laughed. "Oh, Brody, you should see your face. You look like a kid caught with his hand in the cookie jar. Do you really think I'm so petty? I'm glad you had a good time. I'm just a little worried about what Evangeline Madison might have on her mind now. You're practically dating."

"It was one evening, and I just gave her a ride."

"I understand. But does she? Brody, you might need to do a little clarifying before you break that woman's heart."

"I'm breaking no one's heart."

She looked at him in the dim light, suddenly not so playful. "Is that so?"

The words had been there, almost in his throat, his confession of all the sin he'd been hiding for so long. He'd almost been free. Now he shoved them back down inside, back into that dark place.

"I didn't do it to hurt you, Garnet. I wouldn't do anything to hurt you."

"Is that true, Brody? Tell me you don't find her attractive."

"Do we have to have this conversation now?"

"We don't have conversations in any other way, Brody."

"And whose fault is that? I'm not the one who won't leave my marriage."

"You have no idea how complicated it is."

"And you don't know me at all, do you?"

He sat up and watched a moth flutter about the lantern on the loft floor. A moment later, he felt her hand on his back.

"You're the best thing about my life, Brody. If I lost this, I don't know what I'd do."

It was what she always said. It was like a little key to the lock that secured the chain around his heart, that kept him hers. But deep down, Brody knew it wasn't true. He'd seen the look on Garnet's face when she was with her children, and it was anything but unhappy. He'd heard his mother speak so very often of how cheerful Garnet was, how much joy she brought to the house. And not all that long ago of how happy she made Tom. Maybe the marriage itself wasn't always a wellspring of perfect happiness, but it didn't seem to Brody to be at all an awful thing. It was her life. And really, truthfully, painfully, Brody understood that she was content with it.

She kissed his shoulder. Kissed the scars on his back, one by one, as if each was beautiful to her. Kissed the long rope of knotted tissue along his neck where once a bayonet had cut. Kissed his chest where old cigarette burns stood out like pale stars against a paler sky. Kissed his belly and then slid lower.

They made love again, and this time Brody let the oblivion that Garnet offered with her body swallow him whole.

CHAPTER THIRTY-ONE

THE SECOND FUNERAL in Jewel that week took place on Friday afternoon, only seven days after Jimmy Quinn's chewed-on body had been found caught up in some driftwood along a bank of the Alabaster River. The service was held in the Church of Saint Ignatius, and although it was as grand and solemn an occasion as any held in that sanctuary, those who attended, Charlie Bauer among them, did not seem nearly as grieved as those who'd turned out the day before to mourn Ruth Coffee. James Patrick Quinn might have been the wealthiest landowner in Black Earth County, but Charlie believed that Ruth Coffee, who'd been a simple teacher all her life, had been richer in so many ways. Both the service and the visitation that had preceded it were closed-coffin affairs. The mortician Fred Brown was good at what he did, but he was not a miracle worker.

Charlie went to the funeral, not because she had any final respects to pay James Patrick Quinn but rather from a professional curiosity. Although she wanted to see who was there, she was far more interested in who was not.

Most of Quinn's immediate family were present, though they didn't all sit together. Marta and her children occupied a pew on the right side of the aisle, Terry Quinn and his wife and children on the left. Charlie saw them exchange words but couldn't hear what was said. They didn't appear to be words of mutual condolence, however. Terry Quinn was very much like his father, full of bluster, even in that place that was supposed to engender quiet humility. His wife, whom Charlie had never seen before, wore a fine black dress and pearls and a black hat with a veil that fell across her entire face. Whenever she lifted the veil, Charlie could see that she looked drawn and tired.

There was something that troubled Charlie about the service, and when it was over, she corralled Brody Dern, who had come dressed in his uniform.

"A minute of your time?" she asked.

The casket had been carried out by pallbearers, men who'd been Quinn's fellow parishioners, and row after row, those in attendance were released, some to follow to the cemetery, others to prepare the meal that would be served in the church fellowship hall, after the burial.

"Kind of surprised to see you here, Charlie," he said. He looked a little haggard, and Charlie wondered if he was ill.

"Have you seen Fiona McCarthy?" she asked.

She was talking about Quinn's daughter from his first marriage. As far as Charlie knew, after the young woman had fled town following the scandal of her pregnancy and hurried marriage, she'd never returned to Jewel.

Brody scanned the sanctuary, which was emptying quickly.

"She lives in Des Moines now, is that right?" Charlie said.

"Last I knew."

"Only three hours away. An easy drive for anyone who'd care to come. Have you heard from her at all since her father's death?"

He shook his head. "But maybe she's been in touch with Terry or Marta."

Someone else called his name, and Brody said, "I have to go."

Charlie stood there until the sanctuary was empty. She considered why Fiona McCarthy might have missed this important ritual in the cycle of a family's life. Charlie hadn't attended her own father's burial, and at the time had felt her reasons were sound. She wondered now about the reasoning of Fiona McCarthy.

THE QUINN FAMILY had burial plots together in the Catholic cemetery, which topped a small rise overlooking the Alabaster. James Patrick Quinn's plot was marked with a tall monolith, his name chiseled in great scrolled letters into the granite. Many of Brody's family were also buried in that cemetery, but they lay scattered among all the other plots. Although the gathering of mourners in the cemetery was smaller than it had been at Saint Ignatius, there were still a great number of cars parked along the tendrils of road that threaded through the cemetery. The sun was high and hot by then, and Brody stood far back in the shade of a tall hackberry tree. He listened for a while as the priest performed this final ritual, then he drifted away to another grave with a small, nondescript headstone that read ROBERT DERN. LOVING HUSBAND AND FATHER. 1896–1941.

Loving. Brody had always wondered about that. His father had never been a cruel man, never raised his hand against Brody. But in Brody's opinion, that was setting the bar pretty damn low for love. If loving was indeed what his father had been, he'd kept it well hidden. At least from his younger son.

"I remember the day we put him there."

Brody turned and found his brother standing behind him. Taller than Brody by a couple of inches and broader in his chest, Tom had been a football and baseball star in high school and had played a year as tight end for the Cyclones in Ames before damaging his right knee in a way that had ended his collegiate sports career. The sudden death of his father a year later had ended any other hopes he might have had in Ames.

"It was raining cats and dogs." Tom stared at the gravestone steadily, as if it wasn't that marker he was seeing but instead the relentless downpour seventeen years before.

"I remember the mud," Brody said. "Ankle deep. Ruined the only good pair of shoes I owned."

"And Mom's and mine and Amy's. And probably everybody else's who was here.

"A lot of folks turned out despite that rain. People thought the world of Dad."

Brody made no reply and the brothers stood together, silent. Brody could hear the distant drone of the priest and the periodic responses from the gathering. He was uncomfortable in his brother's presence. Guilt, he well knew.

"A shame about Noah Bluestone," Tom finally said.

"You know him well?"

"He's kept to himself since he came back, but I knew him pretty well in the old days. We graduated from high school the same year. Played football together. Never saw a more fearless competitor. A guy you definitely wanted on your side. Spoke his mind. Honest to a fault. You always knew where you stood with Noah Bluestone. That's a rare quality these days." He glanced at his brother with a look that made Brody wonder if he ought to interpret it as an accusation.

Brody said, "He won't speak a word in his own defense."

"So I heard," Tom said. "Have to ask yourself why. Here's a story about Noah Bluestone. Even though he didn't wear moccasins or feathers or anything, he still took a lot of crap for being Indian. I remember he was always in fights when he was a kid. Then he started playing football. We'd never had good teams, but all of a sudden we were winning games. And you know what? Him being Indian wasn't a big deal anymore. I remember he had this fine head of black hair that he wore slicked back. Girls loved it. Then his mother died, and he cut all that hair off, almost all the way down to his scalp. An Indian mourning tradition, I guess. His head looked like the backside of a bristly hog. They threatened to kick him out of school because of it, but he stood his ground. Lot of iron in that man."

"Your point?" Brody said.

"It's not easy, what you do. Trying to get to the truth of something like Quinn's death."

"You don't think it was Bluestone?"

"Here's something you might throw into that cement mixer you call a brain. Years ago, Terry Quinn was all set to get married and buy his own place. He'd saved his money and found the land, the old Ingersoll farm out by Eddington. Made an offer, a good offer, I understand, and the deal was looking done. Then you know what? Jimmy bought it right out from under him. Paid way more than it was worth. Took away his son's farm. That was after you'd gone into the service, so you probably don't remember it."

"Why would he do that?"

"Who knows?" Tom ran a finger under the tight collar of the white shirt he wore, then undid the top button and loosened his tie. "Terry talked a good game at the service today. Built up his old man pretty good. But you have to wonder what's really in his heart. He's not like Noah. Never has been."

The service had ended, and the gathering was breaking up. Tom turned from his father's grave and made ready to rejoin the others. "We'll see you for dinner on Sunday?"

"I'll probably be there."

"Mom counts on it."

As those who'd come that afternoon filtered away, Terence Quinn remained behind, talking with the priest. Brody waited until their business seemed completed, then he approached Quinn, who appeared glad to see him.

"Thanks for coming," he said, shaking Brody's hand. "I meant to tell you the other day after Bluestone's arraignment that I appreciate what you've done."

"I haven't done anything but my job, Terry."

"Well, you just keep on doing it."

He looked from Brody toward the opened grave, where the expensive coffin lay in shadow at the bottom. He stared as if he wanted to say something final to his father. If that was so, Brody thought it might be the first and only time Jimmy Quinn's son had ever been able to get in the last word.

Then Brody asked a question, one that clearly caught Terence Quinn by surprise. "You raise hogs, don't you?"

CHAPTER THIRTY-TWO

DEL WOLFE'S COUSIN was from Minneapolis and was city-girl pretty. She was fifteen, with long chestnut hair and violet eyes. She wore makeup and nail polish, a little gold ring on a gold chain around her throat, and on her wrist a gold charm bracelet. To Scott Madison, she was the most sophisticated girl he'd ever met. Her name was Holly Coleridge.

She'd brought a friend with her on this visit to Jewel. Nicole Blake wore dark eye shadow and a black beret and spoke in beatnik phrases like "I'm hip," and "Cool," and "You're one crazy cat." As smitten as Scott was with Holly Coleridge, around Nicole Blake, Del was like a kite that had finally found the wind.

All the mothers had agreed to the plan for that Friday afternoon, a float trip on inner tubes down the Alabaster from the Stoughton Bridge north of town to the spillway in Jewel. The kids would disembark there and picnic in Veteran's Park. Angie would supply the food. Del got the tubes from the garage run by Creasy's family in the hollow, and Tyler Creasy hauled them—kids and tubes—in the back of his pickup to the bridge. The boys wore shorts and T-shirts. The girls wore bathing suits. Nicole's suit was black and Holly's a scarlet that lit a fire deep in Scott. In the shade under the bridge, he waded into the water and held Holly's tube while she positioned herself in it. Del did the same for Nicole, and then the boys got into their tubes, and the current carried them away.

Their day together had begun with a lie. Del had told Holly that

Scott was fifteen, the same age as she, and would be a sophomore in high school in the fall. A small lie, but Scott felt uncomfortable with it. Del also told her that Scott played the guitar and was thinking about starting his own band someday, which was not exactly a lie, but far enough from the truth of his current musical ability that it felt like a lie to Scott. Del had told her something else, too.

"Del says you have a hole in your heart," Holly said as they floated together, only a foot or so separating their tubes. "Is that true?"

This wasn't something Scott particularly wanted to talk about, and he wasn't happy at all that Del had revealed this terrible physical flaw. "Yeah," he admitted.

"So, do you notice it? I mean, can you actually feel it?"

He shook his head. "It's just there."

"How do they know?"

Scott looked up at the sky, which was mottled with clouds that were partly gray, like dirty cotton balls. "I was kind of blue when I was little. It's one of the signs."

"Is it . . . ?"

He glanced at her in the tube beside him. Her face was pinched as if it pained her to be asking these questions. "Is it what?"

"Is it big?"

"It's just kind of a leak."

Del and Nicole had drifted ahead, and Scott could hear Del talking about *Peyton Place*.

"Can they fix it?" Holly asked.

"Maybe. I see this specialist in the Twin Cities sometimes."

"Could I . . . ?" She looked at him shyly, her eyes peeking from beneath strands of chestnut hair fallen across her face.

"Could you what?"

"Touch your heart?"

"You can't feel anything."

"My mother says I'm psychic. You know what that means?"

"Sure."

"My father—my real father, not my stepfather—had a heart attack just after Christmas. I told him he would because, when we hugged goodbye on Christmas Eve and my heart touched his heart, I felt it. I really did. And I told him, but he didn't believe me."

"Is he okay?"

"He died. This"—she fingered the gold ring on the chain around her neck—"was his. And he gave me all the charms on my bracelet, one on every birthday. Mom didn't want me to wear them on the river today, but I told her I wear them everywhere. We kind of argued about that. She didn't love him like I did. That's why they got divorced."

"I'm sorry." Scott looked at her and saw that her violet eyes were wet, and his imperfect heart ached for her. "You can touch my heart if you want."

He lifted his T-shirt, exposing his chest. She reached out across the water and her fingers found his heart. Although it was a touch as light as a butterfly, Scott felt branded, a searing of his flesh, a sweet pain, and he closed his eyes to savor it.

"You're strong," she said, and her hand was gone.

He opened his eyes and found her gazing at him seriously.

"Really," she said. "You're very strong. I didn't sense anything but strength."

Which was the loveliest thing Scott Madison thought he'd ever heard. He was so in love he could barely stand it.

The river was higher and faster than usual. Here and there, huge tree limbs from the spring flooding were still embedded in sandbars that lurked below the river's surface. The branches reached out of the water like the talons of some great river creature, and Holly let Scott help her navigate safely around them. Turtles sunned themselves on rocks along the banks, and coming around the bends, the kids startled herons that took flight, much to the delight of the city girls. Del and Nicole drifted farther and farther ahead, and that was fine with Scott, because he wanted Holly to himself. She told him about her father who'd died and Scott told her about his father, whom he'd never really known but had imagined in heroic ways.

"Del's father died, too," Holly said. "And then his mother married that Tyler Creasy."

"You don't like Mr. Creasy?"

Holly scowled at him. "Do you?"

Scott had been well schooled in never speaking ill of people, but he said, "Not especially."

"Have you ever been in that trailer where they live?" she asked.

Scott had not, but he hadn't given the trailer much thought until now. "What's wrong with it?"

"Oh, Scottie"—she'd begun using that variation of his name, which had always seemed childish to him, but from her lips sounded endearing—"it's a tragedy. I don't know how Del and my aunt can even live there."

"Messy or what?"

"It smells like a barroom."

He wondered, briefly how she'd have any idea what a barroom smelled like, because he didn't.

"Mom says Aunt Ramona always had a taste for liquor, but when she married Mr. Creasy, it got way worse. That's one of the reasons we came to visit." She was quiet, staring at the two tubes far ahead on the river. "I'll tell you something if you promise not to tell Del."

"Okay."

"Mom wants Aunt Ramona to leave him."

"Leave Creasy?"

"Mom says she and Del can stay with us for a while, until Aunt

Ramona figures what next. My stepdad wouldn't be too thrilled, I can tell you that."

Scott was a kid divided. He thought it wouldn't be a bad idea at all for Del and his mom to get away from Tyler Creasy and the whole Creasy clan. But then Wolfman would be gone, and when Scott realized this, it was as if he had another hole in his heart.

Something flashed in the water not far from them, leaving rings that vanished quickly in the current.

"What was that?" Holly asked, clearly startled, and maybe a little afraid.

"A catfish, probably. The river's full of them."

He considered telling her about Mr. Quinn but decided it might frighten her too much. The day was hot and the sun was high, and they drifted in and out of shadows under the broad overhang of tree branches.

"Dreamy," Holly said.

Scott saw her close her eyes, and he did the same, feeling the push of the river, his hands and feet cool in the drag of the water. He felt sleepy and happy and wished that the afternoon would never end. His bottom, which was cradled in the hole of the tube, scraped across a submerged tree limb, and he lifted himself slightly.

And then he heard Holly scream.

His eyes snapped open. Her tube was still there, just an arm's reach away, but it was empty. He heard the splashing and flailing at his back. He turned in his own tube and saw Holly in the river, snagged somehow, struggling in the sweep of the current. As he watched she went under, then fought her way back to the surface. He had no idea what was happening, but even in the few seconds it took him to react, the current had carried him many yards downriver.

He rolled off his inner tube and began to swim, battling the sweep of the river, which seemed in the blink of an eye to have become something malevolent, a beast with an angry will. He was a good swimmer and he fought the river and tried to keep his eye on the place where she'd now disappeared. Stroke after stroke he crawled, yard by yard. He felt his heart, that damn faulty organ, hammering in his chest, and he was afraid it would give out before he could reach her.

Then his fingers touched the unseen snag, and he grabbed it and pulled himself into a web of branches lurking beneath the surface. He went under, groped blindly, and found her arm. He grasped it and felt his way to her wrist. His hand curled around the charm bracelet she wore, which had become caught on a fork of one of the submerged branches. He tugged, but it was no good. His lungs were burning by then, but he wouldn't give up. With all the strength he could summon, he pulled her whole body against the shove of that great river and was able at last to slide the bracelet up the length of the fork until it was free and Holly with it.

But the monster the river had become was not finished.

The current swept them downstream, Holly heavy in his grip, a deadweight pulling him under. He kicked to get ahead of the current, and as he did, he drew the girl up and into his arms. He fought to latch her in a cross-chest carry, a lifesaving technique he'd been taught in Boy Scouts. With her head finally above water, he began to swim toward the riverbank. He could feel himself weakening rapidly, his heart working harder than it ever had. His arms and legs felt as heavy as stone. He gulped water, coughed, almost lost his grip on Holly, and then his feet found the muddy bottom. He stumbled up the bank backward, dragging the girl from the water. He laid her in sunlight on a bed of timothy and wild daisies. She wasn't breathing. He cocked her head back, opened her mouth, and breathed air into her. He put his hands together, the heel of his right palm on her chest, and pumped ten times. He breathed into her again, desperately.

She spat water and gasped. Scott turned her quickly on her side, and she vomited into the grass.

"Madman!"

Del was next to him now and Nicole, too.

"Is she okay?" Nicole was in tears as she knelt beside her friend.

Holly's eyes fluttered open. She stared up at them, dazed. "What . . . what happened?"

"I'll tell you what happened," Del said. He slapped Scott on the back. "Madman here saved your life, that's what happened."

CHAPTER THIRTY-THREE

JIMMY QUINN'S FUNERAL resulted in another quiet day at the Wagon Wheel. Angie and Wendell took care of the spotty lunch crowd while Ida represented the Madisons at the service. Then Angie began to work on the picnic lunch that Scott and Del and the two visiting girls would eat when they were finished with their tubing.

In truth, Angie hadn't been thrilled with the idea of the river excursion. Partly, it was because she didn't know the girls. Judging from their makeup, they seemed a little too eager to grow up, something that because of her own past she was terribly sensitive about. But they were polite and seemed excited about the outing. And Scott and Del were both eager, so what could she say?

It wasn't really the girls that troubled her. It was Scott's damaged heart. Every time she saw him run out of sight, every time he looked tired, every time he was absent longer than she'd anticipated, she worried. Even as she cut the ham salad sandwiches she'd prepared and wrapped the chocolate chip cookies and washed the apples, she fought not to listen to the voice of tragedy that always whispered at her back.

Wendell stepped into the kitchen. "Got yourself a visitor, Angie."

"Who?"

"Garnet Dern."

Angie looked up from the prep counter. "I thought she'd be at the Quinn funeral."

"Probably was. She's dressed for it."

Angie came out wiping her hands on her apron. Garnet stood near the register, wearing a simple, beautiful black dress, a string of pearls around her neck, and matching earrings. She smiled radiantly.

"Hello, Angie."

"The funeral's over?"

"The services, yes. Folks will be gathering at the church now for some food and fellowship. You know how funerals are."

"Of course. Is there something I can do for you?"

"I just wanted to remind you that the Women's Guild will be collecting tomorrow for our book drive, and you've promised us a box."

"Oh, sure. I'll put that together tonight."

The smile left Garnet's lips and a look of concern clouded her face. "Mimi Fowler is on the guild, and I was talking with her this morning. She told me that she was at the Wicklows' home for dinner last Sunday night and you were there."

"Loretta and Sam hosted a little gathering in honor of Ruth Coffee."

"Gordon Landis accompanied Mimi."

"That's right."

"Mimi's a little concerned."

"About what?"

"She thinks Gordon is interested in you."

"Ever since his wife died, he's been interested in anything that wears a skirt, Garnet. When I was a girl, we had a saying: A man's like a skeeter; he'll suck on any neck. If I was you, I'd caution Mimi to be careful where Gordon Landis is concerned."

Garnet leaned against the register and asked, a little too casually, "You and Brody, did you have a good time?"

"It was a lovely evening," Angie said.

She smiled, and Garnet smiled, and for a long moment, nothing more was spoken.

"Well." Garnet took a step back. "I'd best be on my way. Me or somebody else from the Women's Guild will drop by tomorrow for that box of books."

"I'll be sure to have it ready."

Garnet left the Wagon Wheel and got into her station wagon, which was parked in the gravel area in front of the diner. She glanced in Angie's direction. Through the glass of the front window, their eyes met once more. Then she backed out and drove away.

If Angie Madison hadn't known it before, she knew now absolutely. Garnet Dern was in love with Brody. .

The phone in the kitchen rang, and as if the thinking of him had conjured his voice, it was Brody on the line.

"Angie," he said. "It's about Scott."

THE HEADLINE IN the *Black Earth County Clarion* the next day would read SCOUT TRAINING HELPS BOY BECOME HERO. It would feature Del Wolfe's glowing eyewitness account of his friend's dramatic rescue of Holly Coleridge and a photo of the girl planting a grateful kiss on Scott Madison's cheek. For his part, Scott's only quote was that he was thankful for all he'd been taught in Boy Scouts.

Brody Dern had been called to the scene by Russ Arnold, whose land bordered the river where Scott had come ashore. Brody, in turn, had called out the paramedics. Holly Coleridge was taken to the hospital ER, where she was examined and pronounced well enough to be released into her mother's care. Sam Wicklow had been alerted and was there to snap the front-page photo of Holly planting that kiss on Scott. There was no picnic in Veteran's Park that day.

Scott's heart had been overworked. When Angie arrived at the hospital, what she saw was a wan boy, her beloved boy, who smiled at her but looked ready to fall over. She brought him home, and he didn't argue at all when she put him to bed. He fell asleep almost immediately and slept through the late afternoon. He woke in the evening, and Angie brought him chicken noodle soup. He ate in bed, and then went back to sleep.

Angie didn't leave the house. She divided her time between Scott's bedside and the bookshelves, considering all the volumes she'd acquired over her years of voracious reading, culling for the Women's Guild those she was willing to part with. She boxed them and put them beside the desk in her bedroom.

That night, she sat at the same small desk. Two journals lay before her—that old worn volume of her earliest years, and the newest, which contained less than a year of entries. She'd scanned the older journal, reminded herself of her current blessings, and now the fountain pen was in her hand poised above the new journal. She stared a long time into the dark outside her window, imagining all the terrible possibilities that day might have held. Finally, she wrote: *The most frightening thing we do in our lives is to love.*

She might have written more, but she heard a knock at the front door, a gentle rapping at first. It was late, well after ten, and she was in her nightgown. She waited, and the rapping came again, more urgent this time. She put the new journal atop the old and stood. But as she turned from her desk, her elbow knocked both volumes to the floor. In her haste, she simply snatched them up and put them atop the box of books she'd set aside for her donation. She grabbed her robe, stepped into the hallway, and hurried down the stairs.

Felix Klein stood in the glare of the porch light.

"It's late, Felix." She tried not to sound as put out as she felt. "I'm not inclined to fix you a meal at the Wagon Wheel, if that's what you've come for."

"Oh no, Angie, nothing like that. And I haven't been drinking, if that's what you think. It's just that I saw your light on upstairs, and I have something for you. Something I would like you to give to Scott."

He held out his hand. Cradled in his palm was a medal hung from a ribbon.

"It's the Distinguished Service Medal. I was awarded this for my service in the First World War. Quite an honor. I heard about what your son did today. It struck me as an act of valor, something that deserved a medal. Would you be willing to give it to him for me?"

She eased the screen door open and stepped outside with her visitor. She took his medal and in return leaned to him and planted a kiss on his grizzled cheek.

"That's just about the sweetest thing I've ever heard, Felix. Of course, I'll give Scott the medal. It will mean a great deal to him, I'm sure."

"Thank you, Angie. That's all I wanted. Good night."

He descended the steps, and she watched as he walked away and blended eventually with the gentle dark.

She closed the door, turned out the porch light, and climbed the stairs to her bedroom. She switched off the lamp on her desk and lay down with the little ribboned medal still in her hand. She began to cry, weeping out of love, purely and simply. She loved this place she'd come to and the people in it. She loved Jewel, Minnesota, and Black Earth County. She loved Felix Klein and all the others who'd entered her life through the door of the Wagon Wheel: the cantankerous, the laconic, the bigoted, the gentle-hearted, the fearful, the horse's asses, the sheltered, the accepting, the broken—especially the broken, who came to her every day. Her life had begun in another way, promised something else entirely, days filled with degradation and despair. But she'd been saved. Salvation had come to her unasked for and undeserved, and it had brought her to this beloved place.

She'd almost lost Scott, but she hadn't. And she held in her hand recognition of his valor. In the morning, she would give it to her son, proof that although his heart wasn't perfect, it was strong in all the right ways.

CHAPTER THIRTY-FOUR

CHARLIE BAUER CHERISHED her mornings. She cherished the first cup of coffee, cherished the solitude in which she drank it, cherished the view from her front porch as the sun rose above the hills east of the Alabaster and for a little while blinded her to everything except the small, lovely piece of land that was her home now.

That Saturday morning, she sat in faded jeans and an old work shirt ragged at the collar. She wore no shoes, and her big feet felt perfectly delighted with that liberation. She hadn't brushed her hair. It was just her and the morning and the mounting sun and a cup of coffee. She was enjoying her solitude when she spotted a ribbon of dust rising along the lane that ran beside the river and led to her home. Her senses went on high alert. She hadn't received any threats directly since she'd taken on the defense of Noah Bluestone, but she'd seen a few vehicles creep up her lane and sit there. It was usually near dark so that she couldn't make out the details of the vehicles or who was inside, but the message they wanted to send her was clear.

No one had been bold enough to come in this way during the day. Still, she watched the station wagon that turned onto her lane with apprehension. It stopped near the shed she used as a garage, and Charlie was relieved to see Sam Wicklow behind the wheel. They'd become good friends over the years as he'd covered events at the courthouse, and every once in a while, he'd drop by to run a legal question past her. That morning, she figured he wanted to talk about Noah Bluestone.

"Morning, Charlie," he called. "Mind if I join you?"

She waved him up and indicated the unoccupied chair on the porch.

With that prosthetic leg, mounting steps tended to be a little awkward for Sam. When he was seated, she held up her mug and offered, "Care for some coffee?"

"Thanks, no."

"Fine morning," Charlie said.

"Indeed," he replied. He gazed at the sun a moment, then launched into what had brought him.

"I've got something here I'd like you to read, Charlie, if you wouldn't mind. It's an editorial I'm thinking of running in the *Clarion*."

"Since when do you need my approval for an editorial, Sam?"

"Just read it, okay?"

He handed her a sheet of typed paper, and she read the paragraph.

I was in the hardware store yesterday, and I overheard a conversation that alarmed me greatly. Two men, two staunch citizens of Black Earth County, were talking about the death of Jimmy Quinn. They both agreed that it would be good to have the man accused of his murder locked up in prison and the key thrown away. Or better yet, why not just string him up? Killing Jimmy Quinn was a savage thing to do. But what else could you expect from an Indian?

She glanced up at Wicklow. "You really overheard two men talking about lynching?"

"I didn't just overhear them. I argued with them. By the time I left, they were ready to lynch me along with Bluestone."

"Who were they?"

"Doesn't matter. I've been hearing similar sentiments since word first got out that Noah Bluestone was a person of interest."

Charlie read on and wasn't surprised by Sam Wicklow's incisive assessment of the prejudices abroad in Black Earth County directed at a man who was Sioux and who'd married a Japanese woman. Wicklow's defense of the precept of innocent until proven guilty was eloquent. He ended the editorial with these lines:

Noah Bluestone is innocent of any crime until a jury of his peers decides otherwise. If I had to sacrifice another part of my body to defend this liberty, I would do so gladly.

Charlie lowered the paper and studied Sam. "If you haven't got enough enemies in Jewel already, Sam, this'll fill the quota. What's Loretta say?"

"Her exact words were 'You'll publish this over my dead body.'"

"She's worried about losing subscribers, advertisers?"

"More about losing respect. She says if I print an editorial like this, she won't be able to walk down the street without people accosting her."

"There are some folks in Black Earth County who will agree with you a hundred percent, Sam."

"And a lot that would likely want to. hang me."

"What is it exactly that you want from me?"

"I could say I'm concerned it might be prejudicial when it comes to picking a jury."

"But that's not really it."

"You're sticking your neck out for Noah Bluestone, Charlie. I admire that. I guess maybe I just wanted you to know that you're not alone."

"So you're really going to publish this?"

"I am." He looked at her then, and she knew there was more. "Any chance you'd let me talk to Bluestone?"

"About his arrest? I'll advise him against that, Sam."

"No, not about that. I want to talk to him about growing up Sioux. For the book I'd like to write."

It was a sultry day. The air in the valley of the Alabaster River hung damp and heavy and unmoving, and over the broad, unkempt field between the house and the river, a hush had settled, empty even of the songs of meadow birds.

"The book about the Sioux uprising?"

"Yes."

"You're really serious about writing it?"

"I'm going to try."

She remembered Loretta Wicklow's cutting reaction when Sam declared this intent during the last gathering of the Prairie Blooms, and everything in her wanted him to succeed.

"I'll talk to Noah. But if he agrees, I'll want to be there when you do the interview, and you'll have to stick to information that has nothing to do with the charge against him. Is it a deal?"

"Deal," he said.

"You mind if I keep this editorial? I'd like Noah to see it."

"Thanks, Charlie."

He returned to his car and drove away, leaving behind him a trail of yellow dust that took a long time to settle in that still morning. Charlie couldn't help thinking that a lot more than dust was being stirred up in Black Earth County and whatever the outcome of Noah Bluestone's trial, it was going to take a long time for everything to return to normal, if it ever did.

CHAPTER THIRTY-FIVE

BREAKFAST WAS WHAT Scott's mother called Cajun Scramble: eggs scrambled with andouille sausage she'd made herself, cheese, hash browns, and Cajun spices. Along with it came a couple of slices of toasted bread and homemade strawberry-rhubarb jam. When Scott walked into the jailhouse carrying the tray, he found Hank Evans, one of the sheriff's auxiliary deputies, sitting behind the sheriff's desk.

"Breakfast for the prisoner?" Evans asked. He was tall, heavily built, jowly. His hair was gray and his eyes a color so dark they seemed black. He held an opened newspaper in his hands.

"Yes, sir," Scott said.

Evans had spent thirty years with the police department in Minneapolis before retiring to Jewel, his hometown. The man sometimes helped the sheriff when one of the other deputies was on vacation or otherwise unavailable. So far, Scott had only seen him on duty in the jailhouse. Because he was never actually certain of the man's official position and whether he should call him Deputy Evans, Scott usually kept his end of an exchange as simple as possible.

Evans put the paper on the desk, folded it so that the front page showed, and tapped the photo there. "You're a hero."

"I guess so."

"Pretty impressive, son."

Scott wasn't used to such praise and found it embarrassing.

"I made the front page once," Evans said. "Up in the Cities. Remember Morgan Gilroy?"

"No, sir, I don't."

"Robbed a dozen banks. I finally cornered him in an alley. Shot it out with him. Got me a medal from the mayor for that one."

Scott wanted to tell him about the medal he'd received but was afraid it might be bragging, so he held his tongue.

"Probably ought to get that food in to Bluestone before it gets too cold." Evans rose and opened the door to the cellblock. He stood aside and watched as Scott delivered the tray.

"Smells good," Noah Bluestone said.

The phone on the sheriff's desk rang.

Evans said, "You stay back from the cell, son, hear?"

Scott said, "Yes, sir."

Evans went to answer the call.

Bluestone set the tray on the cot beside him and lifted the cloth that covered the food. "At least they feed you good in here." He picked up the spoon Scott's mother had sent along and began to eat. "I heard about what you did yesterday. A good piece of work."

"Thank you."

"Mind if I ask you something?"

"Okay."

"Were you afraid?"

Scott looked toward the little window of morning sky at the end of the cellblock. He thought over his answer to the question.

"It all happened so fast, I didn't have much time to be afraid. But . . ." He glanced into the calm eyes of Noah Bluestone, and he wanted to tell this man the truth. "I was afraid I couldn't save her. I was afraid that if she died, it would be my fault."

"You felt responsibility and you acted. A lot of men freeze up in a desperate situation like that, Scott. I've seen them paralyzed with fear. I've seen them run. I've seen them break down and cry. You learned something important about yourself. In a way, it's a gift, and you'll always have it with you."

"It doesn't feel like a gift. It feels kind of heavy. I keep thinking, *What if?* And every time I do that, it scares me more."

"Will you do something for me?"

"I guess so, if I can."

"Next time you come, break off a small stick from a cottonwood tree and bring it with you."

"Why?"

"Bring it and I'll show you why."

Evans returned. "How's that breakfast coming?" he asked Bluestone.

"Almost done."

Bluestone ate the last few bites and slid the tray through the opening in the bars into Scott's waiting hands. "The cottonwood," he said. "Don't forget."

As Scott was leaving the jailhouse, he asked Evans, "Where is everybody?"

"Brody and Asa are out on duty. Deputy Graff turned in his badge."

"He quit? Why?"

"He decided to help Bluestone's wife take care of the farm. Sticking his neck out, seems to me. I can understand why Brody asked for his badge. This whole situation, Quinn's murder, it's got folks upset. Sentiments are running high. Jimmy Quinn was a son of a—" Evans caught himself and quickly shifted direction. "He was a man who made lots of folks around here angry, but he was one of us. Bluestone?" He looked back toward the closed door of the cellblock "Indian," he finished, as if that one word spoke volumes.

—

SCOTT MADISON WAS leaving the jailhouse as Charlie arrived. He carried a tray in his hands, and Charlie figured he'd just delivered breakfast to her client.

"Congratulations, Scott," she said. "A heroic thing you did yesterday. Read all about it in the paper. Nice photograph, too. Pretty girl."

Scott looked down and spoke to the floor. "Thanks."

"How's Mr. Bluestone this morning?" Charlie asked because she'd become aware that over the past few days the boy and the prisoner had struck up a kind of friendship. Noah Bluestone's tone changed whenever he mentioned Scott, went from granite, which was how, from behind his bars, he usually addressed everyone, to something softer.

"He's good, Miss Bauer. Could I ask you a question?"

"Sure."

"He told me that a good man died on Inkpaduta Bend. A man worthy of respect."

"Mr. Bluestone said that to you?"

"Yes, ma'am."

"Worthy of respect?"

"That's what he said. I didn't know Mr. Quinn, really, but I've never heard anybody say anything like that about him."

"Nor have I, Scott."

"So you don't know what he meant?"

"No. But I intend to find out."

"I hope it was okay I told you."

"It's just fine, Scott. I'm his lawyer. Okay?"

"Okay."

He didn't move and Charlie thought he wasn't quite finished. "Something else?"

"Mom says you used to work in California defending poor people. She said you defended them against bullies."

That brought a smile to her lips. "That's an oversimplification, but I suppose it's essentially true."

"Why did you leave California?"

"The honest to God truth is that I got tired and I got lonely. When you're tired and lonely, home's a good place to head for. Jewel has its problems but it's the only place I've ever thought of as home."

He nodded as if that was something he could understand. Then he said, "Bullies, huh?" and gave Charlie a parting look of approval.

Hank Evans let her into Bluestone's cell and she sat, as she always did when she met with him, at one end of his cot while he sat at the other with his back rigid against the stone wall.

"I talked with our county attorney this morning," Charlie said. "He's moved pretty quickly. Your psychiatric evaluation is scheduled for next Tuesday."

"Think I'm crazy, Charlie?"

"What I think doesn't matter, Noah. But I'm sure you'll be found fit to stand trial. Something else. Read this. Then I want to ask you a question."

She gave him the editorial Sam Wicklow was intent on publishing in the *Clarion*. He looked it over, handed it back, and said, "Wicklow's a fool."

"A damn fine one."

"He's just asking for trouble."

"That's all you've got to say?"

"You said you had a question to ask me."

"Sam wants to talk to you. Are you willing?"

"About Quinn?"

"About growing up Sioux in Black Earth County."

That made him think. His face didn't change, but there was a long pause before he spoke again. "What's his interest?"

"He wants to write a book."

"About growing up Sioux? He must not want to sell many copies."

"I think he's after the truth."

"Of what?"

"The history of this place. The whole history. The true history."

"What do you think?"

"I think whenever you begin by believing it's the truth you're after, the journey's already hopeless. I also think there's no reason you shouldn't talk to him. Considering what he's put in that editorial, maybe you owe it to him. But I want to be there when you do, just to make sure he doesn't slip in any questions about Jimmy Quinn's death."

"All right," he said.

"Also, there's something you ought to know. I spoke with a young woman who worked for the Quinns before you and Kyoko were hired. She quit because Jimmy assaulted her. I have a sense it might not have been the only time Jimmy did something like that."

She watched him closely, but he gave no sign that this was important in his own thinking, nothing to indicate that it might have happened to Kyoko when she was working for the Quinns.

"I have just one more question for you," Charlie said. "What was it about Jimmy Quinn that you find so worthy of respect?"

"Respect?" That got him. He reacted as if Charlie had jabbed him with a pitchfork. "What the hell ever gave you that impression?"

"Scott Madison told me that you said a good man died on Inkpaduta Bend, a man worthy of respect."

"Oh." He nodded and settled back. "Bring Wicklow to me, and I'll tell you both what that's about. And one other thing, Charlie."

In the moment of quiet between them, a bird settled on the sill of the east window, a cardinal. It caught Bluestone's eye, and it was as if he drank in the beauty of that little creature. Or maybe he simply savored the sense of its freedom. The bird took wing, and Bluestone turned his attention back to Charlie.

"Thank you" was all he said.

ON HIS WAY back to the Wagon Wheel, Scott Madison stopped at the Western Auto store and stood before the big display window eyeing the Columbia three-speed that was his faulty heart's desire. He believed the bike would be his ticket to riding all over Black Earth County, up and down the hills, and maybe even beyond. He'd saved nearly enough to purchase it now. The question was, considering her fear about his heart, would his mother allow it?

Del Wolfe came out of Gowen's Book and Stationery, two doors down. He saw Scott, hurried to him, and gave his friend a playful shoulder punch. "Hey, Madman, how's the hero?"

"Good," Scott said, though in truth he still felt tired.

"Got something for you." Del slid a small envelope from between the pages of the book he held, which Scott saw was *The Naked and the Dead,* Del's all-time favorite read.

The envelope was pinkish, and the flap was sealed with red wax, into which an imprint of a rose had been stamped. The envelope was also scented, something floral.

"Well, what're you waiting for?" Del said.

Scott tore open the envelope and slipped out the folded stationery inside.

Dear Scottie,

I write this by moonlight. The memory of what you did is still with me, and always will be. I'm alive because of you. Can one person ever be more deeply indebted to another? You breathed life back into me, and

*I don't mean just the air that you filled my lungs with. I don't know
how it will happen, but I want to see you again. I have to see you
again.*

Yours with gratitude and love,
Holly

"So, what did she say?"

Scott gave the note to his friend. Del read it and whistled. "I'll bet you
could get to second or maybe even third base with her now, Madman."

Which was something that hadn't even entered Scott's mind and
sullied the moment for him just a little.

"Hey," Del said. "I've got a great idea. Remember that gun I showed
you? Creasy's twenty-two?"

"Yeah."

"Want to do a little target practice this afternoon?"

"Where?"

"The gravel pit south of town."

"I don't know."

"Come on, Madman. It'll be a blast."

"After yesterday, my mom won't let me out of her sight for more
than an hour."

"Okay, we'll keep it to an hour."

Scott had to admit, the offer excited him. He'd never shot a gun
before, not ever, and the idea of it was a siren call.

"All right," he said. "But it'll have to be after the lunch rush. Mom
and Grandma and Wendell will need me at the Wagon Wheel."

"Okay. Say two?"

And so it was agreed, and the course it would eventually take Scott
Madison and Del Wolfe down was set and the sun went on rising and
the morning went on around them as if the world either had no idea of
the sorrow ahead or did not care.

CHAPTER THIRTY-SIX

THEY QUIT THEIR work at noon, and Kyoko went into the little house to prepare a meal. Connie Graff washed himself at the pump beside the barn, which was the only source of water on Bluestone's farmstead. There was no running water in the house, and Kyoko—or Bluestone when he'd been there—had to carry it to the house in a bucket to heat on the stove for the cleaning of dishes or before filling the washtub for laundry. For cleaning himself and his wife, Bluestone had built a little wooden tower six feet high next to the pump. Atop the tower was a platform on which sat an opaque ten-gallon plastic container filled with water that was heated by the sun. Near the bottom of the container, Bluestone had inserted a spigot to which was affixed the spout of a watering can. Turning the spigot released a little shower of sun-warmed water. The man had also poured a slab of concrete on which to stand and a trough for the water to drain away. There was a little shelf on the wooden tower where a bar of soap sat, and a towel hung on one of the tower's crossbeams. There was no curtain to shield the area from prying eyes, and Graff knew that Kyoko showered in the evening after he'd gone. It was a primitive way to live, and yet Connie Graff felt only a sense of contentment from the young woman Noah Bluestone had married.

She called him into the cool of the house, where the table was laid with simple food—rice mixed with pork and vegetables and flavored with ginger and other spices.

"You are good at farming. You could be Japanese," she said, teasing.

"Too tall," he shot back.

"And too disrespectful."

"To you?"

"To the sheriff."

"Ah. Well, Brody and I go way back. He'll come around."

"You're not like him," Kyoko said.

Graff put down the chopsticks, which he was becoming adept at using. "I beg your pardon?"

"He's a sad man. But you're not."

Graff thought about it and said, "Maybe he's a little unhappy."

"We're all unhappy in some ways. But there is usually balance. I don't sense a balance in Sheriff Dern."

"Maybe he just needs a good woman, Kyoko. Someone like you."

She laughed and Graff marveled at the richness of the sound, because he knew her story now and knew she had little reason for happiness, yet there it was.

Kyoko Bluestone had been born and raised in Nagasaki. Her father had been a colonel in the Imperial army. She remembered that he did not think the war was a good thing for his country, but it was his duty to participate. He'd been killed in fighting in Malaysia. She'd lost one brother in the Battle of Midway and another on Guadalcanal. When she was twelve years old, near the end of the war, she'd left her mother and her remaining younger brother and had gone to help care for her grand-parents, who lived in a village on a small island off the coast. One day, everyone in the village had seen a great fire in the sky, like another sun rising on the horizon. The next day, she'd made her way to the mainland and had stumbled, horrified, among the ruins of what had been a beautiful city. Her mother and brother were gone, obliterated. Later, during the occupation, her hair had fallen out, and the American doctors had told her that it was the radiation. As a result, she would never have children.

She'd been raised Catholic in Nagasaki, had gone to a Catholic school, and learned from the nuns how to speak excellent English. When she met Noah Bluestone, she'd been working as a translator for the government on Okinawa, where he was stationed. He was kind to her; they'd fallen in love. Against the advice and, generally speaking, the wishes of his superiors, Bluestone had married her. Almost immediately, he'd been sent to fight in Korea. When the conflict ended, he'd been assigned to a Marine combat training center in the hostile California desert. It was a continuing punishment, of sorts, and when, after more than twenty years of service, he could draw a pension, Noah Bluestone left the military and returned to Black Earth County, bringing Kyoko with him.

She was right about Brody Dern. And she was right about Connie Graff, who felt happier these days than he'd been since his wife's passing. After Gordon Landis and the other two hooligans had showed up with rifles and Brody had assigned him the responsibility for seeing to Kyoko's safety, Graff had established a new routine. At the end of each day, after helping on the farm and sharing supper with her, he would ask, "Will you be all right?"

To which she always replied, "I say my prayers. And I have Fuji." As if the Christian ritual that she'd grown up with in a Shinto country and the old dog who kept her company were reasonable defenses against all the dangers of the night when she was alone on the farm.

He'd tried at first to argue her into allowing him to sleep in the small barn, but she refused, gently and persistently. So Graff had found a way to be her unseen sentinel. After leaving the farm, he would return to his home, exercise Bogie or Honeydew, riding for an hour along the graveled back roads of Black Earth County. Then he put the horses to pasture, cleaned himself up from the day's work, and returned at dark to the Bluestone farmstead. There, hidden among the trees along the Alabaster River and unbeknownst to Kyoko, he bedded down in his pickup truck for the night.

She poured him more iced tea and asked, "Do you have children, Connie?"

"Myrna and me, we tried but it never happened. That's okay. We were fine with just each other."

"You told me you are a widower. How long?"

"Myrna died four years ago last March," Graff said. "Lung cancer. She never smoked a cigarette in her life. The doctors at Mayo said it could have been from breathing in all that smoke from my cigarettes." And now the guilt that he so often felt in his aloneness settled on his shoulders. "Was me that killed her."

"But I've seen advertisements with doctors themselves smoking cigarettes."

"When money's involved, Kyoko, everybody lies."

She laid a hand gently on his arm. "How could you have known?"

"Doesn't matter," he said. "Can't change the past."

They both heard the growl of a vehicle approaching on the lane. They were always on the alert these days, and Kyoko gave Graff a look of concern.

"Wait here," Graff said. He left the table and went to the window. He watched the car pull to a stop, then he turned to Kyoko and said, "Relax. It's only Charlie."

CHARLIE JOINED THEM at the table where they'd finished the noon meal, and they drank iced tea. Charlie had told them about Jimmy Quinn's funeral. Then she said, "What I found most interesting was that Fiona, Jimmy Quinn's first daughter, didn't attend."

"Lives in Des Moines, doesn't she?" Graff said.

"An easy drive if you cared to pay last respects to your father," Charlie said.

"What are you thinking?"

"That I'd like to talk to Fiona."

"What could she tell you that would help Noah?" Graff asked.

"Jimmy's first wife was ill a long time. I'm wondering if there might have been a girl they hired back then who maybe had the same kind of experience as Sissy Barrows."

"Looking for a pattern of behavior?" Graff said. "Did you talk to Terry Quinn?"

"He told me he didn't remember any girl. I honestly think he was lying. But he did give me Fiona's address in Des Moines."

Kyoko said quietly, "Did you ask him why his sister might not have come to the funeral?"

"I did, Kyoko. He told me he doesn't talk to his sister, and so he had no idea."

"Lying again?" Graff asked.

"Maybe. That's what I'd like to find out."

"And if you prove this pattern," Kyoko said, "how will it help my husband?"

"It's a building block in the defense. Let me get it set in place, and then I'll tell you the rest."

Which was obfuscation. What Charlie really wanted was to be able to suggest to a jury that someone had killed James Patrick Quinn because of an assault. She believed this someone was either Kyoko or Noah Bluestone and believed that they were holding back the truth because they didn't think a jury in Black Earth County would buy their story. She thought if she could prove that Jimmy Quinn was the kind of man who'd attack a defenseless woman, the Bluestones might come around and deliver the details of what really happened the night the big Irishman died.

CHAPTER THIRTY-SEVEN

THE LUNCH CROWD at the Wagon Wheel was large and hungry and boisterous. Angie and Ida scurried like crazy. In the kitchen, in the heat from the griddle and oven, Wendell's face ran with beads of sweat. Scott hustled to bus the tables so that he could load the dishwasher, but he was often held back by folks who wanted to talk to him about his heroics on the Alabaster.

In the middle of the rush, Garnet Dern entered the café. She spoke to Scott's mother briefly, and Angie called her son over.

"Scott, I need you to go up to my bedroom. There's a box near my desk full of books. Bring the box down and give it to Mrs. Dern, will you?"

"Sure," Scott said.

"If you'll excuse me, Garnet," Scott's mother said, "I need to get back to my customers."

"Of course, Angie."

As she hustled away, Scott saw that Mrs. Dern watched his mother go with a look that seemed to him hard and that he didn't understand.

He said, "I'll be right back."

"Meet me outside, Scott," Mrs. Dern replied. "I'll open the back of my station wagon and wait for you there."

Scott knew his absence, however brief, would be tough for his mother and grandmother and Wendell, so he ran. To the house, up the stairs, and into his mother's bedroom. He found the box next to her desk, as she'd told him. On top lay two books with no titles. One was new-looking, the other old and worn. He unflapped the box, slipped the volumes inside with the other books, closed up the box again, carted it down the stairs and out of the house, where he loaded it in the back of Mrs. Dern's station wagon, which was already full of other boxes.

She thanked him and said, "I have to tell you, I'm so proud of you. We all are."

He was almost to the point where such praise no longer embarrassed him. In fact, he was beginning to like it.

Then Mrs. Dern did something unexpected. She leaned to him and kissed his cheek. The fragrance she wore poured over him in a heady, invisible haze. And as the woman drew back, Scott Madison caught a glimpse down the top of her loose blouse at the fleshy mounds barely contained by the white lace of her bra.

She got into her station wagon, waved through the window at him, and drove away.

Scott Madison stood in the gravel of the lot, in the heat of the early afternoon sun, and stared after her as if he'd been smacked in the head with a frying pan.

AN HOUR LATER, as the rush abated, his mother said, "Are you all right? You seem a little unfocused."

"I'm fine," he said.

"I think maybe you should just go lie down for a while. We can take care of things here."

"I'd rather go to the library."

She smiled as if this pleased her immensely. "Of course."

"I'll be back to help with supper," he promised and left.

He almost never lied to his mother, but he wasn't inclined to tell her that he was really going to the gravel pit to shoot a gun with Del Wolfe.

And, anyway, it was the second lie he'd told her in their conversation. The first was that he was all right. He wasn't. He couldn't get the image of Mrs. Dern's lace-cupped breasts out of his mind. They'd been so near to him, inches really. And he'd begun to imagine, even as he'd moved zombielike between tables, what those breasts might look like loosed from her bra. And that imagining was suffused with the memory of her scent and the wet plant of her red lips against his cheek. And Scott Madison, who'd only that morning been in love with Holly Coleridge, found himself—just like that—totally intoxicated with carnal thoughts of a woman old enough to be his mother.

He walked out to Creasy's Hollow. In the year that he and Del Wolfe had been best friends, he'd never visited Del's place. Del had never invited him. The trailer in which Del lived with his mother and Tyler Creasy was mounted on cinder blocks in a stand of old trees behind the gas station–garage that was the source of most Creasy income. There were also several small houses among the trees, accessed by fingers of unpaved, rutted lanes. The hollow was dark and smelled of mud and stagnant water. Scott heard the sound of men's voices coming from the open doors of the garage, and then the sound of a pneumatic machine of some kind. He skirted the building and headed to the trailer, where he climbed a set of warped wooden stairs and knocked on the door. Del opened up, a book in his hand and a surprised look on his face.

"Madman?"

"The gravel pit," Scott said. "Bad time?"

"No, Madman. It's cool. Just wait a second."

Del left the door and stepped out of sight.

Scott could see a part of the inside of the trailer. A living room, with a threadbare sofa the color of pond algae, heavy curtains, and clutter everywhere. His own house—his grandmother's actually, but it was all the home he knew—was always tidy and airy and welcoming.

Del returned with his knapsack hanging heavily on his shoulder. The gun, Scott figured.

They left on Del's motorbike and drove along a country road that paralleled the east side of the Alabaster. A mile outside Jewel, they came to an old excavation where sand and gravel had once been dug. A thick cable was strung across the access road and from it hung a sign that said, NO TRESPASSING. But everyone did, mostly at night. The floor of the pit was scarred with black circles where fires had been built, parties had been held, and drinking and God knew what else had gone on. That afternoon and most others, it was empty.

Del collected beer cans—they were thrown about everywhere—and set up several against a wall of the pit. He pulled the pistol from his knapsack. It was as black and shiny as a scorpion's back, and although it didn't seem particularly large, not like the guns in the Westerns on the screen at the Rialto, on the whole it looked quite sinister.

Del hefted it with relaxed familiarity and said, "Creasy told me some gangster in Las Vegas gave it to him. I don't believe him." He dug a handful of bullets from the knapsack, released the gun clip, and filled it. "Want to shoot first?"

"No," Scott said, suddenly not so eager. "You go ahead."

Del fired all the rounds in the clip and with each shot sent a beer can flying.

"Jesus, you're good," Scott said.

"I come here a lot. Sometimes I imagine each of those beer cans is Creasy. Helps." He reloaded and handed the pistol to Scott. "Give 'em hell. Just keep it pointed that way," he cautioned, waving at the wall where the targets were set.

Scott took a stance in the way he'd seen Del do, leveled the pistol, closed one eye, sighted, and pulled the trigger. The little pistol kicked in his grip, and a shot cracked, but nothing happened to the beer can.

"Takes a while to get the hang of it," Del said. "Keep trying."

They took turns, each shooting a full clip, then passing the pistol. Scott nicked a couple of cans near the end, but Del was like Wild Bill Hickok. He had the knack.

When they'd run out of rounds, they sat down, backs against the pit wall.

"So, what's up with you, Madman?" Del asked. Now that he had no ammunition, he'd taken to throwing rocks at the cans that still stood. "You've been real quiet. Got Holly Coleridge on your mind?"

If there was anyone to whom Scott might confide such a risky truth, it was Del Wolfe. And in a way, he was bursting to share what he'd glimpsed of Mrs. Dern. So he did.

"I've seen her in town," Del said. "Boobs out to here." He cupped his hands a foot away from his chest. "You saw those?"

"She was wearing a bra, but I pretty much saw everything."

"If you used it as a slingshot, I'll bet you could shoot coconuts with that bra. Compared to her, Holly Coleridge's tits are like a couple of Hershey Kisses."

Scott picked up a handful of rocks and threw them one by one at the cans.

"Hey, Madman?" Del turned to him. "How would you like to see a naked lady?"

"You got a *Playboy* stashed somewhere?"

"No, Madman. I mean a real live naked lady."

"What? Your grandma or something?"

"No. A beautiful naked lady, I swear."

"Are you kidding me?"

"Honest to God."

"Where?"

"I'll show you. But it has to be at night. Will your mom let you camp out tomorrow?"

"You and me? Where?"

"The campground next to Fort Beloit."

"I don't know. I could ask her. You got a tent?"

"It's summer. Who needs a tent? I'll bring a bedroll. You're a fuggin' Boy Scout, so you probably got a sleeping bag, right?"

"I can't promise anything. My mom's kind of weird about what she'll let me do."

"You're a hero, Madman. Use it. Get yourself free. I promise you a night you'll never forget. Deal?"

Del held out his hand, and they shook on it. Man to man.

CHAPTER THIRTY-EIGHT

THE HOUSE WAS in an area of relatively new constructions, all single-story, built postwar to accommodate the demand created by the low-interest government loans authorized in the GI Bill. The front lawn was nicely kept, with a crab apple tree almost dead center. Bright marigolds fringed the sidewalk on both sides. The air carried the pleasant smell of freshly mown grass.

A young woman answered, blond, maybe sixteen, with a bit of red at the end of her nose, perhaps a pimple in the making. "Yes?" She smiled graciously.

"I'm looking for Fiona McCarthy."

"Mother's in the backyard. May I tell her who's come to call?"

"My name is Charlotte Bauer."

"Would you like to come in and wait, Mrs. Bauer?"

Charlie was always called "Mrs." Bauer by default. She accepted the invitation and found the home to be as lovely and well kept inside as it was out. The young woman offered her a seat, then went to fetch her mother.

Charlie had fled Black Earth County about the time Jimmy Quinn's daughter Fiona was born, so she'd never seen the woman. But the moment Fiona walked through the sliding door that opened onto the backyard patio, Charlie saw Jimmy Quinn in her features. She was tall, with blazing red hair, and large hands. She carried a sunhat and gardening gloves, and she set these on the dining room table as she passed. Charlie stood to meet her.

"Mrs. Bauer?" Fiona offered her hand.

"Miss, actually."

"Forgive the dirt," Fiona said, indicating the soiled spots on her sundress. "I've been seeing to my roses. What can I do for you?"

"I have a law practice in Black Earth County. I'm representing a man named Noah Bluestone."

She'd been smiling cordially, well-defined laugh lines cutting through the freckles of her cheeks, but the smile fell from her lips. "I can't even imagine what you want with me."

"Just to talk, if you're willing."

"About what?"

"Your father mostly."

"I try never to talk about my father."

"I'd like to know why."

"I don't want to be rude, Miss Bauer, but I'm simply not going to have this conversation with you."

"Will you at least allow me to explain why I came?"

Fiona considered this request and begrudgingly gave a nod. She sat in one of the two matching wing chairs, so stiffly that she couldn't possibly have been comfortable. Charlie took the twin chair.

"What do you know about your father's death?" Charlie asked.

"I've spoken with Marta and with my brother. They've kept me informed."

"I'm not convinced that Noah Bluestone killed your father."

"Obviously," she said in a dead voice. "You're defending him."

"That's not it. I took the case at the request of the court because Noah refused to defend himself."

"How noble," she said.

Charlie ignored her tone and went on. "Fiona, I believe your father may have attacked Noah's wife, a young woman named Kyoko. And I believe it may have been Kyoko who actually killed your father and, if so, she did it in self-defense."

"If that's true," Fiona said after a long moment, "why hasn't she or her husband said as much?"

"Her husband, as you well know, is Sioux. Kyoko is Japanese. People in Black Earth County have long memories and deep antipathies. Noah and Kyoko are certain that no one there would believe their story. So silence is their response."

"They've told you this?"

"They refuse to say anything, even to me. It's what I believe."

"What evidence do you have?"

"I spoke with a young woman who was briefly in your father's employ last winter. She told me that your father assaulted her. This happened after Marta became too ill to meet many of your father's needs. Do you understand what I'm saying?"

She stared at Charlie a long while, then said, "Yes."

"Your mother was also quite ill for a very long time. Did your father hire anyone to help with the housework?"

"He did." Her lips were drawn in a thin line.

"Can you tell me her name?"

"Of course. It was Marta."

Charlie sat back a little, hoping the surprise she felt didn't show on her face.

The patio door slid open, and the young woman who'd greeted Charlie earlier stepped inside. "Mom, is it all right if I take the car to Woolworth's? I'd like to get some bobby pins and hair spray. Danny's taking me to the movies tonight."

"Yes, Susan."

Her daughter went into the kitchen, and Charlie heard the door to the attached garage open and close, the engine turn over, and the car back out of the driveway. In all this time, the woman's eyes didn't leave Charlie's face.

"I'm from Black Earth County myself," Charlie said. "Ran away, if you want to know the truth, when I was eighteen, just as fast I could. I didn't return until seven years ago. Even my father's death didn't bring me back. Sound familiar?"

"What do you want from me exactly?"

"To know if you believe your father was the kind of man who'd assault a young woman. And if so, why do you believe it?"

"I can't help you, Miss Bauer."

"You mean you won't help me."

"I'd like you to leave now."

"Noah Bluestone will probably go to prison. I'm not sure I can prevent that. How long he stays there, that I can affect. But I need your help."

"No, you need his. Or his wife's."

"Even if I convince them to tell their story, it will take a miracle to get a jury to believe it. Folks in Jewel didn't necessarily love your father, but he was one of them. Noah Bluestone is Indian and Kyoko is Japanese. They aren't just the accused, Fiona. They're the enemy."

Fiona rose from her chair. "Good day, Miss Bauer."

Charlie rose, too, and handed her a business card. "I'd appreciate hearing from you if you change your mind."

"I won't."

"A conscience is an interesting thing. I've found that in good people, it usually gets the upper hand."

"My conscience, Miss Bauer, is clear."

"I'm grateful for your time. Thank you." At the door as she left, Charlie said, "One more thing."

"Yes?"

"You knew Noah Bluestone once. He and his father helped work your father's land. What did you think of him then?"

"That was a very long time ago, Miss Bauer. People change."

"Not what's at the heart of them. Think about Noah Bluestone's heart. And then think about your father's. And then look into your own. That's all I'm asking."

Fiona didn't reply. Charlie left her in the doorway of her perfect-looking little house, left her to her perfect-seeming little life, and went back to Black Earth County and the messy business of those who still called it home.

BRODY DERN'S CRUISER was parked in the Quinns' yard when Charlie returned from Des Moines in the late evening. Only the pale blue memory of daylight remained in the western sky, and the big yard light near the barn was already garishly ablaze. All the lights inside the house seemed to be on as well. She got out of her car, and as she did so, Brody emerged from the Quinn home, descended the porch steps, and walked toward her and his cruiser.

"Evening, Charlie," he said.

"Hello, Brody. Just a friendly visit?"

"I wish. The Quinns fired Tyler Creasy this afternoon. He got angry and made some threats."

"Fired why?"

"It was Creasy who accused Bluestone of stealing gas. Bluestone's in jail now, but the discrepancy between the gas going out and what's been entered in the log-book at the pump continues. It has to be one of the hired men, Creasy or Able Grange. Maybe you know the Grange family. Good people. Given a choice between Able and Creasy, it's pretty easy to figure who the real culprit is."

"No proof though?"

"That's right. So no charges. Marta simply fired Creasy. He maintained his innocence, of course, swore Bluestone set him up."

"Where's Creasy now?"

"Took off before I got here. I'll find him."

"And what?"

"I might hold him until Monday, when court convenes."

"On what charge? It's not a crime to threaten someone, Brody. And you have no real proof of theft."

"I didn't think you were fond of Tyler Creasy."

"I loathe the man. We're talking the law here."

"Relax, Charlie. I just want to make sure he's not drunk and that he's cooled off. What are you doing here so late?"

"I'm hoping to talk with Marta."

"She's inside," he said. He eyed the dim glow in the western sky. "I'd best get started. Night, Counselor."

As Charlie mounted the porch steps, the screen door swung open, and she saw J.P. standing in the light. She'd seen him at his father's funeral, but not up close, and she was amazed at how much he'd grown. What had once been just the willowy look of a kid was filling out with the definitions of the man he was becoming. He probably would never reach the full physical stature of Jimmy Quinn, and he didn't have his father's Irish look either. He more resembled his mother and the dark southern Germans from whom she was descended.

"Evening, Miss Bauer," he said.

"Hello, J.P. I wonder if I might speak with your mother."

"Sure. Would you like to come in?"

"Any chance she might be willing to come out? I'd like a private talk."

"I'll get her." He paused a moment, as if wrestling with something, then he said, "Thank you for helping Noah. No way was he responsible for what happened. He stood up to my father, but he didn't kill him."

"How do you know that?"

"Because I know Noah. Because I trust him."

He left her and Charlie settled in the porch swing, where she'd sat so recently with the girls. What a lovely memory that was, of the burned cinnamon bread and the making together of another loaf. The screen door opened quietly, and Marta joined Charlie on the porch. Only the day before, her husband had been buried, but to Charlie she looked surprisingly well. There was color in her cheeks and light in her eyes. She still walked as if she were made of fragile elements, and when she sat beside Charlie, she did so with care. She looked to where the line of trees that marked the Alabaster had turned hard and dark against the powdery blue that was all the light left to Black Earth County. Crickets chorused in the yard. The heat of the day had given way to a cooling breeze, and the stars as they emerged were like tiny, solitary ice crystals.

"I love summer nights," Marta said with a sigh, as if she'd already greeted Charlie and they'd been talking for hours. She settled against the back of the swing and smiled dreamily. "I have taken my medication," she said. "It makes me woozy."

"I hear it's been a hard day."

"We've had our share of those lately. I want to thank you for helping my girls the other day. They told me of your kindness."

"It was my pleasure, Marta."

"They also told me that you wanted to speak with me. About Noah. Is that why you're here?"

"Yes. I'm sorry for the late hour."

She waved it off. "I will be fine for a while. What would you like to ask me?"

"How is it that you came to be married to Jimmy?"

"Ah." She closed her eyes as if gathering her thoughts. "Some women marry for love. The lucky ones, I have always thought. The rest, we marry from necessity."

"Would you tell me about it?"

"That was a long time ago." She smiled in a dreamy way. "I was just a girl, really. I came because there was great trouble in my homeland.

Hitler. We were not Jewish, but my parents were both academics and outspoken, and so we were all at risk. My mother's cousin was Jimmy's first wife, Gudrun. She was very ill and needed help taking care of her husband and children. It was seen as a way to ensure my safety and also help the family here. So I came. Just sixteen at the time. I didn't even speak English. Gudrun died a short time later. And a few months after that, I married Jimmy."

"Not out of love, I take it."

"It was marry him or go back to Germany, where things were much, much worse. Communication with my family had ceased. After the war, I learned that they'd all been killed. I was alone with Jimmy." She smiled. "There was Patrick, of course, who'd come early in the marriage. He was a godsend."

"Terry and Fiona? What about them?"

"They left as soon as they were able. Married and left. Jimmy was not an easy man to live with."

"I have something I need to ask you, Marta. It's difficult but it has to be done."

"Go ahead."

"When you first came from Germany to help with the children, Gudrun was very ill, you said."

"With the same disease that afflicts me. The doctors say there may be a hereditary factor."

"A man has needs. As a woman, you know that."

Marta waited. If she'd been less sedated, she might have tensed, but as it was, she simply remained silent. Until she said, "Yes."

"You were only sixteen."

"You should have seen me at sixteen." She laughed, a small sound, then grew quiet again. "It was a part of the bargain."

"Gudrun knew?"

"Gudrun knew."

Charlie had nothing left to ask, and what was there to say?

The screen door creaked open.

J.P. said, "Are you ready to come in, Mom?"

"A few more minutes, Patrick," Marta said. "It's so lovely out here."

"Call if you need me."

"I will."

He went back into the house.

Marta's eyelids were half closed. "He's such a help."

"He's growing into a good man. And handsome, too."

She smiled in that dreamy, drugged way, her eyes fluttering closed, and she said, "Like his father."

Which surprised Charlie. But she realized that what she saw of Jimmy Quinn was always from a place of profound dislike. Objectively, he probably was a handsome man. And there was probably good in him as well. Maybe if you lived with him day in and day out, if you lived with anyone that way, you eventually saw what good was there, no matter how small a measure that might be.

Marta was sleeping now. Charlie rose from the swing and tapped on the screen door. J.P. came in an instant.

"She's fallen asleep," Charlie said. "Would you like some help?"

"No, thanks. We can take care of her, Miss Bauer."

Charlie wanted to ask him if it was hard taking care of the farm and his mother and being the one his sisters looked to for the advice and guidance that a father might have given. If they'd had one. A real one. Ever. Instead, she simply said, "Good night, J.P.," and left him to the duty she knew he would see to well.

CHAPTER THIRTY-NINE

TYLER CREASY WASN'T hard to find. Brody picked him up in the Blue Bonnet Bar & Grill, a little roadhouse dive a few miles east of Jewel, a place the sheriff knew from past experience was one of the man's favorite haunts. Creasy was belligerent, but not so drunk that he gave Brody cause to consider a charge of resisting arrest or assaulting an officer. He went of his own volition, though not quietly. Brody was forced to listen to his ranting all the way back to town. And when, inside the jailhouse, Creasy realized he was going to be occupying the same cellblock as Noah Bluestone, he spat bullets.

"How can you lock me up with that lying murderer?" he shouted. "Bluestone, if I ever get my hands on you, you're dead, you son of a bitch."

Brody closed and locked Creasy's cell door. "Keep it quiet."

"You put me a stone's throw from that Indian trash and then you tell me to be quiet? I'm gonna scream bloody murder, Dern." He balled a fist and thrust it between the bars in Bluestone's direction. "I'll find a way to get back at you, redskin. You and everybody else in this shithole county." He eyed Brody with menace. "I'll make you pay, goddamn it. Every goddamn one of you."

"I'm more than willing to cuff your hands behind your back," Brody told him, "and stuff a sock in your mouth if that's what it takes to keep you quiet. Your call."

Creasy plopped onto the cot in his cell and gave Brody and Bluestone both a killing look.

"Sorry, Noah," Brody said.

Bluestone responded with a shrug.

Brody left the door to the cellblock open. Hank Evans was at the desk. Brody thanked him for his long day of service and told him to go home.

Evans eyed the open cellblock door. "I don't envy you tonight."

"It'll be fine. Creasy'll sleep it off."

The phone rang. It was Gordon Landis.

"That damn Felix Klein is drunk again, Brody," Landis complained bitterly. "He just pissed all over a car out front of my inn. You come and get him or I swear I'll sweep the street with his sorry little ass."

"Don't lay a hand on him, Gordy. I'll be right there."

Brody hung up. "Mind sticking around another half an hour, Hank?"

"You go do what you have to, Brody. Creasy acts up, I know where I can find handcuffs and a sock."

Felix Klein wasn't at the Alabaster Inn. Landis told Brody that Klein had taken off. Even drunk and with those amputated toes, the little man had disappeared into the night like a bat. Brody cruised Main Street and finally spotted Felix inside the Wagon Wheel, sitting at the counter with Angie Madison. He pulled into the parking lot.

"Are you drunk, too?" she asked with a gentle smile as she opened the door to him. "Or just hungry?"

Brody nodded toward Klein. "Sobering him up?"

"He doesn't eat enough," she said. "There's never food in his system, nothing to help soak up the alcohol."

"I've had a complaint, Angie. I'm taking him in."

"Will you let him finish his sandwich first? I'll make one for you, too, if you'd like."

So they sat together, the sheriff, a slowly sobering drunk, and a woman from the bayou country, sharing a little food and the easy company of people who had a common history. It was part of what had brought Brody back to Black Earth County, part of the reason Felix Klein had stayed after his wife passed on, and one of the blessings that Angie Madison had discovered when, through marriage, she'd migrated there. And the Wagon Wheel? It was one of those places that exists everywhere, in which, small though it may be, somehow there's always enough light inside to go around.

ANGIE SAW THEM off, standing at the door. Brody put Felix in the cruiser and walked back to her.

"Are you doing anything tomorrow evening?" he asked.

"Maybe. Why?"

"I'm thinking of asking Hank Evans to cover the jail. I understand the movie at the Rialto's pretty good. Any interest in finding out?"

"With you?"

"That was my plan."

"Is this an official date, Brody Dern?"

"I guess it is."

"In that case, I'd be happy to go." She kissed his cheek, which was rough from a day's stubble.

"Be ready about seven?"

"Absolutely."

She watched them pull away, then she closed and locked the café door. She spent a few minutes cleaning up from the meal she'd prepared for the two men, turned out the lights, and walked to the house. She stopped at the lean-to her son had constructed a week earlier. That skeleton of a lashed-together shelter might have been of great use in the deep woods somewhere. There on the lawn of the little house in Jewel, it was simply further evidence that Scott was growing into his own interests, his own concerns, his own life. A few more years and he would be gone, off to college. She would insist on this, though it would nearly kill her to see him go. And what for her then? She thought of Brody and smiled.

In the house, she turned off the lights Ida had left on for her. She went upstairs, past Scott's bedroom, peeking in the doorway as she passed. He was sound asleep, the thin sheet that covered him barely disturbed. Good, she thought. He still seemed tired from his ordeal on the river. Deep sleep would do him good.

She put on her nightgown, brushed her teeth, and sat down at her desk to write in her journal. She took the key that always hung around her neck and tried to unlock the drawer where she kept the leather-bound books. The drawer was already unlocked. She slid it open. The old journal wasn't there, or the newest one. Her heart did a leap and dive. She frantically scanned the desk and the area around it. Her mind began searching desperately for possibilities. Who could have opened the drawer? Ida? Scott? No, she had the only key, and why would they anyway?

Then she remembered. The night before. The rapping at the front door. How she'd knocked the journals to the floor and had quickly tossed them atop the box of books meant for donation. In all the distraction of Felix Klein's visit, she hadn't put her scribblings away in the drawer afterward. And then she'd asked Scott to give the box to . . .

"Oh, God," she whispered. "Garnet Dern."

THE FIRST ENTRY in the first journal had been made in tentative script when she was twelve years old. It read: *This book is a gift from Mama Farrah. She told me it's my beginning. I asked her the beginning of what? She said my life.*

She wasn't Evangeline then. Her real name was Jolie Rae LeBlanc. And Mama Farrah wasn't her birth mother, but she was, in all ways, Jolie Rae's true mother. Jolie Rae barely remembered her birth mother. The woman her father brought into the house after that, a thin, hard woman named Delia, had been lazy. Or maybe just sick. She'd lain around the old shack on Bayou Rouge and done almost none of the work of seeing to the men, Jolie Rae's four brothers and her father. When the men came back from a day of hunting or fishing the bayous, or from selling crawfish or pelts or gator skin and meat, or drunk from the cockfights, it was Jolie Rae who was responsible for feeding them and cleaning their muddied or bloodied clothing. She'd done it since she was old enough to have memories.

A week after Jolie Rae turned ten, Delia died. Jolie Rae's father went away for a month. He came back with a new wife. She was big, robust, with hair like a wild bonfire and a long, ugly scar across her left cheek from the corner of her mouth to below her ear. She took control of that ratty old shack on Bayou Rouge and the men in it and became the only real mother that Jolie Rae ever knew. She took the ten-year-old girl under her ample wing and gave her an education. Not only in the things she believed every girl needed to know, but a real education. Jolie Rae barely knew how to read, but Mama Farrah badgered Jolie Rae's father mercilessly until he brought back books with him when he went off to sell the bounty he and the boys had reaped from the bayou. Mama Farrah made certain that Jolie Rae read every day and practiced her writing and knew her manners and how to speak to people in a way that might disguise her bayou upbringing. And for her Christmas present the year she turned twelve, Mama Farrah gave Jolie Rae a leather-bound volume of blank pages and told her to write her life every day as she lived it. Jolie Rae had no idea as to the why of all this. Mama Farrah would only say, *Preparing you, child, for something better.*

Which sounded just fine to Jolie Rae, who wasn't looking forward to a life of taking care of her brothers and father and eventually maybe a husband who was just like them. Mama Farrah gave her hope that there might be something else in her future, something better.

She was fourteen the first time one of her brothers tried to seduce her. When seduction didn't work, Andre tried to rape her. She was strong and lithe and fast, however, and escaped that terrible possibility. When she told Mama Farrah what had happened, Andre got the beating of his life. And Mama Farrah made it clear to all of Jolie Rae's brothers that any other such attempts would net them the same result.

She could have survived on Bayou Rouge under the protection and tutelage of Mama Farrah, but when Jolie Rae was fifteen Mama Farrah got sick and took to her bed. The woman with bonfire hair and a long ugly scar and the heart of a lioness lay dying, and Jolie Rae could do nothing to change that. In the eyes of her brothers, who'd been so cowed by Mama Farrah, Jolie Rae could see what would happen once she was alone and unprotected.

Before the end came to her, Mama Farrah called Jolie Rae to her bedside.

Under the cypress by the well, she whispered. *Dig.*

Jolie Rae found a small metal box containing twenty-dollar gold coins. She counted fifteen.

They're yours, Mama Farrah told her. *You've got to go, girl. You've got to leave this place.*

Jolie Rae begged her, said she couldn't leave her there alone with the men of Bayou Rouge.

They won't do anything to me now but leave me be. Which is what I want, Jolie Rae. But I can't rest until I know you're away from here.

Then Mama Farrah gave Jolie Rae a sealed envelope with a name and address on the outside.

Find her, Jolie Rae. She was my mama, like I've been yours. She'll take care of you. She'll ask things of you, girl, things that might seem hard at first, but she won't mistreat you, I promise.

It was the most difficult choice she'd ever made, leaving Mama Farrah to die among those men who did not love her. But it was what Mama Farrah wanted and what Mama Farrah needed in order to pass away with an easy heart. So, in the middle of a night when the moon was huge and full and had turned the water of Bayou Rouge into a silver highway among the cypress, she took one of the flat-bottomed pirogues and poled her way to a new life, taking with her only the gold pieces and her leather-bound journal.

The address was in Houston, Texas, a lovely old mansion on a street lined with oak trees hung with Spanish moss. It took Jolie Rae two weeks to get there. When she knocked on the door, it was opened by a Negro woman, dressed beautifully and with a warm, welcoming smile. Jolie Rae handed her the letter and was ushered inside. She waited in a grand foyer decorated with old paintings. In a few minutes, another woman came to her, a woman much older than Mama Farrah, but dressed more beautifully than any woman Jolie Rae had ever seen.

Farrah? the woman asked.

Jolie Rae told her story, and she could see the sadness in the woman's eyes.

Did she tell you about me, about this place?

Jolie Rae said she hadn't.

Well, child, I'm going start you in the kitchen, teach you how to please a man there. When you're ready, I'll teach you everything else you need to know about men.

For the clientele of Madame Justine's, the name Jolie Rae would not do. She was allowed to choose her own new name, which she took from one of her favorite poems, from a book that Mama Farrah had given her. She called herself Evangeline. Just as Mama Farrah had said, what was asked of her wasn't easy for her to give, certainly not at first, but she was certain that it was better than the life she'd have had on Bayou Rouge. Once she'd learned the duties in the kitchen, Madame Justine had taught her the refinements and the manners of a lady. She was free to read and to think. The men who visited her room were clean and didn't ill-treat her. She found that many of these men appreciated a lively conversation almost as much as the other activities that drew them there.

This was all during the war, which she'd been only remotely aware of on Bayou Rouge. In the house of Madame Justine, the war was always on the lips of the men who visited. Frequently, they were men in uniform, fliers from one of the many training bases. They were young, often handsome, often inexperienced in what the girls of Madame Justine's house offered. In a way, Evangeline considered her work part of their training and also, in a way, a little solace that she could offer before they left to join the war, perhaps never to return.

They fell in love with her, many of them, and one or two asked for her hand. But it wasn't until, near the end, when she met Christian Madison, a boy from Jewel, Minnesota, who'd been assigned to Ellington Field to train as a navigator, that she thought seriously of the offer of marriage. And why him? At the time, she couldn't have said exactly. She was seventeen, a veteran already of a kind of life that most people couldn't understand or accept. Christian was nineteen, and what was ahead of him was nothing but dire possibilities. Yet there was something about him, light and freeing and accepting and forgiving, something that came from a heart that seemed older than nineteen and stronger, somehow, than even Mama Farrah's great heart. It didn't matter to him who she'd been, who she was. He told her that what he saw in her was something good and beautiful. And so she'd said yes. For a brief time, they'd shared a life. Then he'd gone to England, and she'd discovered herself pregnant and had journeyed to Minnesota. It was there, a month before Scott was born, that the telegram from the War Department had come.

SO EVANGELINE MADISON had made her life in Black Earth County, and a good life it had been. Then, in a moment of thoughtlessness, she'd laid her journals down in the worst possible of places and they'd fallen into what Angie feared were the worst possible of hands. And now she sat on her bed, sleepless, fear carving a terrible emptiness in her belly as she waited for the long dark of that night to end.

CHAPTER FORTY

AT FIRST LIGHT that Sunday morning, Angie Madison left the house and walked to Saint Ignatius. She tried the doors, but they were locked at that early hour, so she waited on the front steps. Although she often attended church on Sundays—Calvary Lutheran on the other side of town—she wasn't much of a praying woman. She'd become Lutheran when she joined the Madison family, all of whom had been baptized and raised in that denomination. On Bayou Rouge, she'd had no formal religion. When Mama Farrah came into her life, the woman had brought with her a Bible, but she'd used it mostly as a tool to teach Jolie Rae to read. She never suggested that it was necessarily a guide for anyone to live a life by. What Jolie Rae had read in the Bible remained just stories to her. And praying? In a way, it was like singing. It made her feel better sometimes, but it didn't change a hard thing and she didn't really believe anyone was listening. What she believed was that goodness and badness came out of people because of how they were treated. And if you wanted goodness from others, that's what you let come out of you. And the badness? Well, sometimes it slipped out, too, because no one was all one thing or another, but you forgave yourself when you were not who you wanted to be and you did the same with others. It was a pretty simple way of being, but it was one she could understand and believe in and follow.

She watched the sun rise over the low hills that formed the eastern edge of the Alabaster River Valley. Then she saw the light come on in the kitchen of the rectory next to the church. She knocked at the back door and Father O'Gara answered. He knew her; everyone in Jewel knew Angie, had eaten at the Wagon Wheel, had been won over by her food and her easy manner and the exotic Cajun accent that ghosted through her speech. She explained that one of the books she'd donated to the charitable drive of the women of Saint Ignatius had been a mistake and that she needed to get it back. Did he know where the boxes of books were being stored? Was it possible for her to look for the book?

The priest unlocked the door to the church gymnasium, which was attached to the classroom annex and was where the donations were being stored. She'd packed her books in one of the cardboard boxes left from a delivery to the Wagon Wheel, a Heinz 57 box, and she'd thought it would be easy to locate. Unfortunately, the citizens of Jewel had been depressingly generous, and the whole west wall was stacked high and deep with boxes and bags and wooden crates and anything else that could hold books.

"What are we looking for?" the priest asked.

She told him about the Heinz 57 box.

"You take this end, I'll take the other," he said. "I'll give a holler if I find it."

She felt guilty pulling the priest into this search. The boxes and bags and crates were numerous and heavy, and even across the length of the gym floor she could hear the old cleric grunt and wheeze as he lifted and moved them and bent and peered. But her desperation overwhelmed her conscience.

Nearly half an hour of digging, and she was almost to the place where she and the priest would meet. She'd given up hope by then and was moving simply to finish the task. Her mind was already going over all the consequences of that thoughtless moment when she hadn't put her journals back into the drawer under lock and key. And she found herself marveling at the way disaster could hit you like a cartoon anvil falling from the sky.

That's when the priest called out, "Eureka!"

She dropped the paper bag she'd lifted, and the books inside spilled out over the box beneath. She ran to the priest, who was, indeed, cradling the Heinz 57 box in his arms and beaming through a stream of sweat that ran down his reddened face.

"Oh, Father, thank you," she said, sounding ridiculously Catholic to herself, but in her gratitude, she would have converted in an instant.

The priest set the box on the polished gymnasium floor. Angie knelt and opened the cardboard flaps. The journals weren't there.

"So," the priest said brightly. "Success?"

She lifted a hardcover copy of Margaret Mitchell's *Gone with the Wind*. "Yes," she said holding the novel up for him to see. "Thank you."

He smiled but looked a little confused. "If you don't mind me asking, what's so special about that book?"

"It was given to me by my husband," she said. Which was a lie, horrible in many respects, not the least of which was that, in her deception, she'd invoked the name of a sweet boy long dead. But she didn't want the priest to feel that all his difficult effort was in vain.

"And now the book is in the hands where God always meant it to be," he said.

Maybe he was right, Angie thought. Maybe all the good that had come into her life had been meant only to prepare her for this moment and all the terrible ones to follow. What did she know of God and his intentions? What did anyone?

She thanked the priest for his help and walked back to the Wagon Wheel. It was seven o'clock. The streets were empty and, except for the ubiquitous singing of the birds, quiet. She walked through long early shadows and through sunlight that, on any other day, would have made her heart leap. She didn't notice at all the beauty of the morning.

On Sundays, the diner didn't open until noon. But Ida was already there, preparing breakfast for the men in jail. Angie stood at the screen door, listening to her mother-in-law at work. Ida was a happy woman, always humming to herself. That morning she was humming "I Got Rhythm." Angie stepped in, and Ida turned, smiling.

"Out for an early walk? It's a glorious day."

"A walk," Angie said. "Yes."

Ida came to her and peered at her face. "Are you all right? You don't look well."

"Just a little trouble sleeping last night."

Ida put the back of her hand to Angie's forehead, as she might have if Angie were a child, her child. "No fever. But maybe you should go on into the house and lie down, rest up."

Angie thanked her and started out. She ran into Wendell Moon, coming in to get the kitchen prepared for later. He, too, was stopped by her appearance.

"Girl, you look like you been run over by a train. You okay?"

She told him she was, then went to the house and upstairs and sat at her desk, staring at the elm tree in the front yard, where morning sunlight dappled the branches.

She could already feel the anvil falling.

CHAPTER FORTY-ONE

SUNDAY MORNING, SCOTT Madison brought breakfast for four men: the three in lockup—Bluestone, Creasy, and Felix Klein—and Brody Dern. It was a pan of Ida's egg bake. He also brought a big thermos of strong, black coffee. And he brought one other item that had nothing to do with food: a small branch broken off a cottonwood tree.

Brody helped Scott divide and plate the egg dish and pour the coffee, and he oversaw the serving of the meal to the three men. Noah Bluestone asked Brody if it would be okay to take the cottonwood branch Scott had brought. Brody leaned against the doorway of the cellblock, arms crossed, and said, "All right."

"I need one more thing, Sheriff," Bluestone said. "A sharp knife."

Brody considered the request, the man who'd made it, and the boy. He said, "Step away from the cell, Scott."

The boy took a step back. Brody reached into his pocket and brought out a folded barlow knife. He handed it to Bluestone through the bars. Creasy gave a snort of disbelief but said nothing. Bluestone drew out the blade and carefully cut the thin cottonwood branch in two. He folded the blade and handed the knife back to Brody.

"Take a look at this," Bluestone said. He turned the cut end of the branch toward the boy. "See the star?"

There it was, inside the branch, dead center. A dark, five-pointed star. Brody could see it, too.

Scott's eyes grew large with wonder.

"There's a story my people tell about that star," Bluestone said. "They say that all the stars in the sky are actually made inside the earth. Then they seek out the roots of cottonwood trees, where they patiently wait. Inside the branches of the cottonwoods, they're dull and lightless, like you see here. When the Great Spirit decides that more stars are needed, the wind shakes the branches of the cottonwoods, and the stars are released. They fly up and settle in the heavens, where they shine and sparkle and become the luminous creations they were always meant to be." Bluestone looked seriously at the boy. "Do you know why I wanted to tell you this story?"

Scott said, "No."

"When you saved that girl, I told you that you'd received a gift. The gift is like this star at the center of the cottonwood. It's inside you now. Someday, when you need it, it will come out, like the stars when the wind shakes the cottonwood trees, and it will shine for you, well and truly."

The boy seemed to think about that.

"What a load of horseshit," Creasy said.

"It's a wonderful story," Felix Klein piped in. "Your people are wise, Noah."

"His people have always been thieving, lying, murdering sons of bitches," Creasy said.

"That's enough," Brody said.

Scott said, "Can I keep the cottonwood?"

"Of course." Bluestone handed the cut branch through the bars.

Brody said, "Eat up, boys. Food's getting cold."

CHARLIE HAD CALLED Sam Wicklow on her return from Des Moines the previous day and had made arrangements to meet with Noah Bluestone at eleven on Sunday morning. When she arrived, Brody had already released both Tyler Creasy and Felix Klein. He'd let Creasy go because there were no real grounds for holding him. He'd never actually charged Klein with anything, just got him to a place where he could sober up. Brody sent him off with the understanding that the little man would abstain that Sabbath Day from drinking alcohol, that he'd eat decently and would apologize to Gordon Landis for his transgression. Felix had solemnly sworn he'd faithfully comply with all these conditions.

Brody brought a chair for Wicklow and locked him and Charlie in the cell with Bluestone, then left them alone. Charlie wasn't at all certain how things would go.

"Thanks for agreeing to talk to me, Noah," Wicklow said.

Bluestone said, "*Hihanni waste.*"

"He honnay washtay?" Sam gave him a bewildered half smile. "I'm afraid I don't understand."

"Exactly my point," Bluestone said. "I've lived in a white man's world all my life. But you have never lived in mine. It's like hearing a foreign language and not knowing any of the words."

"Was that Sioux you spoke?"

"It's a greeting. Charlie says you want to write a book."

Wicklow nodded. "I don't know much yet. It will be about this area, about its history, its people. All of its people."

"Why?"

"Why will it be about these things?"

"Why write it at all? Who cares?"

"I care. It doesn't matter to me if no one else does. I want to try to get at the truth of things I believe are important. I suppose if I were a painter, I'd use canvas. But I'm a writer, so I use words. Does that make sense?"

"You're really going to publish that editorial you wrote?"

"Yes."

"In the old days, they'd tar and feather you. Or worse."

"It's not the old days, Noah. Things are going to change, and I want to be part of making that happen."

Bluestone studied him in the way he might have a piece of land in order to figure what would grow best if he planted seed. "Tell me what you want to know."

"What was it like growing up Sioux in Black Earth County?"

"First off, I'm Dakota. Sioux, yes, but Dakota Sioux. Other Sioux are Lakota or Nakota. There are differences, but to white people it's all the same. So call me Dakota."

"All right. What was it like being Dakota here?"

"Have you read Anne Frank's diary?"

"I have."

"Then you have everything you need."

"Are you saying that's what it was like? Trying to hide?"

"There aren't many full-blood Dakota left in this county and most do their best to look white. It's just too hard to be Indian, obviously Indian. So we cut our hair, wear the clothes everyone else wears, go to church on Sunday. Art Garrison owns the feed store in Jefferson. Bob Odegard drives forklift out at Peterson's Concrete. Maggie Green teaches kindergarten at Morningside. You'd hardly notice them on the street. And there are others, not necessarily full-blood. I could name a dozen who'd rather cut their throats than admit they've got Indian blood in them. Because what happens when you show you're Indian? You get called all kind of names. You get beat up maybe. Hell, you even get arrested for murder. There's hatred in a lot of hearts here. It goes way back."

"You could have stayed away, but you returned," Wicklow pointed out.

Without hesitation, Bluestone said, "In spite of everything, it's home."

"Are you saying you love this place, then?"

"A big part of growing up here was working the land with my father. I loved that. He was a good man, kind, strong. He taught me to pay attention."

"To what?

"Everything. The beauty of it all. The way the earth smells wet and raw when it's first turned in the spring or after a summer rain. How the wind bends a field of tall grass into a moving sea. The creak and moan of trees, like they're talking to one another, or to us if we listen. Everything about the river, the Alabaster. I grew up fishing it, swimming it, watching it flood the fields again and again. My father had great respect for that river. He had great love for the land that he tended, and so do I."

"Why work for Jimmy Quinn? Do you love his land, too?"

Those dark eyes, which had been focused on the blue sky outside the cellblock window, shifted to Wicklow. "A lot of white folks in these parts, their ancestors were killed in what your history books call the Great Sioux Uprising. In schools, they teach that the Dakota were savages, that we rose up against our neighbors and slaughtered them. The only thing the history books don't have is a photograph of John Wayne leading a cavalry charge against Little Crow."

"The Sioux—Dakota—here probably have ancestors killed by whites."

"But the Dakota didn't win that war. In the end, a war is always about who wins. My people had no chance. It doesn't matter that they had every reason to be angry and desperate. They'd been lied to, cheated, starved, their land and everything on it stolen. So they fought. And they lost. But the history has been written by the whites. In Black Earth County, it's the whites who believe they were set on unfairly, cruelly, and have the right to carry all that hatred in their hearts.

"You asked why my father and I worked for Quinn. It's because there was a time no white person in this county would hire an Indian. It was that way when I was a kid. But Quinn would. The man had his reasons, I know, and they weren't about tolerance and being Christian. The bottom line was that he paid my father and he paid me, and we needed the money. My mother was real sick and required treatments. It was Quinn's money that paid for those treatments."

"One of your ancestors first owned the land Jimmy Quinn's family owns now. That's true, isn't it?"

"We have never owned land."

The answer seemed to confuse Wicklow. "You own that farmstead outside town, don't you?"

"Do you know what Crazy Horse said? He said, 'How can anyone own the land we walk?' It's like owning the air we breathe. I have a white man's document that says I own the land, but that's not how I feel about it."

"All right. But this ancestor of yours, he farmed, didn't he?"

"His name was Takoda. It means 'friend to everyone.' He was my great-great-grandfather. He understood the white ways and saw the future and knew everything was changing for the Dakota. He farmed, farmed well."

"I've heard that Quinn's family stole the land he farmed. Is that true?"

"I can only tell you what I've been told. Takoda, as his name implied, had many white friends. When he learned that the intent of some Dakota was to kill white settlers, he left his wife and children and went to spread the warning. He never came back. His family was among those rounded up and sent to Fort Snelling. And then the trials began. You're a lawyer, Charlie. You know the truth about those trials?"

She knew only too well, and although it was long ago, that cruel miscarriage of justice still made her angry.

Wicklow said, "What do you mean?"

"After the army brought the war to an end," Bluestone explained, "they rounded up every Dakota they could and marched them to Fort Snelling, up at Saint Paul. A military commission tried those accused of killing white settlers. They were mostly warriors. They weren't allowed defense counsel or witnesses to testify in their behalf. The trials were shams that resulted in the death sentence for over three hundred men. Abraham Lincoln commuted the sentence of all but thirty-nine. At the last minute, one of these warriors was granted a reprieve.

"So, at ten o'clock in the morning on December 26, 1862, thirty-eight

Dakota men stood together on an enormous scaffolding constructed for the occasion, the largest legally sanctioned mass execution in American history. At a given signal, the warriors dropped to their deaths at the same moment. A crowd of spectators estimated at four thousand had gathered to watch and to cheer."

Although Bluestone recounted this tragic history in almost a monotone, to Charlie it felt as if a great stone had been laid on all their hearts, and a long silence followed.

At last, Bluestone went on. "After the executions in Mankato, Takoda's family was shipped off to North Dakota. Years later, they made their way back, but the soil they'd broken and the house and barn they'd built, all that had been taken over by Quinn's ancestors, documents filed legally. So my great-grandfather settled on a small parcel of land too wet and too rocky to be attractive to white farmers. He made a life there, where the house I live in sits. It's not an unusual story. Most Dakota in Minnesota lost everything."

Wicklow said, "Did you ever wonder if it might have been Quinn's great-great-grandfather who killed yours?"

"That speculation has been made from time to time by lots of folks here. To me it's never much mattered."

Charlie had been silent, but now she spoke, addressing an issue that had been puzzling her no end. "You told Scott Madison that a good man died on Inkpaduta Bend, a man worthy of respect. Frankly, it surprises me that you'd think about Jimmy Quinn in that way."

"I didn't."

"Then why did you say it?"

"I wasn't talking about Quinn."

"Who then?"

"Takoda."

"I don't understand. You said he went away to warn the settlers and never came back."

"I didn't say he was never found, Charlie. Word reached his wife that she would find his body on what was even then called Inkpaduta Bend. She went with her children, my great-grandfather and his sister. They found his body hanging from a cottonwood tree. He'd been tortured, mutilated. They cut him down and took him home and buried him. Then they were taken themselves. It was never clear who'd killed him, the whites or his own people."

"His own people?" Wicklow was clearly surprised.

"It was a divisive conflict, even among the Dakota. To this day, there's often bad blood between the families of those whose ancestors fought the whites and those whose ancestors befriended them. People in Black Earth County swear that you can hear a woman crying out on the Bend. They say it's the ghost of a white woman killed there by Inkpaduta's band. I've heard that crying myself. My family, we've always believed it's the sound of my great-great-grandmother weeping for her dead husband. Want to know something strange? It's a sound I've heard in a lot of the places I've been where people were killed."

"You've seen a lot of war," Wicklow said. "When did you leave Black Earth County to join the Marines?"

"Nineteen thirty-nine. I was twenty."

"If your father needed you to help earn money for your mother's treatments, why did you take off?"

"My mother died. Doesn't surprise me that you don't remember. Never any mention of it in the *Clarion*."

"I'm sorry," Wicklow said.

Bluestone shrugged off the apology. "Water under the bridge. After that, there was nothing holding me here."

"What brought you back, Noah?" Charlie asked.

He thought about this, and while he did, his dark eyes studied that patch of blue sky at the end of the cellblock. "It was time to come home," he finally said. "That's all. It was time."

"To a place where people hate you?"

"This county's got no monopoly on hate, Charlie. I came back because of the land, because of my good memories of it, because it's in my blood, I suppose."

Brody stepped into the cellblock and said, "I've got a call to go out on. Sam, Charlie, I need you both to leave."

Wicklow had been taking notes on a little pad. He closed it and put it in his shirt pocket, along with the pencil he'd been using. "I'd like to talk with you some more, Noah, if you're willing."

"I'm not going anywhere soon," Bluestone said. "And as long as we stick with the past."

Brody unlocked the cell door. Charlie and Wicklow walked out. Hank Evans was on duty at the sheriff's desk and he gave them a hearty "Good morning."

Brody locked the door to the cellblock. "Sorry I had to cut you short in there, Sam."

"Okay if we come back sometime?" Wicklow asked.

"If Bluestone's willing."

Charlie and Sam Wicklow left the jailhouse together and stepped into the late morning sunshine. Wicklow stood a moment, hands in his pockets, leaning a little on his good leg.

"You okay, Sam?" Charlie asked.

"I've heard it, too," he said.

"What?"

"The crying where people have died. During the war. Faint, coming in on a soft wind over a patch of jungle that had been obliterated, all stumps and charred vegetation and bodies torn apart. I chalked it up to frayed nerves. But it wasn't. I knew it even then." He looked back at the jailhouse. "I'm sure he's killed people, Charlie, but that man's no murderer."

"Going to put that in your book?"

"If you're any good at what you do, maybe I won't have to."

CHAPTER FORTY-TWO

SUNDAY DINNERS WERE always the same. Brody arrived at the Dern farm a little before one. Sean Cassiday, Brody's brother-in-law, and Tom were on the front lawn with the kids playing touch football. They called to Brody to join them, but he begged off for the moment, citing his desperate need for some ice water first.

He found the women in the house, in the final stages of preparing dinner. His sister, Amy, kissed him on the cheek and told him to stay out of the way. His mother said he looked too thin and that this whole Jimmy Quinn mess was wearing on him. Garnet gave him a terse hello and a mysterious look that he couldn't interpret.

When he went back outside, the game was over, and Tom and Sean were sitting in chairs in the shade of the porch. Brody joined them. They asked about the Quinn case, and he filled them in on what he could, which wasn't much more than they'd already heard through gossip.

"Got to tell you, Brody," Tom said. "I thought Terry Quinn might've had something to do with his dad's death. That's why at Jimmy's funeral I told you about him stealing the land out from under his son. Thought it might be a motive. You ever follow up on that?"

"Right there in the cemetery. I asked Terry where he was the night his father was killed. Turned out he had a rock-solid alibi. He was sitting up all night with a cow who was calving. Difficult situation, and their local vet was there with him a good portion of the night. I confirmed it with the vet. Terry wasn't one bit happy about being a person of interest, even for a day. I'm pretty sure I'm at the of top his shit list."

"No doubt," Tom said. "I heard he's looking to come into a lot of that property Jimmy left behind, but the whole of Jimmy's own farm is going to J.P. Is that true?"

"I heard the same," Brody said. "As far as I know, it's still just a rumor."

"I could have predicted," Tom said.

"Oh?"

"Never heard Jimmy Quinn say one good word about Terry. Always running him down."

"I don't remember that."

"You were younger. Noah and Terry were my age, same class in school. Let me tell you, there was bad blood between those two from the moment Noah started helping his dad work Quinn's land. I remember sometimes after church listening to Jimmy Quinn cut into his son. But, you know, when it came to Noah, Jimmy never had a bad word to say. Back then, anyway."

"Why?"

"I always figured Noah was the kind of kid Jimmy wanted his own son to be. Athletic. Hardworking. Iron in his constitution. Terry? Now there was a kid hard for anyone to like."

"Hasn't changed much," Brody said.

"I know. But cut him some slack. It had to be tough growing up always being compared unfavorably to another boy."

The children ran past the porch in a game of tag and the men paused for a moment in their conversation to watch.

Tom said, "Dad was always telling me I should be more like you, Brody, live a little, be willing to take chances."

Which caught Brody completely by surprise. "I never heard him say that."

"That's because he said it to me. He probably didn't want you to hear. You gave him a hard time, sure, but you were always your own man. He respected that."

Brody turned to his brother. "Hell, Dad was always telling me I should be more like you."

Tom nodded, looked wistful. "You could have used a little more balance probably. You always went headlong into everything. Reckless, I thought then."

"And now?"

Tom stared a long time out of the shade of the porch across the sun-drenched fields he tended every day. "You want to know something, Brody? I always imagined that I would be the hero, the one coming back from war with all the medals. But someone had to run the farm and that was never going to be you."

Amy pushed open the screen door and said, "Dinner's ready, boys." Then she called to the children.

SUNDAY DINNER WITH his family was always a lively, noisy affair, but this day Brody was quiet. When the meal was finished, his mother said to Garnet and Amy, "Girls, would you mind cleaning up today? I'm going to take a walk. Brody?" She beckoned him toward the door.

They strolled the lane between the barn and outbuildings, then between the fields of young corn and soybeans. Beneath the broaden-ing leaves and rising stalks lay the rich soil from which the county took its name, and the beauty of all the fresh green against the bed of deep, black earth on that sunny afternoon made Brody's heart ache for the kind of peace it seemed to promise.

"Tom and Sean, they're good with the kids," he said.

"The kids love it when the men'll play with them," his mother replied.

"Dad never did that with us."

"That's not true. He played ball with you and Tom all the time."

"When we were just kids, maybe."

His mother stopped and turned to him. Her face was sunstruck, hard gold, but her eyes were soft. "You were the one who pulled away, Brody. Your dad, he just couldn't understand it. Hurt him."

"Dad?"

"He loved you."

"He loved Tom."

"Not more than you. Or less. But you, well, he knew you needed him more than Tom did. He just didn't know how to help you. You were so angry. Your dad and me, we used to lie in bed at night and talk about it. I'd tell him to be patient, that you'd come around. And you did. But by then he was gone."

"When did I come around?"

"When you returned from the war. You were different. I didn't see the anger anymore, but you'd become quiet. And you've stayed that way. We've never talked about it, the war, you and me. But if you wanted to, I'd listen."

Brody knew if he told her the truth, spilled his heart, what he offered might break hers.

"Thanks, Mom. I'm okay," he said.

They walked on until they reached the creek and the little wooden bridge that spanned it.

"I was remembering the other day when you and that band you were with—what were they called?"

"Sons of the Prairie."

"That's it. Sons of the Prairie. I was remembering when you used to play at the county fair. Don't know what brought it to mind. I remember those country tunes. Roy Acuff, Bob Wills. You were good. Shall we sit?"

The bridge was an ancient but sturdy construction. His mother sat with her feet dangling above the run of creek water. Brody sat beside her. He could hear far away the hum of some piece of heavy farm equipment, which had always been for him part of the voice of that land and part of its song. In a way, it was what had brought him back to Black Earth County, the knowledge that despite the horror he'd seen and the horror he himself had created, this place went right on singing its old, old song.

"When are you coming home, Brody?" his mother asked.

"I am home."

"You're here in Black Earth County, but I've never got the feeling you came home, not completely. There's some part of you that you left somewhere else. It must have been real bad."

"What?"

"The war."

"Yeah, Mom, it was real bad."

"I wish you'd tell me about it. I've asked you again and again, but you always say the same thing, that it's something I don't really want to hear. When you hurt, Brody, I hurt. That's the way it is with people you love, especially your children."

Brody looked down at the creek, at the rivulet of reflected sky. "I'm not who you think I am, Mom."

"Oh, I know who you are, Brody. I know things about you that you think no one does."

He glanced at her, wondering what she meant exactly.

"I know, for instance, there never was a woman in Worthington. No schoolteacher named Lilah."

Oh, God, he thought. This was about Garnet and him. She knew. She knew everything.

"I've wanted to ask you something for a while," she went on. "Are you . . . ?"

She hesitated, and he tensed, afraid that all those lies on which his life was built were about to come tumbling down around him.

"Are you homosexual, Brody? Because if you are, it's all right. I'd still love you with all my heart."

THE RIVER WE REMEMBER

"Homosexual?" He laughed, laughed in relief. "No, Mom, I'm not homosexual."

"Then why don't you have a girl?"

"I just haven't found the right one yet."

"What about Angie Madison? I hear you've been seeing her. I've always thought she was a nice girl."

"Could we talk about something else, Mom?"

"All right." She put a hand gently on his leg. "Tell me about the war, then."

Which was something he wanted to do. He wanted to tell someone. Wanted to let go of the crushing weight of all those memories that Jimmy Quinn's death had dredged back up. Wanted to be done with it. Wanted it known to everyone exactly what he was. A liar. A coward. A murderer.

"Tell me," she said again, so quietly it could have been the wind speaking.

THE WORST HAD begun long after he'd entered the war itself. He'd already fought his way across North Africa and become inured to the sight of bodies and half bodies and burned bodies lying beside the roads like things discarded in thoughtless haste. He'd seen men whose names and stories he knew well torn apart by hot shrapnel or machine-gun fire and all that they were and all that they'd hoped to be spilled out there with their blood and entrails on sand and stone for the desert scavengers to feast on. He'd moved beyond the point where he thought of pulling the trigger of his BAR as the slaughter of other human beings. He was good at what he did, and what he did was kill. But the worst began after his second wounding, when he was convalescing in an Allied hospital near Constantine, Algeria. He'd already been awarded a Silver Star and now his second Purple Heart.

Whatever it was that had driven him to take so many chances was still eating at him inside when he heard about a call for volunteers for a new outfit that was going to fight the Japanese in Southeast Asia. He knew about desert heat and fighting on bare sand and rock. He wondered what it would be like to fight under the cover of jungle in a place where water was plentiful. He knew what it was to fight the Germans and the Italians. Were the Japanese a different kind of enemy? In the end, he thought, what the hell, did it really matter? He was there to fight.

He trained in India, in northern Assam near the town of Nazira, at the base camp for what was called OSS Detachment 101. Their mission was to infiltrate Burma, gather intelligence, organize resistance, and in general, do all they could to harass the Japanese, who'd easily taken control of that country and were threatening the vital links between the Allies in India and Chiang Kai-shek's Nationalist government in southern China. By the time he was sent into Burma in the last week of December 1944 with William "Mac" McMillan and a Kachin Ranger who called himself Ho, he'd been on a dozen missions. Their objective this time was to assess the Japanese strength in the Hukawng Valley, in preparation for an objective to further clear the way for construction of an important overland link with China, what would come to be called the Ledo Road.

Things went horribly wrong from the beginning. Three days out, deep in jungle near the Torung River, the Kachin Ranger, their guide and interpreter, was killed in a skirmish with a small Japanese patrol. McMillan was wounded badly in his right thigh, but Brody managed to get him safely away. Over the course of the next week, as they tried to navigate their way back toward India, they encountered increased enemy patrol activity and were forced time and again to alter their route. Worse, McMillan's leg wound became gangrenous. Mac could barely walk, and they both knew that if he didn't get treatment soon, there was no hope for him.

Their last night together they huddled under an overhang of rock along a small river. In his lucid moments, Mac urged Brody to leave him and go on alone. But Brody would have none of that. Mac pointed out that if they were both captured, he'd be killed anyway and Brody would probably be tortured for information and end up dead or in a Jap POW camp, which was maybe worse than dead. The poison in Mac's blood caused him to burn with fever, and he'd begun lapsing into periods of delusion in which he cried out to people Brody could not see. It was in one of these periods that Brody heard the voices of a Japanese patrol moving along the far bank of the river. Horrified, he watched as the soldiers set up camp for the night almost directly across from the overhang. They built a fire, and Brody could see their faces in the flickering light. He tried to keep Mac quiet, but the man was out of his head, beyond reason. Brody lay on top of him and clamped his hand over Mac's mouth, pressed himself hard against his comrade to silence him. Mac fought desperately with what strength he had left. Brody pushed harder and harder, and finally Mac went limp. But still Brody didn't let up on that killing press, hating himself for what he was doing even as it was done.

When it was over, he cradled Mac's body a long time in his arms. He listened to the soldiers across the river, talking and laughing in a language he couldn't understand. They didn't sound like monsters. But because of them, he'd done a monstrous thing, and he hated them for it. In the early hours, as the jungle filled with the noise of birds and the sky hinted at gray, he left Mac's body beneath the overhang and sneaked back into the jungle, away from the river and the soldiers camped there.

He was lost. Absolutely. For several more days, he stumbled through jungle and struggled up high hills, heading west toward India. He had no food, and though he'd been hastily trained to live off the land, he wasn't, as it turned out, very good at that. His water purification tablets were gone. It was the dry season. There was no rain. He sometimes drank from stagnant, foul-tasting pools, and he began to be sick in every way.

He wasn't sure how long he'd been lost and alone when he woke one morning to find a young girl standing above him. He was too tired and too weak to be afraid. He smiled and said, "Hello."

She was small, Asian in her features. She smiled back at him and spoke in a language that Brody assumed was a local dialect. She beckoned him to follow her. With some difficulty, he rose, and she led him a short distance to a tiny village. The people there took him in, gave him food and water, made gestures for him to lie down on a mat in one of the huts. He thanked them and, for the first time since he'd left Nazira, slept soundly.

He was awakened by a kick to his ribs. He opened his eyes to the sight of two Japanese soldiers, their rifles pointed at his chest. They spoke harshly and gestured for him to get up. He rose, and they ushered him outside, where more soldiers waited. The villagers were gathered there, too, and didn't seem frightened by the soldiers. Among them was the young girl who'd smiled at him and led him, he'd thought, to safety. They all stared at him now, and he understood that he'd been nothing to them but an item for barter.

He was taken on foot to a large clearing at the edge of a river where rows of bamboo huts stood surrounded by barbed wire. Inside, he passed stick-thin men in rags, who glanced up at him and then quickly back down to their labor. He was shoved into one of the larger structures and made to stand in front of a desk while one of the soldiers fetched an officer. The man who came and sat behind the desk and removed his cap was bald. He had a great, amoeba-shaped burn scar across the left side of his face. His eyes reminded Brody of the black cutworms that, back home in Minnesota, could destroy a farmer's entire corn crop. With him was another man, not a soldier. He was, Brody would learn later, Burmese. His name was Kyaw. He did the speaking directly to Brody.

"American," he said.

Brody said, "American."

"We don't see many Americans here."

"Doesn't surprise me," Brody said. "You're not very welcoming."

The man spoke to the bald officer in Japanese, and the officer with the worm eyes replied.

"On the contrary," the Burmese man said to Brody. "We are very glad to see you."

And by that, it turned out, the bald man, whose name was Colonel Himura, meant that he believed Brody could supply important information about American intentions in the region. Himura knew about Nazira and OSS Detachment 101, but he wanted to know more. Over the course of the next weeks, he did his best to get what he could from Brody. Which was very little, because all that Brody told him under duress Himura somehow already knew. That didn't stop the Japanese colonel from torturing Brody and continuing the questioning.

In his first few days, Brody was kept from the other prisoners in the camp, tied to a tree, beaten with clubs, burned with cigarettes, threatened with beheading. He was denied food, water. When he was finally cut down, he couldn't walk and was dragged to a hut no larger than a doghouse and thrown inside. He was pulled out at irregular intervals and subjected to more torture, more interrogation.

Eventually, Brody was placed with the other prisoners, who turned out to be Aussie and British. The camp—it was called Shwenwa, after the nearest village—had a small prisoner population, under two hundred men. Every day, those prisoners who weren't already deathly ill were marched out to the river, where they worked breaking and sluicing rock for gold. His new comrades told him they believed Himura wasn't operating in the interests of his home nation but intended to enrich himself. It was grueling, brutal work, and the men, who were fed barely enough to keep them alive, suffered long hours in the humid jungle heat.

Rumors circulated widely about the Allies advancing into northern Burma soon and about orders to kill all prisoners of war before liberation could occur. Like everyone else, Brody slept with the knowledge that, one way or another, he would probably not leave Shwenwa alive.

The day came when all the fears—Brody's and the other prisoners'—were realized. They'd noticed an agitation among the Japanese soldiers that they'd never seen before. Word spread that Chinese and American forces were sweeping down from the north and out of the west, closing in on Shwenwa. That final morning, the men weren't marched out to the river but instead were directed to use their shovels and picks to dig a long trench outside the wire. They were told it would be used in defense of the camp, if necessary. The men bent to their labor, and as they eyed their captors closely, they saw great fear in the faces of the Japanese. When the trench was several feet deep, the men, all two hundred, were ordered to toss away their tools. To their great alarm, they watched the Japanese roll out barrels of gasoline and position them beside the trench.

And the slaughter began. At first, the Japanese soldiers didn't waste bullets. They set upon their prisoners with bayonets. Those men who tried to flee were shot down like dogs. The POWs fought back. Amid the mayhem, the barrels were tipped and gasoline covered the bottom of the trench and was set ablaze. Before the flames reached him, Brody leapt clear of the trench. Immediately a bullet tore into his left calf, and he went down. A Japanese guard was on him in the blink of an eye, bayonet fixed. But someone grabbed the guard from behind and Brody rolled away, free. He was up and running toward the wall of jungle fifty yards away. Behind him, he could hear the screams of men as they burned and the cries of those who were still fighting back and the crackle of rifle fire and then he was in the trees and still running and he didn't stop until he was so far away he couldn't hear the war anymore.

They were true, the rumors. Unit Galahad—Merrill's Marauders—out of India, and two Chinese divisions out of the north, had swept through the region on their way to capturing the important airfield at Myitkyina. Brody stumbled into them, the only piece of luck he'd had in weeks. He led a small force back to Shwenwa, but all they found was a long mound of dirt outside the camp wire. They didn't have to dig deep to hit the charred remains.

—

HE'D LIED WHEN they debriefed him. Lied about Mac and lied about running from that burning trench to save his own skin. In the end, they gave him another medal.

Now, as he sat on the bridge over the small clear stream in the middle of a field he'd dreamed about in the worst moments of the war, he understood, as always, that these were terrible secrets he couldn't share, not ever, not with anyone. He looked at his mother, smiled in a reassuring way, and said, "Don't worry about me, Mom. I'm okay."

He heard the children running down the lane, the sound of their laughter and their voices, high and happy. Before they arrived, his mother said, "I'll know when you're okay. It's a day I pray for."

The children came up the lane, thundered over the bridge, and ran on toward a broad field of alfalfa, beyond which lay a small acreage of trees.

"We're going on a snipe hunt," Jack cried as he passed. "In the woods."

Amy and Garnet came strolling behind. They joined Brody and his mother on the bridge.

"We've been worried about you two," Garnet said.

"No need," Brody's mother said. "We were just catching up. But I guess I'm ready to go back now." She stood up. "Are you coming?" she asked her son.

"I think I'll stay a little longer," he said. "It's peaceful here."

"Want company?" Garnet asked.

"That'd be all right," he said.

"Come on, Amy." Brody's mother took her daughter's hand. "Let's get that strawberry shortcake ready for the kids when they come back."

Garnet sat on the bridge, and her feet dangled alongside Brody's. She rested her hand on his thigh. "I wish we were alone here."

Brody's eyes followed the creek to a place where it curved out of sight between low cornstalks. "We need to talk," he said.

"I don't like the sound of that." She smiled, as if they were both only joking.

"We have to stop, Garnet."

She took her hand away.

"It's Angie Madison, isn't it?" she said.

"No, Garnet. It's the situation. We've been lucky no one's found out. Just so damn lucky. Because it would break this family apart. You know that."

"What I know is that I can't live without you."

"I'm not going anywhere. But this part of our lives is over. It has to be."

"I don't want it to be over."

"Do you love Tom?"

"Of course I do," she said.

"Do you want to hurt him?"

"You know I don't."

"Then we have to stop this."

Now the stone of her face cracked, and she seemed ready to fall apart. "You don't want to hurt him but you're willing to devastate me?"

"I don't want to hurt anyone, Garnet. I'm tired of being afraid of doing just that. We can't go on like this forever."

"Why not, Brody? We're careful. And you love me, you know you do."

"There's so much more to consider than you and me. So much hurt. Let me go, Garnet. Just let me go."

And now she would not look at him. She turned her face away toward the small patch of woods where the children had disappeared. He could tell from the quiver of her body that she was crying. Everything inside him wanted to reach out and hold her, comfort her, to feel the familiar contours of her body against him. It took all his strength to refrain.

At last she seemed to gather herself. She turned to him, her eyes red from weeping, and said, "There's something you should see."

CHAPTER FORTY-THREE

ON THAT FATEFUL Sunday, Angie Madison was like a woman with a terrible fever, drifting in and out of awareness, time lost to her. She worked the Wagon Wheel but walked leaden through her duties, waiting for the world to collapse around her. At five that afternoon, Ida told her to go to the house and get herself ready for her evening with Brody Dern.

"I think I need to call him and cancel," Angie said.

"Are you sick?" Ida asked for the umpteenth time.

"Not sick, no."

"What then?"

"I just . . ." Again, she couldn't answer.

"You're just nervous. Go bathe, clean yourself up, put on something pretty. You'll be fine," Ida insisted and ushered her out the back door of the Wagon Wheel Café.

But all her preparations seemed like playacting, as if she were going through the movements of something that wasn't real. It had always been a dream, she knew, this life she'd been living. She looked at herself in the mirror and saw the aged face of a girl from the bayou country, a girl who, before she met Christian Madison, had given herself to so many men she had finally ceased to count them, almost none of whom she'd remembered. But she could see them now, a legion of ghosts parading naked before her. For so long now that had been another life, had happened to another woman. But the curtain that had hidden her sins was about to be drawn aside. For Evangeline Madison, it felt like Judgment Day.

She heard Scott come in from his work at the diner. He came upstairs and began rummaging in his room. She left her bedroom and stood in his doorway, watching him roll and tie his sleeping bag.

"Where are you going?" she asked.

"I'm spending the night with Del at Fort Beloit, remember? I asked and you said it was okay. We're going out as soon as we've changed the Rialto marquee."

"That's right," she reminded herself. "Can I fix something for you to take to eat?"

"Grandma already made us some sandwiches."

"Oh. Good," she said.

He tried to walk past her, but she stopped him, leaned down, and kissed his forehead.

"Jeez, Mom, I'm not going away forever. It's just an overnighter."

"Be careful," she said.

"You know I will."

He bounded down the stairs and outside, and she returned to her bedroom and her preparations for an evening she'd begun to dread.

The knock at her front door pulled her from her dreary thoughts. It was still too early for Brody, and she considered simply ignoring the visitor, whoever it was. But the knock came again, insistent.

Felix Klein, she thought wearily, and descended the stairs and opened the door.

On the porch stood Garnet Dern.

SCOTT FELT A little guilty about the way he'd secured his mother's permission to spend that Sunday night away from home. She'd clearly been distracted, and he'd purposely asked her in a moment when she seemed completely lost in thought.

He met Del at the Rialto Theater, where they changed the marquee to reflect the next week's new film, *The Vikings*. He and Del had seen the trailer, and both boys thought it looked like a great movie, full of strong, dirty men and lots of sword fighting. It starred Kirk Douglas and Tony Curtis, and when the big Viking ships filled the screen, Del had leaned to Scott and said, "Fuggin' cool."

When they'd finished their work at the theater, they mounted Del's motorbike. Scott shouldered his Boy Scout backpack, in which he'd put his sleeping bag, flashlight, and the sack with chicken salad sandwiches, apples, and cookies his grandma Ida had prepared for their dinner. He'd tied Del's rolled-up blanket on top. They took off for Fort Beloit as the sun hung on the horizon, a tired, bloodshot eye ready to close for the night.

Fort Beloit stood at the river's edge just south of town. It was a re-creation of an enclosure that had been used to protect families just prior to and during the Great Sioux Uprising of 1862. Scott had been inside so many times that it had lost its allure for him. Attached to it, however, was a campground where tourists could spend the night in tents or park their Airstreams and where, on occasion, his Scout troop had practiced their camping skills. The Petersons, who owned the property and ran the attraction, said they wouldn't mind if any of the Scouts wanted to throw out a sleeping bag there beside the river, so long as a site was available. On that Sunday evening, there was plenty of room.

They picked a spot overlooking the river a safe distance from anyone else, bought Cokes at the little concession the Petersons ran, and ate the dinner Ida had prepared. Scott wanted to ask Del more about the true nature of their outing that night, the possibility of actually seeing a naked woman, but he didn't want to appear too eager. He knew this was something that his mother, if she'd had the slightest inkling, would have disapproved of absolutely. In truth, he was a little ashamed of himself for being so ready to be involved in something that seemed not at all in keeping with the "clean and reverent" part of the Boy Scout Law.

But he'd been unable to get rid of the image of the bare slopes of Mrs. Dern's breasts and the lacy white cups of her bra. That single glimpse had engendered a kind of hunger inside him that begged to be fed.

"MAY I COME in?" Garnet Dern said.

Angie stepped back and let her enter. She closed the door, and the two women stood in the simple living room, facing each other across a space empty of any decent purpose Angie could imagine. She didn't allow herself to look at the two journals the other woman held in her hands. Instead, she gazed into Garnet Dern's unreadable eyes.

"Brody was at the farm this afternoon," Garnet said.

"Like every Sunday," Angie said, because everyone in Jewel knew that.

"We had a long talk," Garnet said.

"I'd guess you did."

"Why did you write it down? I mean all of it."

"Because it was the truth. Or the truth of my experience anyway. I thought maybe it would help me understand."

"Has it?"

"I work on that every day, Garnet." Angie didn't really know the woman with the damning journals in her hands, and because she was afraid and defensive, she let fly the one truth about Garnet Dern that she did know. "You're in love with Brody."

Garnet looked surprised, then another look came into her eyes, a look that communicated fear, and in that instant Angie knew the whole truth.

"How long has the affair been going on?" she said.

Garnet's posture changed. She moved to clasp her hands protectively over her chest, but the journals got in the way. "I never . . ." she began.

"How long?" Angie said in a hard voice.

Garnet held rigid for a moment more, then melted. "I've loved him since I was seventeen."

"Yet you married his brother."

"I love him, too. I do." She looked down at the journals. "We all do things in our lives that we'll never really understand. I thought about showing these to Brody. I was going to, in fact."

"But you didn't?"

"No."

"Why not?"

Garnet looked up again, and now Angie believed she saw a softening in all the features of the woman's face, especially her eyes, and believed she could read sadness there. "Did you love Christian Madison?"

"He was sweet and kind and gentle," Angie said. "I loved him as much as I was able in the short time we were married. And in the time since, I've loved him through Scott, if that makes sense to you."

"Do you love Brody?"

"I believe I could."

"Do you think if he knew who you really are he could love you?"

"Only Brody can answer that."

Garnet glanced down at the journals she held. "He deserves to know. But if it came from me, it wouldn't do Brody or me any good. I thought it might even turn him against me. He has a good heart and I know that somewhere in that heart is a love for me. Whatever else I might give up, I don't want to lose that."

Garnet held out the journals.

Angie took them and asked, "Does anyone else know?"

Garnet shook her head.

"If I tell Brody, will that be the end of it?"

Garnet stared at Angie, as if this was a question she wasn't prepared to answer yet. "Tell him," she said at last. "That's all I want."

Garnet turned and reached for the doorknob, in a hurry, it seemed, to be done with this business.

"Thank you," Angie said.

Garnet hesitated, then turned back. "If he wants you, you do right by him, do you understand?"

Angie nodded. "If he wants me."

Garnet Dern walked out the door and closed it behind her.

BRODY DIDN'T COME, not at the time they'd agreed on. Angie sat waiting, worried that Garnet Dern had lied to her and told Brody everything, and now he wanted nothing to do with her. What man would?

He pulled his cruiser to the curb a few minutes after seven. Angie watched him through the front window. He wore dark slacks, a short-sleeved blue shirt, a broad indigo tie. He came up the sidewalk and knocked on the screen door. Evangeline Madison stood frozen and couldn't ever remember having been so afraid.

When his knock wasn't answered, Brody called, "Angie? Ida? Anybody there?"

"Just a minute." Angie took three deep breaths.

Brody smiled as she opened the door. "You look beautiful."

"Thank you."

"Sorry I'm late," he said. "Got a last-minute call I needed to see to. We might miss a few minutes of the show, but we can still make most of it."

"Brody?" Her mouth was so dry that, for a moment, she couldn't speak. "Would it be all right if we skipped the movie? I'd like to go somewhere and just talk."

"Well, sure. That's fine by me. We could talk here."

"No, not here. How about . . ." She thought a moment. "What if we went down by the river and sat for a while?"

"If that's what you want," he said.

He drove the cruiser to a small wayside north of town. There were a few picnic tables and grills and the broad run of the Alabaster. The only other car was a green station wagon that had disgorged a family who stood gathered around a fire they'd built in a grill and were roasting marshmallows. Angie didn't recognize them, and Brody paid them no heed. She left the car and walked to a table near the river. The sun was low in the sky, caught in the branches of the trees on the far bank. Broken sunlight dappled the surface of the water. Angie sat down on the bench of the picnic table.

"I've always wondered," she said as Brody sat quiet and patient beside her, "why this river is called the Alabaster. Alabaster is white."

"Under a full moon, in the right light, it looks pure as snow."

"Doesn't everything . . . in the right light?"

"Something on your mind, Angie? Something you want to say?"

"People can fool you, can't they, Brody?"

"Probably. But only for a while. Their true nature usually slips out. At least, that's been my experience."

"You're such a good person."

"I wouldn't say that."

"That's all I've ever seen. And if what you say is true, if you were something different, I'd know it by now."

Brody didn't reply.

She felt as if she were standing on the edge of a great cliff, trying to gather the courage to leap. She could barely breathe.

"There's something I have to tell you, Brody."

AT FORT BELOIT, the boys had rolled out the sleeping bag and the bed-roll and had lain awhile watching the sun descend. Del told Scott about the book he was reading yet again, *The Naked and the Dead,* and said he thought maybe he'd go into the army as soon as he graduated from high school, make a career of it, like his dad. He punched Scott playfully in the arm and said, "You should have brought your guitar. We could sing 'Kumbaya' and those other songs you Girl Scouts sing around the campfire." He laughed but Scott knew it wasn't malicious.

Then Del looked around carefully and said, "Dig this, Madman." He reached under his shirt and drew out the .22 pistol they'd used in target practice the day before.

"What's that for?" The presence of the gun made Scott nervous, especially there in the campground, with other people so near.

"I thought maybe tomorrow we'd see if we could flush out some rabbits and try our luck."

Target practice was one thing; shooting an animal was something else. Scott didn't push it, but he figured that in the morning he'd find an excuse not to join in the hunt.

When the sun had set and the sky had begun to slide toward a dark, moody blue, Del stood up and said, "Time to go, Madman."

THE WHOLE OF the time she spilled her history, Angie refrained from looking at Brody. She watched the sun drop lower and lower, the light reflecting off the Alabaster in shatters of gold. She heard the doors of the station wagon slap closed and the family drive away, leaving her alone with Brody and the truth of who she was. Brody said nothing. Because she couldn't bring herself to look at him, she had no idea if patience was the reason or horror. She didn't cry. She didn't want to offer Brody anything but the naked truth, because she knew Garnet Dern had been right. He deserved to know, to make his own judgment and decision, and she didn't want to influence him with her tears.

When it was done, she sat and waited. Finally she risked a glance at him.

Now it seemed that Brody was the one who couldn't look. She thought it was over then, anything they might have shared, the life with him she'd briefly let herself imagine. She tried to hold back the tears, but they would not be denied.

"I'm sorry, Brody," she said.

He turned to her, his face a wonder of compassion. "Sorry? Oh, Angie, you've got nothing to apologize for. We do what we have to, all of us. We survive. Do you think I care about all that in the past? That's not who you are now. That's not who you've ever been. Not to me. Not before, not now." He took her hands in his. "To me, you're the Alabaster in moonlight. That's how I'll always see you."

"Oh, God, Brody." She laid her head against his chest, and now her tears were from gratitude and relief and joy.

He held her for a long time that way, then she could feel a change in his body, a stiffening. She drew away.

"What is it, Brody?"

He looked deeply into her eyes, as if searching for the answer to a question he hadn't yet asked.

"Now I have something to tell you," he said, and his own confession spilled forth.

Even after the sun had set and the sky had gone from bruised purple to an indigo full of stars, they talked. There beside the silent flow of the Alabaster River, they split open the darkness inside both of them in which too many secrets had lain hidden.

"I was so afraid, Brody, so sure you wouldn't understand."

"We're all broken. I've heard you say it a hundred times."

"It's that easy?"

"Why not?"

"Garnet knows everything."

"You know about her, too, now," Brody pointed out.

"I wouldn't use it."

"She won't either."

Angie settled in his arms and they watched the Alabaster begin to take on a white evanescence with the rise of the moon.

"Now you know the worst about me, and I know the worst about you," she said. But she felt him tense. "Don't I?"

"There's one more thing, as long we're sharing secrets."

"What?"

"The night we found Jimmy Quinn's body, I destroyed evidence."

"Why?"

He stared at the river a long time. "Holden Caulfield, I guess."

"I don't understand."

"I looked at everything out there on Inkpaduta Bend, and I knew something wasn't right about the way it all sat. In my gut, I knew someone had killed Quinn."

"Why did you destroy the evidence?"

"I couldn't help thinking that there are a lot of good people here who had good reason to hate Jimmy and wouldn't mind seeing him dead. What if it was one of our neighbors? This is the kind of thing that can tear a place apart, Angie. I thought that no one in this whole county would grieve Jimmy Quinn, and if I got rid of evidence that might say it was anything other than a terrible accident or, hell, even a suicide, we could all get back to our normal lives pretty quick, and things could just go on the way they always have. Maybe even a little better without Jimmy, you know?"

"Holden Caulfield out there in that rye field protecting the innocent," she said.

"Something like that."

"Do you think Noah Bluestone really did it?"

"If it wasn't him, it was Kyoko. I don't know the truth of it, but I know Quinn somehow drove them to it. That damn Connie Graff. If he'd just been willing to let it go, let me call it an accident, this would all be over now."

The radio in Brody's cruiser crackled, and they heard the voice of Hank Evans. "Base to Unit One. Do you read me, Brody?"

Brody slid his arms free. "I better take this."

She stood up with him and, for the first of so many times that it would become impossible to count, she kissed him.

"You there, Brody? Come in."

He pulled away reluctantly and went to the cruiser. When he came back, all the softness was gone from him. "We have to go, Angie."

"What's wrong?" she said, frightened by what she saw in his face.

"Trouble," he said. "A shooting out at Noah Bluestone's place."

CHAPTER FORTY-FOUR

THE BOYS FOLLOWED the river south. Scott began to think that they were headed once again for Inkpaduta Bend, but Del turned off before that, at a place where the railroad tracks crossed the river. They dismounted, and Del walked the bike across the trestle and parked it among the trees on the other side of the Alabaster.

"This way," he said and waved for Scott to follow.

The light in the west was mostly memory now. Along the horizon lay a thin strip of red and a few scraps of cloud that were the color of flamingo feathers. Scott could see Fordham Ridge, a dark wall that cut off the view of everything beyond. He followed Del across a field of young corn and slipped through a fence of loosely strung wire. On the far side of the next field stood a small barn and a house and outbuilding. In the gathering gloom, the boys loped to the back of the barn, where Del put his finger to his lips for silence. He opened a narrow door and they slipped inside. The dim twilight offered enough illumination for Scott to see a tractor and tools and the stairs that Del took quietly up to the hayloft. Scott's heart had begun to beat faster as he realized they were trespassing in a way he hadn't considered in his imaginings.

Hay bales stood stacked against a wall of the loft. Del crouched near a dusty window that overlooked a little wooden tower next to the barn.

Atop the tower sat a big plastic container with a spout. A neat, square slab of concrete had been poured on the ground next to the tower.

"What is that?" Scott asked in a whisper.

"A shower," Del whispered back. "Creasy told me about this. Said Quinn blabbed all about it once when they got stinking drunk together. Just watch."

Creasy? Quinn? The names felt dirty to Scott. And then the whole thing felt dirty. He could see the house and the front door and illuminated windows. He thought that someone was in there who felt safe, who had no idea of this trespass. He decided that he wanted no part of whatever it was that Del had in mind.

But by then it was too late. The front door opened. A little slice of lemon-colored light fell across the grass and a shadow entered that light. He watched a woman cross the yard. A dog, an old Saint Bernard, trotted along at her heels. He couldn't see her well in the early dark and through the dusty window, but he could tell that she wore a robe and carried a towel. She approached the little tower, reached toward the barn wall, and an outside light snapped on. He could see her now, clearly, and he recognized her.

He felt like the worst kind of criminal. He wanted to leave, to run, but he knew he couldn't do this without giving his presence away and Del's. He told himself not to look at the wife of the man he'd come to know and admire in the jailhouse in Jewel. But when she slid the robe off her small white shoulders and reached to open the flow of water from the plastic container, he saw her breasts lift and their brown areolas and the dark triangle of hair between her legs, and he couldn't pull his eyes from the sight. He watched her step into the flow of water, take a bar of soap from the little shelf attached to the tower, and lather herself. He watched her hands run over her whole body. He watched long fingers of soapsuds feel their way down the curve in the small of her back. He wanted to look away but could not, and even as he stared, he hated himself for it.

She rinsed completely and turned off the water. As she reached for the towel that she'd hung on a crossbar of the little water tower, Del moved—God knows why—and an old floorboard under his foot collapsed with the loud snap of breaking wood.. The dog looked up, went rigid, and began barking furiously. The woman froze and looked up, too. Scott prayed she couldn't see him in the dark of the loft and through the dusty window. But in the glare of the light on the barn wall, he saw terror on her face, and she turned without bothering to grab her robe and fled toward the house.

The boys raced from the loft. Del went first, thundering down the stairs. Scott was hard on his heels. They hit the dirt floor and were just turning for the back door of the barn when the old Saint Bernard leapt from the darkness and blocked their escape, teeth bared and barking furiously. The boys backed away and the dog came at them. Before he knew what was happening, Scott heard the crack of Del's .22 pistol and the yelp of pain as the dog went down. Del sprinted past the animal and Scott didn't hesitate in following. The boys burst from the barn and sprinted across the fields toward the waiting motorbike and neither of them looked back.

CONNIE GRAFF LAY on a mattress in the bed of his pickup truck, which was parked among the trees along the Alabaster River where he could watch the lane that led to the Bluestone place. He'd done this every night since Noah Bluestone's arrest. He was worried about the enmity abroad in Black Earth County since the murder of Jimmy Quinn. It wasn't just the general concern of a decent man but also the concern of a man who'd taken a deep, almost paternal interest in the young Japanese woman. In this way, he eased his own unsettled mind about her safety.

He was smoking a hand-rolled cigarette and watching the stars emerge above Fordham Ridge when he heard the furious barking followed by the crack of a gunshot. He threw the cigarette away, leapt from the bed of the pickup, and hopped into the cab. He kicked the engine over, swung the pickup onto the dirt lane, and sped to the farmhouse. The light above Bluestone's makeshift shower blazed and there were lights on inside the little farmhouse. Graff parked, grabbed his rifle from his gun rack, ran to farmhouse door, and knocked hard.

"Kyoko! It's Connie Graff! Are you in there?"

A moment later, the lock released and she swung the door wide. She wore a flowered kimono that she clutched about herself. Her eyes were huge and terrified.

"In the barn," she said. "There was someone in the barn when I was showering."

"Stay here. Keep the door locked."

The light above the outside shower gave only a bit of illumination inside the barn. Graff stood in the open doorway a moment, an ear cocked toward the dark, a bullet already chambered in his Winchester. He heard a soft whimpering and he reached for the light switch. When the bulb came on, he spotted the old Saint Bernard lying on the floor, bleeding into the dirt. His first impulse was to see to the wounded animal, but his training pushed him to make certain the barn was not still occupied by the intruder. Kyoko Bluestone had been right to be terrified. Anyone who'd shoot a dog was the worst kind of unpredictable scum.

Graff slowly circled inside the barn, then cautiously mounted the steps to the loft. He moved to the window that overlooked the makeshift shower. He saw the wild disturbance of the dust on the floor there and the broken floorboard and he figured he understood the trespass. He worked at keeping his anger in check, his senses on alert. He left the loft and descended the stairs. He turned out the barn light, crept past the wounded dog, and eased open the door in the back wall. He slipped outside and crouched and let his eyes adjust. He could see the empty field and far away the dark, uneven outline of the trees along the Alabaster. From that distance came the sound of a little motor, like the whine of a mosquito, vanishing into the deepening night.

CHAPTER FORTY-FIVE

BEFORE THEY'D GONE a mile in Brody's cruiser, Hank Evans radioed and redirected Brody to the animal hospital on the west side of town.

"Graff'll explain everything to you there," Evans said.

As they pulled into the parking lot of the animal hospital, the cruiser's headlights swung across Graff's pickup. Brody and Angie found Connie Graff inside the hospital, sitting in the waiting area with Kyoko Bluestone. The old deputy held her hand as a father might have. It was clear the woman had been crying, but now her eyes were dry. Next to the tall, lanky man, she looked small and childlike.

"What happened, Connie?" Brody said.

"Somebody snuck out to the Bluestone place and shot their dog."

Angie sat down in the plastic chair on the other side of Bluestone's wife and laid a hand gently on her arm. "I'm so sorry, Kyoko."

Brody studied Kyoko Bluestone and thought about her alone and vulnerable at the farmstead. "They were just out there to shoot the dog?"

Graff said, "Why don't you tell him everything, Kyoko."

Brody listened to the woman who, only a few days earlier, had sparked in him an unreasonable anger simply because she was Japanese. What he felt now was a different anger, one directed at the kind of man who was cowardly enough to want an eyeful of a naked woman and then shoot her dog.

"You couldn't tell who it was?" he asked.

She shook her head.

"You can't stay out there, Mrs. Bluestone," Brody said. "We need to figure out something different for you until this is all over."

Kyoko, who'd been looking mostly at the floor, lifted her face and raised her dark eyes to Brody. "When I was a girl, I left my home and I lost it. I won't leave my home again."

Brody hadn't learned her whole story yet, of the war and the terrible bomb, and so he didn't understand what she was talking about. But it was clear that she was dead set against leaving the farmstead.

Graff said, "I'm staying out there with you, Kyoko. No arguments."

Her smile was small, grateful. "Thank you, Connie."

They all heard a door open and close down the hallway, and a moment later Mike Kearney, the veterinarian, stepped into the waiting area. Kyoko Bluestone looked up at him, her face awash with fear of the news he might have to deliver.

"Fuji'll be sore for a good while, Mrs. Bluestone, but he'll recover." He nodded to the newcomers. "Figured you'd be here eventually, Brody. Evening, Angie."

"Tell me about the dog, Mike," Brody said.

"One bullet. Entered his left haunch. I've removed it and patched him up. I'll be keeping him here a day or so to monitor his recovery."

"You have the bullet?"

"Yeah. Looks to be from a twenty-two. You want it?"

"I'd appreciate that." Brody turned to Kyoko. "I think it's best for you to go on home, Mrs. Bluestone. It's late and I'd prefer to explain all this myself to your husband. I'll make sure he understands that you're safe. If you'd like to talk to him, come by tomorrow morning. All right?"

He could see that she was disappointed, that she would have preferred to deliver the story herself, but Brody had much to do that night, and he wanted to get to it as soon as possible. He was grateful that she didn't argue with him.

He took Angie home and saw her to her door. It had been both a marvelous evening and a hard one. He wasn't certain if a kiss good night was appropriate, but she solved that question for him by pressing her lips briefly to his.

"You have work to do. Come by the Wagon Wheel for breakfast, okay?"

"I'll be there," he promised.

HE PULLED INTO Creasy Hollow and saw that Tyler Creasy's trailer was dark. But there were lights on in the derelict-looking house where Creasy's mother lived. He knocked at Creasy's dark trailer, expecting no response, but in a moment, a light came on inside and the door was opened.

Del Wolfe stood there, rubbing his eyes as if he'd just awakened. Brody wasn't fooled. The kid was hiding something.

"Is Tyler here, Del?"

"No, Sheriff. Just me and my mom. She's sleeping."

Brody had been to the trailer a number of times in the past, seeking Creasy for questioning or to deliver a summons. *She's sleeping* was often the way Del had got around saying that she was drunk and passed out.

"Know where he might be?"

"No idea, sir."

"Mind if I come in?"

The kid stepped aside, and Brody spent a minute making sure that Del Wolfe's story was true. His mother lay on the ratty sofa, snoring softly, so dead to the world that Brody's intrusion didn't register at all.

"Last Halloween, I cited Tyler for shooting out some streetlamps with a little twenty-two pistol. Does he still have that firearm, Del?"

"Yes, sir."

"Know where he keeps it?"

"I do."

"Mind if I take a look at it?"

Del left the disheveled living room and came back a minute later with the handgun. Brody sniffed the barrel, smelled burned powder.

"Is something wrong?" Del asked.

"There are a few questions I'd like to run by Tyler."

"Is he in trouble? Again?"

"I'm going hang on to this pistol, Del. You go on back to . . . whatever."

Brody left, placed the .22 in his cruiser, then crossed the bare ground between the trailer and the first of the decrepit houses nestled in the trees. He knocked at the door, and the old woman opened up immediately. He figured she'd been watching since the moment he pulled into the hollow.

"I'm looking for your son, Velma."

"Tyler?" Her gray hair was in rollers, and she clutched an old quilted robe about her. "What'd he do this time?"

"I just want to ask him a few questions."

"Like I said, what'd he do this time?"

"Have you seen him this evening?"

"He's been in and out."

"Know where he is right now?"

"Drinking, most likely."

"Bars are closed on Sundays, Velma."

"A man who wants to drink finds a place."

Brody looked past her, into the darker recesses of the old house.

"I'm not hiding him," she said.

"I think he might have shot a dog tonight. With that little twenty-two he owns."

"He owns lots of guns." Her face, if it was possible, went even more sour. "A dog, huh?"

"That's right."

"Whose dog?"

"Noah Bluestone's."

"He the one married the Jap?"

Brody didn't answer that. He said, "'Night, ma'am," and started away. But she spoke again. "He was the best of all my boys."

Brody turned back. "Beg your pardon."

"Tyler. He was the best of 'em all. The sweetest. The softest. Then they called him up to fight. It was them damn Germans, they done something to him."

He could see the sorrow in her sagging face, the loss in those sad, dark eyes. He'd never paid her much attention when he visited the hollow except to ask about her wayward son. She'd always seemed to him a woman whose heart was as dry and wrinkled as her skin. Now he saw a mother who long ago had lost the son she'd loved.

"The war killed what was best in a lot of men, Velma," he offered.

"You want to know something, Sheriff? Sometimes I wish they'd just shipped him back to me in a coffin. And I told him that to his face."

"Good night, Velma."

"You find him and you take him in, don't call me to bail him out."

"I'll keep that in mind." Brody gave a nod in parting.

HE DIDN'T FIND Tyler Creasy. In the end, Brody drove back to Jewel, the whole way trying to figure someone like Tyler Creasy, who'd gone to war a quiet kid and had come home the kind of man who'd shoot a dog. Who'd steal gas and blame it on somebody else. Who'd throw a fist at the least provocation.

Them damn Germans.

Maybe Tyler's mother had been right. Or maybe it was something more than just the war. He thought about what the woman had said, that she wished her son had not come home alive and that she'd told Tyler so. He thought that if he'd heard such a thing from his own mother, the cut would have been too deep to heal. There were many ways of being wounded, Brody understood. Tyler Creasy? Maybe he knew them all.

CHAPTER FORTY-SIX

SLEEP WOULD NOT come, and for hours Scott Madison lay awake watching moonlight inch across his bedroom floor.

After the terrible incident at the Bluestone farmstead, he and Del Wolfe had sped away as quickly as possible. They hadn't stopped at Fort Beloit to gather their things but had gone straight home. They hadn't talked about what had occurred, a series of missteps more horrible than any nightmare Scott could ever have imagined for himself. When they'd parted, Del had said only "You can't tell anyone, Madman. Not anyone. Not ever. Promise."

He'd given his word, even though he knew it was unnecessary, because how could he ever admit to what he'd been a part of?

He heard his mother come home from her evening with Sheriff Dern. She lingered in the rooms below for a while, then turned out the lights and came slowly up the stairs. She paused as she passed his doorway and finally stepped in. He pretended he was sleeping, but she sat on his bed, so he looked at her.

"Anything wrong?" she asked.

"No." He wondered if she could see on his face the lie in that word.

"You and Del decided not to spend the night at Fort Beloit?"

"Mosquitoes," he said.

She leaned to him, kissed his forehead, just as she had before the whole terrible evening began. "All right, then. Good night."

"'Night."

He watched her go, longing to tell her, wanting to be free of the burden he carried now. He couldn't understand how everything could change so quickly. Only yesterday he was a hero. And now? Now he was the worst kind of person imaginable.

He heard the clock on the living room mantel strike midnight, and he could no longer lie there suffering. He slipped from his bed, dressed, and so quietly that he might not even have existed—and wouldn't that have been best, he thought miserably—left the house. Spring field crickets chirred in the darkness but stopped as he passed, and their sudden silence felt to him like censure. The moon poured silver over the town, and his black shadow kept company at his side. He walked without particular purpose, walked because he couldn't be still, walked mindless, walked dead.

The river, when he came to it, was a milk-white flow between trees ghosted with moonlight. To his right, the Alabaster ran smooth and fast. Left was the old spillway that had been built to hold back the river in order to power a mill that had been the town's first large enterprise. Below the spillway, the water churned and foamed and eddied in dark currents. He stood a long while, staring down as if all that turbulence called to him.

"Different, isn't she?"

He spun, startled. The voice was near and familiar, but at the moment, he could neither see nor identify the speaker. It was as if the words had come out of the night itself.

"Who's there?" he said.

"Down here."

He saw then, on the riverbank below the spillway, a form that was ghost-white in the moonlight. He knew the voice now, knew the man who'd spoken. Felix Klein sat with his feet in the water of the Alabaster. As Scott watched, the small man gathered himself and climbed laboriously to where the boy stood. He carried his shoes and socks, and in the glow from the moon, Scott saw how misshapen his bare feet were from the amputation of all those frost bitten toes.

"Different, isn't she," Felix said again.

"Beg your pardon?"

"The river. Under a big moon. She's different from the day. Beautiful, don't you think?"

"Sure." His answer was polite and vague, because the river's beauty wasn't at all what he'd been contemplating.

"I come here a lot at night because I don't sleep too well. Haven't since Hannah died. My wife," he said.

Scott knew who he meant. Sometimes in the Wagon Wheel, when Felix Klein had been drinking, Scott had listened to him hark back to the days of his marriage. Sometimes the man spoke of them fondly, sometimes not.

Behind Felix, the sky was lit occasionally with broad, bright explosions, lightning from a storm still too distant for the thunder to be heard. But that storm was coming. Scott could smell it in the wind blowing out of the southwest now, something brittle and electric.

"The Indians in these parts used to call this Spirit River," Felix said. "Because of the color under a full moon. It changes to white. Something about the minerals from one of the springs that feeds it. Makes it appear to luminesce, like a specter, I suppose." His eyes followed the broad, smooth flow upriver, which did, in fact, seem to glow. "Spirit River," he said again, more softly.

Scott knew the Indian name for the river. It was a part of the long history of the land. But out of politeness he remained quiet and let the man go on.

"Sometimes I drink before I come down here. I admit, I do. Sometimes I have to." Felix spoke more to himself than to the boy. "They found her down there, my Hannah." He nodded toward the roil of water below the spillway. "But you probably know that. Something you may not know though. It was no accident. The truth is she killed herself." He was quiet a long moment. "The river was high that year, just like now. She wore her long, black wool coat. She used to collect rocks, beautiful reminders of the places we'd been. Big pieces of quartz and pyrite and copper ore and geodes. She filled her pockets with those rocks and threw herself off the George Street Bridge."

Scott wondered if the man had been drinking, though Felix didn't sound drunk.

"She wasn't an easy woman to live with. Never very happy. I don't know why. I did my best. She always told me I would be better off without her. Well, she was wrong. I loved her, unhappiness and all. She thought, I guess, that she would be freeing me. Or, I don't know, maybe she wasn't thinking of me at all. I wish she had. Because the honest to God truth is that she hasn't left me. She's in all my wondering, all my regret. She haunts my every moment." He fell quiet and seemed to think. "Or maybe it's me and I just can't let go of her. Either way, I'm in a pickle."

"Why don't you let me help you home, Mr. Klein," Scott said.

But Felix wasn't listening. He was staring at the Alabaster. "She's still in there, I think. Her spirit anyway. Hers and Quinn's and everyone else who ever died in that water."

Scott didn't know Mr. Klein's wife, but he knew Mr. Quinn, and because of the kind of man Quinn had been, Scott didn't much like that idea.

"It's not just this river," Felix said. "It's wherever you are when you die. The place takes you in, all that energy, all that life. The land feeds us, then we feed the land."

Scott said again, "Maybe it's time to go home, Mr. Klein."

Felix considered it. "I think you're right."

The man sat down and worked his socks on and then his shoes.

Scott helped him up, and together they made their way slowly back to Felix's house.

At the door, Felix turned to him and put a hand on his shoulder. "Everybody says there's something wrong with your heart, son. Well, the truth is that none of us has a perfect heart. But you've got a good one, and that's more important." He smiled. "The apple doesn't fall far from the tree. Give your mother my best."

"Thank you for the medal," Scott said. "It means a lot to me."

"You deserved it." Felix turned and went inside.

Scott walked home slowly. The storm in the southwest drew nearer, and he could hear the first distant rumbles of thunder. He thought about the things Mr. Klein had said. The ghosts of the Alabaster, of Black Earth County. He remembered the words: *The land feeds us, then we feed the land.* He dropped his clothes onto his bedroom floor, climbed into bed, thinking sadly that lately what he and the others in Black Earth County had been feeding to the land was mostly poison.

WHEN BRODY WALKED in that Sunday night to relieve Hank Evans from his long day's duty at the jailhouse, Hector leapt up from where he lay in his favorite corner and trotted to greet him, tail wagging madly.

"Hey, boy." Brody ruffed the dog's fur lovingly, then asked Evans, "Did you say anything to Bluestone?"

Evans shook his head. "Didn't see a need until I knew what was what. Then I figured you'd fill him in."

"Thanks, Hank."

Evans gathered up his newspaper and the book he'd been reading. "I understand folks being upset with Bluestone for bringing home a Jap wife. A lot of good boys from this county dead because of those slant-eyed little bastards. But shooting a dog? Only pond scum would stoop that low."

Evans left the jailhouse, and Brody went into the cellblock with Hector at his heels. Bluestone was asleep.

"Noah?"

He spoke quietly, but the man was instantly awake, up and alert in the blink of an eye. A lifetime of military training, Brody figured.

"There was trouble out at your place tonight."

"Kyoko?" Although his face was stone, Bluestone's eyes betrayed his fear.

"She's fine. But your dog took a round from a twenty-two. He's hurt, but he'll recover."

"Do you know who did it?"

Brody shook his head. "As nearly as we can figure, somebody was up in the loft of your barn, watching your wife shower. She spotted him, he ran. Your dog just got in the way."

Brody couldn't believe the iron in the man, the way his body and face held still. But those dark eyes showed everything.

"Not the first time someone's gone after our dog," Bluestone said.

"What?"

"Not long after Kyoko and I got married. This was in Okinawa. Wasn't a popular thing to do, marrying a Japanese woman. I took a lot of grief for it. So did Kyoko, from her people, for marrying an American soldier. We got us a little shih tzu. Had him six months. Then somebody poisoned him. Never knew if it was my people or hers. Truth is we didn't have a people, either of us."

"When did you get Fuji?"

"After my transfer to the Marine Combat Center in Twentynine Palms. He'd been abandoned. Kyoko took him in. I think mostly because she knew what it was to have no home. Gentle dog, really, unless somebody or something threatens Kyoko."

"You say you don't have a people. Then why'd you come back here, Noah?"

Through the open window at the end of the cellblock came the sound of distant thunder. Bluestone glanced that way, and then Brody, but all they saw was the glow of moonlight.

"Tired of killing," Bluestone finally said, "and tired, too, of making sure we had boys trained to do it. Thought maybe back here on my farm we could start new, a different kind of life." His gaze returned to Brody. "Think it was Creasy out at my place?"

"I can't say."

"He said he'd get back at me. And it's the kind of thing he'd do." Bluestone looked down at Hector. "You probably ought to watch your dog close."

Brody put a hand to one of the cell bars. The metal was cool against his palm. He leaned nearer to Bluestone. "You know, Noah, you could save everybody a lot of trouble if you'd just say what happened with Jimmy Quinn that night. Who are you protecting? Is it Kyoko?"

Instead of answering, Bluestone said, "You're sure she's safe?"

"Connie Graff's out there with her. I don't know a better man in this whole county."

Bluestone seemed satisfied. "I hear you playing the guitar and singing upstairs at night. I remember when you were a kid, playing at the county fair. Sons of the Prairie, wasn't that what you called your band? Still play with them?"

"No," Brody said. "We broke up when the war broke out."

"You ought to think about getting back together. You're still pretty good."

"I'm going for a walk," Brody said. "I'll be gone ten minutes. I'll lock the jailhouse door behind me." Bluestone went back to his bunk, and Brody said to Hector, "Let's go, boy."

He walked the streets of Jewel, past the lamps that lit the sidewalks in front of the shops on Main, into the darkness where the Alabaster ran. He came to the George Street Bridge, where Hannah Klein had thrown herself into the river. He'd known her well, and her husband, and he knew that Felix, because he'd loved her, had done his best to protect her. And still she'd died. He looked down at Hector and considered Bluestone's warning. Then thought of the others he loved and all those for whom, as sheriff, he felt responsible. In a town where the hatred from wars long past and wars more recent still had hooks set in so many hearts, was anyone safe?

He was startled by a roll of thunder from the west, and he looked there and saw the black clouds rising, swallowing the stars. Once again in his life, he found himself thinking like a soldier: *Find Tyler Creasy. Neutralize the threat. Whatever that takes.*

IN HIS OWN war, what had once been called the Great War, Connie Graff had become used to lying awake listening for the enemy. In the last months of his marriage, he'd lain awake listening to his wife suffer. Now he lay awake listening because of Kyoko Bluestone.

She'd made a bed for him on the sofa in the living room. As Graff lay there, he thought that everyone had come from somewhere else. Even the Sioux had not always lived on the land along the Alabaster. They were all travelers. But he appreciated the idea that Bluestone's people had never claimed to own the land, that they understood they were like the birds and the buffalo, all of them just passing through. There had been a time, a very long time, when there'd been no humans on this land, and Graff believed that someday it would be that way again. All that men had done to prove their ownership, their mastery, would be undone. In time as it was reckoned by humans, this might be a long while coming, but it would come. In the reckoning of the earth, it would take place in less than a heartbeat.

In the war, he'd seen castles and great monuments that had been built centuries ago. He'd witnessed the kind of carnage that had, time and again, waged around them. In the end, no matter the rhetoric, it was always about the land, about wanting more of it. He thought about Jimmy Quinn, who'd acquired more acreage in Black Earth County than any man before, and where had it got him? Behind his back, people had spoken of him with distaste and often with open hostility. Had he ever been a happy man? Had all that land ever made him content? Graff still didn't know the truth of Quinn's death, but he absolutely believed that at its heart was the unhappiness of a man who'd labored and fought and connived to gain the world, and in all that effort had lost everything of real value.

At this simple farmstead, Noah and Kyoko Bluestone had cultivated more than the crops they'd planted. They'd cultivated love, cultivated happiness. Graff believed this because it was what he'd experienced in his own life with Myrna. They'd never been rich by Jimmy Quinn's standards, but during his years with Myrna, he had harvested an abundance of happiness, which he'd stored in the silo of his heart.

He lay a long time listening to the storm move in over Black Earth County and finally closed his eyes and let himself slip under the thinnest blanket of sleep, ready, at the smallest sound of threat, to rise and stand between Kyoko Bluestone and danger.

NO ONE BOTHERED to call Charlie Bauer. So in ignorance, she sipped good whiskey that night and went over once again the photographs that Sam Wicklow had shot of Jimmy Quinn's ravaged body, and thought about Fiona McCarthy's adamant refusal to speak to her, and considered the evidence gathered so far, which included an expensive sapphire ring with no adequate explanation. All the evidence against Bluestone was circumstantial, but it was still compelling, and she'd seen juries convict with even less. She tried to construct a reasonable scenario of self-defense, though it was all speculation because Noah and Kyoko were still no more forthcoming than Fiona McCarthy had been. What was it about Jimmy Quinn that, even after he was dead, scared people so much?

That's when the storm rolled in.

Charlie had heard it coming for a long while, thunder rumbling across the fields and down into the narrow valley of the Alabaster. She stepped onto her porch. Beyond the big, open meadow that ran down to the river, the trees along the bank flared white in the lightning flashes. Charlie stood at the railing of the porch and recalled another storm, forty-five years earlier, the summer she was fourteen.

Charlotte Bauer's mother had died birthing her. Her father never remarried, and he incessantly reminded Charlotte as she grew up that the reason he remained a widower was because he considered her a punishment and didn't need any further suffering. Charlotte's first transgression was her mother's death. Charlotte's second was that she didn't resemble her mother at all but took after her father, hence her big nose, wide face, and ungainly frame. Also, she was a disobedient child. She challenged her father at every turn. And finally, she was, as he was fond of saying, too smart for her own good. He was an old Mennonite with a crusty heart, and although he put a roof over Charlotte's head and made certain that she never wanted for food or clothing, he never gave any visible sign that he loved her. She couldn't recall a single comforting word or gesture.

In the summer of her fourteenth year, they had a terrible confrontation. Her father didn't believe that a woman needed an education. He allowed her to go to school only because it was the law, but at home, he would not tolerate the sight of a book in her hands, unless it was the Bible. Charlotte used to sneak books home, however, and read them at night by the light of a candle. The summer she was fourteen, he found her out. He came into her room late one night and discovered her reading *Jane Eyre*. He tried to snatch the book from her hands. Charlotte would not yield and clutched it to her breast. He pulled her from the bed, book and all, so furious she thought he would beat her, a thing he'd never done. They screamed at each other, and he finally muscled the novel from her grasp.

There was a storm that night. When her father finally succeeded in taking the book from her, Charlotte fled the house and ran in her bedclothes into the storm. She stumbled to the meadow and stood there, the tallest thing for a hundred yards in every direction, weeping bitter tears. Lightning illuminated everything in brilliant, angry flashes. She saw, in those moments of electric explosion, her father standing under the safety of the porch roof. As he watched, she raised her hands above her head to make herself a better lightning rod, a show of ultimate defiance. But she also did it with the hope, so deep-seated she couldn't even acknowledge it then, that he might risk his own safety to come into the field and bring her home. It was a hope unfulfilled; he simply stood there. Across the whole of her life, Charlotte had no idea why. Was he proving he could be just as stubborn as a fourteen-year-old girl? If so, what kind of victory was that? Maybe he was too afraid of the lightning. That, at least, would have been forgivable. But what Charlotte truly suspected was that deep down he wished her dead for not being the child he wanted.

It seemed to Charlie, standing on the porch now, watching the storm break over the Alabaster River, that what anyone knew of love began early and the lessons stayed with them a lifetime. She'd learned from her father that she was somehow unworthy of love, that no matter what she did, she could never win it. For a long time, that's how she'd lived her life. It had often been a lonely existence. But there was more to life than love, she'd told herself. There was camaraderie, and many times, in the midst of some battle for justice, she'd found herself steeped in the affection of her comrades. There was gratitude, and she'd received her share. Of course, there was friendship, which was perhaps the purest form of love, and she'd certainly known friendship. So all things considered, Charlie had never assessed her life as a particularly empty one. It hadn't been easy, but it also hadn't been without reward. And there was something else. As she'd grown older and had put so many battles behind her, she'd come to a different understanding about herself. Although she had never been a beauty, she'd finally learned to see what was beautiful about her, and she tried to look at other people with the same forgiving eye, and this had made a vast difference in how she embraced what life offered her.

The night the Bluestones' dog was shot, the sky cleared quickly after the storm and the moon returned. Charlie still didn't feel like sleeping. On impulse, she did something that she'd often done as a child. She found a path worn long ago through the trees to the bank of the Alabaster. She sat on a rock whose contours she knew by heart and took off her shoes and put her feet into the cool water. Under the bright moon, the river lived up to its name and flowed white before her.

She thought about everything that had happened in Black Earth County, all the death associated with the Alabaster, and she understood that there had been no intent in the river, either good or evil. If the river did possess spirit, as the Sioux believed, then that spirit seemed to Charlie so vast that it was probably blind to all the small things that occurred along its course. If the spirit was aware that she dangled her feet in its current, it gave no sign of caring. And Jimmy Quinn and Hannah Klein and Noah Bluestone's great-great-grandfather and the nameless white woman whose life, legend said, had been lost on Inkpaduta Bend, none of this mattered to the spirit of the Alabaster. What mattered was the serving of its ultimate purpose, which God alone knew. And what was the point of Charlie's life or anyone's but to run its course and serve its purpose, though that purpose might remain a mystery?

Yet the deaths mattered to Charlie. They mattered to a lot of good people in Black Earth County. And her guess was that no one who cared about these things was sleeping well that night. Which was unfortunate. Because the next night, they were to get no sleep at all.

CHAPTER FORTY-SEVEN

IN THE MORNING, Brody Dern gave an early call to Asa Fielding and filled him in on the events of the previous night. Though the sun was barely peeping above the horizon, Fielding came in immediately to cover the jailhouse. Brody took Hector and drove to a wooded rise overlooking Creasy Hollow. He let the dog run free while he used a pair of binoculars to observe the sad-looking constructions that housed the families there. Eventually Creasy's brothers and an uncle drifted out, all of them looking unkempt, and they went about opening the gas station and garage. He could see no sign of Tyler Creasy or the mold-colored, rust-chewed truck the man drove. But he was pretty sure that Creasy would, at some point, try to contact his family. A man might leave his home, his wife, his livelihood, but he would need something to tide him over, some cash and whatnot. For that, Creasy had nowhere to turn but the people in the hollow, the people of his blood.

The sun had climbed well above the lazy roll of the eastern farmland when the sheriff finally decided to take the bull by the horns.

"Come on, boy," he called to Hector.

He drove into the hollow and pulled up to the garage. Creasy's uncle, a man named Luther, came out, wiping grease from his hands with a dirty red rag.

"Heard about my nephew," he said to the sheriff. The man needed a shave, always needed one, in Brody's experience. He could have used regular visits to a dentist as well.

"Seen him, Luther?" Brody asked.

"Nope. But his wife has and that boy of hers." He gave a sly smile, the kind that made Brody want to slap it from his face.

The other Creasys stood watching from the dark of the garage. They made Brody think of hyenas in a cave. He tried to let go of the enmity he felt toward the clan, tried to tell himself most people had no control over the forces that shaped them, but it was a hard sell.

"You've seen them this morning? Ramona and Del?"

"Oh, yeah."

Brody had wasted enough time with half answers, and he headed to the trailer and knocked. When the door was opened to him, his stomach gave a fierce twist.

Del Wolfe's face was agate colored, a mottle of red and purple bruising. His left eye was swollen nearly shut. His lower lip bore a clotted wound like a leech.

Brody said, "Jesus, son. Did Creasy do that?"

"Yeah." It seemed to hurt Del even to speak that one word.

"Your mom?"

Del gave a jerk of his head, indicating that Brody should come inside.

Ramona Creasy lay on the couch where she'd been when Brody visited the night before. She didn't bother trying to rise but stared at him out of a face that was twin to her son's.

"I'm calling an ambulance, Ramona."

"No." She shook her head. "No money to pay for it."

"You need to be seen by a doctor."

"Can you take me?"

"All right. Del, give me a hand."

They helped her up. She winced at every move. They eased her outside and onto the backseat of the cruiser. Brody called Hector up front, and Del got in beside his mother. Brody hit his siren and shot toward the hospital.

"HE CAME HOME early this morning, before sunup," Del explained after he'd been examined in the emergency room. "I heard his truck pull up. He got out, went to Velma's place first, then came to the trailer. I don't know what Velma told him, but he was worse than I've ever seen him. He lit into me. Mom tried to get between us, so he lit into her."

"Any particular reason?"

"Screaming about that twenty-two of his. Then he started screaming about everything and everybody. He went crazy, said he was going to settle accounts, make everyone pay."

"Everyone? Did he mention names?"

"If he could, he'd shoot the whole fuggin' world."

"Any idea where he was headed when he left?"

"No. But I'll tell you this. If I ever see him again, I'll kill him."

Del Wolfe was all of fifteen years old. Brody looked into that beat-up face, into eyes as full of hate as he'd ever seen. As inured as he believed himself to be because of all the brutality that he himself had been a part of, Brody's heart nearly broke.

"I'll find him, Del. And the law will deal with him, I swear."

Ramona Creasy's injuries, though ugly and painful, weren't life threatening: bruised ribs, lots of contusions. The ER physician recommended she stay overnight, just for observation, but she refused. Brody was pretty sure that money—or the lack of it—was the main reason for her decision.

"I'm not taking you back to the hollow," he told her.

"I'm never going back there," she said.

"Where do you want to go?"

"My sister in Saint Paul."

Brody said, "Greyhound leaves this afternoon."

"I don't have any money," the woman said.

"I'm buying you two tickets courtesy of Black Earth County. In the meantime, I'm taking you someplace safe."

Which was the home of Ida and Angie Madison. Brody called and explained the situation, and when his cruiser rolled up in front of the house, the women were waiting. They'd closed the Wagon Wheel for the rest of the day, and gentle as saints helped Ramona inside their home. Del hung back in the yard, Scott with him, and Brody let the two boys be.

After they got Ramona settled, Angie accompanied Brody to his cruiser. "He's a man with a lot of anger in him, Brody," she said. "It's going to keep exploding from him until someone helps him through it."

"Or kills him," Brody said.

"Is that your job?"

"If it comes to that, yeah, Angie, it is."

"Oh, Brody, be careful."

Though Brody would not himself have kissed her there, in such a public way, she stood on her toes and lifted her face and pressed her lips to his.

"Take care of yourself," she said.

SCOTT COULD BARELY bring himself to look at Del. He'd never seen such brutality. To have it visited on his best friend made him hurt, too. He didn't feel the pain in his face, but he certainly felt it in his heart.

"Fuggin' Creasy," he said.

"Fuggin' Creasy," Del echoed.

They sat on the lawn inside the frame of Scott's lean-to. He'd built it visualizing himself on a mountainside far above the rest of the world. In his imagination, it had been a kind of refuge, protection from all that nature might throw at him. But he understood now that there was another kind of fury, the human kind, and how did anyone protect themselves from that? Laws could punish, but laws kicked in only after terrible things had been done. In a way, they were like that lean-to, a promise with no substance.

"I'm going to kill him, Madman."

Scott had never heard his friend speak so quietly or so cold.

No you're not, Scott wanted to say. Because he hoped Del's thinking was another thing that was like the lean-to. How could a kid—and that's what they were, still just kids—do something so terrible, so destructive, so utterly final? It happened on the movie screen in the Rialto, maybe, but not in real life. Not in Jewel, Minnesota.

"Honest to God, Madman, I thought he was going to kill me. Probably would have if Mom hadn't clobbered him with that big glass ashtray. Didn't drop him, but it dazed him enough we pushed him outside and he drove off."

"Why didn't you call the sheriff?"

"I wanted to, but Mom . . ." He shook his head. "I don't get her, Madman. So I grabbed one of his guns in case he came back."

"Where is it?"

"I put it under the sofa when the sheriff showed up this morning. I'm going back to get it, then I'm going after Creasy."

"You don't know where he is."

"I'll bet the rest of the Creasys do. They're like snakes, all balled up together." He stood abruptly. "I'm out of here, Madman."

Scott leapt to his feet. "Wait, Wolfman. You're not really going to do this?"

"Just watch me."

"You sound as crazy as Creasy."

"Don't you ever compare me to that bastard."

"That's not what I meant. I meant you can't go out there looking to shoot someone. There's no way that can end well."

"It sure as hell won't for Creasy."

"Let the police deal with him."

"And what? They lock him up for a while? Then he just comes knocking on our door again. I want him out of our lives for good."

Del moved to leave but Scott stepped in front of him. "Wolfman—"

Del pushed him aside. "Out of my way."

It was crazy thinking, all of it. Scott couldn't let Del go, not like that. But he knew, too, that he couldn't stop his friend and also that he couldn't tell anyone. It seemed to him that he had only one choice.

"I'm going with you," Scott said. "Wait here."

"What are you doing?"

"If my mom looks out and we're gone, we won't get far. I'm going inside and make up something."

"You say anything—"

"I won't," he promised.

The women were in the living room. Del's mother lay on the sofa, her shoes off, a pillow beneath her head. She looked awful, worse than Del. And Creasy was still out there, still a threat.

"We're going for a walk," he said to his mother. "Del and me."

"I don't think so, Scott," Angie replied.

She sat in an easy chair with flowered upholstery. It looked so normal, so comfortable, so familiar. So why did it all feel so alien to Scott at that moment?

"Just around the block," he said. "Del's kind of upset. He can't sit still. I'll be with him. It'll be fine."

She considered him carefully and at last gave a nod. "Not long, though."

"Not long," he said. Because he was already steeped in lies. And how much worse could one more be?

CHAPTER FORTY-EIGHT

UNTIL SAM WICKLOW called Charlie Bauer that Monday morning to ask if he could talk to Noah and Kyoko Bluestone, the lawyer was completely in the dark about what had happened the night before at the Bluestone farmstead. Sam filled her in on what he knew, and she got herself together and ready to speed off to the jailhouse. Just before she left, however, the telephone rang. She was in such a hurry that she almost chose not to answer it.

"Miss Bauer?"

Charlie recognized the voice right away. "Good morning, Fiona."

"Miss Bauer, I wonder if I could talk to you."

"I'm listening."

"Not over the phone. I need to talk to you in person."

"All right. Would you like me to come there?"

"No. Not here."

"Would you prefer that we talk in Jewel?"

"It's too far, and I don't have that kind of time today. Would you meet me partway?"

"Of course. Where?"

"Do you know Pilot Knob? In northern Iowa?"

"Of course."

"Meet me there. At the observation tower. Can you make it by one?"

"I can. And thank you, Fiona."

In Des Moines, their brief time together had ended on such a sour note that Charlie had expected never to hear from Jimmy Quinn's daughter again. She replayed their phone conversation, tried to recall the timbre of the woman's voice. Afraid, Charlie thought. Whatever it was Fiona had to say, it scared her.

But there was much to do to in Black Earth County first, and Charlie headed quickly to the jailhouse. Connie Graff was there with Asa Fielding, and when Charlie arrived, Kyoko was in her husband's cell. Asa told her about what Tyler Creasy had done to Ramona and Del. He said that Brody was out talking with the state police about getting some help tracking Creasy down.

Charlie went to the door of the cellblock and waited for the deputy to get the key. What she heard as she stood there surprised her. In a very low and angry voice, Kyoko Bluestone was arguing with her husband. She couldn't hear most of the words, but Kyoko was clearly upset. Then she said something that Charlie did hear: "I don't know if I can go through with this. I don't know if I'm strong enough."

To which Bluestone replied, "The truth will only make everything worse. Trust me, Kyoko. I wouldn't be able to live with myself. And I don't think you could either."

Asa fumbled the key in the lock of the cellblock door and the voices inside died abruptly.

When Charlie entered the cell, she could see that Kyoko was still upset, but Noah Bluestone's face, as usual, revealed nothing. She wondered if his stoicism was a part of his Native heritage or his training as a soldier, or maybe both. When the world throws at you nothing but stones, maybe to survive you simply become stone yourself.

She stood inside the cell and leaned against the bars. "You know about Tyler Creasy?"

Bluestone said he did.

"Noah, I wish to God you'd just tell me the truth. Maybe I could have you out of here. Wouldn't you prefer to be able to protect Kyoko yourself?"

Which was unfair, she knew, playing on his inability to protect his wife while those iron bars kept him penned.

"Connie's been very helpful," Kyoko said.

"I'm sure he has. But it's going to be a long time before your husband is a free man, if he ever is. And, Noah, I hope you don't expect Connie Graff to spend his life seeing to the safety of your wife and your farm."

Bluestone considered this intentional salvo. "In war, I learned to accept my life one day at a time. It's the only way I know."

Charlie gave up. "Sam Wicklow would like to interview you both about what happened last night at your farm. What would you like me to tell him?"

"He can talk to me," Bluestone said. "But he stays away from Kyoko."

"Fair enough. I'll let him know."

If she was going to make it to her meeting with Fiona McCarthy by one o'clock, Charlie had to leave. But she felt there was more she should be able to do. She was more convinced than ever that Kyoko Bluestone had killed a man who'd tried to perpetrate some terrible violence against her and more convinced than ever that her husband's silence was the only way he believed he could protect her now.

"Charlie," Bluestone said as she prepared to leave. "Thank you. I know that you're doing your best to help, and I appreciate it."

"Save your thanks for the day you walk out of here a free man."

THE DRIVE TO Pilot Knob State Park in Iowa took almost two hours. Charlie wove through rolling farmland beautiful in its profound fertility. For millennia, this had all been tall prairie grass, which had created rich black soil so deep that the blades of the first plows could not find an ending.

Fiona was waiting for her in the gravel parking area of the stone observation tower atop Pilot Knob. Although it was a time of year that usually drew tourists, Charlie and Fiona were alone that Monday afternoon. In greeting, Fiona said only, "Let's climb."

The tower itself was thirty feet tall. The sun was high overhead, the sky a relentless blue, the day hot. Fiona stood at the wall of the observation platform, staring at the vista, which stretched miles and miles in every direction, a patchwork of farm and field.

"It wears a coat of many colors, this land," she said.

"Like Joseph," Charlie said.

"Like Joseph." Fiona took a deep breath and sighed. "I never go back to Black Earth County, but I can almost see it from here. This is the second highest elevation in all of Iowa. That's not saying much, but still, it's lovely, don't you think? Bob used to bring me here sometimes, before we were married, when I needed to escape. Thank you for coming, Miss Bauer."

"Call me Charlie, please."

"Charlie, then. I want to apologize for being so rude the other day. You caught me off guard."

"I was just trying to understand a few things."

"Of course."

Fiona turned away and once again studied the land below the knob.

"Did you know this was an important gathering place for Indians before white people came?" she said. "The Winnebago, the Pottawattamie, the Meskwaki. Bob told me that. He knows everything about this area. When we left Jewel, he couldn't get a job teaching anywhere, because of the scandal. He sells John Deere equipment now. He's very good at it, but history is still his first love." She glanced at Charlie. "You know the story, why Bob had to marry me? Of course you do. Everyone in Black Earth County knows that story. Or thinks they do."

"I was gone from Jewel a very long time," Charlie said. "All of that took place before I came back, so I only know what I've heard."

"He was the most handsome teacher. He had a way of making history seem important and interesting. He'd lived in the East and seemed so sophisticated. He was smart and kind and funny. And unmarried. We all had a crush on him, all of us who were just girls then."

A breeze came up, cooling, and she lifted her face as if to welcome it.

"The story is that he seduced you," Charlie said.

"Nothing could be further from the truth. I did all the seducing." She smiled, but it was worn and sad.

"Why?"

"I wanted to get pregnant. I wanted to punish my father."

"For what?"

Fiona had been wearing sunglasses. Now she removed them, and Charlie could finally see her eyes. They were deep green and, in a way, threatening. "What I'm going to tell you, I have told only one other person. I need to know that you'll keep it to yourself. You can't use it to defend Noah Bluestone. If you say anything, I will deny it. I will deny it to my grave. Do you understand? And do I have your word?"

Charlie wondered what her word was worth to this woman. What did Fiona know of her, professionally or personally, of her ethics? Although Charlie was still in the dark about so much, there was one thing she understood at that moment: a heavy weight lay on Jimmy Quinn's daughter and she was desperate to be relieved of it. Across all her years of defending the accused, Charlie had come to understand that was the way of our darkest secrets. As much as we fear their revelation, we pray to be able to bring them into the light, to unburden ourselves to someone who might understand. Charlie wasn't Catholic, but the ritual of confession had always made sense to her.

"You have my word," she pledged solemnly.

Fiona turned away and addressed the rest of her remarks to the wind. "When I was twelve years old, my mother became ill. She was diagnosed with ALS. You know what that is?"

"I do," Charlie said.

"She got weaker and weaker, became bedridden. We had to do everything for her, and we had to do all of the things for ourselves that she could no longer do. My grandmother Quinn helped some, but she was a dry, bitter old woman, and I didn't like her. Terry didn't either. So more and more I took on a lot of responsibilities. Adult responsibilities."

She paused, and Charlie could hear the leaves of the trees around the base of the tower rustling with a liquid sound as if a river were running past. Far away she saw smoke rising where a farmer was burning some kind of debris, and the smoke lay in a long gray smudge across the pale blue sky.

"The first night my father came to my bedroom, I was thirteen. He'd been drinking. He'd been doing a lot of that over the weeks before this, wrestling with something. That night, he came to me smelling of whiskey. He sat on my bed in the dark and explained to me why he was there. He told me that because of my mother's illness, it was my duty. He told me it would be a special thing that we'd share. He told me it wouldn't hurt. Promised me. He told me there was nothing to be afraid of. But I was afraid. Absolutely scared to death."

Her voice was thin and rigid and seemed on the edge of breaking.

"I didn't understand, really. What child would? I knew it was a terrible thing. I couldn't tell anyone. But I didn't have to. They all knew. They all knew and they all looked away. My mother, my grandmother, Terry. They were weak people. In my father's shadow, we were all weak people."

Her hands gripped the tower wall, as if she were afraid she might fall.

"It's a strange thing about adversity, Charlie. You can get used to anything, no matter how difficult, if it's the same sort of difficulty each time. So I got used to my father's visits. I even made myself believe that it was, just as he said, something special between us. Because he treated me very nicely, so much better than he did anyone else. Whenever he visited me, he would bring me a gift, an expensive little piece of jewelry.

A bracelet, a necklace, a ring. I wore them and offered no explanation for where they came from. Terry hated me, but he never said a word. My mother would look at me when I came into her room, and to this day I'm certain that what I saw on her face was a mixture of grief and guilt, because she was helpless. Or so I thought. Because in the end, she did do something, the only thing she could. She arranged for a distant cousin to come from Germany to help with the work."

"Marta?"

"Yes, Marta. She was sixteen, the same age I was by then. But she was very different from me. Stronger. Her parents had been important people in Germany but outspoken opponents of Hitler. I suppose they saw the writing on the wall and wanted to get their daughter to safety. Sending her to a family in America must have seemed the way." She looked down from the height of the observation tower and shook her head. "They had no idea."

"What happened, Fiona?"

"My mother died a short while after Marta's arrival. My father stopped coming to my bed. A few months later, he and Marta were married. The following summer, she became pregnant with their first child."

"Patrick," Charlie said. "J.P."

"Her belly swelled. She lost her figure. I saw my father looking at me again, in the old way. By then, I wanted nothing to do with him. I hated him. For what he'd done to me, of course, but also . . ." She paused. "Also for casting me off in favor of Marta."

She stopped then, was quiet for a long while, and eyed the distant smudge of smoke as if it were a thing she couldn't comprehend.

"It was all so complicated, so unbelievable, the things I felt. Mostly I wanted to get away from him, from that place, from those circumstances. So I seduced Bob and got myself pregnant and . . ."

Now she broke. That great dam she'd built just gave way, and she bent and wept tears that fell onto the white stone. She sobbed uncontrollably, and Charlie wanted to hold her, comfort her but was so unsure of everything at the moment that she simply let Jimmy Quinn's daughter weep.

At last Fiona wiped her cheeks with the back of her hand, then dug into her pocket and brought out a tissue and blew her nose. "It cost Bob terribly, and I've always felt responsible for that. But I've tried to be a good wife to him. All those expensive little pieces of jewelry my father gave me? I sold them and we used the money for a down payment on our home."

"Does Bob know any of this?"

"I've never told him. He knows there was something bad between my father and me, but neither of us has ever broached the subject." She looked at Charlie again, her face dark with concern. "When I heard that Marta was ill, I became afraid for Colleen, terribly afraid about what might happen, if it hadn't already. But I . . . I still feared my father, feared the past, feared what the future might hold if the truth were known. So I did nothing. Just like my mother and my grandmother and my brother."

"Why are you telling me this now?"

"Because I think there's a good reason my father is dead. And I think you may not have to look any farther than that farmhouse I grew up in."

"Are you saying someone killed him to keep Colleen safe?"

"Marta's stronger than I ever was. If I were that strong, it's what I'd do."

"But the sheriff found a tarp at Noah Bluestone's place. It was covered with blood that matched your father's type."

She blew her nose again. Her eyes were red from crying. She said, "Have you ever been in love, Charlie, and lost that love? Because when that happens, I think love sets a hook in your heart that will always be there. Marta was a very pretty girl. Easy to fall for. Just ask Noah Bluestone."

"There was something between Noah and Marta?"

"A very long time ago. They tried to hide it, but I could see. We all could. Everyone except my father. He was blind to everything but his own selfish needs."

A little yellow bus wove its way up to the top of the knob, pulled into the parking area of the observation tower, and disgorged a number of children and several adults. Fiona put her sunglasses back on, signaling, Charlie knew, that their time together had come to an end.

"I understand that Noah Bluestone refuses to say anything about what happened the night my father died. If you want the truth, Charlie, maybe you should ask Marta."

As she turned to leave, Charlie said, "Who else?"

Fiona's face was eyeless behind those dark lenses. "Who else what?"

"You said there was only one other person you'd told all this to."

Charlie could hear the children coming up the stairs, eager and noisy.

"I've been seeing a therapist forever," she said.

"And so you know that what happened when you were a girl wasn't your fault."

"You're not my therapist, Charlie."

The children burst onto the tower platform and raced to the wall.

Fiona turned and waited until the stairs became clear, then she left. From the top of the tower, Charlie watched her get into her car and drive away.

The lawyer thought again about truth, something she'd never believed was an absolute. What Fiona had told her was a terrible story and took courage. Knowing Jimmy Quinn, Charlie could believe there might be truth to it. But she also considered Fiona's motive in arranging this meeting and couldn't help but wonder if the direction in which the woman had pointed her might, after all these years, be a form of revenge against Marta, who'd stolen her father's affections. Charlie had listened to people on a witness stand swear to a lie that they believed in their hearts was necessary in order for justice to be done.

There was, however, a detail in Fiona's story that made Charlie lean powerfully toward believing her. Charlie thought about the sapphire ring Brody had found in Jimmy Quinn's pants pocket, a ring he believed was meant for a small woman, someone like Kyoko Bluestone. But now Charlie had a different idea about that ring.

CHAPTER FORTY-NINE

BRODY SPENT AN hour at the jailhouse talking by phone with the state patrol and law enforcement in adjacent counties, enlisting their help in locating Tyler Creasy. He phoned the Quinns and talked to J.P., cautioning him and urging him to call immediately if Creasy showed up. He phoned the Bluestone farm and spoke with Graff. When he'd finished his calls, he headed back to the Madison home. As he rolled his cruiser up to the curb, Angie came running to meet him.

"They're gone," she said.

"Who?"

"Scott and Del. They went for a walk, just around the block. That was a couple of hours ago. They haven't come back."

"Have you looked for them?"

"I've been all over the neighborhood, Brody. Nothing."

"They're boys, Angie. They've lost track and gone farther than they intended. It's how boys are."

"Not Scott. He promised me."

"Did you see which way they went?"

"I didn't. Oh, Brody, I wouldn't worry, but so much has happened. And with Tyler Creasy gone crazy out there—"

"You don't need to apologize, Angie. And don't worry, I'll find them."

But he didn't. He drove every street in Jewel and saw no sign of the boys. Then Hank Evans raised him on the cruiser's radio.

"Base to Unit One. Brody, are you there? Over."

"Unit One here. What's up, Hank?"

"Got a call from Velma Creasy. Scott Madison and Del Wolfe were out at the hollow. They had a gun, made some threats."

"What kind of threats?"

"Not sure exactly."

"Are the boys still there?"

"Negative. They took off on a motor scooter."

"Did Velma have any idea where they were headed?"

"Another negative."

"Thanks, Hank. Things quiet there?"

"As the grave."

Brody swung his cruiser in a wide arc and headed east across the Alabaster.

The old woman answered the door. She wore a ratty sweater that was the same dismal gray as her hair. Her face was white and pinched, her eyes dark and penetrating.

"Yes," she said. "They were here."

"What did they want, Velma?"

Her right brow curled up like an inchworm. "My son."

"They're looking for Tyler?"

"Hunting Tyler more like it. They took off on Del's motorbike."

"I was told they had a gun."

"You bet they did."

"Where'd they get it?"

"My son likes guns. He keeps them in his little trailer over there."

"Do you know where your son is?"

"My guess? Standing in the doorway to hell."

"Is he still in Black Earth County?"

"I don't know."

"For his sake and the sake of the boys, if you know, tell me."

"I don't. And that's God's truth."

"If Tyler comes back here, I hope you'll let me know. This is already way out of hand, Velma."

"I said goodbye to my son a long time ago. The man he is now is a stranger to me, and I don't care about him one bit."

AT THE MADISON house, Brody found Wendell Moon sitting in a chair on the front porch, strumming a guitar.

"Sheriff," the man greeted him.

Brody listened for a moment as Wendell played. "Don't know that one."

"Big Bill Broonzy tune. 'Looking for My Baby.' You find them boys?"

"Not yet."

"How 'bout that Creasy fella?"

Brody shook his head.

"Big place, Black Earth County."

Brody nodded toward the house. "You acting as sentry?"

"Something like that. Seeing me here, I figure it might make a man think twice if he's got no good on his mind."

"Thanks, Wendell."

The man shrugged and went on playing.

The front door opened, and Angie stepped out with a glass of iced lemonade in her hand, which she offered to Wendell. He laid the guitar beside his chair and took the glass.

"Thank you, Angie."

To Brody, she said the obvious: "You didn't find them."

"I just came from Creasy Hollow. We got a call that the boys were out there."

"Doing what?"

"They had a gun, Angie. Made threats."

"A gun? Where would they get a gun?"

"It belongs to Tyler Creasy. The boys were looking for him."

"What happened?"

"According to Velma, they took off on Del's motorbike."

"Headed where?"

"She didn't have a guess. Or at least one she was willing to share."

"Oh, God, Brody. What do we do?"

"You just keep doing what you're doing. The state patrol is watching the main highways for Creasy. I've got the sheriffs' departments in all the adjacent counties here in Minnesota and in Iowa patrolling the back roads. We'll round up Creasy and we'll find the boys."

"I don't understand, Brody. This isn't like Scott at all."

Wendell said, "To him and Del this probably feels like war."

"But they're just boys, Wendell."

"It's always boys who go to war, Angie."

"Find them, Brody. Find them before something terrible happens."

"I will," Brody said, and hoped he sounded convincing.

INSIDE, ANGIE RELAYED what Brody had told her to the other women. Ramona Creasy slumped where she sat and began to cry. "I'm sorry. I'm so sorry. This is all my fault."

"It's no one's fault," Angie said.

Ramona lifted her face, tear-streaked and battered. "Tyler wasn't always like this. There was sweetness to him once. It's just . . . it's been like watching him sink into quicksand. He just goes deeper and deeper, and he can't seem to pull himself out."

"Then you need to save yourself and your son," Ida told her.

"I know. Christ, I know. It's not too late, is it, Angie? Our boys will be okay, won't they?"

"Brody will find them," Angie assured her. "Ida, let's fix tea for us all. You relax, Ramona. We'll be right back."

In the kitchen, Angie ran water into a kettle and, under the sound of it, confided, "I'm scared to death, Ida."

The older woman sagged against the counter, as if her strength had deserted her. "This is what it was like in the war, worrying about Christian. Do you remember, Angie? Oh God, I hoped we'd never have to feel this way again."

"He'll be all right," Angie said, as much for herself as for Ida.

But she recalled only too well that they'd all said the same thing to one another when Christian Madison had gone away to war.

The kettle began to whistle. Angie made tea, and the two women put on brave faces and went to comfort Del Wolfe's mother.

CHAPTER FIFTY

WHEN CHARLIE PULLED into the Quinns' farmyard, she could smell the evening meal on the air, the good aromas of baking biscuits and something fried drifting out through the kitchen windows, being carried on the currents of the breeze. She spotted J.P. exiting the huge barn and coming down the slope to the house. He would never be a big man physically, and there was none of Jimmy Quinn's swagger in his step or Jimmy Quinn's all-consuming selfishness in his eyes. He would grow up to be a good man, she thought, despite his father. She knew this was because of his mother. Fiona had been right. Marta was a strong woman, and neither her illness nor Jimmy Quinn's bullying had been able to break her.

"Evening, Miss Bauer," J.P. called out. He held a pair of well-worn work gloves in his hand and slapped them gently against his thigh as he came. His boots were caked in what looked and smelled like cow manure. "Me and Able, we were just mucking out the cow pen. With everything that's gone on, it's been a while."

"I'd like to talk to your mother again, if I could."

At the front door, he removed his dirtied work boots and entered the house sock-footed, ahead of Charlie. "If you'll wait, I'll get Mom."

"Thank you."

He climbed the stairs. Almost simultaneously, Colleen came from the kitchen, wiping her hands on the apron she wore. "Hi, Miss Bauer. Did you come for supper?"

"That wasn't my intent."

"Oh stay, please. There's plenty, and we'd love to have you."

"It does smell wonderful."

Little Bridget stepped in behind her sister, and she, too, gave Charlie a lovely smile. "Miss Bauer!"

They all turned at the creak of the stairs and watched J.P. help his mother descend. When she saw Charlie, Marta's face, like those of her children, warmed in welcome. Charlie felt a great weight on her heart, knowing what she had to do there. She didn't relish this duty, but it had to be done.

"Hello, Charlotte." Marta took Charlie's hand in both of hers, which were cold despite the summer heat. "What a pleasant surprise."

"I was passing by, Marta, and hoped I might have a word with you."

She looked into Charlie's eyes and seemed to understand that what was going to be said was for her ears alone. "Shall we sit on the porch swing?" she suggested. "It's such a lovely day."

"Supper in a few minutes," Colleen said. "We'll set an extra place."

Marta and Charlie walked outside, and J.P. followed with a knitted afghan that, once his mother was seated, he placed around her shoulders.

"Iced tea, Miss Bauer?" he offered. "Or lemonade?"

"I'm just fine, J.P. Thanks."

"I'll call when supper's ready." He vanished into the house.

"He's a good son. You have wonderful children, Marta. So much to be proud of."

"Thank you."

"Was it difficult?"

"Difficult?"

"Raising them in the shadow of a man like Jimmy. I'm sorry if that sounds like I'm speaking ill of the dead."

Marta didn't appear to be offended. "We had an understanding, James and me. I never interfered with the farm and his business, and he let me run the house. The children had their farmwork. My husband oversaw that. They also had chores they did for me. James had his way of doing things. I tried to show them something different, kinder."

"It's no secret that a lot of people in Black Earth County were afraid of your husband. Were you, Marta?"

"Despite what people say, he never raised a hand to me."

Which didn't exactly answer the question, but Charlie let it go.

"The children, were they afraid of him?"

"I never allowed him to raise his hand to them either."

Which again was an evasion.

"This isn't exactly the conversation I'd anticipated," Marta said, but not unpleasantly.

In the distance, the slope of Fordham Ridge lay in late afternoon shadow, but the sunlight along the crown gave everything there a soft look as if it were dusted with yellow pollen. It was such a pleasant, pastoral scene and so completely at odds with the subject Charlie needed to broach.

"I've just come from speaking with Fiona McCarthy," Charlie said. "There are some things I need to ask you. Difficult things."

Marta waited, her eyes steady on Charlie's face.

"I know what Jimmy did to his daughter when she was a girl Colleen's age, Marta. I'm guessing you know, too."

Marta blinked, looked down at her hands on her lap, took a deep breath. "It is a large house, but not so large that secrets are easily kept."

"Are there more recent secrets?"

The woman didn't look up from her hands.

"Who killed your husband?"

Charlie could hear from the kitchen the low murmur of the children talking as they worked on the evening meal. The cattle in the fenced yard behind the barn lowed now and again, sounds like notes from a tuba. The sun seemed nailed to the same place in the sky and the shadows it cast seemed permanently embedded in the ground.

"It is a long story," Marta said, finally lifting her eyes.

"I'm a patient woman."

"And a kind one. I have seen this. So I will tell you, and I will rely on your kindness." She seemed chilled and drew the afghan more tightly around her. "I came from Germany," she began, "in a terrible time. My parents saw what was happening to those who opposed the Nazis, and they didn't want me to be caught up in that. James's wife was a cousin to my mother. The two made an arrangement. I didn't want to come here. I didn't want to leave my family. But my parents insisted, and so I obeyed.

"I saw immediately what was going on. The illness of my mother's cousin. What was happening between James and Fiona behind her closed bedroom door. The terrible silence of them all. I understood very quickly the true reason I'd been sent for, not a reason that my mother or father could ever have imagined."

"Why didn't you just go back to Germany?"

"Only days after I left, my parents were arrested. Much of my family, in fact. I had no one to go back to. And here in America there was no one I knew. I had nothing and nowhere to go."

Charlie could visualize her, the girl she was then, lost, trapped.

"I decided there was only one choice and James was it. But I was not going to enter meekly into what he wanted from me. I demanded two things before he came to my bed. I told him I knew about Fiona and that it sickened me and must end. And I told him that I needed a wedding ring. He denied what had been going on with his daughter, but it stopped. And he found the patience to wait until his wife died, which was soon enough, and he put this wedding ring on my finger before he took what I'd promised him. Think what you want of that, but it kept me alive while so many of my people in Germany were being killed."

"After the war, you didn't consider returning?"

"To what? I had a child here and another on the way. I had a life.

Despite what you may think, it was not a terrible life. James was a bully, yes, but he was not cruel to me. I didn't allow him to be cruel. To me or my children. I have always kept a sharp eye. James was a man of appetites. Land, money, power, sex. As long as those appetites were fed, he was not a dangerous man." She'd been holding herself erect. Now Charlie could see her bend a little, as if under a weight. "But then . . . This." She indicated her weakened body. "This, I didn't plan on. To stand up to my husband took strength, and I felt that strength draining away. I could no longer feed his appetite in the bedroom. I began to see the hunger in his eyes and I became afraid."

The screen door opened and Bridget stepped out. "We've set a place for Miss Bauer. Colleen says less than five minutes, Mama."

"Tell her to give us a little more time together. I'll let her know when we're ready."

"Okay." Bridget went back inside.

"You hired a girl," Charlie said. "To help here."

"I didn't hire her. James did that. To help me with the house, he claimed. I hoped it was true. Maybe it was at first. But then James—" She broke off, and her eyes searched the distance, as if the right words, like the sun, might be hanging above the horizon. "James attacked her. I intervened and took her home and told her not to return."

"You said that the hunger you saw in his eyes made you afraid. For Colleen?"

She nodded. "I tried to send her away, did you know that? To a Catholic school for girls in Saint Paul. James absolutely refused. He told me that we needed Colleen here. I could not fight him on this. Then over the months, I saw him slide more often into that hopeless place he sometimes went, and I knew that when he was there he was battling demons, and I was certain I knew one of them."

"Did you say anything to him?"

"I told him I was sorry for what was happening to me. I also told him that if he ever tried to do to my daughter what he'd done to Fiona I would kill him."

It was time, Charlie thought, to ask the question that had brought her there. "Marta, what really happened the night your husband died?"

It took Marta some time to gather herself. She didn't look at Charlie but stared across the fields toward Fordham Ridge.

"Bridget was at a sleepover," she finally began. "Patrick had a date with his girlfriend. The hired men were gone for the day. It was just me and Colleen and James here. We had an early supper. It was an odd meal, James so quiet. He looked pale. He wouldn't talk. I thought maybe he was ill. He didn't finish his food. He just left the table. I watched him walk away, up the lane to the old shack where sometimes he drank. He tried to kill himself there last fall, drunk. Patrick found him with a noose around his neck."

Which was not news to Charlie. Connie Graff had told her this, and she'd been considering how she might use it in her defense of Noah Bluestone.

"I should have been more vigilant," Marta said. "But I was tired, so I lay down on the sofa in the living room while Colleen cleaned up from supper." Her eyes closed, and she shook her head in regret. "God forgive me, I fell asleep. When I woke up, the house was empty and it was almost dark outside. I called for Colleen. She didn't answer. I found a pitcher of lemonade on the kitchen table and two glasses, but no sign of Colleen or James. I stepped outside and called again. And then I knew something was wrong. I could feel it and I was certain what it was. My worst fear. Why had I been so careless?

"James kept his guns in a case in the den. I took one, the biggest, and loaded it. He'd shown me how to do this, for my safety if I was alone on the farm. I went to the shed. I could see a light on in the window. I threw the door open." She stopped speaking. Her breath came in choking sobs, and tears began to run down her cheeks, gold in the late afternoon light. "A long time ago, he put a cot in the shack and slept there some-times when he'd been drinking. Colleen was on the cot, lying there like she was in a deep sleep. He'd taken off her jeans and underwear. He'd removed all of his own clothing except for his undershorts. I screamed. Oh God, did I scream. Colleen didn't move at all. But James turned to me. Red-eyed and red-faced and stinking drunk. He stared at me, at that big shotgun I held. I screamed at him again, screamed at him to get out."

The still of the afternoon was profound and the air felt close and Charlie held her breath, waiting for Marta to go on. Although neither of them moved, the chains of the porch swing gave a small groan.

"He spoke to me," Marta went on. "Two words. Only two. He said, 'She's mine.' As if she was just like his land and his money and his power. He was drunk, yes, but it was not the whiskey speaking. And I knew. I knew she would never be safe."

"What did you do, Marta?"

She turned to Charlie. The tears down her cheeks streamed onto the afghan, but there was something hard and enduring and powerful in her aspect.

"I shot him."

THERE ARE MOMENTS that stay with you forever and the details are burned into your memory as if etched with acid. Charlie would always remember the moment of Marta Quinn's confession, not because it startled her—by then she'd pretty much put together that part of the mystery—but because she understood Marta's action so clearly and there was, odd as this may seem, a beauty to it. Death is as ordinary in this world as birth or breathing. Though we may fear that journey and what awaits us there, it's a revelation that will come to us all someday. To Charlie, the truly interesting aspect was the manner of the death itself. That great gaping hole Marta Quinn opened in her husband shattered the sixth commandment, went against all the law of most lands and, in reality, tore a hole in Marta herself. But to Charlie's way of thinking, it was justice.

"Does Colleen know?"

Marta shook her head. "I don't know how it went with his first daughter, but with mine, he had knocked her out, drugged her somehow, probably with the Seconal he took for his insomnia. He must have put it in her lemonade. She didn't see anything, doesn't remember anything. If she suspects at all, she's kept it to herself."

Charlie thought a moment, imagined the woman in that shed, her husband on the floor, destroyed at her feet. Then she thought about Jimmy Quinn's body eventually turning up in the Alabaster as fish food, and she was about to ask how Marta had managed that when J.P. stepped onto the porch and saw his mother crying. There was such compassion in his young face, such an absence of brutality. And that's when the final piece fell into place, and Charlie saw what had been in front of her the whole time.

"Are you okay, Mom?" He knelt and laid his hand gently on her knee.

"Fine, Patrick. I'm fine." She patted his hand and wiped at her tears. "Just tired," she said.

J.P. looked at Charlie, and, although he didn't speak, she knew he was asking her to end the conversation because, whatever the topic, it was clearly distressing his mother. But Charlie wasn't finished yet. There was one final part of this story that she needed to hear, an important part.

"We'll just be a minute more, J.P.," she told him. "Promise."

He stood. Charlie knew he would never be tall like Jimmy Quinn, but she suspected that he would always be strong in his heart like his father. His real father.

He went back into the house, and Charlie said to Marta, "Does he know that he's Noah's son?"

Marta stared. Charlie thought she saw both surprise and relief there. "How . . . ?"

But the how of it didn't really matter to her. That Charlie knew was enough.

"James was my husband," she said. "What was between us was never love. Noah"—and here she smiled sadly—"he was beautiful and kind." She took a deep breath and let it out slowly. "Patrick doesn't know."

"But Noah does."

She nodded. "He came back on leave after the war, to see his father's grave and to see to legal matters related to his land. He visited. The moment he saw Patrick, he knew."

"Your husband never suspected?"

"I'm not big myself. None of my family in Germany was big. I told James that there was a good deal of southern European in our blood, and it was not unusual for our people to be of dark complexion. But the truth is his world was always so much about him that I believe he never once considered there might be another explanation. And thank God for that."

"I understand why Noah would want to work for your husband—"

"To be with his son," Marta said with a nod. "Finally to be with his son."

"But why did Kyoko agree to work here?"

"Noah asked her. When he understood how it was for me here, and the children, he asked if she would help."

"Did she know Patrick was Noah's son?"

"Yes. It made no difference. She is a woman with a wonderful heart. We became friends."

Which made perfect sense. Two women who'd lost their homes and families and who'd become strangers in this strange land, outsiders, alien.

"So after you'd shot your husband, you called Noah and asked for his help."

"I didn't know what else to do. He came and brought Kyoko with him."

"What happened?"

"He carried Colleen to her bedroom. She was still knocked out. Then we talked. I told them to call the sheriff, but Noah said no. He said it didn't matter what James had done, the people here would put me in jail anyway."

Charlie thought he was not necessarily wrong.

"Why didn't Noah tell the truth when he was arrested?"

"After the sheriff found that tarp with James's blood on it, we talked again. Noah said that if he was arrested, he would not fight it. I argued with him, but he said I didn't have much time left to be with the children. You see, the doctors have told me maybe two more years. He said it wouldn't be right if I spent that time in jail."

"He was willing to go prison for the rest of his life to protect you? And Kyoko agreed?"

"It was not going to be like that. Before he was arrested, Noah took photographs of everything in James's old shack, the whole mess there. I have that roll of film. And I wrote a confession, too. When I die, those pictures and my confession will free Noah if he's been convicted. Two years, Noah said. If it came to that, he would spend two years in jail for my sake, so that I could live out my days with my children. Kyoko agreed, though I knew it was very hard for her. I have been in Black Earth County for almost twenty years. No one has been as kind to me as Noah and Kyoko."

Charlie understood now why Noah Bluestone would not plead one way or the other to the charge of murder. A guilty plea or even a plea of nolo contendere might cast a deep shadow of doubt on everything when the real evidence was eventually presented. And a plea of innocence might result in the truth coming to light too soon and Marta being put on trial. Better to hold to silence.

"Would you really let Noah go to prison, Marta?"

The sunlight was shattered by the branches of a great elm in the front yard, and Marta stared at the bright, broken pieces. "What time I have left, I would like to spend with my children."

Yes, it was selfish, but in Marta's place, Charlie thought she might well have made the same choice.

"Mom." J.P. was on the porch again.

"We'll be there in just a minute," she said.

"No, Mom. Look." He pointed toward the barn.

Marta and Charlie turned and saw what had so alarmed J.P. Standing in the shadow cast by that great structure was a man. Because of the distance and the darkness of the barn shade, Charlie couldn't make out who it was at first. She figured it must have been Able Grange. It took a moment to realize that she was wrong.

"Tyler Creasy," she said.

"That's a shotgun he's holding," J.P. said.

Creasy stood looking their way, as if trying to make a decision.

"Go inside," Charlie said to J.P. "Call the sheriff, get him out here."

The young man vanished with a slap of the screen door.

Charlie stood up and stepped to the railing, and that movement seemed to push Creasy to action. He began walking toward the house.

"Tyler," Charlie called to him. "The sheriff is on his way. The best thing for you to do now is just turn around and go back where you came from."

He cradled the shotgun in his hands the way Charlie had seen hunters do when they were watchful for the flight of quail or pheasant. She heard the springs on the door squeal at her back and felt the boards on the porch quiver, then J.P. was beside her, a rifle in his own hands.

Marta said, "No, Son. No."

"That's far enough, Creasy," J.P. hollered.

The man stopped.

The screen door opened again, and Marta said, "Girls, back inside."

Colleen said, "We're staying with you, Mama."

Charlie glanced back and saw the daughters huddled against their mother.

Creasy considered them all a long time. Then he took another step forward. J.P. raised the rifle to his shoulder and fired a shot, aimed high.

"The next one won't miss," he called. "You go on and get out of here. Now!"

Creasy slowly lifted the shotgun as if preparing to return fire, then lowered it. He stared awhile longer, finally turned, and walked back the way he'd come. But he didn't go away. He disappeared into the barn.

"Inside, girls," Marta said. "You, too, Patrick."

"I'm staying out here," her son said. "I want to make sure he doesn't come back."

"I'm staying, too," Colleen said.

"And me," Bridget chimed in.

"Better all together," Charlie said to Marta.

So they stood huddled on that porch, watching the barn as if it were the lair of a monster.

It wasn't long before they saw black smoke roll out the windows of the loft and tongues of flame begin to lick at the walls. In the stillness of the late afternoon, they heard the boom of a single shotgun blast from inside that burning building.

CHAPTER FIFTY-ONE

WHEN HE GOT the call, Brody was driving slowly just south of Jewel, along a dirt road paralleling the Alabaster River and running through a thick stand of mixed hardwoods. It was a place he thought a man on the run might considering hiding a truck.

"Base to Unit One. Come in, Brody."

"This is Unit One. What's up, Hank?"

"Just got a call from the Quinn farm. Creasy's there. He's got a shotgun."

"What's he doing?"

"Nothing so far. Just threatening."

"I'm on my way."

Asa Fielding broke in on the transmission. "Unit One, this is Unit Two. Over."

"Go ahead, Asa."

"I'm at the north end of town, Brody, but en route now to the Quinn farm. ETA fifteen minutes."

"Ten-four. Call Noah Bluestone's place, Hank. Tell Connie I want him on this, too."

"Roger that, Brody. Base out."

Brody was still a good two miles from the Quinn farmstead when he saw black smoke rising in the sky above the green fields. Almost simultaneously, Hank Evans hailed him on the radio.

"That son of a bitch Creasy set fire to the barn, Brody."

"Get Norm Castle and his guys out there," Brody said, speaking of the town's fire chief and his men.

"Called 'em before I radioed you."

"Good work. Did you get hold of Connie?"

"He's on his way."

Three minutes later, Brody rolled his cruiser into the Quinns' yard. He leapt out and ran to the porch, where Charlie Bauer and the Quinns stood together. His eyes quickly took them in, especially Charlie, whose presence surprised him.

"Everyone okay?" he asked.

"We're fine," Charlie said.

"Creasy?"

"He's still in the barn," J.P. said. "But, Sheriff, before Creasy got here, Able Grange and me, we were mucking out the cattle pen. I came in to have supper, but Able stayed up at the barn. He wanted to sharpen the blades on the disc harrow before he went home. He hasn't come out."

"After the fire started, we heard a shotgun go off inside," Charlie said. "Creasy wasn't shooting at us."

Brody stepped to the railing and studied the barn intently. "You all stay here," he said. "Deputy Fielding and Deputy Graff are on their way."

He left the porch and returned to his cruiser. He opened the trunk, bent inside, and came up with a shotgun in his hands.

A moment later, Connie Graff sped up the lane. His truck skidded to a halt near Brody's cruiser, and the old deputy jumped out, bringing a rifle with him. He met Brody and they talked strategy for a moment, then Graff headed toward the big equipment shed that lay on the other side of the lane directly opposite the burning barn, where he took up a position that would allow him to fire into the open barn door, if necessary. Asa Fielding arrived moments later, and Brody sent him to a position behind the long feed trough of the cattle yard, which gave the deputy a clear view of the back of the barn. Then Brody got into his cruiser and drove within thirty yards of the flames.

When he got out, he felt the scorch from the heat, smelled the char of the burning wood, heard the flames speaking in their crackling voices. He'd been to fires before in his capacity as sheriff, lots of them. But he'd never had an armed man inside a burning building. He thought about that single shotgun blast that had come moments after Creasy started the fire. Had the man killed Able Grange? Or had he finally turned the corner on sanity and ended his own life?

Brody crouched behind the cover of his cruiser, shotgun to his shoulder, aimed at the barn doorway, where all that came forth were rolling heaves of thick smoke. "Creasy!" he shouted. "Tyler Creasy! Come out now with your hands up!"

He got no response.

"Able Grange, you in there?"

There was no reply to that either. He glanced toward Graff and nodded at the barn door. Graff gave him a nod in return. Brody rose and ran.

He pressed himself against the wall next to the broad barn doorway. He breathed hard and fast and it had nothing to do with any physical exertion. He was simply scared. Scared so bad his legs threatened to buckle.

"Tyler! Able!" he called again. "Can you hear me? It's Brody Dern."

The only reply came from the fire and now included the sound of collapse from inside the building. Brody knelt and peered around the edge of the door opening. He couldn't see anything except smoke. He signaled to Graff that he was going in and moved forward. Almost immediately, a burning board from the collapsing loft fell only a few feet from him, and he backed out quickly.

The barn was built into a hillside and constructed on three levels: the loft, the main level with its heavy-beamed floor, and the lower area, which was basically a pen and opened onto the large cattle yard in back. Brody slipped along the side of the barn, down the steep slope, and climbed the fence into the cattle yard. Asa Fielding rose to join him, but Brody waved him back. The livestock had all moved to the far railing, where they stood milling and bawling. In a separate, smaller pen, the bull that J.P. called Big Bastard paced back and forth, bellowing as if he'd love nothing better than to lower his great head and charge the fire. Brody eased to the wide rear entrance of the barn.

The fire was still above him. The lower level was relatively clear of smoke. Brody moved carefully inside. Except for the support posts and the long feed troughs, the area was unobstructed. A wooden stairway at the far end led up to the main level. Brody made for the stairway, climbed the steps cautiously, paused, then, with great reluctance, poked his head through the opening above.

The heat was intense, the barn a chaotic roil of gray and white and black smoke. At first, Brody could see almost nothing. Then he spotted what appeared to be a human form lying on the barn floor, partially obscured by the blades of a disc harrow.

"Able!" he called. "Able Grange!"

The form didn't move. Brody left his shotgun on the stairs and crawled on all fours, trying to keep as low as possible in order to find breathable air. He did a poor job of it, and his lungs felt seared. Bits of burning debris rained down around him. He reached the body, his vision blurry, his eyes watering from the smoke, and grabbed blindly. His fingers wrapped around wrist bone, and he tugged. As he dragged the body across the floor, the air he sucked in felt as if it had come from a blast furnace. He tumbled down the stairs onto the dirt floor, hauling the body with him. He managed to pull himself up and drag Able Grange into the fresh air of the cattle yard. Then he coughed himself sick.

"You okay, Brody?"

It was Asa Fielding at his side, a hand on his arm in support.

Brody coughed a good deal more, spat up black sputum, and said, "How's Grange?"

"All I can see is a bad bruise on the side of his face and his eye's all swoll up. No gunshot wound. Looks like Creasy just clobbered him good. You see Creasy in there?"

Brody shook his head.

"Norm Castle wants to know if it's safe to fight the fire."

Brody brought himself upright and looked toward the farmyard, where two pumpers sat, lights still flashing. The firefighters stood ready, keeping at a distance that ensured a load of buckshot from the barn would have no effect.

Brody nodded. "If Creasy's in there, he won't be causing any trouble. Help me get Grange up to the house."

Fielding waved an okay toward the fire trucks, then turned to give Brody a hand.

BRODY SAT ON the steps of the big Quinn house. To Charlie Bauer, he looked like a man who'd crawled through hell. His face was red, as if he'd been badly sunburned. His hair was stiff and he had no eyebrows. His clothing reeked of smoke. His shadow on the porch steps was black, like the burned man he might have become in risking himself to pull Able Grange from the barn.

Sam Wicklow was there, shooting photos of the fire, the firemen, and now of Brody as he sat hunched on the steps.

Tom Dern knelt before his brother, asking Brody questions, treating in a preliminary way the damage Brody had sustained in his ordeal. Tom had long been a member of the volunteer fire brigade out of Crescent, a small community south of Jewel that serviced the surrounding area and that often joined the Jewel firefighters on rural calls. Garnet was there, too, as were a number of the Quinns' neighbors, who'd seen the smoke and had hurried over to do whatever they could to help. Charlie stood with them in the farmyard, watching the fire being fought.

Wicklow gestured to Brody and Tom. "You two boys mind looking this way?" His camera clicked. "Good shot," he said. "Caption: Brothers Fight Blaze."

Tom turned his attention back to Brody. "You need to get yourself to the hospital. You inhaled a lot of smoke. Those burns'll need treating, too."

Brody waved him off. "I'm okay." He stared at the barn, where the flames had been pretty well dealt with. Although the loft and roof had collapsed, the walls were still mostly intact. Smoke and white steam rose up from inside, and firefighters were still pouring streams of water over the debris there.

Before they took him to the hospital to be treated, Able Grange had regained consciousness. All he could remember was that one minute he was bent over the disc harrow in the barn and the next he was lying on the grass in front of the Quinn house.

Charlie stood with Connie Graff, who'd finally left his position covering the front door of the barn.

"What do you think, Connie?" she said.

"About what?"

"Tyler Creasy."

"One shot and it wasn't to take out Grange. I think the man came to the end he wanted. Maybe deserved."

Charlie wondered aloud if his end had been from that single shotgun blast they'd heard, or if the fire had been the agent of his demise.

"Does it matter, Charlie?" Graff said. "His misery's over, and the misery he caused."

Brody stood up. "I need to get inside the barn."

"What for?" Tom said.

"To make sure Creasy was in there."

"Nobody saw him leave."

"People miss things."

"Wait here." Tom walked toward the pumpers.

Graff said, "He's done for, you know that, Brody."

"I need to be sure," the sheriff replied.

Tom came back with Norm Castle, the fire chief, who was looking none too happy. "I understand you want to go in there, Brody," Castle said.

"Yeah. And now."

"I'd prefer you wait until I'm sure everything's cooled down and we've got no hot spots. I also don't know how damaged that floor is and what kind of weight it will or won't hold."

"I'll be careful, Norm."

"If you go, I don't want you going in there alone."

"I'll go with him," Tom said.

"Okay," Castle said. "I guess we're ready when you are."

Brody, Tom, and Castle headed to the barn, with Sam Wicklow trailing behind, moving that stiff leg as rapidly as he could to keep up. Castle gave orders to the firefighters, and the streams of water that arced against and into the barn were cut off. Castle handed Brody and Tom each an ax, then accompanied them as far as the barn door, or what was left of it, and stood watching as they entered. Wicklow positioned himself in the doorway, camera raised. Charlie and everyone else stood watching, holding their breath. Smoke still curled up from inside the charred walls, vining tendrils glowing electric in the late sunlight.

"If they get themselves hurt," Charlie heard Garnet whisper, "I'll kill them both."

They emerged a few minutes later. Brody came out at a run. He went straight to the Quinns.

"He's not in there, Marta. You're sure you didn't see him leave."

"No." She looked at her children.

"We couldn't see the back of the barn," J.P. said. "He could've gone down the stairs and out through the cattle yard, I suppose."

"Why did he fire the shotgun?" Marta asked. "If he was just going to run away?"

"Obfuscation, maybe," Graff said. "He may have wanted you to think he was still in there while he hightailed it. He's gone off his rocker, but that doesn't mean he doesn't have a plan."

"He threatened to get back at the people in this county he had a grudge against," Brody said. "Maybe he figured burning the barn took care of the Quinns." He thought a moment, then looked at Graff. "He threatened Bluestone, too."

"Marta," Graff said in a tense voice, "I need to use your phone."

"Of course. Colleen, will you take him inside to the telephone?"

Asa Fielding had been at his car, using the radio to keep Hank Evans apprised of what was happening at the Quinn farm, and Evans, in turn, had been giving updates to the other law enforcement agencies involved in the hunt for Tyler Creasy. Brody signaled to him, and Fielding hustled over.

"Asa, tell Hank that Creasy's still out there. Have him alert the other officers. Let them know he's armed and dangerous." Brody turned to Marta. "I'm going to leave Deputy Fielding here with you and the kids. I don't imagine Creasy'll come back, but just in case he does." He looked to Tom, who'd come with him from the barn. "I need a favor, a big one."

"You've got it."

"Scott Madison and Del Wolfe are out there somewhere hunting Creasy. They're armed and they're boys, Tom. I've been looking for them all afternoon. No luck. It's more important than ever that we find them."

"Got a suggestion?"

"Creasy likes to drink and he likes to do it in the company of cock-roaches. I want you to hit the bars in the county where decent folks don't go, see if Creasy's been there or the boys. You know the places I'm talking about?"

"I've lived here all my life, Brody. I don't frequent them, but I sure as hell know where they are."

"If you happen to run across Creasy, no heroics. Just call the jailhouse. Hank'll let me know."

"What about the boys if I find them?"

"You'll figure something."

Graff came from the house, looking worried. "Kyoko's not answering, Brody. I'm going over there."

"Go ahead," Brody told him. "And let me know."

"Will do." Graff sprinted for his truck.

"I'm going with him," Charlie said. She turned to Marta. "You're safe, I promise."

Anyone who heard would have thought she was talking about the situation with Tyler Creasy. But Marta knew the truth and thanked her with a nod.

CHAPTER FIFTY-TWO

BRODY DERN HAD been correct in his final speculation about the two boys. Scott Madison and Del Wolfe had, indeed, gone hunting for Tyler Creasy in the crossroads bars where the decent folks of Black Earth County seldom set foot. These were places with dark interiors and names like the Pickled Pig, Robber's Roost, and the Lion's Den. They rode the motorbike. Though Del hadn't put a speedometer on his little makeshift machine, he'd always judged top speed to be maybe fifteen miles an hour. They filled the tiny gas tank three times. The last was in the village of Carthage, on the Alabaster well south of Jewel, almost to the Iowa border. Del stopped in front of a bar called Willy's, and the boys went inside.

It was late afternoon by then. The place was nearly empty. Somebody had put a nickel in the jukebox and Buddy Holly was belting out "Peggy Sue." The barkeep gave the boys the evil eye, and when they approached, he said, "Don't serve kids here. Come back when you've growed face hair."

Scott stood beside his friend. He found himself trying to identify the chords in the song on the jukebox, and in his head, he was watching his fingers slide over the strings of his guitar. He was also wishing he were home and sitting with Wendell and they were playing music together. The bar smelled damp and sour, and he knew it was no place for them. It scared him. The surly look of the man behind the bar scared him, too.

Maybe what scared him most was that all afternoon Del had seemed oblivious to the hostility they'd encountered in every dive they'd entered. It wasn't fearlessness, Scott believed, but recklessness. Yet scared as he was, he was glad to be there. If he were in Del's place, he'd want a friend at his side when confronting a man like the one who glared at them now.

"Looking for someone," Del said.

"Yeah? Who?" The barkeep had beefy arms with tattoos whose outlines looked like gangrenous veins.

"My old man." It wasn't exactly true, but Del had been using the line all day.

"And who would that be?"

"Tyler Creasy."

"Creasy? That son of a bitch has a kid?" The barkeep gave a laugh, and his breath carried foul across the bar to where Scott stood, wishing only to be gone. "He the one messed up your face? Yeah, he was here. Got himself a snootful, left. Couple of hours ago."

"Did he say where he was going?"

"Didn't say and I didn't ask."

"Come on, Del." Scott took hold of his friend's arm.

Del shook him off. "If he comes back, do me a favor."

"Yeah, what?"

"Tell him from me to go to hell."

The barkeep smiled in broad approval. "I just might do that, kid."

Outside, the sun had sunk low in the sky. Although all he'd done much of the day was ride on the motorbike, Scott was tired. In fact, he was exhausted, that faulty heart of his working hard. He wanted to be home and resting.

"Let's just go back to Jewel, Del."

"I'm not going back. They'll make me take that fuggin' bus to Saint Paul. I'm not leaving until I find Creasy, or someone has."

"Maybe they've already found him."

The boys stood in the long shadow of Willy's, in a town that was a gathering of a couple of dozen houses, one gas station, a small grocery store, and the bar. But for them, the street was empty. The loneliness of the place weighed on Scott, and he still had no idea what, exactly, Del might actually do if they found Creasy. He didn't like thinking about that.

Del considered the possibility of what Scott had suggested, that Creasy had been found. "Maybe, Madman," he said.

"Let's go back and find out."

"I'm not going to your house."

"We can call from a pay phone."

"Where?"

"Fort Beloit. We've got to get our stuff anyway, and that way we don't even have to go into town."

Del looked at the sky, which at the moment was an immense, washed-out, cloudless blue. He gave a nod. "All right."

They kept to back roads. A few miles outside Jewel, they saw a column of black smoke against the horizon.

"Big fire somewhere," Del called out, and he turned west to avoid trouble.

According to the clock on the wall of the concession stand at Fort Beloit, it was nearing seven when the boys arrived. They each bought a Coke and a hot dog, then Scott dropped a dime into the pay phone on the outside wall and called home. His mother answered, and the relief in her voice nearly shattered his resolve.

"Oh, Scott, you're all right."

"Of course I am, Mom."

"Where are you?"

"Safe," he said and hated himself for what he knew was cruelty. "Have they found Tyler Creasy yet?"

"They haven't. You come home. You come home this minute."

"I can't, Mom. Del needs me."

"This isn't a game, Scott."

"We have to do this."

"Do what?"

"Find him."

"And then what?"

The question of the day, and one for which he had no answer.

"I'm sorry, Mom. I've got to go."

He hung up before she had a chance to say anything more, a chance to talk him out of what he'd known from the beginning had been a very bad idea.

"Creasy?" Del said.

"He's still out there."

"Then we still have work to do."

"Look, it'll be dark soon. What're we going to do then?"

Del's mouth set in a grim smile, and Scott knew he'd been thinking about this and had an answer.

THE SUN WAS setting when Del drove the motorbike off the main road and onto the track that led to the bloodstained ground at the tip of Inkpaduta Bend. They came to a small gathering of birch trees along the western edge of the Bend, where Del killed the engine and they both dismounted. Del pushed the bike into the trees. Scott followed, carrying the things they'd retrieved from the campground at Fort Beloit—a bed-roll, a sleeping bag, and a pack, which held, among other things, snack food they'd purchased from the concession stand.

"We can build a fire here and nobody'll see it," Del said with satisfaction. "Tomorrow, we'll look for that fuggin' Creasy again."

Scott didn't say anything. What he hoped was that a night out in the wild like this might cool Del off and, in the morning, he might listen to reason.

They laid the bedroll and sleeping bag beneath the birches on the bank of the river. The base of Fordham Ridge lay in shadow now, but the sun, as it set, poured red-gold over the fields on top. Inkpaduta Bend was a pretty place, Scott thought. And quiet. And far from the menace of the bars they'd spent the afternoon invading. He was tired and ready to lie down for a while and rest, and he told Del so.

"That's okay, Madman. You go ahead. I'll gather some firewood."

Del walked off, and Scott lay down. He hated himself for what he was doing, the worry he knew he was causing his mother and grand-mother. But he believed that he had no choice. What concerned him even more was the question of what Del might do, or try to do, if they actually found Tyler Creasy. He hoped the man had fled Black Earth County, even if that meant Creasy would still be out there, a threat that might come back into Del's life. But maybe, because of the man Creasy was, he'd get himself into trouble somewhere else and it would fall to others to bring him to justice and put him away where he'd do no harm. Scott closed his eyes, thinking that if he were Creasy, he'd just run as far as he could from the trouble he'd caused. That thought gave him some measure of comfort, and before he knew it, he was sleeping.

He was awakened by a shaking of his arm and Del's harsh whisper in his ear: "Madman! Madman!"

Scott looked up into Del's face. "Wha—?" he began, trying to clear his brain.

"He's here, Madman," Del whispered. "That fuggin' asshole Creasy. He's here."

That woke Scott completely. He sat up. "Where?"

Del put a finger to his lips and signaled for Scott to follow.

In the darkening twilight, they crept through the tall grass and wild-flowers. They came to a narrow thicket of sumac, and Del went down on all fours. Scott did the same and they crawled forward.

Among the trees on the other side of the thicket, Scott saw what Del had already seen, a pickup truck, the same truck that only a few days earlier had hauled them both, along with Holly Coleridge and Nicole Blake and four inner tubes, to the Alabaster for the float trip that had made Scott a hero.

"Where is he?" Scott whispered.

"Gone," Del said. "At least for now. Wait here."

Scott watched his friend run to the truck and open the passenger door. Del rummaged inside for a minute, then closed the door and came quickly back. He held out his hands to Scott, and in them was a shotgun.

"Take it," Del said.

"I don't want to, Wolfman."

Del shoved it at him. "Take it," he ordered.

Scott did. The firearm felt so heavy he wasn't sure he could hold it up for long. "What are we going to do?"

"Wait for Creasy to come back."

"And then what? Just shoot him?"

From where he'd shoved it in the waist of his jeans, Del took the pistol he'd carried with him all day. He looked at his friend, eyes like ice. And Scott knew that was exactly what he intended to do.

CHAPTER FIFTY-THREE

IN HER CAR, Charlie followed Connie Graff as he maneuvered along the roads to the Bluestone farmstead. He went fast, his concern for Kyoko giving his driving a reckless edge. Noah Bluestone's land lay in the shadow of Fordham Ridge, four miles north of the Quinn farm. Graff crossed the Alabaster on County 13 with Charlie close behind and turned up the long dirt lane that led to the farmhouse and outbuildings. He skidded his truck to a stop in the bare dirt in front of the little barn. He leapt out and ran to the house. Charlie parked and hurried to where he was pounding on the front door and calling Kyoko's name. By the time Charlie joined him, Kyoko still hadn't answered. Graff threw the door open and rushed inside, Charlie hard on his heels.

"Kyoko!" he called.

"Kyoko!" Charlie echoed.

The house was empty.

Outside, the last light of the sun bathed the land and everything on it in a blood-red hue. The pigs, blood red in their muddy pen, seemed restless and milled about and gave out grunts like disapproving old men. In the chicken yard, blood-red hens ran about in pointless lurchings, as if startled by things Charlie couldn't see. She and Connie Graff called Kyoko's name again and again, looked in the barn and in the loft. With each failure in finding her, they grew more afraid.

Graff said, "I'm going to call Brody on the radio, see if anybody's got anything."

There didn't seem much use in this, but Charlie figured Graff needed to do something and that was it. Charlie walked around to the back of the house because it was the only place they hadn't looked yet. The tiny orchard was there, the apple trees where Graff and Brody had dug up the tarp with Quinn's blood on it. Charlie had always thought of the orchard as a symbol of promise. Noah Bluestone and Kyoko had planted it with the idea that it would bear fruit for many years, and they would be there, year after year, for the harvest. For a long time, neither of them had had a place they called home, but this was going to be it.

The people of Black Earth County had never been welcoming of the Bluestones, Charlie thought. Many, in fact, had carried in their hearts a deep enmity from wounds that neither Noah nor Kyoko had had any part in delivering. These weren't bad people. They simply did not forgive easily. In Charlie's experience with human beings, that was the rule, not the exception.

As she stood looking out across the rows of young trees, she heard a long, low keening, like a mother cat calling for her lost kittens. She saw movement on the ground at the far end of the orchard. She began to walk toward it. Then she began to run.

Kyoko lay in the short grass that had grown beneath the fruit trees. She'd been beaten. The shirt she wore was torn open. Below her waist, her body had been stripped bare of clothing. It was clear to Charlie what had happened.

Kyoko stared up into the evening sky and sobbed uncontrollably.

Charlie spoke gently: "Oh, sweetheart, I'm sorry. I'm so sorry."

Graff came loping toward them. Charlie wore a light beige sweater over her blouse. She removed the sweater and, as best she could, covered that part of Kyoko's body that was bare and had been violated.

Graff slowed as he neared. Charlie looked at him and saw the devastation in his face. He knelt beside Kyoko. "Who?" he said. When she didn't respond, he said, "Creasy?"

The young woman closed her eyes, as if the name itself conjured an image she couldn't bear to see. "He said hateful things about my husband. He said he was going to ruin us both."

"We need to get you somewhere to be treated," Graff said.

"I don't want to see anybody."

"A doctor—" Charlie began.

Kyoko shook her head, violently flinging tears off her face. "No one. I want to see no one."

"All right," Graff said, soothing. "All right. But let's get you back to the house, okay?"

Her jeans and underpants lay thrown in the grass. Charlie said, "Turn away, Connie. I'll get her dressed."

They helped her to the farmhouse and inside to the bedroom, where she lay down.

Graff stepped back. "I've got to call this in." There was raw menace in his voice. He left and went outside to his truck and its radio.

Kyoko had finally stopped crying but wouldn't speak. Although the window was open, not a breath of wind came through. Outside, the land reflected the light that had spread across the sky, a rash-red hue that put Charlie in mind of contagion. Inside that small room, the air felt too dark and too close.

Graff returned. "Brody's on his way."

There's a hardness in men that Charlie had always wondered at. A part of them seemed always stone or ready to turn to stone. An evolutionary necessity, perhaps, in the face of all that a hostile world might throw at them. To stand before the walls of Troy and hack away at another man or be hacked at required, Charlie supposed, a certain granite resolve. And that's what she saw in Connie Graff on his return. His face was a mask of gentleness, for Kyoko's sake, Charlie figured, but in his eyes, she saw the stone look Achilles must have given Hector before slaughtering him and dragging his body ignominiously around the city walls. She knew that Tyler Creasy, if Graff were the one to find him, stood no chance of surviving that encounter.

Charlie's heart went out to Kyoko, but she understood that Bluestone's wife was resilient, because that's what a woman had to be to survive. What Charlie knew when she looked at Connie Graff was that his own heart was broken. And that was the problem with stone. It could not yield. It simply shattered.

CHAPTER FIFTY-FOUR

ANGIE MADISON STOOD outside in the waning light of day, her arms crossed pensively. Wendell Moon still occupied the porch chair in which he'd sat all afternoon. He had a paper plate on his lap and was eating a turkey sandwich Angie had prepared for him. Leaning against the wall at his side, next to his guitar, was a squirrel gun, an old .22 long rifle. After Brody got the call about Tyler Creasy waving a shotgun around at the Quinn place, Wendell had gone to his room above the garage and pulled the old piece from the closet where he kept it. It was clean and oiled and loaded.

"Beautiful sunset for such an ugly day," Wendell said and wiped his mouth with a paper napkin. "Like God puttin' icing on a cow pie."

"Do you believe in God, Wendell?" Angie didn't look at him when she asked. Her eyes were on the street, watching for Scott or Del, or for Brody to come with some word of the boys.

"Seen too many miracles to say no to that one, Angie."

"What kind of miracles, Wendell?"

"Birth of my son, for one."

Now she looked at him, and it was with surprise. "Whenever I've asked you, Wendell, you've always said that you've got no family. Why haven't you ever told me you had a son?"

"No reason to."

"Where is he?"

"Lost him in the war, in some jungle. Missing in action first, then presumed dead. Nothing after that. Presumed," he said, as if the word were an affront. "You don't hear from someone for fifteen years, it's a pretty good bet he's not coming back."

"I'm sorry, Wendell."

"So am I. But that's the way it is, and that's why I never told you. Nothing to be done about it. You asked about miracles. I believe in 'em, I do. Yeah, I'd love to see that son of mine come walkin' down Main Street here in Jewel someday. I know it ain't gonna happen. But there is a miracle in the way things are."

"What would that be?"

"What I said about not havin' any family? That's not true. I'm sittin' here on this porch, with a woman that's family to me, and another woman in this house that's family, and a boy out there that's family. When I lost my son, I pretty much thought I lost everything. Then I stumbled onto you and Ida and Scott." He looked up at her and smiled. "You asked me if I believe in God. You know what I think, Angie? I think you're God. And Ida is. And Scott. And you know what else? Me, too, this old black Okie. If that makes any sense to you."

She went down on her knees and wrapped her arms around Wendell, who still smelled of fried onions from the kitchen. "It makes perfect sense to me."

She stood up and Wendell said, "Now if I can just line up a bead on that Tyler Creasy, I'd happily send that man's soul into the arms of the angels for a little redemption."

"I don't want anyone dead," she said. "Not even Tyler Creasy. I just want my son back."

Wendell considered that, gave a nod, and returned to eating his sandwich.

She spotted Brody's cruiser approaching from far down Main Street, and her heart made a fist in her chest. Brody pulled to the curb. She wanted to run to him but held back. He didn't look happy as he came up the walk.

"Have you heard from Scott?" he asked before he reached her.

"He called but wouldn't tell me where he was. Have you had any word?"

He shook his head. He smelled of smoke, and his face was bright red, and his eyebrows had been singed nearly clean off.

"What happened?" she asked. "You look like you've been in a fire."

"Creasy tried to burn down the Quinns' barn."

Wendell said, "And maybe did that barn burn the man up with it?"

"He managed to slip away," Brody said.

All of Angie's fears welled up, nearly choking her. "He's still out there, then. And Scott's still out there. Oh, Brody, I don't know what to do."

The radio in Brody's cruiser crackled. "Base to Unit One. Come in, Brody."

He lifted a finger to Angie, a signal to be patient while he took the call. The radio was loud enough that she heard the information Hank Evans relayed: Tyler Creasy had attacked Kyoko Bluestone.

Brody came back.

"I heard," she said.

"I've got to go out to there, Angie. But listen, we've got lots of folks looking for Scott and Del right now. If I hear anything from them, I'll let you know. If the boys show up here—and I'm still believing they'll be back by dark—give the jailhouse a call. Hank'll relay that to me."

"What if they don't come back? What if they just stay out there hunting Tyler Creasy?"

"Then pray that we find Creasy before they do."

AN HOUR LATER, Brody walked into the jailhouse. Hank Evans was on the telephone, writing down something on a pad of paper. He looked up when Brody entered and said into the receiver, "He just came in. You want to talk to him?" Evans held out the phone. "Your brother."

Brody took the call. "What have you got, Tom?"

"I'm in Carthage, at Willy's. You know the place."

"Sure. Are the boys there?"

"They were. The barkeep says they came in a couple of hours ago looking for Creasy. Left pretty quick."

"Did they say where they were going?"

"Not to the barkeep, but he saw them take off on a little motorbike heading toward Jewel."

"A couple of hours," Brody said. "If they were coming home, they'd be here by now."

"I'll keep looking."

"Thanks, Tom. I appreciate it." He handed the receiver back to Evans. "Did you say anything to Bluestone about his wife?"

Evans said, "You told me not to."

"Good."

"How is she?"

"Beat up pretty bad. Doc Porter's out at Bluestone's place now. She won't leave the farmhouse." Brody looked toward the cellblock door.

"Going to tell him?" Evans asked.

Brody said, "Let me have the keys."

A soft padding came from the stairs that led to the upper floor. A moment later, Hector trotted in. He came to Brody eagerly, and the sheriff bent and ruffed the dog's fur. "Sorry, boy, it's been a busy day."

"I let him out a little while ago so he could do his business," Evans said. "He's pretty easy."

"Come on, Hector." Brody rose and headed toward the cellblock.

Bluestone was lying on his cot, staring up at the ceiling, which was lit with the last sad light of that sad day. Bluestone sat up at his approach.

Brody stood at the barred cell door. "We need to talk, Noah. Tyler Creasy's been on a kind of rampage today. He set fire to the Quinns' barn."

"That son of a bitch."

"That's not all of it," Brody said. "He attacked your wife."

Bluestone was off the cot and to the cell door, his hands squeezing the bars. "Attacked? Is she all right?"

"He roughed her up pretty bad, but she's okay. Doc Porter's with her and Charlie and Connie Graff. But, Noah . . ." Brody gathered himself before going on, before delivering the worst. "He didn't just rough her up. He raped her."

Brody watched the man's face change. A moment before, there'd been fear. Now there was something else. Stone.

"I want to see her," Bluestone said.

"She's not ready for that, Noah. Not yet anyway."

"I want to see her." And what was in his face was in his voice now.

"I don't think that's a good idea."

The two men stood with the bars between them, both unmoving in their resolve.

Then Bluestone said the one thing that could make Brody crack: "If it was the woman you loved, would you stay away?"

Brody thought of the woman he loved, the women, and he unlocked the cell. "Let's go, then."

Back at the desk, he said to Evans, "Give me a pair of cuffs, Hank."

Evans opened a drawer in the desk and pulled out handcuffs and a key, which he handed to Brody.

"We're going to the Bluestone farm, Hank," Brody said. "You hear anything about Creasy or those two missing boys, you let me know."

"I will. When this is over, you should talk to Doc about that face of yours. So red you're looking Indian." He glanced at Bluestone, shrugged a kind of apology.

The sheriff cuffed Bluestone, then knelt and ran his hand over Hector's head and down the soft fur of his back. "Got to leave again, boy. You be good for Hank." He stood. "Let's go, Noah."

By the time they arrived, night had descended and the moon was on the rise. Graff met them at the door. He eyed Bluestone, and it was clear that he thought the man's presence wasn't a good idea. But it was Bluestone's home and Bluestone's wife and Brody's call, so Graff stepped aside. They met Doc Porter coming from the bedroom.

"How is she?" Bluestone asked.

"Bruised mostly. I've given her something for the pain and to help her relax. It would be good, though, if she went to the ER or to my office."

Bluestone turned to Brody and held up his cuffed wrists. "Best if she doesn't see me like this."

Brody took off the cuffs and walked Bluestone into the room, where Charlie Bauer sat with Kyoko.

KYOKO HAD HEARD his voice in the house, heard him coming, and she'd whispered, "Oh, God, no."

But there he was in the doorway, and Charlie saw in him the same kind of stone that she'd seen in Graff. Shattered. The moment he saw Kyoko, his heart had broken. His face betrayed nothing, but his eyes, those windows on his soul, showed everything.

Kyoko must have seen it, too. Because now she was not weak. She was not weeping. She said, "Come here, Noah."

From the doorway, Brody looked at the room's open window, then he looked at Charlie. She gave him a nod, letting him know that Noah Bluestone would not depart that way. He stepped back and disappeared, leaving them alone.

Noah walked to his wife and sat on the bed, and Charlie wasn't sure she'd ever seen a man try so hard not to cry.

Kyoko reached up and touched his face. "It will be all right." She smiled gently. "They've tried in every possible way to ruin us, but we are not ruined, Noah."

"I should have been here," he said.

"You're here now."

He dropped his gaze, as if he could not meet her eyes.

"Look at me, Noah." She waited until he did. "Everything passes. We know this, you and me. Everything. This will pass, too."

"Do you hurt?" he asked.

"Not much." She squeezed his hand. "Mostly when I look at you."

"I love you," he said. And all the tears he could not cry were in those three words.

"Still?" she asked.

"Forever."

"You see," she said. "We are not ruined."

Noah leaned down and kissed her forehead.

Then Brody was in the doorway again. "We need to go back now."

Noah said to Charlie, "You'll stay?"

"Of course I will."

He looked up at Brody. "And Graff?"

"Graff stays," Brody said.

"I'll come back," Noah said to Kyoko.

She smiled at him again. "I know you will. I'll be waiting."

Noah stood and walked out the door with Brody.

In the quiet of that windless evening, Kyoko said, as if to reassure herself, "We are not ruined."

IN THE FARMYARD outside, Bluestone held out his hands. Once again, Brody placed the cuffs on his wrists. The moon was climbing above Black Earth County and the Alabaster River, and the three men—Bluestone, Brody, and Graff—cast long black moon shadows on the ground.

Bluestone said, "Creasy slipped away at Quinn's. On foot?"

"I'm guessing so," Brody said.

To Graff, Bluestone said, "And here? How did he approach my wife?"

Graff said, "She told me she didn't hear him coming, so on foot I'm guessing."

Bluestone said nothing more. Brody opened the back door of the cruiser and Bluestone got in.

"You're okay here tonight, Connie?" Brody asked.

"I've got it covered. Any word on those missing boys?"

"Nothing yet."

"Long night, looks like."

"Looks like." Brody got behind the wheel.

He'd driven only a couple of hundred yards down the dirt lane when Bluestone said from the back, "Pull over."

Brody glanced into the rearview mirror. "What?"

"Pull over. I'm going to be sick."

Brody slowed but didn't stop.

"I'm going to be sick," Bluestone said again. "You want me to puke in your car?"

The man had held himself together at the farmhouse, but now Brody saw the impact from that emotional trauma, the physical effect, the unraveling, which often came in the form of vomiting. He braked, got quickly out, and opened the back door.

Bluestone slid from the cruiser, then launched himself. Before Brody knew what hit him, he lay facedown on the ground with the full weight of Bluestone on his back, the chain of the handcuffs digging into his throat, his air cut off. He clawed at Bluestone's arms, tried to push himself up, flip his body over, somehow blunt the attack. But Noah Bluestone, who'd spent the last twenty years killing and training others to kill, knew his work. Brody's head tingled, and he saw honest to God stars, and just as he began to black out and go limp, the chain came away, and he could breathe again.

He felt Bluestone rifling his pockets and he tried to protest, but the chain that had choked off his air had done something to his vocal cords as well, and he couldn't speak. He rolled over and watched as Bluestone used the key he'd found to free himself. He threw the cuffs down next Brody in the dirt lane.

"I have to do this," Bluestone said.

"Creasy?" Brody managed to croak.

"Creasy," Bluestone said.

Brody swallowed hard and it hurt, but he said hoarsely, "Know where he is?"

"Pretty sure."

Bluestone got into the cruiser, which Brody had left running, and drove away.

GRAFF SAT ON the bench beneath the Dutch elm tree in the yard of the Bluestone farm, smoking a cigarette he'd rolled. In their pen, the pigs were quiet now, unmoving and white under the risen moon. In that windless night, the old deputy stared across the fields of strange crops that Noah Bluestone had planted. Not the corn and soybeans of the neighboring farms, but crops with names like amaranth and millet, and what the hell could you make from those things? Why had a man with nothing to pull him back returned to Black Earth County? Why had he brought a beautiful woman like Kyoko to a place that didn't want her and where men like Jimmy Quinn and Tyler Creasy could prey on her? Connie Graff was angry with Noah Bluestone, angry with himself, angry with Brody. Men were supposed to protect those they loved and those they were responsible for. A lawman especially. But what had he done? Or Brody or Asa Fielding or anyone else?

He'd never truly felt murder in his heart, but that's what he felt now. There was a man somewhere out there in the dark who was better off dead. He could name a hundred unfortunate reasons why Tyler Creasy was the way he was, but that didn't change what the man had done and still could do.

If only he hadn't gone on the call to the Quinn place. If only the Bluestones' dog had not been shot and could have barked a warning. If only Noah Bluestone had not been arrested for a crime he was probably guilty of but which Graff understood completely and could pardon. If only . . . if only . . .

When he heard the shuffling in the dirt of the lane behind him, he threw his cigarette down and stood quickly, ready for battle if it was Creasy returning. He saw the dark figure against the white moon and immediately recognized Brody Dern.

"He jumped me," Brody said in a strange, rasping voice.

"Bluestone?"

"Took my cruiser." Brody spoke not only strangely but breathlessly, as if he was having trouble drawing air. "He must know where Creasy is."

Which amazed Graff. "How could he know that?"

Brody leaned against the back of the bench and sucked hard and didn't answer.

Graff thought a moment and the answer came. "We gave it to him."

Brody looked up, uncomprehending.

"Think about those last questions he asked us, about Creasy on foot. We haven't been able to find the man, so it's a good bet he's hiding somewhere, somewhere he'd be pretty certain not many people would go. Think, Brody. Where would that be? Somewhere walking distance from here."

Graff watched Brody's eyes and saw the knowledge come into them, watched them turn to the south where Fordham Ridge stood like a dark wall against a tide of moonlight. Below that great formation lay Inkpaduta Bend.

CHAPTER FIFTY-FIVE

HE CAME AFTER the moon had risen. The boys heard him breaking through undergrowth along the river, then saw him, ghost-white in the moonlight, enter the clearing. He crossed the Bend in the same way they had crossed, following almost the same line they had followed through the tall wild grasses. Scott was afraid Creasy might notice the crushed ground cover and bent stalks they'd left in their wake, which was something Scott had learned about tracking from the Boy Scouts. But Creasy seemed oblivious. Scott figured this was probably due to the dark, or the man's ignorance of such things, or maybe the liquor, because Del had found empty bottles in the cab of Creasy's pickup. When Creasy passed near the boys, who were lying prone in the stand of sumac, Scott saw that he cradled a rifle in his arms in the way of a hunter, and the sick feeling that had been with him all day and all evening worsened, and he felt like puking.

The birds had ceased their calling and their songs, but now a spring field cricket began to chirp. Scott had heard that you could tell the temperature from the sound of a cricket. He tried to remember the equation, to take his mind off the awful reason they were there, but he couldn't concentrate. The cricket chirped and chirped, and the incessant sound began to feel like a little chisel working at Scott's resolve. He didn't want to be there. He didn't want Del to be there. He thought about home, about his mother and Ida and how worried they probably were. He felt awful for them, but there was nothing to be done about it now. Now there were only Creasy and Del, and what was going to happen between them, one way or another.

In the moonlight, through the broken view afforded from within the sumac, Scott watched Creasy throw some wood together and start a fire. He kept waiting for Del to give some kind of indication of what they should do, but Del held rock still, watching. Creasy was never more than a step away from that rifle of his, and Scott thought maybe that's what Del was waiting for. In his hand, Del gripped the pistol he'd brought from the trailer in the hollow. It was a Luger, which Tyler Creasy claimed to have taken off a dead German officer. Del said that Creasy was always full of crap, so who knew if the story was true.

For a long time, the moon had seared a white hole in the indigo sky. But now an errant cloud moved across its face and the light vanished. Creasy sat by the fire he'd made and opened a can of some kind and began to eat with his fingers. Scott thought it might be Vienna sausages. He realized he hadn't eaten in forever, but his sick stomach made the idea of food repugnant to him.

Del moved, just a slight adjustment of his position. It made a sound, a brittle crackling, and Creasy looked up. Del froze, and Scott's heart went into a gallop. Creasy's face flickered red-orange with reflected firelight, and his eyes, as they scanned the sumac, seemed to flame. Creasy set down the can he held and reached for the rifle. At that same moment, the cloud moved on and the moon returned, bathing everything in brilliant silver-white light. Then Scott heard another sound. Weeping. It was the same ghostly voice he and Del had heard when they'd come to Inkpaduta Bend the night after James Quinn had been found dead. Creasy must have heard it, too, because his eyes swung away from the sumac. He stood up with the rifle in his hands, left the fire, and walked along the riverbank toward the crying sound.

Del finally made his move. He tapped Scott on the shoulder, gestured for him to stay where he was, and crawled on all fours out of the thicket. He dashed through firelight and moonlight to Creasy's pickup, slipped around to the far side, and disappeared.

The crying sound died as suddenly as it had begun. Creasy stopped, held still, an alabaster statue as he waited for the sound to come again. But it never did. He finally turned back toward his truck and the campfire.

Beside Scott lay the shotgun Del had given him. Scott's hand rested on the stock. The weapon felt hot under his touch, as if he'd already fired it. He was more afraid than he'd ever been in his whole life. Even worse than on the river when Holly Coleridge had almost drowned. Because with Holly he'd had no time to think. He'd simply acted. Now his brain worked and worked, trying to find some way out of what he'd signed on to do here. Which was nothing less than to kill or be killed. He was afraid, too, that he was going to throw up or soil himself, because all his guts were in turmoil. He knew that whatever was going to happen that night was going to happen when Creasy reached the campfire. And the man was almost there.

Ever so slowly, Scott eased the shotgun closer and gripped it with both hands.

Creasy sat down by the fire, laid his rifle at his side, picked up the can of sausages, and began eating again.

That's when Del made his move. He came out from behind the pickup, the pistol in his hand raised and aimed at Tyler Creasy. Scott could see them both clearly in the firelight: Del tensed with the gun pointed and Creasy frozen with his mouth open, ready to receive a little sausage. Behind them both, the water of the Alabaster River, in the remarkable way that it responded to moonlight, had turned milk white.

"Go to hell," Del said, and Scott saw his hand stiffen as his finger pulled the trigger.

But nothing happened.

Before Del could move again, Creasy was up and had swung a fist and knocked Del back against the pickup's grille. He swung again, and Del fell to the ground, nearly senseless. Creasy bent and swept up the dropped Luger.

The man stood breathing heavily. He looked at the pistol, shook his head, and laughed.

"You picked the wrong gun, boy. This piece of shit always jams."

Del stared up from where he lay, still dazed by the blows he'd received. Creasy fiddled with the Luger, cleared the jam, pointed the barrel toward the night sky, and fired.

"Works fine now," he said. "Boy, if you didn't have bad luck, you'd have no luck at all."

Move, Scott told himself. *Do it. Now.*

But he could not. His faulty heart hurt in a way it had never hurt before. His head pounded, and he could barely breathe. And there was something else, a paralysis that was pure fear.

"You never liked me," Creasy said. "Well, Delbert, I never cottoned to you neither."

He held the Luger at arm's length, poised with the barrel slanted down at Del's head.

Now Scott rose, at last unthinking, ignoring the pain in his chest, the pounding in his head. But before he could act, something else happened.

From the blind side of the pickup flew another figure, a swift dark shape that collided with Creasy and took the man down. They rolled together across the campfire in an explosion of embers that spread the flames and dimmed the light. Scott could see only a dark tangle writhing in the moonlight on the riverbank. The gun fired, but the struggle continued.

Del staggered up and stumbled toward the fight. He grabbed at a shape and tugged, and now it was like a ball of black snakes coiling and uncoiling against the white curtain of the Alabaster. One figure finally separated itself and sprang up and backpedaled a dozen feet. In the silver-white moonglow that bathed Inkpaduta Bend, Scott saw that it was Tyler Creasy. The next figure that stood was Del. And the last was Noah Bluestone, who held a hand to his stomach, where his shirt was stained dark. He placed himself purposely between Del and the gun that Creasy held.

Scott stepped nearer, but Creasy didn't notice, so focused was he on those in front of him. Creasy spoke no word. He simply fired, then fired again. Scott saw Bluestone drop to his knees and fall face forward onto the ground.

Del looked at Creasy, and there was nothing between them now but the barrel of that Luger.

Something in Scott finally broke loose, broke wild. He lifted the shotgun to his shoulder. "Tyler Creasy!" he yelled. When the man swung his way, Scott pulled the trigger. The recoil was the kick of a mule, and for weeks afterward Scott would carry the bruise. Creasy's face and neck were obliterated by a bloom of black, wet and shiny in the moonlight. The man stumbled backward from the impact of all those searing pellets. Scott readied himself to fire once more, but it wasn't necessary. Creasy dropped the Luger, tipped back, and fell with a splash into the river.

Across the course of his whole life, Scott Madison would never forget that scene. It would play itself out in unexpected moments, in dreams and in nightmares, in those solitary reveries he couldn't share, in the parade of all his regrets. Noah Bluestone lying dead on a riverbank that was so white in the moonlight it was like a bed fitted with a clean sheet. Del above him, still stunned and swaying, but alive and shining as if he wore clothing spun of moonbeams. Tyler Creasy falling backward into the milky flow of the Alabaster River. And from a place Scott could never quite fix in his remembering, the sound of someone crying.

BY THE TIME Graff and Brody drove up, it was all over. Death had come again to Inkpaduta Bend, reaped its harvest, and gone. Scott sat on one side of Noah Bluestone's body and Del on the other. In the headlights of Graff's pickup, they reminded Brody of soldiers who'd refused to abandon their downed comrade, and their faces, when they turned to the glare, brought back to him a gallery of hollowed faces from another war.

Brody left the truck and walked to the boys. He knelt on one knee next to Bluestone's body, put fingers to the neck, checked the artery there, found no pulse.

"Creasy?" he asked the boys.

Scott spoke without inflection. "The river. I shot him."

Graff stepped to the bank, bent, and reported to Brody, "He's in there. Current's about to take him away."

"Snag him," Brody said. He walked back to the truck, killed the headlights, then returned to the boys and sat with them. The scattered sticks from the fire still burned and gave a little illumination. The moon gave more, and Brody studied the boys in that light. He could see that more damage had been done to Del Wolfe's face, a swelling that might have been from a broken jaw. The damage he saw in Scott's face was of a different kind.

From the distance came the whine of sirens. Asa Fielding, Brody figured, and officers from the other agencies who'd been involved in the manhunt that day.

Graff returned from the river and said, "Creasy's going nowhere now."

"Get on the radio, will you, Connie? Let Hank Evans know that we've found the boys and that they're safe. Have him call Angie." He said to Del, "We're going to take you to the hospital and get you checked out, okay?"

The boy gave a weak nod.

Brody wondered what he could say to Scott that would make any difference and finally offered the only the thing he had: "It's over now."

But he knew it wasn't, and it never would be.

CHAPTER FIFTY-SIX

THE DAY KYOKO Bluestone left Black Earth County for good, Charlie gathered at the farmstead with the others who'd come to know, to respect, and even to love the young woman. The pigs and chickens had been sold. The land itself Kyoko had deeded to James Patrick Quinn, Jr., for reasons she never explained to anyone. But Charlie knew. And Marta Quinn knew. All the belongings she cared to take with her were packed in the back of Connie Graff's pickup. She was headed to California, where she had distant relatives near Sacramento who would take her in. Graff was going to drive her there, deliver her safely. Angie Madison had prepared lunches for them to eat on the road that first day.

The morning sky was soft blue and nearly cloudless. Beneath it, the young plants in the fields were deep green and promising. Kyoko stood in the farmyard and turned in a slow circle, taking in her final view: the outbuildings, the empty hog pen, the fields of amaranth and millet, the line of trees that marked the Alabaster River, Fordham Ridge, the young orchard, the Dutch elm tree with the iron bench beneath it, the small house.

"It's a fine place," she said.

"J.P. will take care of it well," Graff assured her.

Sam Wicklow was there. Kyoko had been especially grateful to him because of the way he'd championed Noah Bluestone in a number of pieces in the *Clarion*. She knew the reason for his scars and that prosthetic leg, and she had thanked him many times for not holding anger in his heart and for speaking out so eloquently in defense of her husband's character.

Brody, of course, was there. And Hector, who played gently with Kyoko's old dog, Fuji.

Scott Madison had come, too, accompanying his mother. But he held back a bit, as if terribly uncomfortable with the emotion of the moment. There was more to it than that, of course, much more, a great deal of guilt, but Charlie didn't know the whole story then and just thought him shy. He'd agreed to take care of Graff's horses until the old deputy returned. His plan was to ride his new Columbia three-speed out to Graff's place twice a day. Such a physical exertion concerned Angie and Ida, but Scott was determined, and with the recent events in Black Earth County, he'd become older than his fourteen years and independent in many ways.

"Are you ready?" Graff finally asked.

Kyoko and Charlie hugged goodbye. Then Kyoko called to her dog and they climbed into the cab of Graff's pickup.

"Take good care of her, Connie," Charlie said.

"Like she was my own daughter," Graff promised.

They stood together, those who'd come to see her off, and watched Graff's truck raise a little rooster tail of dust as it sped down the lane. Black Earth County might not have welcomed her well, but those who were there that day were sincere in their sadness at seeing Kyoko Bluestone leave. Sam Wicklow, who'd taken photos, wrote in his little pad, notes for yet another editorial he would compose about the whole Bluestone affair. Brody Dern and Angie Madison held hands and were quiet. Scott stared off into the distance, and Charlie couldn't say whether the young man was seeing the past or trying to see the future. Charlie just felt tired in the way she used to feel when fighting battles she knew she could not win. But then, that's one of the beauties of life. That we still fight on.

EPILOGUE

OUR LIVES AND the lives of those we love merge to create a river whose current carries us forward from our beginning to our end. Because we are only one part of the whole, the river each of us remembers is different, and there are many versions of the stories we tell about the past. In all of them there is truth, and in all of them a good deal of innocent misremembering.

Charlie Bauer still sometimes thinks about the death of Jimmy Quinn and the part she played in the events of that long-ago summer. These days she's staring her ninetieth birthday in the face. Her skin is covered with liver spots and her hands shake a bit. Her eyes are good, and her thinking clear. She spends most days sitting on the porch of her little house, reading and admiring the view across the fallow field where once, in the middle of a raging storm, she'd stood like a lightning rod. Beyond are the trees that curtain the Alabaster River, and beyond that, the gentle roll of the land all the way to the horizon. To the south stands Fordham Ridge and below it Inkpaduta Bend. Not far from that is the acreage once farmed by the Bluestones, now turned and planted every year by a good man who calls himself Patrick Quinn. There's a little orchard, too, which produces some of the sweetest apples you'll find in Black Earth County. Charlie can't help but think how wrong that early explorer Stephen H. Long was when he stood atop the ridge and surveyed the land below and called it the Great American Desert, deeming it unfit for cultivation. There is a profound tenderness in this land, she understands, and life has been brought forth from it in wondrous measure.

Stories are like those seeds we plant in the soil. They just grow and grow. So this story, which began with a man found eaten by catfish in a river, is not yet finished. Some of the players are no longer part of it, but the story goes on. The river continues to flow.

Over all these years, Angie and Brody Dern have been Charlie's good friends, and on occasions of legal necessity, Charlie has acted as their attorney. Because of that special relationship of client privilege, and also because of their deep friendship, Charlie has sometimes been their confessor as well and has heard the truth of their past, or the truth as each of them remembered it.

Whenever he returns to Jewel, Scott visits her, too. He's a lawyer, lives in Saint Paul, and works for the public defender's office there. When he was twenty, he was admitted to the Mayo Clinic for a new procedure to repair his faulty heart. The surgery was gloriously successful. During his recovery, he had two constant visitors who weren't family: Del Wolfe and Holly Coleridge. In his first year of law school, he and Holly married.

On Scott's trips to Jewel, Holly and their two children usually accompany him. Sometimes Scott and Brody have hauled out their guitars and put on a bit of a hoedown on Charlie's front porch, playing new tunes together and old ones and, as a tribute, a song or two Scott learned from Wendell Moon, who left this earth long ago. Across these years, Scott has slowly revealed to Charlie the events of that summer in which he played a part and which still trouble him. He's still plagued by the demons of *if only*. If only he hadn't befriended a boy as troubled as Del Wolfe, maybe none of it would have happened. If only he and Del hadn't gone to the Bluestone farm and shot the dog, who would have later barked a warning, Kyoko Bluestone might not have been raped and Noah Bluestone might yet be alive. If only . . . if only . . .

After graduating from high school, Del Wolfe attended the University of Minnesota. He had little money, so to help foot the bill for his education he joined ROTC. On graduation, he went directly into the army, figuring to make a career of it, as his father had. A year later, he was deployed to a faraway place barely on the radar of most Americans at that time, a small Southeast Asian country called Vietnam. When he finally returned home, it was in a coffin draped with an American flag. Every Memorial Day, Scott puts flowers on Del's grave at the Fort Snelling National Cemetery, along with one page of text torn from an old paperback copy of *The Naked and the Dead*.

Kyoko Bluestone settled in Davis, California, first living with relatives, then marrying a Nisei farmer named David Kimura. She sent Charlie letters and Christmas cards, and sent them to Connie Graff, too, until lung cancer took him. Kyoko passed away a year after Connie, succumbing to leukemia, the seeds of which were probably planted in her by the bombing of Nagasaki long ago.

Here's something that always makes Charlie smile. Seven years after the deaths of Jimmy Quinn and Noah Bluestone, Sam Wicklow published his first novel, a fictionalized account of the events of that fateful summer. He titled it *Spirit River,* and it enjoyed great success. He didn't know everything that Charlie knew, the secrets revealed to her over the years, but it was nonetheless an epic story. In Charlie's opinion, it should have won the Pulitzer Prize. Sam has written a number of other fine novels since, all of which he's signed for Charlie and are now shelved beside her inscribed Steinbeck, a position they occupy well.

Brody Dern died a year ago. He was atop his brother's barn, helping repair the roof, when the scaffolding plank gave way. Brody grabbed Tom and kept him from falling, but in the moments that followed, Brody lost his own footing and plunged. He was in a coma for two days, then slipped away. Shortly after his funeral, Angie visited Charlie and brought something from the safe deposit box that she and Brody kept at the bank. It was a sealed manila envelope with Charlie's name written on the front.

Charlie broke the seal and tipped the envelope. A ring fell into Charlie's palm, small and silver and set with a sapphire. She looked at Angie, and it was clear that the ring was unfamiliar to her. Although Charlie had never actually seen it, she knew that piece of jewelry. A slip of paper was also in the envelope. Written in Brody's hand was this: *Colleen Quinn.*

Whenever she looks back at the summer of Jimmy Quinn's death, she's certain that somehow Brody understood the truth of Quinn's murder, and he knew that Charlie understood it, too. That ring was the telling clue. At some point after his official investigation, some moment he never revealed to anyone, the light must have dawned. Charlie recalled visiting the Quinns sometime after that tragic night on Inkpaduta Bend and noticing that the old shack where Jimmy Quinn had died was gone. When she asked J.P. about it, he told her the sheriff had ordered it dismantled because he considered it a fire hazard. Marta simply said she was glad to see the thing torn down. But with that ring in the palm of her hand, Charlie wondered if, after he finally grasped the truth, Brody had approached Marta, and she'd told him everything. If so, he'd sworn her to absolute secrecy and had made sure any evidence that might have soaked into the boards of the old shack was gone forever. Charlie recalled *The Catcher in the Rye,* the last book they'd read for the Prairie Blooms so many years ago, and she imagined Brody, during his lifelong silence, envisioning himself standing alone out there in some great field of rye, protecting the innocent.

She spends her days much in solitude, but never really lonely, awaiting that end which comes to us all. She will be buried in the cemetery in Jewel, on the hillside that overlooks the Alabaster River. You may find it strange that she's purchased the plot next to her father's grave, a decision she made because of a small, beautiful piece of wisdom Jimmy Quinn's death offered her. And here it is: We all die, but some of us—those who are blessed or maybe just lucky—have the opportunity before that end to be redeemed. We can let go, forgive others, and also forgive ourselves for the worst of what we are or have been. Jimmy Quinn didn't have that chance, and even given the opportunity might not have had the inclination. For Charlie, Quinn's death has always been a reminder that we need to be kind to each other and ready to forgive. Brody Dern understood this, and Angie. Charlie believes that Scott will, too, someday, where his own guilt is concerned. Charlie Bauer doesn't intend to leave this life filled with rancor or regret or plagued by the demons of *if only*. She intends to lie down in peace.

And so, she sips her whiskey and reads her books and every once in a great while allows herself the pleasure of a cigar, and she awaits without fear her own passing, when she will be lowered into the soil of Black Earth County and laid to rest forever beside the moonlit, milk-white flow of the Alabaster, a river she remembers fondly as an old friend.